Praise for *Death of a Musketeer*

"Delightful . . . Sara D'Almeida is a gifted writer who brings new life to our old friends, D'Artagnan, Athos, Porthos, and Aramis. Medieval France comes vividly to life in this intriguing adventure."
—Victoria Thompson, author of *Murder in Little Italy*

A Murder in Disguise

Aramis bowed.

"I have brought Monsieur D'Artagnan with me because after the fight with the guards, we stumbled upon . . ." He realized he would have to tell Violette the whole thing.

"Violette, when did you last see the Queen?"

"The Queen?" Violette looked surprised.

"Please, tell me, when did you see her?"

"An hour ago, or little more," Violette said. "I spent the afternoon with her, reading, and then I retreated to her prayer room with her to pray. And now, will you tell me why?"

Aramis nodded. "Because the corpse we found in the alley looked exactly like Her Majesty."

"The corpse?" Violette asked.

Death of a Musketeer

A Musketeers Mystery

Sarah D'Almeida

BERKLEY PRIME CRIME, NEW YORK

THE BERKLEY PUBLISHING GROUP
Published by the Penguin Group
Penguin Group (USA) Inc.
375 Hudson Street, New York, New York 10014, USA
Penguin Group (Canada), 90 Eglinton Avenue East, Suite 700, Toronto, Ontario M4P 2Y3, Canada
(a division of Pearson Penguin Canada Inc.)
Penguin Books Ltd., 80 Strand, London WC2R 0RL, England
Penguin Group Ireland, 25 St. Stephen's Green, Dublin 2, Ireland (a division of Penguin Books Ltd.)
Penguin Group (Australia), 250 Camberwell Road, Camberwell, Victoria 3124, Australia
(a division of Pearson Australia Group Pty. Ltd.)
Penguin Books India Pvt. Ltd., 11 Community Centre, Panchsheel Park, New Delhi—110 017, India
Penguin Books (NZ), Cnr. Airborne and Rosedale Roads, Albany, Auckland 1310, New Zealand
(a division of Pearson New Zealand Ltd.)
Penguin Books (South Africa) (Pty.) Ltd., 24 Sturdee Avenue, Rosebank, Johannesburg 2196, South
Africa

Penguin Books Ltd., Registered Offices: 80 Strand, London WC2R 0RL, England

This is a work of fiction. Names, characters, places, and incidents either are the product of the author's
imagination or are used fictitiously, and any resemblance to actual persons, living or dead, business es-
tablishments, events, or locales is entirely coincidental. The publisher does not have any control over
and does not assume any responsibility for author or third-party websites or their content.

DEATH OF A MUSKETEER

A Berkley Prime Crime Book / published by arrangement with the author

PRINTING HISTORY
Berkley Prime Crime mass-market edition / November 2006

Copyright © 2006 by Sarah Hoyt.
Cover art by Gregory Manchess.
Cover design by Steven Ferlauto.
Interior text design by Tiffany Estreicher.

ISBN: 0-425-21292-0

BERKLEY® PRIME CRIME
Berkley Prime Crime Books are published by The Berkley Publishing Group,
a division of Penguin Group (USA) Inc.,
375 Hudson Street, New York, New York 10014.
The name BERKLEY PRIME CRIME and the BERKLEY PRIME CRIME design are trademarks belonging to Penguin Group (USA) Inc.

PRINTED IN THE UNITED STATES OF AMERICA

10 9 8 7 6 5 4 3 2 1

To my father,
Antonio Marques de Almeida,
whose love of mysteries proved contagious.

Prologue,

or

How I Came by the Other Diaries of Monsieur D'Artagnan

MY first encounter with the gentlemen known to all the world as Athos, Porthos, Aramis and—of course—D'Artagnan came at a young age when, searching through the shelves of my grandfather's library, I was called by several leather-bound volumes bearing the name DUMAS on the spine.

I hardly need to tell anyone who has had the good fortune of reading Monsieur Dumas's works at an early age with what rapt attention I followed the actions of the brash young man from Gascony and his three daring companions.

Over the years, I've returned to the same book—and its companions, *Twenty Years After* and *Viscount de Bragelone*—every winter, when the snow first fell. I reread the adventures of the four charming rogues, again and again, by my cozy fireside. But I knew I'd never encounter them in any other writing.

I was wrong. This year, when snowflakes first danced on the thin mountain air of Colorado, and while my slippers and my hot chocolate waited with a leather-bound book by my comfortable chair, a delivery service dropped an unpromising battered cardboard box on my front porch.

Inside it was a brief note from my father-in-law, some of whose ancestors immigrated to the New World at the end of the seventeenth century.

Not a French speaker, he said he thought it best if I were given these papers, found in an elderly relative's estate.

I confess I perused them, at first, with some distaste. The pages had mildewed to an unappetizing shade of grayish-yellow and I had to turn them with the greatest care to prevent their falling apart. I picked a word here and there, amid decay and mildew. The spelling was quite the oddest I'd ever encountered.

However, on page two I encountered the name D'Artagnan; on page five the name Athos and on page ten the names Porthos and Aramis together. By page fifteen I realized these diaries referred to murders investigated, solved and often avenged by the three musketeers plus one. I was hooked.

After that, I devoured the twenty mildewed diaries with the eagerness of one too long separated from a childhood friend. Woven around the events that Dumas told the world of in his books, the diaries started with the fateful duel at the Barefoot Carmelites. However, they very quickly turned into a series of murder mysteries often involving the highest nobility of France.

The main of it was written in ink that had faded to brown, and in an assured, angular handwriting that marched across the pages with the certainty of a military officer on campaign.

However, over it all, there were notes in other hands, squeezed in the margins and scribbled between the lines. I soon learned to identify the small, sharp, inclined hand with Athos; the round, well-formed ecclesiastical one—still with a hint of violet to its tints—with Aramis and the laborious printing with Porthos. The notes gave details that the writer of the main diaries—certainly D'Artagnan—couldn't have known at the time he wrote them.

I do not know how his friends came to editorialize D'Artagnan's diaries. And I have no idea how or by what crooked lines of descent and inheritance or happenstance and luck those diaries passed into the hands of my family.

The only thing certain is that those diaries, which I edited for coherence and adapted to our modern storytelling mode, reveal murders as intricate and fiendish as any writer could dream, and that these crimes could only be solved by Athos, Porthos, Aramis and D'Artagnan.

To whose spirit, nobility and courage I hope my retelling will do justice.

Sarah D'Almeida
January 2004, Colorado Springs

The Duel That Wasn't;
Where the Cardinal's Guards Are
Taught a Lesson; A Handy Guide to
the Taverns of Paris

D'ARTAGNAN knew he was going to die.

It was April 1625 and the spring sun, fierce and blazing, shone like an unblinking eye over the bustling city of Paris. Henri D'Artagnan, aged seventeen, a slim, muscular young man with olive skin, dark hair and piercing black eyes, had arrived in town just the day before.

Now, under the noon sun, he stood outside the convent of the Barefoot Carmelites, a religious house situated in a conveniently deserted spot on the outskirts of town.

Around him spread fields of green wheat. The wind being still and no breeze stirring the sheaves, the only sound was the drowsy droning of insects, drunk with midday languor and heat.

And D'Artagnan thought this was the last day of his life.

If D'Artagnan weren't himself, if he were not the only son of nobleman Francois D'Artagnan, a hardened veteran soldier, D'Artagnán could have turned and taken off running through those fields, relying on his young, agile legs to get him away from death.

His mind cringed away from such an unworthy thought.

His opponent, with whom his sword was crossed, scraped the sword lightly along the length of D'Artagnan's—just enough to call the young man's attention.

And D'Artagnan turned toward him, at the same time his

opponent's second, who served as their judge in this case, dropped the white handkerchief signaling the beginning of combat.

D'Artagnan's opponent came at him like a tiger, his sword pressing D'Artagnan close, and demanding all of the young man's concentration.

The man was called Athos, and he fought like a veteran duelist. Which he was, being one of the older and more experienced, and—as far as D'Artagnan could determine—one of the most feared members of His Majesty Louis XIII's corps of musketeers. Other things D'Artagnan had heard, once he'd given himself the trouble of checking: that the man had the personal friendship of Monsieur de Treville. That he was of noble birth. That Athos was a nom de guerre, picked up to hide disgrace or guilt.

Athos attacked, driving the young man back and back and back, till D'Artagnan's shoulders were solidly against the whitewashed wall of the convent and only his quick wit and quicker reflexes permitted him to step sideways and avoid being skewered.

D'Artagnan flitted and skipped, danced away from trouble and contorted away from tight spots, but his mind became oddly detached.

His body moved and seemed to think with a reasoning of its own while it parried and thrust, and made Athos back away. Meanwhile D'Artagnan's mind—what his mother used to call his quick and lively mind—had gone away, to some place at the back of himself. Someplace away from the battlefield, where it could do its thinking.

When Henri D'Artagnan had left the paternal abode, his father had given him only one substantive piece of advice: that he fight often, that he fight well and that he never tolerate any insult from anyone but the king or the Cardinal, who was, truth be told, as powerful as any king.

Henri had tried to follow his father's advice and, on the road to Paris, in the small town of Meung, had challenged a nobleman who laughed at his attire and horse. This had cost him dearly, as his opponent had his servants hit Henri from behind. While Henri was unconscious, the stranger had stolen Henri's letter of recommendation to Monsieur de Treville.

The letter that would have got him into the musketeers this very day.

But I don't learn, do I? D'Artagnan thought to himself as he pushed hard with his sword arm, forcing Athos's sword away, shoving the musketeer back at the same time.

Athos fell away and tripped and bent down upon his knee.

I had to challenge three musketeers for a duel today. Three. Musketeers. Today, D'Artagnan thought, as he jumped nimbly back, ready to parry Athos's next thrust.

No, he didn't learn. He'd continued following his father's advice, until he'd managed to challenge the three men who the rest of the corps called the three inseparables. Athos, Porthos and Aramis. One of whom would kill him today.

D'Artagnan's mind was so preoccupied with its gloomy thoughts that he didn't at first realize that Athos hadn't got up from his position, half bent over his knee.

"Monsieur," he said, when he did notice it. "Monsieur, if it would suit you to adjourn our appointment to another time . . ."

He noticed Athos's hand pressed hard at his right side, and he remembered the scene, that very morning, in Monsieur de Treville's office, where an obviously wounded and ill Athos had come in to present himself to his captain and to deflect Monsieur de Treville's anger at all of the three musketeers who'd been bested in a skirmish with the Cardinal's guards.

"Monsieur, if you are in too great a pain . . ." D'Artagnan said. He'd got in this duel with Athos by careening against the musketeer and making him bleed. And failing to apologize sufficiently for the hurt he'd caused.

But Athos only shook his head. He took a deep breath, audible in the midday stillness, and he rose slowly from his knee. "It's nothing," he said, his face ashen. "It is nothing. I didn't want to distress you with the sight of blood you haven't drawn." A red stain showed on the side of his doublet. He changed his sword to his left hand. "If you don't mind, I will fight with my left hand, though. It will not put me at a disadvantage, as I can use either hand to equal effect. But it might be harder for you to defend yourself."

D'Artagnan nodded. He knew he would die anyway. And if he was going to die, perhaps it would be best if it was at Athos's hands. Of his three potential opponents, he liked and admired Athos the most. It certainly was no dishonor to be killed by such a man.

Athos straightened and pulled back a stray lock of pitch-black hair, which contrasted glaringly with his alabaster-pale complexion.

D'Artagnan had heard that Athos was considered handsome by many men and even more women in Paris. This opinion baffled D'Artagnan.

Athos's face was spare, with high cheekbones and intense, zeal-burned eyes. The rest of his features, precisely drawn and finely sculpted, made the man look less like a living being and more like those caryatides of Greece and Rome—columns given human form and forever holding aloft the white marble roof of a temple or palace.

Athos's character, like his appearance, seemed as spare, as certain, as controlled as those columns. Rightly or not, he gave the impression of a man who served a cause greater than his own whims, purer than his own advancement.

And this, D'Artagnan thought as Athos raised his sword, was what D'Artagnan would have liked to be—if he ever got to live beyond his present seventeen years.

Aramis, Athos's second and D'Artagnan's next arranged opponent, stepped up. He was a blond man, so dainty looking that one might fail to notice he was almost as tall as Athos, and just as muscular. Accounted a gallant by all who knew him, he was said to be popular with the ladies and rumored to be entertaining duchesses and princesses by the score.

D'Artagnan, who had challenged him to a duel over an argument started on a point of honor, had at first thought him just a dandy and nothing more. But Aramis's bright green eyes showed such a keen appreciation for the irony of D'Artagnan's situation, perhaps there was more to him.

As Aramis stepped up, picking up his white handkerchief from the ground where it had lain, he said, "You must restart the duel."

D'Artagnan, noticing that Athos was very pale still, his skin tinged with the gray of a man fighting extreme pain and realizing that Athos's old-fashioned Spanish-style doublet was laced tightly over his musketeer's tunic, said, "I would not object if you undo the ties on your doublet, since the sun is so devilishly hot."

But Athos shook his head. "I thank you for your courtesy," he said. "But really, I'm afraid if I do it will restart the bleeding. The wound is bothering me."

"Do not misunderstand me, I am eager to cross swords with you," D'Artagnan said. "But if you wish to wait and perhaps drink something for your present comfort . . ."

Athos smiled, a flash of genuine amusement. "Your sentiment does you credit, but I believe in collecting my debts promptly and drinking afterwards. And then, it is not the first time I've fought while wounded." He shifted his feet and tilted the upper half of his body forward, baring his teeth slightly, as if allowing the animal to peer out of his noble features.

"Come, come," Porthos spoke, from where he stood by the white wall of the convent, hands the size of hams folded over the guard of a very substantial sword. A redheaded giant, he dwarfed other men with the size of his lean, muscular body. Each of his arms looked to be the size of one of D'Artagnan's thighs, each of his legs like an oak tree trunk. And yet he gave the impression of suppleness, of not a wasted ounce on his huge frame. "You are all talk. Less talk and more fighting. Remember, Athos, he owes me satisfaction after you and Aramis have your turns. He offended me most horribly on a matter of fashion."

Did D'Artagnan fancy that a smile crossed both Aramis's and Athos's lips when Porthos spoke?

Aramis raised his eyebrows and, still holding his handkerchief aloft, turned toward Porthos. "When you wish to be so rude, you should speak for yourself only, Porthos. I have no objection to the noble and proper sentiments these gentlemen express. Indeed, I will gladly listen to them for as long as necessary, before they feel it fit to cross swords."

And now another flinch of remorse came to join D'Artagnan's regret that he would die so early, leaving so much untasted of life's joys: that he would never get to know these men better. There was such an easy comradery between the three of them, so devoid of the formality of most friendships, that he imagined they could have been his friends.

"Only," Porthos said, pulling a large red handkerchief from his sleeve and mopping at his forehead with it, "it's too blazing hot."

"It doesn't matter," Athos said, and leaned forward, displaying his teeth again in that expression that was more animal threat than human smile. "For we are ready." He pushed his sword against D'Artagnan's and said, "En garde," between clenched teeth.

Aramis dropped the scarf.

A throat was cleared, nearby—but neither by Aramis nor Porthos.

Their swords still crossed, D'Artagnan and Athos turned to look. Five men stood near them—so near that they could only have approached unnoticed while the musketeers and D'Artagnan were distracted with talk and worry for Athos's wound. All of them wore uniforms similar to those of the musketeers, but where the musketeers wore blue, the group's knee breeches, tunics and plumed hats were bright red, like freshly spilled blood.

They were guards of the Cardinal, sworn rivals of the musketeers, their enemies in a thousand brawls, a million street skirmishes.

"Well, well," said the leading guard, who had a suntanned face and a Roman nose. "What have we here? Dueling Musketeers? What? In open and defiant contravention of all the edicts against dueling?" He smiled unpleasantly, revealing a wealth of very large, yellowed teeth. "I'm afraid we'll have to arrest the lot of you."

"Leave us alone, Jussac," Athos said, without turning to look, his sword still crossed with D'Artagnan's. "I promise you if we found you in like amusement, we'd sit back and let you proceed. Enjoy and amuse yourselves, have the profit of our injuries with none of the pain."

Jussac smiled wider. "That's as it may be, Monsieur Athos. But the thing is, there is an edict against dueling and our master, the Cardinal, wants laws obeyed."

Athos lowered his sword. He turned to Jussac and, with an air of strained patience, said, "Nothing would please me more than to oblige you. But, you see, our captain, Monsieur de Treville, has forbidden us from being arrested."

Jussac sighed in turn. He lifted his hat and scratched under it at his sweat-soaked hair. "Think about it," he said. "There are only three of you, one of you wounded. Three of you and a child who was dueling you. If you force us to fight you, they will say it's murder."

The three musketeers formed a circle, from within which their worried voices reached D'Artagnan's ears.

"I'm afraid he's right, you know," Aramis said. "There are only three of us, one of us wounded. And there's five of them: Jussac, Brisac and Cahusac, the three fiercest fighters in the Guards, and two of their companions. They will slaughter us."

Athos paled yet further and glared, his zeal-burned blue eyes seeming to flame. His features hardened into a harsher pose of dignity. "I would rather die than appear before Monsieur de Treville defeated again."

"Me too," Porthos said.

D'Artagnan remembered the scouring reproach that Monsieur de Treville had inflicted on the three musketeers that morning. Everyone waiting in the captain's antechamber had heard it. He didn't blame the three for not wishing to face such humiliation again.

"Very well, then," Aramis said. He straightened a little and squared his shoulders. "We'll die here."

"You, the child," Jussac said, pointing at D'Artagnan. "Save yourself. We'll allow you to go."

D'Artagnan looked at the three musketeers, who were so calm, so resigned, gallantly preparing themselves for death rather than face dishonor. He looked over at Jussac, who smiled benevolently at him, showing long, yellow teeth.

He pushed himself into the musketeers' circle, shoving his sweaty face between Aramis's and Porthos's shoulders. "You are wrong," he said. "When you say there are only three of you. I count four of us."

They looked back at him and for a moment it looked as though Porthos were on the verge of asking who the fourth one might be. But before he could, Athos smiled. "You're a child," he said. "And someday you'll be a man I'd be proud to call a friend. But right now, you're a boy. And this is suicide. Or chosen death. Save yourself."

"No," D'Artagnan said, his certainty growing with the rebuff. "No. I'll stay and fight by your side."

"But you're not a musketeer," Aramis said. "Why would you want to die with us?"

"Though I don't wear a musketeer's uniform," D'Artagnan said, "in my heart I am a musketeer. And though I might only be able to give you very little help, if I leave and save my life, I'll never be able to live with myself."

For a moment Aramis stared at him, Porthos frowned at him, and Athos furrowed his brow as if in deep thought.

And then Athos smiled. "You're right," he said. "There are indeed four of us. Athos, Porthos, Aramis and— your name, my friend?"

"D'Artagnan," D'Artagnan answered, as his heart hammered faster and faster in his chest, and once more he was sure he was going to die.

This time he knew he was going to die at the end of the guards' swords. But he would die next to musketeers. He would die almost a musketeer. His father would be proud.

"Well, then, Athos, Porthos, Aramis and D'Artagnan. One for all and all for one. If death is to come for us, let us not keep her waiting. Let us go out and meet her halfway, like gallants, and receive her kiss proudly."

"We grow impatient," Jussac thundered, outside their circle. "Will you save yourself or not, boy? Because if not, we're coming to get you."

The circle broke apart as though they had rehearsed, and the four of them faced the five guards.

"We've made a decision," Athos said, his voice steady and calm.

"Oh," Jussac said. "I hope it's a sensible decision."

"Very," Athos said, and removed his hat, bowing with a deep flourish. "We're going to have the pleasure of charging you."

Before the guard could snap shut his mouth, which he'd let drop open in his astonishment, Athos's hat was back on his head, and Porthos and Aramis had unsheathed their swords.

"One for all and all for one," they shouted, as they fell on the guards.

By the rational odds of combat and war, they should have lost. There were but four of them, one of whom was severely wounded, and the other little more than a child.

D'Artagnan's only experience of dueling had been his mock duels with his father in the field behind their house, in the calm Gascon countryside.

If that duel had been decided on body count, or on experience, or even on the relative size of the opponents, surely the guards of the Cardinal would have won.

But wars and duels are fought with the mind, the heart and that other thing—that thing that is neither loyalty nor comradery, but which has hints of both.

That thing allowed D'Artagnan to know and come to Athos's rescue when his breathing grew too labored. That thing allowed him to go away when Athos had recovered enough to resume his own battle.

And duels are also fought with pride and fear. The three musketeers were too proud to surrender, too fearful of Monsieur de Treville's wrath to allow themselves to be arrested. They fought like fury unleashed.

Porthos fought and defeated two enemies at once.

And so, fifteen minutes later, the only one left standing of the small army of Cardinal Guards was de Brisac—like D'Artagnan, a Gascon, and like D'Artagnan, ill-suited to surrender. Surrounded by all the musketeers, he broke his own sword upon his knee to avoid losing it.

But then he gave up. He helped the musketeers and D'Artagnan take the wounded and dead to the convent's door. And stayed behind with them, while the musketeers and D'Artagnan rang the bell and walked away.

Years later, D'Artagnan would try to recall the rest of the afternoon. All he would remember was Athos's promising that he would show D'Artagnan the best taverns in Paris.

And then they'd gone to the Louis, where there were ten musketeers and where, when Porthos had told their story, people had rushed to buy them strong, sweet, fiery liquor. From there, they'd walked a block to The Maiden's Head, where the seven musketeers present had listened to their story with awe. And then to The Head and Bucket, where, at the telling of their tale, musketeers and sympathizers had bought them a sparkling white wine.

D'Artagnan remembered there had been a pause between The Grinning Corpse and The Coup de Grace while he leaned against a wall in an alley and lost most of the wine he'd drunk in the preceding hours.

But then they'd taken him to The Drinking Fish for a few mugs of house special, and from there to The Drunken Lord for something that tasted like molten fire.

Night had fallen when D'Artagnan found himself stumbling along the back alleys and narrow staircases of the working-class neighborhoods of Paris, one arm thrown over Aramis's shoulder, Porthos's huge hand on his other shoulder, singing softly a song about the Queen, the King and the Musketeers that would surely be treason if they weren't all drunk and all so loyal that they'd just risked their lives to ensure the King's own musketeers suffered no defeat.

"We should take the boy home first," Athos said. He had to be drunk. He'd drunk more of all the various liquors than all of them combined. He had to be dead drunk. But he walked steadily and his voice sounded, if anything, a little slower and calmer and more controlled.

Porthos giggled. "'s right," he said. "It is past the time schoolboys should be asleep."

"Where do you live, D'Artagnan?" Aramis asked.

"Rue des Fossoyers," D'Artagnan said, glad he'd rented lodgings before going in search of his fate outside the Barefoot Carmelites. Looking back, it had been presumptuous to think he'd survive three duels. But at least he'd have a place to sleep tonight.

"Good," Athos said. "That's just around . . ."

He turned, as if to get his bearings, and as he turned, and they with him, they all saw a figure in the uniform of a musketeer cross the alley right in front of them.

"Oh, I say, wait," Athos said. "Wait, friend. King's Musketeer, hold. Have you heard that we defeated Jussac outside the Barefoot—"

The musketeer jumped, as if touched with hot iron, and took off running, the sound of his steps echoing and reverberating through the maze of narrow streets.

The musketeers stopped and frowned at the space where the unknown musketeer had been.

"That's abominably rude," Aramis said.

"Musketeer or no, someone should teach him some manners," Porthos said.

"He should buy us a drink to make up for it," Athos said. "After all, there must be a place still open."

As one man, the three musketeers ran, pursuing the fugitive. D'Artagnan followed the sound of their steps.

They ran down so many blind alleys, careened precipitously down so many worn staircases that D'Artagnan was sure they'd never find the runaway musketeer. He'd be lucky if he didn't get separated from his friends.

But at last, they all surged into an alley. And there, on the ground, the musketeer lay.

The three musketeers had been calling and jeering and laughing, but now all their noises stopped.

It was suddenly very quiet, in that alley. Far away, an owl hooted, chasing prey in some attic. D'Artagnan drew a deep breath, which sounded too loud in the silence.

"It can't be," Aramis said under his breath.

Though D'Artagnan had never seen a dead body, he knew the musketeer lying on the muddy, smelly ground of the alley was dead.

If asked, he could have given no more justification than a certain angle of the arm protruding from under the body and the stillness, the eery stillness of whole body.

"He's dead," he said.

Aramis crossed himself and Athos stepped forward, toward the corpse.

The Many Complications of a Dead Musketeer; Where the Corpses of Queens Are Different from the Corpses of Commoners; What One Owes the Dead

ATHOS was suddenly, startlingly sober.

One moment he'd been laughing and running with his friends, his head muddled, his vision blurring scenes and places.

The next breath he was stone-cold sober, standing in a narrow alley, his nose full of the stink of mud and the human waste that housewives daily emptied into the common street from their windows. His head hurt a little with something that was not so much a hangover as the distant echo of a hangover. His shirt and hose stuck to him with dried sweat and felt prickly and cold against his skin. His tightly laced doublet made his shoulder wound throb.

He lifted his hand and wiped his forehead. His side hurt with burning, insistent pain. The wound he'd received from Jussac the night before was still bleeding and perhaps starting to become infected.

Surely Athos's reactions showed a touch of fever. Because he'd seen death many times. Death, in the battlefield or in private brawl meant very little to French noblemen used to and encouraged to quarrel over matters of honor, over matters of the heart, even over trivial matters.

It had been a long time since Athos had learned how quickly the flame of life could be extinguished in combat.

But it had been even longer since he'd seen the body of one killed dishonorably. A *murdered* corpse.

And without being able to point to anything specifically, he was sure this man had indeed been murdered. There had hardly been time for him to challenge anyone, to engage in a duel with anyone.

Athos stepped forward, a prickle of uneasiness at the back of his neck. He knelt by the body, ignoring the smells that accompanied death.

The dead man must be very young—there was so little breadth to his shoulders. Short too, shorter than their new friend, D'Artagnan. The hair that escaped from the broad-brimmed musketeer hat was as pale white as moonlight.

And the light of the lantern hanging at the door to a tavern three doors down was enough to see that the left hand, extended to the side of the body—palm up as if in supplication—was white and pale and unmarred by calluses.

This meant that not only was the man young and, undoubtedly, had led such a sheltered life as only certain wealthy families could afford, but also that he'd been a musketeer for a very little time.

Because the wielding of the sword, the gripping of the oft-ornamented pommel, the force necessary to parry and thrust with the blade, soon turned the hands of those sons of the nobility who made the sword their profession as callused, as blistered and as rough as the hands of any farmer's son.

From beneath the neck, on the right side, a little pool of thick liquid—dark under the insufficient lighting—spread sluggishly on the muddy ground.

Athos put his hand on the back of the boy's head. It still felt warm.

"Help me turn him," Athos said.

Porthos stepped forward, put a hand on each of the boy's shoulders and easily, like turning a rag doll, flipped the body so it was faceup.

In the effort, the corpse's hat went flying. Athos flinched as the corpse's blue eyes appeared to stare at him.

It was not a boy, but a young woman.

She could be any age between sixteen and twenty, but

Athos did not need to notice the gentle swell of breasts beneath the musketeer's tunic to know that it was no man.

Her forehead was too smooth, her nose too small and tilted slightly up. Her eyes were too wide. Her lips too soft and pliable. Lips that would have made many a suitor tremble.

Her eyes looked puzzled, as if she couldn't quite understand what had happened, and there was a small crease of worry on her white forehead.

Without thinking, Athos brought out his handkerchief from his sleeve and wiped the mud and blood from the side of her face. Then he gasped, in turn.

She looked like . . . it was . . .

He jumped back, unconsciously tracing the sign of the cross over his own forehead—not in the careful, deliberate way Aramis did, but in the frantic way of a child warding off evil.

From either side of him, in Porthos's booming tones and Aramis's half-sighed ones, he heard the words his mind whispered: "The Queen. It is the Queen."

Athos shook his head reflexively. D'Artagnan pushed forward and stopped at the feet of the corpse, looking hesitant.

"It can't be the Queen," Athos said. "It would never be the Queen. What would our Queen be doing here, in musketeer attire, in the dark street?"

A half groan from Aramis answered him, a wordless crescendo of worry. It ended fast and, without turning, Athos was sure his friend had bit his own tongue to stop the sound.

And then in a fearful whisper, because this wasn't an antechamber or a salon where such things could be said and bandied as a joke, Aramis said, "It is said Buckingham is in town."

"Aramis!" Porthos said.

Athos didn't say anything. He hadn't heard the rumors of Buckingham's visit. But then, he wouldn't have. Other than his two friends who knew better than to gossip to him, he spoke to very few people. Most of his days were spent in silence. Even his servant, Grimaud, had been taught to answer a gesture or an expression, which saved Athos the trouble of talking.

He'd joined the musketeers as other men would join a cloistered order. In fact, it was only the consciousness of be-

from the idea of this dead body in an alley to the trouble that would ensue in the world at large if this were, indeed, the Queen of France.

Porthos, the direct man of action, found words a slippery adversary who wouldn't meet him openly.

Athos sighed. Again he rubbed his forehead with his fingertips. Sober, he might be. Startlingly and suddenly sober. But the alcohol he'd drunk remained with him—a dull ache behind the eyes, a confusion of the tongue. "I meant that if this is the Queen and she is dead, the world will tremble for this. Our King will say she was out for unknown motives, probably dishonorable, and that no one can ever find out who killed her. Her relatives abroad, though—her very powerful relatives, the Hapsburg Emperor, her brother, and her cousins and siblings, in the various thrones of Europe—will not be satisfied. They'll say our own king contrived her death." Athos shook his head, unwilling to speak further of all the things that could be said in this regard. "And then there is, as Aramis mentioned, Buckingham. He too is unlikely to believe the Queen's death was a murder committed by a mere footpad. He will want revenge. All of them will. There will be war."

"Let them make war, then," Porthos growled. "They will break their teeth on the nut of France."

"Shhhh," Aramis said.

And Athos looked around, at the still-closed windows of the upper floors, at the deserted street, the lantern burning out the last of its oil in front of the tavern three doors down. Aramis was right. All the merchants in the street might be asleep, snug in their beds over their shops. But make enough noise and they would wake. And if they wakened . . . If they wakened, the scandal would be out in the open.

"She looks younger than the Queen," D'Artagnan said. He blushed furiously as Athos looked back at him. "I know all I've seen of the Queen are woodcuts and a portrait, once. But this woman looks like she can't be twenty, yet."

Athos grunted. He knelt and examined, as closely as the tavern light allowed, the small, white, flawless hands, and the corners of the eyes of the corpse.

He rose, shaking his head. "I can't tell for sure," he said. "She looks somewhat younger than our Queen, that is true.

But then, our Queen has led a sheltered life. And she has no children. Both of these can make a woman look younger than she truly is. And then, I've never been that close to Her Majesty, though I've often seen her at court."

Porthos sighed. "Well, well," he said. "I'll go alert the guard then, right? No use our going on like this."

Aramis gasped. "Porthos, I've said it before, but I'll say it again. You can be a fool."

"A fool? I? How?"

And there, they would be off on another round of the endless bickering they enjoyed as much as other men enjoyed chess games.

"He's not a fool," Athos cut. "He's simply not seeing the whole thing. If the murder of Anne of Austria leads to an invasion of our country, what are we as men of honor and musketeers to do?"

"Defend France," Porthos said.

"Exactly. But, Porthos, by the time the armies of Europe converge on us it might be a little late to defend our country."

There was a silence. "Er . . ." Porthos said. "Er . . . how are we supposed to defend France, then?"

"By stealth," the young man, D'Artagnan, said. "By not telling anyone who this woman is, or that we found her, or that she's been murdered. By hiding the murder."

"That's despicable," Porthos said. "To hide a murder and let the murderer go free?"

"Hush, Porthos," Athos said. "No one said anything about letting the murderer go free, but our friend the Gascon seems to know my mind better than I do, so I'll let him speak."

D'Artagnan looked up at Athos and met his gaze with a half smile. The small man straightened himself in response and turned away from the corpse to face the other two musketeers. His hat, carefully clutched to his chest, was of an uncertain color between blue and black—as if the fabric had suffered one too many colorings. The two plumes were broken and half bald, as if they had been played with by countless generations of toddlers.

"The thing is, if we say nothing and investigate the murder, then when we know who the murderer is, we can present it to someone—Monsieur de Treville, for example—who will then present it to the King. With proof and a well-reasoned explanation. So that when the King announces Her Majesty's death to the crowned heads of Europe, he will be in a position to prove he did not cause her demise."

"Exactly," Athos said, relieved he didn't have to find the words to explain it. "Exactly what I was thinking."

Porthos sighed. "But we'll have to hide the body. For . . . days."

Aramis sighed. "I know a man," he said.

Athos smiled but managed not to say that this was strange as, in fact, Aramis normally knew women.

Aramis glared at Athos, as if he knew the thought that had crossed his friend's mind. "He is a curate in a little church near here, in the street of the Holy Martyrs. He has a cellar . . . where he often keeps the bodies of people who die in Paris and whose relatives will come from the provinces to fetch them for burial. Or people whose names and relatives no one knows. He keeps them a while and if they're not claimed, he pays for their burials himself. I suppose if the curate were another person, of different means, his basement would be a wine cellar, for it keeps amazingly cold even in this heat. And he keeps the bodies in coffins. All that could be holy and proper. It is his ministry, his vocation. Just as I feel that mine is to preach to those too comfortable in their sphere and with their wealth . . ."

Athos nodded, forbearing to say anything about the methods Aramis used for that preaching. Aramis seemed to first demonstrate the sin so he could more easily bring the lady—it was always a lady—to repentance. "That would do," he said. "Yes, that would do, handsomely."

"But we'd share a dreadful secret," Porthos said.

"And have we not in the past?" Athos asked. His friends nodded. D'Artagnan, their new acquaintance, looked wide-eyed at them but said nothing.

"Well, then," Aramis said. "I live close by. I'll go home and send my servant, Bazin, with a message for my friend, the curate, to come with his wheelbarrow to collect the corpse, shall I?"

"Yes," Athos said. "That would be—"

"No." It was D'Artagnan, his voice full of urgency. "No," he continued as all of them turned to look at him.

"You don't want us to solve this murder?" Athos asked.

"You don't want us to hide the body?" Aramis asked.

"You are too cowardly to aid in this?" Porthos asked.

D'Artagnan shook his head. He looked from one to the other of them but, at last, he faced Athos.

Athos felt as if the young man wanted to talk to him alone, as though having decided that Athos was the most likely to understand him. Or perhaps the least likely to shout him into silence or cast aspersions on his courage.

Athos smiled a little, in encouragement, and the young man took a deep breath.

"What I meant," D'Artagnan said, "is that before we do this, there is something else we must decide. What if this isn't the Queen? What if she's just someone who died because she resembled the Queen? Or someone who was killed by a jealous lover, or a controlling husband, or a refused suitor?" He took another deep breath, and looked around at them.

Athos, confused as to why this mattered, was sure that D'Artagnan met with equally blank expressions from Aramis and Porthos.

D'Artagnan sighed. "Like this," he said. "If this woman was murdered for some reason that has nothing to do with the King or the security of France, we're doing her a disservice by hiding her body. It might be some time before her murder is revealed to the guard, and even a few hours might allow the murderer to get away."

"But . . ." Athos hesitated, not knowing how to explain it to the youth. "Surely the security of France—"

"Yes," D'Artagnan said impatiently. "Yes, but. There is this woman too. If she's neither the Queen, nor murdered because she looks like the Queen, then we should let the law catch her murderer. If we don't, we're wronging this woman." He gestured broadly toward the corpse.

"Oh," Athos said, understanding it. Into his mind crept the memory of another unavenged murder—a Countess of France left swinging from a low branch in the forest, her murderer unpunished. "Oh," he said. "I think I see your meaning. If we hide this body, we're committing ourselves to solving this murder, whoever the victim is."

He looked around at Aramis and Porthos. "Do you understand?"

Surprisingly Porthos nodded, one second before Aramis.

He swallowed audibly. "It would be damnable," he said. "To leave this woman's murderer free and unpunished."

"Yes," Aramis said.

"Yes," Athos said, wondering if her ghost would join the other by his bed in the middle of the night. "Assuredly, D'Artagnan. You have the right of it. We will investigate this murder, no matter who the victim is."

"Or the murderer," Porthos said.

Athos looked toward him, wondering what was in his friend's mind. But Porthos's blue-gray eyes were unreadable. Athos inclined his head. A half nod. "Or the murderer," he said.

Before he quite knew what he was about, he pulled his sword out and extended it over the corpse. A salute of sorts.

The Gascon seemed to understand what Athos was doing and pulled out his sword too, holding it so that the tip just touched Athos's. Aramis was next. And finally, Porthos.

"On our honor as gentlemen and musketeers," Athos said. "We will find this woman's murderer. Whether the woman be a Queen or a beggar, we will see justice done," he said.

"One for all," Aramis said.

"And all for one," the others completed in a chorus.

A Musketeer's Servant; The Many
Guises of a Seamstress; A Little Desecration
in the Proper Place

ARAMIS sheathed his sword. He wasn't sure why they'd done that, but he was the first one to admit that Man—a fallen and fallible creature—often had need of ritual to steel his weak self to great decisions.

Look how even God had condescended to create ritual with which mere mortals could worship him. Surely it wasn't because God needed the ritual, but because humans needed it.

Aramis knew better than to give voice to these thoughts. He knew that his friends would just stand astounded looking at him. Or worse, Porthos would laugh and Athos would let that little ironical smile—more insulting than any laughter—slide across his lips. As for the boy, Aramis wasn't sure. But Gascons had a reputation that preceded them, and it was neither for piousness nor for quietly listening to pieties.

The problem was that no one, save his servant, Bazin, believed Aramis was sincere in his devotion and anxious for the day when he could lay his sword aside and take on the habit.

"I'll go for Bazin, then," Aramis told Athos, keeping his voice even and soft. His mother had told him early on that a good cleric never lets his voice rise and fall with his emotions.

Shouting displeased God and scared the faithful. And besides, Aramis had found that women preferred soft-spoken men. Although he doubted his mother meant to teach him the best way to attract women, considering his own father had died in an affair of honor when a lady's inconvenient husband had surprised him in showing the new court dances to the lady.

Aramis shook the thought from his mind. "And I'll come back here, so I'll be with you when my friend arrives to collect the body."

"We'll wait," Athos said. "And keep guard and scare away anyone who might see the resemblance."

D'Artagnan picked up the hat from the ground, and gently set it over the corpse's face. He looked up and flashed Aramis a smile. "No one will mind," he said. "If musketeers keep watch over a dead musketeer. Probably a duel, you know, or an accident."

Aramis nodded. He would have to watch the boy. Until now, he'd been the only one in his group of friends capable of cunning or willing to employ deception. Athos disdained it and Porthos couldn't understand it.

But this Gascon bore watching. He was young, yet, and it was sometimes hard to tell from the seed what the fruit would be. Yet Porthos and Athos had accepted him, and both Porthos and Athos were good at accessing character.

Aramis turned and walked down the narrow alley to the left, and then down another, southward and under an arch, where two houses, on each side of the street, had become one by linking to each other with a little enclosed corridor-bridge.

Down three houses to his own austere residence, where he lived as quietly and spartanly as the monk he hoped to become.

Up two flights of stairs, he opened the door. And was greeted by the steady drone of the rosary being muttered just under one's breath. Beads clicked. The only light burning was a tiny candle at the foot of a vast, ornate iron crucifix that took up most of the wall of the narrow entranceway.

At the foot of the cross, kneeling on a padded knee rest that, like the crucifix, had belonged to Aramis's mother, was Aramis's servant, Bazin.

Bazin had been born into the household of Aramis's father, and had, from early childhood, showed the kind of easy and unquestioning piety that Aramis envied. When Madame D'Herblay, Aramis's widowed mother, had decided that her two-year-old son would go into the church, Bazin had been overjoyed. He had immediately attached himself as personal servant to the young man, ten years his junior, and vowed to go along and become a lay brother in whatever order the Chevalier D'Herblay graced with his vows.

Now, twenty years later, Bazin outweighed his youthful master two to one. He wasn't so much fat as spherical—a short man as broad as he was tall. He had, in fact, the ideal build for a monk. And his hair had started falling out in such a way that it gave the impression of a tonsure.

Disappointed with the sudden change in their fortunes, shocked at the affair of honor that had chased Aramis from his novitiate and into a musketeer's uniform, Bazin refused to admit he was now the servant of a musketeer. He dressed all in black, spoke in a small voice well suited to monastery halls and spent most of his time on his knees, praying.

Aramis suspected that Bazin, still clinking his beads and whispering frantically the words of the Ave Maria, was either praying for his master to have a change of heart and finally return to his vocation, or for God to forgive Aramis his many sins.

Probably both.

"Oh, Bazin," Aramis said.

The beads clinked more ferociously and the whispering became slightly louder.

"Bazin, I have need of you," Aramis said, this time more firmly as he closed the door behind himself.

The beads fell, with a clinking sound, and Bazin turned around, crossing himself as he did. "You're not wounded, are you?" he asked, as he stared at his master, widening his eyes to see more clearly by the light of the small candle.

Aramis reached for the candle at the foot of the crucifix. He removed the glass that shielded the lantern on the wall and lit the wick. Then he replaced the glass, blew out the candle and set it back down.

Bazin blinked in the sudden light, like a mouse coming out of a dark hole into the noonday sun. "Monsieur—" he started.

"No," Aramis said. "Listen. I'm not wounded, nor is either of my friends wounded, if you were going to ask."

"Them? I don't care about them. Sinners all, leading you astray. The Bible says—"

"Yes, Bazin, I know the Testament quite as well as you do. But right now I need your help. I need you to go to Father Bellamie and ask him to come with his wheelbarrow. There is a body for him to take care of."

Bazin crossed himself again. His mouth normally was small and puckered anyway, now puckered further, into an expression of extreme displeasure. "You killed your opponent at the duel today." He opened his hands, palms up, then clasped them together theatrically. "I knew it. And it will be some provincial lord whose relatives will make a lot of noise, and it will be years—years yet—before any decent order will take you."

Aramis shook his head. His irreverent mind insisted on asking what Bazin disapproved of the most in his imagined scenario. Was it the fact that Aramis would have tainted his soul with yet another killing? Or merely the fact that this inconvenient killing would delay their entrance into orders?

"I did not kill the person who's dead and in fact I'd never met . . . um . . . the person. It is a matter of some secret and—"

"The person," Bazin echoed disdainfully. "The person." He raised his hands to heaven. "Don't you think I know if it were a man you'd say so? Clearly, it's a woman who's dead." Bazin raised his hands to his head. "It was some woman who killed herself for love of you, wasn't it? Oh, the women you've condemned to eternal—"

"None that I know of," Aramis said hurriedly. And that was true. His abominable sin of lust, which he couldn't seem to control, might have stained souls, but not with the sin of self-murder. His mistresses usually continued to love him long after he'd tired of them, but not one of them had been so foolish as to kill herself. "And look, I truly don't know this woman. Bazin, this is a matter of the highest secrecy, a matter on which the fate of nations might hang. So, not a word. Not one word. Tell Ettiene Bellamie only that there's a corpse for him to pick up and we'll tell him the rest when he arrives. As much as he needs to know. Tell him to meet me and my friends where the Street of St. Antoine meets St. Catherine Alley. If he's at the crossroads and looks around, he'll see us easily enough. We're three doors down from The Pistol."

Bazin opened his mouth once or twice. Bazin's abiding sin was his love of scolding, as though his piousness liked best to display itself against the background of others' sins. But this time, even he couldn't make too much reply. He bowed once, and let the stiff way he held himself serve to reproach Aramis.

And then he turned and headed out the door, closing it behind him and leaving Aramis alone in his rooms.

Aramis crossed quickly through Bazin's room—a spare cell, bare of all save a thin mattress and the blanket on the floor, a wooden cross on the wall and a suit hanging from a peg on the wall—and entered his own, which was little different save that his mattress was set upon a very spare wooden frame and that, instead of the peg on the wall, Aramis had a wardrobe filled with his fifteen or sixteen spare breeches, tunics, cloaks and doublets. Also, he had a narrow desk, at which he worked at his Biblical study and his correspondence.

From a secret place at the bottom of his wardrobe, a compartment he was sure that even Bazin hadn't found, he retrieved blue linen paper of the best quality, quite different from the white paper he used for his everyday correspondence.

The top of the page was graced by Aramis's coat of arms, which he'd relinquished when he'd become a musketeer and taken on the name of Aramis.

He picked up the ink and the quill from his desk, and wrote quickly, in the hand of one trained to the church from childhood. *Madam, a matter of the greatest importance requires that I visit you tonight. Could you make the usual arrangements?* He signed it Aramis, though this woman knew his true name.

She was no passing lust and he knew not how to rid himself of the spell she cast over his body, heart and soul. He could not enter an order while his whole being was permeated by desire for her.

She was just older enough than Aramis for him to be interesting, exotic and seductive to her. And just young enough to still look like a woman in the prime of her life. Her hair was as golden blond as his own, and her eyes just as sparkling blue.

Were it not for the inconvenient matters of a husband and a high-born title, which she had and he lacked, they would have made a very pretty couple. But she had her duty and he had . . . the church.

Aramis sighed heavily, as he swung out of his door and ran down the two flights of stairs to the front hall of the house. There were two doors there; one led to the stairs and to his own apartment and the other, to the right, led to the bottom floor where the landlord's family lived.

Aramis knocked on the latter door with perhaps more force than could be expected of an apprentice priest, even one turned musketeer.

The response was surprisingly fast, as if they always listened for him. Which they might well do. Aramis had some vague idea that the family was happy to have him living with them. He was a musketeer and therefore he kept them safe. And he would one day be a priest or monk, so he certainly wouldn't dally with their two very pretty teenage daughters.

The youngest of whom, Yolande, now opened the door. The girl was maybe seventeen, and wore her chestnut-brown hair free over a threadbare white nightshirt just worn through enough to allow a glimpse of her pink flesh beneath.

Aramis felt his knees go weak and bucked up against the demon of lust, as he looked at the girl's steadily redder face and said, "Yolande, please, if you'd call your brother."

Yolande curtseyed and went inside. Her brother, Pierre, came out shortly, fully dressed except that he was still fastening his ratty red velvet doublet.

Even if Aramis had not had a vocation and wasn't keeping his eyes steady on the prize of ordination, Pierre would have made an excellent argument against Aramis's having any amorous intents toward the landlord's daughters.

Pierre was shorter than Porthos. Also, smaller. But Porthos was probably the only person who could claim that distinction.

Broad of shoulder with huge arms and legs like columns,

Pierre towered over Aramis by a good head. He wore a red velvet jacket and bright blue breeches, which went very well with the gold hoop in his ear, but quite badly with his blunt features, greasy black hair and droopy moustache. The scent of spices and sweat rolled off him, as he lowered his head toward Aramis and said, "Yes?"

"I would like you to run an errand for me, Pierre."

"What?" Pierre asked. "The usual?"

"The usual. If you'd take my note to the royal palace and ask for Monsieur LaPlace of the royal guards. He will take the letter where it belongs."

Pierre blinked. One of the reasons Pierre was so eminently suitable to this duty was that he could not read. The mysteries of letters, the idea of words written upon the paper, remained closed books to the brave Pierre. More, he would probably be afraid that if he learned or tried to decipher the writing, he would become instantly emasculated. Aramis had long ago told him these letters were to a seamstress to whom Aramis gave spiritual advice.

"I find it odd," he said, "that a seamstress lives in the palace. And even odder that she would need spiritual advice at this hour."

Aramis sighed and smiled, the ineffable smile of a saint who can divine the mysteries of heaven. "Yes," he said. "But you're not instructed in religion. A crisis of faith can happen at any time."

Pierre looked at Aramis and raised an eyebrow, but then, probably remembering the reputation of the musketeers, he shrugged his massive shoulders and said, "I'll do it."

Aramis obligingly handed over the small silver coin that was Pierre's usual fee for this service.

And then he returned to St. Catherine Alley as fast as his feet would carry him. Just in time. Father Bellamie had arrived with his wagon and looked a little puzzled, finding only two unknown musketeers, a bellicose-looking young man and a corpse.

At Aramis's arrival, the priest turned to him with an expression of relief. "Ah, monsieur, I'm glad you're here. I was afraid I had the wrong place altogether."

Aramis glanced at the corpse and almost asked how it could be the wrong place when there was a corpse right there. But then he remembered that corpses would be quite usual in this priest's life, since he made it his duty to care for all the anonymous corpses in Paris. And often paid for burial out of his own pocket if no family claimed the body.

It was an odd vocation, and yet Aramis felt a sudden stab of envy. He would have liked to be engaged in that kind of work, doing good with no doubts and none of the tormenting demons of lust.

Bazin appeared behind the little priest. They couldn't be more of a study in contrasts. Where Bazin was rotund, the little priest was thin to the point of looking ill. Where Bazin's face was red and florid and—right then—covered in perspiration, the little priest was wax-yellow, had only a few hairs clinging to the top of his scalp and seemed quite un-tired by his journey. He now looked at the corpse and crossed himself. "The poor thing," he said. "A musketeer?"

Athos nodded. His look cautioned all the others against saying anything else.

Aramis said, "Bazin, that will be all. You may return to my lodgings and resume your devotions. I know you hate your prayers to be interrupted."

Bazin bowed. His mouth twitched, as though he longed to protest, but he couldn't quite bring himself to say anything. He walked away as slowly as possible.

He was the greatest gossip alive but gossiping was a sin, and Bazin would never admit to sinful impulses. And it befit Aramis, a caring master, to keep Bazin from corrupting his soul.

Porthos and Athos set the corpse in the wheelbarrow with such care that even if it jostled, the hat would not fall off the face.

The priest put his arms to the posts of the wheelbarrow and started to lift.

"Father, I'll do that," Porthos said.

The priest looked myopically at Porthos, as if the very large musketeer had appeared out of nowhere. "Bless you, son," he said. "Very kind of you."

He stepped aside and let the giant push the wheelbarrow while he walked alongside.

"I live just up ten blocks and to the left," he said. "Beside the Church of St. Peter the Fisherman."

Porthos nodded as if he knew the way.

Aramis doubted it. It would be more Porthos's style to attend mass at a cathedral, where he could see the great ones of the land and be seen and admired by them. Of course, perhaps some maid, some laundress, some seamstress Porthos was courting attended mass at the Fisherman's.

Though Porthos often bragged about bedding with duchesses and being disputed over by princesses, Aramis was sure that his friend's lovers lived lower in the order of society. Principally because those who truly had lovers at the highest levels didn't ever, ever, talk about them. Powerful husbands had powerful henchmen. Why risk one's life for bragging rights?

They walked a while in silence, and then the priest spoke. "This . . . body, it is not of your making, is it?"

"No," Aramis said firmly.

The priest nodded. "Good. You know what the Lord says about those who live by the sword."

"Yes, Father," the four of them said automatically.

Aramis wondered if it was true. For years now, he'd fought and dueled. Ever since an enraged husband had found him explaining the lives of the saints to his wife and challenged Aramis to a duel; ever since Aramis had taken lessons from Porthos and learned enough to kill the man—ever since he'd taken a musketeer's uniform to escape the consequences of what the law would view as a crime—he'd been living a violent life.

Just this morning, he'd been ready to kill D'Artagnan because the man had been stupid about picking up a monogrammed handkerchief and giving it back to Aramis.

Did that mean Aramis would one day die by the sword?

Soon they arrived at the tiny church, the sort of church where the poor people in Paris worshipped. It was small and dank, and whitewashed, with a little tower that didn't climb any higher than two floors.

However, Aramis, touched by the true devotion of the priest, had often come to rosary or mass here, and he knew how the thin, reedy tolling of the bell in that tower called everyone from the hovels and narrow rental rooms hereabout.

Shoemakers and apprentices, printers and lace makers

and embroiderers. They packed the pews and bowed their heads to the tiny priest's words.

The priest turned sharply to the house to the left of the church, and motioned for them to help him carry the corpse down a narrow flight of stairs to a basement.

Porthos and Athos accommodated his request and carried the girl's body down, the hat still over her face.

The priest opened the door and lit an oil lamp, whose light revealed a large, square space where a bank of coffins stood arrayed against the wall.

"There's one there they fished from the Seine," he said, speaking conversationally, as a man might discuss his neighbors. "I might have to pay for that burial myself. Even if the poor man's relatives are looking for him, they'll never recognize him after what the water has done to him."

A smell of must and spoiled meat stung Aramis's nostrils as he hastened forward. The sooner they got the body into a coffin, the sooner they could be out of here.

"That coffin there is empty," the priest said, pointing to a coffin a little ways away from the others. It was a simple pine box.

Aramis opened the coffin, D'Artagnan helping him.

The other two laid the corpse within it, the hat still over her face.

The priest crossed himself. "I notice you keep the face covered," he said. "Is there some great treason here?"

Aramis felt a warm tide of blood climb up his cheeks. "There might be," he said. "It is something we cannot tell."

The priest looked as if about to admonish them. But D'Artagnan hastened forward. "Could you leave us alone a moment?" he asked, taking the lantern from the priest's fingers. "There is something we must do."

"You can't—" the priest started

"That is abominably rude, D'Artagnan," Aramis said.

"No, listen," D'Artagnan said. "No disrespect for either you or the dead is intended, but we haven't searched the corpse yet."

"You can't mean to rob from the dead," the priest and Athos said, in perfect unison.

D'Artagnan shook his head. "No. Only—" To the priest, "We also don't know who this is. There might be something on the corpse—a note, a letter—that might allow us to find his relatives."

The priest raised his head as if to nod but looked doubtful.

"However, we think he might have been killed as the result of some treason," D'Artagnan said. "We don't know for sure, but we don't want to expose you to any trouble, if there is trouble. So we'd rather do this alone."

The priest stared at D'Artagnan a while, then crossed himself. "Well, I'll trust you, my son. May the Lord illuminate your judgment."

As soon as the priest had closed the door behind himself, Athos said, "I must agree with the priest. This is not decent. We cannot search the body."

"Even if it means it's the only way we find the murderer?" Aramis asked.

"Not you too, Aramis. I thought you were pious," Athos said.

"Pious but not stupid. Let's suppose—just suppose—this is not the . . . not Anne. Then who can it be? We'll only discover that through a distinctive piece of jewelry, a note, something that tells us who she is."

Athos stared at Aramis. Aramis held his head up, staring back into his friend's stern gaze. Truth was, Aramis knew he often allowed servants and people like Pierre to talk back to him and to carry on as if they were his peers. The same people would never dare raise their voices to Athos, who could silence them with a single look of disdain. And they would be in mortal fear of Porthos's size and girth.

But they would talk back to the mild-mannered future-priest. And Aramis allowed them to. Life was too short to impose discipline and demand respect from people who did not matter to you.

However, in things that mattered, Aramis knew he could scare even Athos. He now engaged in scaring Athos—by staring back at him steadily and allowing his features to harden, expressionless. "I know it's right, Athos. I know it's moral. It is stupid to swear to find this girl's murderer and then not to follow through."

Athos sighed. He groaned, a groan of defeat. He stepped back and took the lantern. "Fine, but be quick about it, and no disrespect."

Aramis was not absolutely sure what Athos meant by disrespect. Did Athos think Aramis's lustful blood burned so fiercely that he would nurture an interest in even a dead woman?

He knelt and started going through the places where someone might hide possessions—inside the boots, within the sleeve of the uniform. D'Artagnan knelt opposite him and lifted the corpse now this way, now that, making it easier for Aramis to search.

Aramis flashed the young man a smile, which helped distract him from the grim task at hand. He'd never touched a dead woman before and the cooling flesh felt unpleasant to his hands. It reminded him all too clearly of the end to which all of them were hastening, even Aramis and his fair seamstress.

Around the neck of the corpse, he found two things—a chain and a leather strap.

Undoing both of them, he brought forth first a gold chain, from which hung the medal of a saint. Saints coined into the face of a medal looked all alike. The profile looked like a man's and there might be a halo, but Aramis could not be sure. Tilting the medal to catch the light of the lantern Athos held, Aramis read the inscription. "St. Jerome Emiliani," he said. "An Italian Saint."

"Does this mean she's Italian?" Porthos asked.

"I don't know what it means yet," Aramis said. "I can't remember where I've heard the name. I'll have to ask someone."

"And this," he said. Lifting the leather strap, he pulled out the purse that hung from it. It was almost empty, but he poured its contents out onto his hand.

There were two things inside—a letter, which he passed to D'Artagnan—and a small braided silver ring with a pinkish stone, an inconsequential bauble that would only fit the finger of a child or a very small woman. Even this girl's fingers were too thick for it.

He showed it to the others. They shook their heads. It seemed to Aramis that Athos hesitated a moment, but Athos was over thirty years old and perhaps his vision was not so keen as to discern the jewel in the semi-gloom. It didn't bear questioning Athos, who would take offense at being doubted.

Aramis slipped the jewel into his own pocket. "It might be of use in finding who she is," he said, at Athos's indignant glare. And added, "We'll return it to her family as soon as we know who they are."

Meanwhile, D'Artagnan had opened the letter and looked puzzled. "It seems to be in a foreign language, only neither Spanish nor English, as I know some of both." He unfolded the letter and showed it to Athos. "But this I can't make sense of at all."

Athos glanced over. "That's because it's in cipher, D'Artagnan. Meant to say something that only those who know the cipher can read."

"Well," D'Artagnan said. "How in damnation are we to decipher it?"

Porthos's huge hand shot out of nowhere and grabbed at the paper. "I know a duchess," he said, putting the folded paper in his sleeve. "Whose secretary is most wondrous with ciphers. I'll take it there now and it will be solved."

"Now?" Athos asked. "In the middle of the night?"

Porthos shrugged. "She's mad about me. She'll see me at any time."

"But . . ." Athos said. "We are in the midst of an affair that could maybe plunge our country into war. Who knows what conspiracy we've been caught up in? Who knows who might be following us? Porthos, it would be madness for you to go alone. I shall go with you."

"But . . ." Porthos said.

Athos smiled, his superior smile. "Ah, Porthos, you know I'm the soul of discretion."

Aramis felt uncomfortable. He cleared his throat. What Athos said was true. Aramis should not go to the royal palace without someone to watch his back.

If he had to have company, he would have chosen Athos. Who else could he ask?

He cleared his throat again. "I meant to go see a seamstress I know," he said. "Who probably can tell us whether the Queen is alive or dead."

"A seamstress?" Athos asked, with his cursed ironical smile. "Who knows the Queen?"

"She often works for the Queen," Aramis said but felt himself blush. "She lives at the palace."

"Would this be," Porthos asked, "the same seamstress who writes on perfumed violet paper and seals her letters with a ducal crown?"

Aramis shrugged, telling himself that with such friends he truly didn't need enemies. Nonetheless, D'Artagnan's wide-eyed, amazed look made Aramis smile. Ah, the boy had a lot to learn about life in Paris.

"Look, she knows the Queen," Aramis said. "Personally. It will remove one of our doubts, at least. But I meant to ask Athos to come with me. If he's going with you, Porthos, we won't be able to check with the seamstress till tomorrow."

"Take D'Artagnan," Athos said.

Aramis looked doubtfully at the young man so recently arrived from Pau or Bearn or some other godforsaken town in Gascony, which was, of itself, godforsaken. He was dark and silent, with little fashion sense and those disturbingly keen dark eyes.

"I too," the young man said, "can be discreet. And silent as the tomb."

For a moment Aramis hesitated but, after all, the young man needed watching. And who better to watch him than Aramis, who understood cunning and its workings?

He nodded. "Fine, you may come with me. But keep your eyes open and your mouth closed."

The young man smiled, a smile disturbingly like Athos's.

As they set the coffin lid back on, Porthos said, "We should find out where she got that uniform."

"Good idea, Porthos. We'll find out among our comrades."

And with that, they sealed the coffin and left, up the narrow stairs, where they found the priest waiting in his garden.

"Please, Father," Athos said. "There might be treason in this case and there might be danger if anyone else knows this corpse is here. I beg you not to show it to anyone. Even if someone comes looking for a dead musketeer."

"But—" Father Bellamie said.

"Please, Father, trust us," Aramis said. "On my faith we're only trying to find out who killed this person and return the body to the family."

The priest looked long and hard at Aramis then, as if having read truth in the musketeer's gaze, and nodded. "I will keep silent for now and show him to no one. And what you're doing is for good," the priest said. "May God help you."

They bowed their heads as if for a blessing, and left, Athos and Porthos to the north, Aramis and D'Artagnan to the south, headed toward the royal palace and a seamstress who called the Queen her sister.

How One Ascends the Bedchamber of a Disguised Duchess; Where Two Musketeers Might Be Too Much of a Good Thing; A Woman of Judgment

PORTHOS started off on his way with a great sigh. He did not like this at all. First of all, he didn't like the deception, the hiding of the death and that corpse—whether the Queen or commoner—hidden away in a cellar while the four of them, alone, knew of the murder.

Porthos knew, had always known, that his mind worked differently from that of his friends, from that of most people.

As far as Porthos could understand, it seemed to him other peoples' minds were full of words that echoed and resounded in there. And from being close friends with Athos and Aramis these last five years, he'd come to believe it was very easy to fool yourself with your own words. Look at Aramis, who kept saying he wanted to be a priest while dueling and seducing every woman that crossed his path. Look at Athos, with his silences, his sudden furies. It was as if a beast lived beneath Athos's polished, cultivated exterior and only Athos's words and thoughts, reading and quotations, kept it caged.

Porthos's thoughts, on the other hand, were in images and feelings, in sounds and smells, connected only by the thinnest of word bridges.

It didn't leave him much to hide behind, nor much to convince himself that the corpse of that girl in the alley needed to be hid.

He kept seeing her lying in blood and mud, and wondering if she were the Queen. He knew, he just *knew*—as surely as the sun rose in the morning—that the four of them were insufficient to solve this murder if this were truly the Queen of France.

He gritted his teeth and let his feet stomp on the ground.

Athos, by his side, pretended not to notice.

And of course that was the other problem: that Athos was by his side.

For years now, Porthos had bragged of his duchesses, his princesses, his countesses. He knew those were lies, but it had seemed so inoffensive.

Devil take it all, what else was he to do, when Athos was so noble that, with a toss of the head, a step forward, he could make kings look like pot boys? When Aramis, delicate and hesitant and claiming to be destined for the church, was pursued by women of the highest nobility?

What was left to Porthos, if he wanted to fit in, but to wrap himself in gold and brocade and to claim conquests amid the court?

Truth was—and he didn't understand it—when he stood before his mirror and contemplated his broad shoulders, his muscular arms and legs, his coppery hair, he could not understand why the crowned heads didn't swoon over him. But if he had to admit it, he also didn't swoon over them. Their talk of lace and gowns, their petty envies and giggling gossip made him impatient. The few times he'd attracted the attention of one of them and kept it, he'd found himself sighing with impatience and wishing he was on the field of honor, plying his sword, or out riding freely upon his horse, or yet eating a good meal.

But then there was Athenais Coquenard . . . and Athenais . . . Well, she was different. Not a princess or a duchess or anyone Porthos could brag about. A mere solicitor's wife, she might be, yet she could talk of things that interested a man. And she liked to hear Porthos's stories of his exploits at battle and duel—and never failed to make some shrewd observation on the circumstances.

He sighed again. None of Athenais's qualities made it easier for him to drag Athos through these narrow streets and staircases, to a home that was as far from a palace as it could be. What would Athos think? Athos, whose every word and gesture showed him the best-born of them all? Perhaps Porthos could convince Athos that Athenais's husband's home was not her real abode, but a hideout, a place of rendezvous?

"These duchesses," he started. "Well, as you know, these duchesses, often like to be hidden for their assignations. To find a place where no one will suspect them."

The words fell flat into the silence of the night. By Porthos's side, Athos walked steadily on, without hesitation, and Porthos was sure that if he looked just a little to the side, he would see his friend looking at him with that gaze that was not quite reproach and certainly not disdain but which betrayed that Athos knew. He knew of Athenais's true condition, but, more important, he knew why Porthos felt the need to lie.

Porthos did not turn to look. He heard the leather of Athos's soles creak against the cobblestones. He heard a cricket chirp somewhere from within the walls of a nearby house. The night sky above was dark and punctured with stars. It seemed distant and indifferent to the human beings below, particularly to this man who called himself Porthos.

A wind, blowing from somewhere on the outskirts of town, brought with it the smell of ripe fields and flowers. Porthos expanded his deep chest in breath and thought of another time, of other dark nights and of the young provincial nobleman he'd once been and the plebeian girl with whom he'd fallen in love.

It had damned them both, that love, and yet he wouldn't take it back for all the duchesses and princesses in the world.

And with that, he stopped in the middle of the street and said to himself, "Damn it all."

Athos stopped beside Porthos and looked at him. He did not, as Porthos had feared, appear all-knowing or all-understanding. Instead, the expression in his blue eyes was pure bewilderment, and only the slight upturning of his lip showed that he was more amused than vexed by this.

Startled at seeing Athos openly puzzled, Porthos sought to explain. "Damn it all," he said again. "Is it my fault if princesses and duchesses, countesses and their ilk all bore me to tears?"

Athos's lips contorted upward in what was, in him, the equivalent of a guffaw. "They bore me too," he said, in a flat tone. "When I . . . If I ever seek to marry, I'll look for purity and honesty, not for titles." Then all levity disappeared from his face, and his features became more than ever like those of a marble statue. Looking at the sky, he seemed to have been dead many centuries and memorialized in stone looking blindly upward to the indifferent heavens.

It seemed to Porthos that Athos was quite capable of staying like that forever, and these abstract absences of the mind made Porthos feel even worse than did the giggles of duchesses and princesses. He knew less of Athos's mind than of the behavior of noblewomen, and understood it less. In fact, Athos scared him a little, notwithstanding the qualities of mind Porthos admired, and the great honor he felt in having Athos's friendship.

Porthos cleared his throat and stomped his foot. "Right. Very well then."

Athos shook himself as though waking, and the distant expression vanished from his features, but he did not smile, nor say anything, just resumed walking beside Porthos.

They proceeded in silence, up through gently sloped streets and sudden staircases, to streets slightly larger and a better area of town than the one where they'd left the corpse.

The houses were taller in this area. They rose five stories high and almost obscured the sky above. These had fresh coats of whitewash, and were all inhabited by one family, or one family and its dependents, instead of being hives of ill-assorted couples and individuals and wild-running children, such as those who infested the slums.

Number 31 Rue Aux Ors was much like the other houses on either side. In fact, it seemed to Porthos that it was the aim of these lawyers and clerks to never stand out, to always look exactly like one another. He cocked a dubious eyebrow at the house. He'd never stomach it. If this were his residence, he'd have to paint a red stripe around the middle, or hang cloth of gold on the windows. Anything but being anonymous and dull amid the anonymous and dull. How could Athenais stand it?

He glanced at Athos, who was looking bemused at the house.

"I can't hardly knock at the door at this time of night," Porthos said, under his breath, as though talking to himself.

"I assume you have other means of calling on your . . . ah . . . duchess."

Porthos sighed. Of course he had other means, but all this felt a little strange in front of Athos, who was the soul of probity and honor. Porthos looked at his friend a little under his eyelids, as a dog who spies an opportunity to steal a bone.

Athos's returning look remained impassive and a little amused.

"There is a path," Porthos said. "Between the houses." What he didn't add was that this was what the maids used to access the public fountain down the block and that Porthos had initially stationed himself here to watch them come and go—healthy rosy-cheeked wenches being a pleasure just to watch. Their mistress, alerted by the giggling girls to the presence of the musketeer, had come to scold them, and stayed to talk. And though Athenais was neither rosy nor young, her sharp mind had kept him guessing until the pursuit itself made the object of it beguiling.

Porthos sighed. Perhaps he'd spoken too hastily when he's volunteered Athenais Coquenard's clerk, Planchet, as an expert in cyphers. Oh, the boy was that, and more. Porthos had often heard Athenais describe how he could both solve intercepted coded messages from other attorneys and create the most complex ciphers in the blink of an eye. But how would Athenais react to being awakened in the middle of the night? And how would Athos—who disdained even the noblest-born women—react to Athenais?

Nothing for it but to step into the narrow alley, with mire underfoot and their vision obscured by tall walls too close together on either side. Their boots squelched in mud and household refuse.

Porthos ran his hand against the wall, at shoulder level— below that and he'd risk finding it wet from the many gentlemen who used this secluded spot as a public lavatory.

During daylight and in full sun, the alley was dim. Now, it was pitch-black. He did not trust his memory to lead him to the right gate. Instead, he followed his fingers, along the rough stone, till the stone changed to wood.

"Ah!" he said, pleased to have found it. It seemed to him

that he could never be sure nighttime reality would match daytime remembrance, so he had to trust his touch to guide him. His fingers fumbled for the catch, his heart speeding up a little.

Hopefully it wasn't locked. Hopefully . . . It had been at least a month since he'd tried it, at least a month since he sought Athenais. Not that he thought less of her, but a man had other concerns—duels and gambling and following Athos and Aramis in intrigues that Porthos barely understood all over town. After all, a man owed loyalty to his friends. A soldier, moreso.

But women . . . He sighed again. Women were what they were, and Athenais might very well have taken it into her head to lock this back gate. To show to him she didn't need him any more than he needed her.

Just as he thought all was lost, his fumbling fingers found the secret spring that made the catch fly open on the other side.

He let his breath out in relief and pushed at the gate, slowly, slowly. If pushed too hard the metal was capable of letting out a sound that would make any cockerel jealous.

When the gate had opened enough to let him through, Porthos looked over his shoulder. Athos's face was a mere white oval in the gloom.

"Come," Porthos whispered to his friend, and crept into the garden. Where the sudden light of the moon falling on the relatively open space looked like the illumination for a ball—like torches and burning lamps.

Porthos blinked at the white harshness of it and made for cover under the orange trees that surrounded the garden, just inside the wall. That way, he went around the house circling a space planted in neat plots of vegetables and herbs, when no space allowed for more than a wild flower here and there. He came to the other side, where he counted windows, to find Athenais's in the middle.

Normally, when he came here, there was a light burning at that window. A small, hesitant light, but enough to tell him that she was awake, she was within, she waited for him.

But when he'd come here before, there had been a meeting at church, a sign and countersign, and something to let Athenais know that he'd be visiting. Now . . .

Porthos picked up a handful of gravel, and threw it, gently, at the window. That is to say, he threw it as gently as his huge hand could. The pebbles fell like hail upon the glass, the wall and everywhere around.

Quite a number of them rattled off the broad brim of Porthos's hat, causing him to take cover. When he looked up again, both Athenais's window and that next to hers showed faint, wavering lights. From the other one came a reedy, complaining voice, perhaps talking about storms or possibly robbers. Monsieur Coquenard, the attorney.

Porthos grabbed for Athos's arm and pulled his friend under the shade of the trees. Presently, the window next to Athenais opened, and Athenais's blond head appeared, beside her husband—a balding, trembling wreck of a man.

"You see, my dear," she said, as she looked down. "There are no robbers and no hail. You dreamed it all."

"I did not dream. There were taps at my window."

"My dear, perhaps the wind carried some pebbles."

It seemed to Porthos that Athenais looked down and saw him. He could barely see her features, yet he felt as though the physical weight from her gaze rested on him. His heart hammered and he ducked further into the shade, pulling his hat down to cover his face. What if Athenais was sleeping with her husband? Spending the night with him? Impossible. The man had to be well over seventy. But what if she was?

He had just swallowed a lump at his throat, which was composed of jealousy and fear and he didn't know what else, when the light went out in the attorney's window.

After what seemed like an interminable interval, Athenais's window creaked open and she looked down from it. Porthos hurried to stand in the moonlight. He swept off his hat at her.

Athenais tilted her head sideways. He saw her blond locks sway but could not read the expression on her face. Yet, he didn't need to see it to know she was pursing her lips and deciding whether to let him up, after his monthlong absence.

He clasped his hands over his chest, hat and all, hoping she understood his undying love for her. Discussing things out here was not sensible, particularly as it would require him to speak loudly to be heard above, and as her husband was probably not asleep yet.

After what seemed like an eternity, Athenais moved, and the welcome rattle of the ladder sounded as it was let down from her window. It was a cunning construction, all of chain and rope and wood, so ably designed it took even Porthos's weight without buckling. She had once told him that it was similar to what sailors used at sea.

He slapped his hat on his head so as to leave both hands free for climbing, and clambered up the ladder more eagerly than any sailor headed for the crow's nest.

Closer and closer, he could see Athenais's fair face—perhaps a little sharp and spare when compared to her rosy-cheeked maids, but not unlike some ancient statues in a ruined temple in the estate where Porthos had grown up. Porthos's mother had once told him that these were statues of Athena, whom the Greeks had worshipped for her wisdom and, indeed, Porthos believed Athenais was named after that divinity by her father, a minor nobleman fond of antiquities. And she was appropriately named. For though her features might be sharp, her cheekbones prominent, though her lips were more straight than the curved bow that in youth promised Cupid in every kiss, her dark gray eyes showed understanding and wisdom beyond what Porthos ever had seen in any man and woman.

Or at least, they normally did. Now they looked doubtfully at him, as he reached the top of the ladder, as though not sure she should let him in or slam the shutter in his face.

Then they widened in shock as she looked over Porthos's shoulder.

Porthos turned his head and looked down. Athos was at the bottom of the ladder—invisible except for the broad rounded hat of a musketeer and the uniform beneath—and reaching for the ladder.

Athenais grabbed for the shutter, ready to slam it shut, and Porthos sighed. How could Athos be such a smart man, acquainted with Greek poetry and Roman orators, with the marvels of Persia, the history of the Orient, and so dumb when it came to women? What could he expect but that Athenais would be alarmed to see two musketeers where she expected one? She would think her house become a place of debauch and Porthos her defamer.

He reached for her hand, unsettling himself and making

the ladder rock. He held her hand, her skin warm. "Athenais—" he whispered. "It is not what you think."

And that was enough to arrest her movement, to turn her gray eyes to him, expectantly. She knew her lover was slow of tongue, slow to assemble words, but that he did not lie. If he said it was not what she thought, then it was not. This was one of the reasons he prized her over all others, even those rare noblewomen who'd fallen to his lot.

She waited. She stared, eyebrows raised.

"We come . . . we have need to consult you. On a matter of great importance. We . . . are in some danger. Athos is protecting me."

"Protecting you?" she asked, her whisper managing to convey sharp annoyance. "From me?"

Porthos shook his head. The feather of his hat tapped at her window. "It's not like that." He tried to explain, but only managed to shrug and say, "We need to see Planchet."

Athenais frowned. "Planchet?"

Porthos looked down at where Athos was now halfway up the climb, looking up, clearly unaware of having done anything against etiquette, custom and even logic. "Athos," Porthos whispered urgently to Athenais, "doesn't understand women. He doesn't like women much."

And then, seeing Athenais's eyes open wide in shock and her mouth open, to say, "Planchet?"

He realized where her mind had gone, and shook his head. "We have a cipher. A cipher we need solved. And . . . it might be dangerous. We need Planchet to solve it."

Like that, Athenais hesitation disappeared, her shock was gone. She nodded once, and extended her hand to him, to help him in. It was largely ceremonial, as her little hand could never support his much larger weight, but he took her hand nonetheless, and, holding onto the windowsill with his other hand, he vaulted over it and into the room, landing in a surprisingly silent way, the fruit of much assiduous practice at just this maneuver.

Athenais's room was small—a cubicle that contained just her bed and a clothes press upon which rested a candle holder and a lit candle.

It always seemed to Porthos as if there was barely enough space for him in this room. But he always managed to fit.

And the bed didn't creak, a tribute to Athenais's house-keeping.

Now the lady backed into her room to stand beside the clothes press, and Porthos backed with her. Athos vaulted into the room with much too great an ease, landing on his feet like a cat, and pulling in the ladder and closing the window—without needing to be told—as if he too had practiced this maneuver much too often.

He removed his hat and bowed low to Athenais, and Athenais's eyes widened with shock, bringing a quick stab of cold, painful jealousy to Porthos's heart. Athenais was, he judged, just a couple years older than himself. Athos's age. And Athos had his grand-seigneur manner. How could he fail to charm?

In fact, Athos's gaze, sweeping Porthos's lover, didn't show any of the derision or amusement Porthos expected. It lingered on Athenais's eyes and Porthos wished he could be sure it was just noting the fine netting of wrinkles on the corners of her eyes.

"Monsieur Porthos tells me you come on an important mission," Athenais said, speaking in her sharp murmur and managing to imply scrutiny of her was not expected nor would it be tolerated.

Her words and tone were balm to Porthos's heart. And the look of admiration and something else—surprise? envy?—that Athos gave him made him smile a little.

Athos bowed and whispered, "The circumstances are much too involved, the case too perilous to involve a lady such as you, madam."

"I'll judge my own peril. Surely you don't mean to have me involve my husband's clerk in something of uncertain motives and unforeseeable outcomes."

Again, Athos looked surprised, then glanced at Porthos.

In circumstances such as this, and having known and enjoyed the lady for far more than a couple of years, Porthos had learned that evasion and obfuscation did not work. Athenais wanted to know why they came here, and the best thing was to tell her.

"You see, my pigeon," he said and saw her flinch just in time to remember that she did not like that name. "Tonight we found a body. Dressed in a musketeer's uniform. He . . .

it wasn't a he but a she. And she had a ciphered letter on her, which we must solve, if we are to find who killed her."

Athenais frowned. "There is more in this," she said. She glanced at Athos, as though begging him to untie the knot between Porthos's thoughts and words. "Else you'd have called the guard."

Porthos sighed, and was about to explain that the corpse was probably the Queen, but before he could open his mouth, Athos spoke. "It is indeed something, milady, but I hope you won't demand we tell you, but will only be satisfied with knowing that it involves a possible intrigue at court."

As Athenais opened her mouth to speak, Athos bowed. "Milady, please. I beg you that you don't force us to endanger France's security by speaking to you on this. And even if you should promise to be silent as the tomb, there are those who could get you to say anything at all, through means fair or foul."

He straightened and said, "And, Lady, even if you do not mind your own health and safety, mind my friend Porthos's heart. Think how he would suffer without you."

Porthos frowned. He'd never thought of losing Athenais. A soldier's life was an uncertain one, and if he'd thought of one of them dying, it had been himself and not her. But he felt his features fall in unaccustomed gravity when he thought of Athenais dying. Damn it all—he needed her company and the comfort of her being there. Many was the time in duel and battle that he felt better knowing she was at home, going about her daily pursuits.

He realized Athenais was staring at him, as she smiled a little in sympathy with his expression. Did she know what he thought and felt? Was he that transparent?

"I won't," she said. She looked at Athos. "I won't require you to explain further. I understand that if I need to know, you will tell me." She stood there for a minute, in deep thought. The light played on her features, and on the blond hair spilled down her back. It fell in such a way that it softened the fine wrinkles and hid the white threads amid her hair, and made her look like a young angel.

Porthos grabbed her small hand in his huge one and kissed it, and she blushed deep, like a young maid, and lowered her eyelids. She pulled her hand away gently. "Gentlemen," she said. "I will get Planchet, but if all three of you should be discovered in my room, it will be scandal indeed. I will leave first, and then it is up to you to make it down this hallway to the right, and down the next flight of stairs. Downstairs, you'll find another hallway with doors. Take the second doorway to your left. It will take you to one of the store-rooms. Should anyone wake, I'll say you are suppliers of grain and called at an unusual hour, perhaps drunk. And that I called Planchet to avoid waking my husband."

"A capable head," Athos said, and an illusive smile played upon his lips, making Porthos feel very uncomfortable indeed. He bowed to Athenais. "We will follow your instructions."

A Musketeer's Obsession;
In Which One Discusses Queens;
The Ultimate Plan

ARAMIS was not, fortunately, the type of person who mutters to himself. Which, he thought, was very well, all things considered, because if he muttered he would be talking about how Athos had saddled him with the company of this provincial nobody, this creature they'd just barely met, this cipher, who, for all his willingness to face off against the guards, might very well be a spy of the Cardinal.

In fact, Aramis thought—casting a covert look from under those long lashes that so many women admired, at the somber countenance, the sharp features of this strange young man— if D'Artagnan were a spy of the Cardinal, his eminence who was—like his master, the devil—the father of all cunning, would surely have instructed the Gascon to throw his lot in with the musketeers at every turn. In fact, that instruction might be the only thing that justified such a young man, so newly arrived in Paris, casting in with the musketeers whom he had, just seconds before, been ready to engage in a duel.

Aramis realized that the object of his intent study was studying him in turn with a frankly curious look and a vague smile playing upon the corners of his lips. He looked away, quickly, and at the facade of a tall house past which they were walking—a five-story-tall house, every window shuttered against the night and footpads. *Sangre Dieu.* Who knew what a creature like this was thinking? So young, so full of cunning.

Aramis wished that Athos had come with him. He knew

he could trust Athos with his life. Close-mouthed Athos would never reveal anyone's secrets, certainly not the Queen's. Not that Athos was unthinkingly loyal. No. Aramis squinted as though trying to focus his vision, as he ran the problem of his friend's position through his mind.

The fact was, Aramis couldn't understand Athos. He could anticipate Athos—sometimes—and he could persuade Athos—sometimes. But at the back of it all, at the bottom of his friend's actions and character there was a principle he did not quite grasp. For instance, Athos was quite capable of smiling at mockery of the emotional Queen and the incompetent King. When done in private, between the three of them, Athos could find it amusing. He might think Aramis couldn't see the fleeting smile that crossed his lips, but Aramis did, and made note.

But at the same time, he was loyal enough to King and Queen and even to Monsieur de Treville that he would rather—and had often risked—get himself cut into ribbons than disobey the most casual of their orders.

And among the strangeness of Athos's ideas and beliefs, sending this stranger with Aramis to the Palais Royale had to be counted highest. What was Athos thinking? Why would he want D'Artagnan with Aramis on this errand? Was it that Athos had seen or read something in the boy that meant that Aramis's secret, the secret of Aramis's mistress, the Queen's secrets, would all be safe? Or was it because he thought that D'Artagnan was a part of this game and that, by watching and keeping the youth close, Aramis could find out what was behind it all? Or was it simply that Athos accepted the boy at face value and liked him for his intemperate courage?

For all his cunning, Aramis could not decipher this puzzle. He walked alongside the youth, making no effort to walk slower so that D'Artagnan, with his much shorter legs, could catch up. D'Artagnan would slowly fall behind, then take three steps at a half run to catch up, but he never complained.

Aramis climbed narrow staircases, walked along alleys, hurrying on a route he knew so well that he could traverse it in the dark, blindfolded, by the smells in his nose, by the feel of the ground under his feet.

Here, the ground was paving stones so old that the alley they now walked had probably, once, been part of those ubiquitous Roman roads that crisscrossed Europe like the tracery of a spiderweb. Oh, the stones had become buried in refuse and dirt, as the inhabitants of the tall houses on either side daily discarded their leftovers and waste into the alley. But Aramis's feet, in thin-soled boots which made it easier to walk quietly through the corridors of the palace, felt the rounded, time-polished surface of the Roman stones beneath it, even as his nostrils smelled the acrid covering.

At the end, the alley turned to another flight of stairs, these ones descending, and he took them, rapidly, hearing D'Artagnan behind him, struggling to keep up.

Jumping to the relatively solid ground of a larger road at the bottom of the stairs—a road large enough to be surrounded by more respectable houses, some of which had a lantern burning in front of their doors, lending a half-light to the scene—Aramis turned to D'Artagnan.

"I would like you to not speak unless you're spoken to," he said.

D'Artagnan looked shocked for just a moment and his fingers strayed toward the pummel of the great pig sticker the boy seemed to believe was a sword; Aramis wondered if the Gascon hothead was about to challenge him to a duel for speaking sharply.

And perhaps that was all that Athos had meant to happen. Perhaps Athos thought that the secret of finding the woman's body had been compromised by having this upstart among them, and simply wanted him dispatched without much trouble.

But no. Aramis must remember that Athos was not himself. He, himself, might create such a convoluted plan. But if Athos thought the boy a danger, he'd have challenged D'Artagnan to a duel himself.

"I know when to speak and when not to," D'Artagnan said. "If you believe I am a fool, you are proving yourself no great judge of men."

Oh, there was an insolent pup. But at least he wasn't challenging Aramis for a duel. "I am sure you know quite well how to behave, Monsieur D'Artagnan, in Bearn or Tabres or Pau. But we're in Paris now, and we're about to go . . ." He pressed his lips together. "We're about to go to a place for which all your learning and all your cunning has not prepared you."

D'Artagnan gave Aramis a sidelong glance and straightened himself up to his full height, which is to say, he now came in just above Aramis's shoulder, his ridiculous, disreputable plumes swinging up at Aramis's eye level. "Let me tell you a story," he said. And continued, despite Aramis's inward groan that was probably quite visible in his lowered eyebrows and outward grimaces. "I am the son of a reputable nobleman who, nonetheless, has such a small holding that it is smaller than the Cemetery of the Holy Innocents in Paris. This holding is honorable because it was won by the strength of his own arm, fighting in the King's musketeers in his youth. However, his older brother inherited a much larger holding, as did all his cousins. When I was very young, my father took me to visit all of that far-flung family. And while you would be right that I was at first so intimidated as to be speechless, I soon got over my embarrassment and, by observing the manners of those around me, found it easy to act as if I had been born to that station." He looked at Aramis with what he no doubt thought was a hard, serious look. "So do not underestimate me, monsieur. Only behave yourself as you would have me behave."

Aramis raised an eyebrow. "Sometimes it might not be seemly for you to act as I do." He thought of Violette's firm flesh, her pale skin, and wondered if he could keep from betraying the depth of their relationship with a touch, a kiss.

D'Artagnan laughed. "If you think . . ." he started, and hesitated.

Not sure how anyone could finish that sentence without being offensive—did he mean *if you think I would avail myself of your mistress*? Or *if you think you're so far above me*? Aramis himself reached toward his sword.

But the boy cackled and said, "If you think I'm too much of a fool not to realize there is a difference between our birth stations and therefore our expected behavior, then you've not read me right, Monsieur Aramis."

And at this, Aramis, feeling guilty about his own hot head, had to move his hand away from his sword and grudgingly concede the boy was no fool. He nodded and lamely added, "Well, guide yourself by my behavior in all things, then, even if you don't imitate it."

And D'Artagnan, for his only answer, bowed slightly, which was the best response that could be expected.

While they talked, they'd walked along the broader street, to an even broader one, so broad in fact that two carriages could pass each other along its length.

Here there were no facades facing the street but rather, tall walls from above which trees and flowers waved in the summer breeze. The houses proper were somewhere, past the greenery and the flowers, so that the people in them would smell nothing but the scents of their gardens and no city noise would disturb them. Here the nobility lived when they wished to be near the court, but were not important enough to get quarters in the royal palace itself. Here lodged the great merchants who lived more opulently than the nobility.

He quickened his pace, hearing D'Artagnan pick up speed behind him.

Another turn and another, and the huge bulk of the royal palace came into view. Aramis wondered how it would seem to D'Artagnan who, almost surely, came from a village with a lower population than that of this large square stone building.

But a look back at the youth failed to reveal any awe in D'Artagnan's features. Curiosity glinted in his black eyes, a desire to probe.

Biting his tongue, cursing Athos, and hoping the boy didn't probe too deeply, Aramis approached the door he normally used, the one at which Violette would have left instructions to admit him.

Indeed, barely within sight of the guard, and just as the young man, one of Monsieur des Essarts's guardsmen, started to lower his halberd, Aramis found himself saluted. "Monsieur," the guard said.

"You have your orders?" Aramis asked.

"Indeed," the guard said. "I have been told by Monsieur LaPlace that you are expected and to tell you to take the little south door."

"Thank you," Aramis said, as he walked past the guard, only to see, out of the corner of his eye, the halberd come down in front of D'Artagnan.

For a moment there was the temptation to leave the boy stranded and to go on with his own business, and never mind. Pretend he didn't see, pretend . . .

But at the back of Aramis's mind, the disquieting thought remained that he didn't fully understand Athos's plan or intention in sending D'Artagnan with him. What if Athos had spoken plain the truth? That they should be careful? That they should go in pairs? What if Aramis got in trouble and there was no one to assist him? What if Athos had read the boy plainly, or in some other way knew the boy was trustworthy?

All of these thoughts went through his mind for what seemed like an eternity, but the halberd had no more than descended in front of D'Artagnan and D'Artagnan had not yet had the chance of registering true surprise, when Aramis turned around. His voice issued from his lips in as smooth a tone as though this internal battle had never taken place.

This much at least, living with his restrained, ever-watching mother had taught him. "He is with me," he said.

"But, monsieur," the guard said. "The lady—"

"I'll explain it to her," Aramis said. "Please let him through. He knows some fine points of Leviticus, which he wishes to debate with her."

The guard raised his eyebrows and looked puzzled. He knew very well that Aramis pretended to be spiritually counseling the duchess, in the same way the musketeers knew they should pretend she was a seamstress. Now he must be wondering what exactly advising her on Leviticus signified.

Before he could hazard a guess, though, D'Artagnan had ducked under the halberd, to stand near Aramis. He gave the guard a bow with Gascon exuberance, then looked at Aramis expectantly.

Well, Aramis had brought him here. Got him into the precincts of the royal palace, so what was Aramis to do now? Of course, if D'Artagnan was an agent of Richelieu, he would have had access anywhere in the royal palace that he might have wanted to go. So, there Aramis hadn't lost anything.

At worst, he would let the Cardinal know what they had found out. As many spies as His Gray Eminence had, he probably knew all already. Sometimes Aramis thought the rats themselves spied for the Cardinal.

He opened the little door to which the guard had directed him. It led into a narrow, evil-smelling passageway, a place used only by servants and tradesmen. Aramis saw D'Artagnan look at him curiously, and tried to rally himself to mentioning that his acquaintance was, after all, only a seamstress and the niece of his theology professor. But somehow he couldn't find his voice. He knew no one who saw Violette could believe her anything but what she was—one of the highest-born women in any land.

They emerged through a small door on the side of a staircase, and Aramis made his way, loping up the stairs two steps at a time and feeling what he knew was a childish satisfaction in listening to D'Artagnan struggle to follow him.

At the top of the stairs, he waited for the young man, though, for there was only one thing worse than going about the royal palace with D'Artagnan, and that was to allow D'Artagnan to explore where he might wish to all alone after having gotten in on Aramis's recognizance.

When the boy caught up with him, out of breath, Aramis started through a back corridor, toward Violette's quarters. It wasn't all that strange for him to be here. For one, musketeers were common at the royal palace. And besides, many people— with varying degrees of grinning behind their hands—knew him for Violette's spiritual advisor. The boy was the only issue. He did not dress as someone who should be in the royal palace, and for this he would be remembered. His clothes, a Spanish doublet short to the waist and stiff, and his breeches, so short they ended above the knee, were a faded russet to which the addition of a lot of lace added only an impression of greater age. He looked like the ghost of fashion past.

He hurried through, hoping no one would cross his path, and he met only with a couple of servants—which was to say, with no one who would speak of meeting him or not to anyone of consequence.

Aramis plunged madly from corridor to corridor until he stopped and knocked on a narrow door upon the wall. He knocked carefully, two knocks, then one, then two again.

From the other side, there came a rustle of fabric, a low whisper of voices.

Violette's maid opened the door. If she hadn't been Violette's maid, and therefore not near a greater splendor, Aramis might well have considered her beautiful enough to merit attention on her own. As it was, he registered that she had golden hair, a pale, clear complexion, high, pointed breasts and that she smiled warmly at him as he walked past.

But his eyes, his attention, his very soul turned to Violette, who lay on a chaise in the middle of the room with a book open on her lap. As he came close, he saw pictures in the book—pictures of gowns and lace.

He drew breath in, staring at her. As always in her presence, he felt his head spin, his knees go unsteady.

Women were Aramis's weakness, as he would be the first to admit. In fact, there were few women so old and so ugly that Aramis couldn't guess or find some trace of beauty in their features or demeanor.

It might be past beauty, faded beauty or maltreated beauty, but if he looked long enough at any woman, Aramis could convince himself that she was as beauteous as an angel.

With Violette, he didn't need to convince himself. Just being in her presence was to be overwhelmed.

She was blond and blue-eyed, but saying so did not describe her. In her case, even poetry comparing her eyes to a cloudless summer sky, her hair to a shimmering, pure golden halo, fell short of the reality.

She looked like an angel captured but briefly in this earthly plane before her nature would, perforce, whisk her up to where she belonged, beside the eternal throne.

Each of her features were more perfect than the features of any fallen creature should be. Put them together and it was hard not to think her supernatural.

Sometimes, in his lonely nights, in his lodging, with only Bazin veiling outside his door, Aramis would wake up bathed in sweat and trembling, having dreamed that she was truly a holy angel and that what they'd done together was the defiling of one of God's own, for which he would burn forever in hell.

Even her smell was heavenly, a scent of roses and lavender that made him feel as though he were in the midst of a delicious and secret garden of which only he knew.

Now her features lit up with pleasure at his arrival and it seemed to Aramis as though the sun had risen to pour into the room, blinding him.

The room itself was a work of art. Aramis remembered being struck speechless the first time he'd been allowed in.

He'd seen palatial rooms, filled with the painted likenesses of gods and nymphs. He'd seen gilded chambers and chambers with marble columns.

But he'd never before quite seen a room like this one, Violette's study and sitting room.

Its walls were covered in blue satin, gathered at regular intervals with a perfect ivory bead as large as Aramis's thumb. This made the walls look wholly made up of small, square satin pillows held up by large, unearthly pearls. The ceiling too continued this motif. At each corner of the room slim, reeded gold columns shone.

The room looked, in fact, like the inside of a jewelry box. And the furnishings looked like jewels, from Violette's gold-and-velvet fainting couch, to the gilded tambourette near it, at which her maid, or lady companion would sit when they read together, to the desk in the corner, covered from top to spindly legs in painted scenes of centaurs and fauns.

And amid it all, Violette shone as the most precious jewel—her satin dress matching the walls, her pearl necklace falling upon her creamy bosom, an echo of the ivory beads on the wall.

She leapt to her feet, grasping her skirt. Her chest, which the dress just barely covered from the nipples down, rose and fell rapidly, in evident alarm. "What is this?" she asked. "What is the meaning of this, Chevalier?"

Aramis realized that Violette was looking behind him at D'Artagnan just in time to halt her words with a sharp, "Madame," before she let his true name slip her lips.

She stopped, but looked at him, her eyes wide, her hand now at her chest as though attempting, by resting on the skin, to halt the disordered beating of the heart within.

"Madame," Aramis repeated, now in a normal tone. "I beg to introduce to you a young man recently arrived from Gascony, whom I have had the honor of aiding in a fight against His Eminence's guards, a fight, moreover, in which we were completely victorious."

Violette frowned slightly and he knew that given a half a chance she would scold him for fighting.

He did not give her that chance. "Monsieur D'Artagnan,"

he said. "I present to you Violette, an accomplished seamstress and the niece of my theology professor."

Violette's eyes widened, and her mouth trembled upward at this introduction. Aramis wondered if the boy would be foolish enough to believe it. Truth be told, it mattered little. Neither was he experienced nor well known enough at court to know her true identity. And Athos and Porthos already suspected that Violette was far more than a seamstress.

If only he could teach her to write her letters in plain paper and not seal them with a ducal crown.

And then perhaps the boy was not totally stupid. At Aramis's words, he'd flourished the hat from his head and flowed to kneel at Violette's feet, reaching a hand for her hand, upon which he deposited a kiss so reverent that she might well have been a holy image.

"I did well," he said. "I did very well in deciding to come to Paris to seek my fortune. A town in which even seamstresses look like angels cannot but bode well for my future."

Violette giggled and looked at Aramis, her gaze just the slightest bit teasing. "I would beware, Chevalier," she said. "You can see you have a rival in flattery here."

"Only the merest truth," D'Artagnan said, standing up again, but still holding his hat.

Which only went to confirm that—as Aramis had initially suspected—the boy bore watching.

Aramis bowed again, in his turn, refusing to follow the bait and proceed to heap more praise on his fair lover's head. Oh, he wanted to. He longed to. In fact, he longed to grasp her in his arms and do far more than that.

Seeing Violette was like suffering from a fever, and he was having all he could do to keep from touching her, seeking cure by feeling the exquisite newly blossomed–rose softness of her skin.

But it could not be helped. There was more important business here, no matter how much his body protested at the very thought. "I have brought Monsieur D'Artagnan with me because after the fight with the guards, we stumbled upon . . ." He remembered the corpse in the alley and realized he would have to tell Violette the whole thing. There was no other way around it, no way he could afford to tell her a half-truth and hope that she would still cooperate with them. And her cooperation was essential, if they were going to identify the woman as the Queen or not as the Queen. "We found a murdered woman in an alley," he said. "A woman wearing a musketeer's uniform."

"A musketeer's uniform?" Violette asked, so far showing nothing but the mildest curiosity. "A woman?"

Aramis nodded. "Violette, when did you last see the Queen?"

"The Queen?" Violette looked surprised. "What can she have to do with this?"

"Please, tell me, when did you see her?"

"An hour ago, or little more," Violette said. "When I received your note. I spent the afternoon with her, reading, and then I retreated to her praying room with her to pray, when I got your note and came here to wait you. And now, will you tell me why?"

Aramis nodded. "Because the corpse we found in the alley looked exactly like Her Majesty. At least as exactly as I can determine, having rarely been nearer her than three arms' length."

"The corpse?" Violette asked. "Like the Queen?"

Aramis nodded. "Are you sure . . . Are you sure the person with whom you spent the afternoon, the person with whom you were praying, was the Queen?"

"I am," Violette said assuredly. Then hesitated. "At least . . . At least that is she looked like the Queen and acted like the Queen, but . . ."

"But?"

"Nothing was said or discussed that a skilled impersonator, perhaps coaxed by you know whom would not know."

Aramis raised his eyebrows. "Would His Em— Would he want to replace the Queen with someone? Why?"

"Who knows why?" Violette said. "Save that he longs to be rid of the Queen so that he can make the King a new marriage according to his new politics, and a ringer in place of my Queen could give him plausible reason for a divorce. In which case the Queen might have been killed to prevent her from finding her way back and showing the other woman for an impostor."

"But that would make no sense," Aramis said. "Because if he had replaced the Queen, he could spirit the real one away to the Bastille and have her hidden there in such a way that not even her jailors would know who they were keeping."

"That is true," Violette said. "But perhaps they tried to take her to the Bastille and she struggled?"

Aramis inclined his head, conceding this could be true, though truth be told, he could not imagine the guards of the Cardinal being so tested by just one frail woman as to have to kill her to prevent her escape. However, it was true that accidents did happen. As it was true that the Queen might have arranged this to meet a lover and that she might never have got to whatever assignation she was hurrying toward and that a common footpad or drunkard had killed her.

"Would the Queen have a reason to be out?" he said, weighing each word carefully so it came out imbued with unspoken meaning but not necessarily full of treasonous innuendo. "Would she have a reason to be about in the dark of night, wearing a musketeer's uniform?"

All of France spoke of the Queen's attraction for Buckingham and of Buckingham's obvious devotion to her. But since the Queen had yet to give the King of France an heir, talk of her meeting another man was treasonous and implied that she might give birth to a bastard. Even in front of fair Violette, Aramis must mind his tongue.

Violette started to shake her head, then sighed. "I can only tell you," she said, "that yesterday Madame received a letter from . . . from England. And it said that she had agreed to meet . . . with him." She looked up, allowing the full molten blue of her gaze to meet Aramis's. "Chevalier, you must understand that whatever you hear in court or on the street about the Queen and . . . this person . . . is the merest calumny. I'm not saying that she's not moved by his handsome appearance or his great devotion to her. What woman wouldn't be? She would need to be made of iron or stone to turn him away empty-handed. And that, the Queen isn't. But she has never allowed him any liberties nor even ever consented to meet with him in secret. He has asked, in the past. And he's been refused in the past.

"So receiving a letter from him talking as if she'd agreed to meet him and he was all too happy to collect his reward left her shaken. She said she wouldn't go, she wouldn't dream of going, and has since spent her time in prayer."

"But then it couldn't be her," Aramis said.

Violette shrugged, causing her breasts to sway most prettily. "A full night and almost a full day have passed since then," she said. "Who knows what she could or could not have done. I do not spend every moment of the day and night with her, though I am among her favorite companions."

"Could she have left the palace? Who could have procured a musketeer's uniform for her?" Aramis asked.

Violette shrugged. "Many people could have done that," she said. "There are many entrances in the palace, many tunnels, many secret passages. She could have left without my knowing, perhaps even with her own agreement, leaving behind a double who looks just like her. What better way," she asked, looking straight ahead and speaking as if she were speaking to herself, "of fooling her guard and escaping for a few moments from this palace that so resembles a prison?"

"Are you telling me," Aramis asked, "that you have no way of telling whether the person whom you saw an hour ago was the Queen?"

Violette sighed. "I am not telling you that. Of course not. I grew up with the Queen. I call her my sister, and she calls me her sister. There are secrets of childhood we share, from the times when we were little more than girls, little more than children, and knew everything about the other. But to find out for sure whether she is the Queen or not, I would need to talk to her, to lead her into intimate talk."

Aramis cast a quick look at D'Artagnan. If the boy was surprised at a seamstress who called the Queen her sister, he didn't show it. Aramis turned his attention back to Violette. "Would you do it, Violette, and call me when you have come to a conclusion?"

"You want me to do it later?" Violette asked. "Alone?"

Aramis didn't answer, but his green eyes looked intently at her and spoke volumes in the silence.

Violette sighed. "What if the person in there, so prettily crying into the Queen's handkerchief is a member of a plot designed to kill her, to subvert the kingdom of France, to . . . What else would they *not* do, Chevalier?"

Aramis sighed. "I do not know," he said.

Violette nodded. "Then what am I to do if I find out that

woman is a mere impostor? What if she, having a bad conscience, perceives what I am trying to do and has her accomplices waylay me? What if I never get to tell you about it?"

"But . . ." Aramis said. "What else can we do?"

Violette searched for the oil lamp, which rested on the tambourette. "You can watch our meeting," Violette said. "And be on hand, should I be in danger."

"How?" Aramis asked.

"Well, I have told you there are warrens of secret passages and dozens of secret doors in this palace. I propose you should be in one of these secret rooms, listening in, while I ask the Queen questions only she could answer."

She lifted her arm, showing the pearl bracelet on her wrist. "If she answers wrong, I shall remove this bracelet and set it upon her praying table."

"And?"

"I will have to count on your weapons, monsieurs, and your willingness to defend France." With this, Violette stepped forward, resolute and no less decisive than any soldier, for all her soft skin and pink-and-white beauty.

An Attorney's Cellars; Porthos's Doubts;
How D'Artagnan Acquires a Servant

"THE devil," Porthos said.

It seemed to Athos that his friend was possessed of one of those sorts of passions that sometimes inflamed this tallest and most impulsive of the musketeers to anger on someone else's behalf.

Right then, the passion had been brought about by the sight of the storeroom and food cellar of the Attorney Monsieur de Coquenard.

Athenais, the worthy gentleman's wife, had left them a candle stuck on a bottle, on one of the shelves in the huge, dark room.

"You understand, monsieurs," she had explained before leaving her room ahead of them, "it might take me a while to summon Planchet. He sleeps in a room with all the others of my husband's clerks, and I need to wake him without rousing anyone else. Heaven knows how this is to be managed, but I will do it somehow." She'd cast Porthos a look of devotion and determination, as though hoping that he would recognize her sacrifice and her courage. "Meanwhile, you wait there in the storeroom. It is unlikely anyone could go in there, as only I have the keys." And she'd displayed the ring hanging from her waist, the symbol of her mastery over the household.

But now it appeared that Porthos was dissatisfied with the household that she was the mistress of.

The candle she'd left behind was of the cheapest manufacture—a deal of pig fat and whatever other grease could be scraped together from weeks of cooking. It cast a flickering light upon bare, dusty shelves, and tinged the air with a smell of something resembling food—the only such thing in the vicinity.

Most of the storeroom was bare, and the few jars and boxes upon the shelves seemed for the most part empty. Porthos prowled the room like a caged tiger, from one end of the shelves to the other, opening pots and boxes and making sounds of disappointment.

Athos suspected it had started—if he knew his friend—as a search for some food with which to while away the wait. Porthos, taller and more muscular than normal men, appeared to be in constant need of more sustenance than the income of a soldier granted. But as he opened jars and reached disconsolately into empty boxes, he grew more agitated, till he let his disappointment be known in that exclamation.

"The devil," he said. Stomping back to Athos, he said, "They call this a storeroom? I couldn't feed myself from it for an hour, much less a household of a dozen apprentices and servants for months. It's despicable. They must all be starved, even Athenais."

Athos smiled, indulgently. "Perhaps this is only a storeroom and they have others?"

Porthos shook his head. "No. You heard her. She said this was the storehouse and larder. Not that they've stored much. Even mice and rats can't live here." He paused. "You know, I've always imagined that Athenais, living in this house and with servants enough at her command, must live as I have always hoped to—you know, with enough food and drink and more to gladden the day. Perhaps some special wine or some comfit. But, Athos, this is dismal."

"Perhaps it is by thrift that they can afford the house and the servants," Athos said. He had known very few bourgeois, but he'd never known them to be people of spendthrift tastes. That Porthos found this amazing amused the older musketeer.

"The devil," Porthos said again, and smiled. "If her husband would die, and you must know he has to sooner or later, because he's well over seventy, I would show Athenais what life truly is. I would take her back to my father's estate, in the country. With her savings, we'd clean up the old house and get enough servants to look after it properly. And then . . ."

But before he could articulate the idyllic dream of a future with Athenais and her husband's money—a dream clearly shining forth from his gaze—someone knocked at the door.

Athos gestured for Porthos to shut up, but it might be too late. The knock had been timid and small, but who knew if the person outside might not have been there for a while?

They kept quiet while the handle turned and the door opened. Athenais looked in.

Following her was a scarecrow of a boy—thin, small, with a crop of ratty orange-brown hair and a full complement of zits on his ravaged features.

Athenais stood aside to let him in the room, then spoke severely to his back. "This," she said, "is Planchet. He is my husband's clerk, and he has some facility with ciphers." Then to Planchet, her voice yet more stern, "And these are the gentlemen I told you about, Planchet, the ones who need a cipher worked. This is an affair at the highest levels of the kingdom and only the best-born people in the world know about it. It is also dangerous, so you're not to breathe a world of it to my husband."

Planchet nodded and swallowed at each injunction, as though he were too afraid to speak. Athos wondered if they'd come here on a fool's errand. How good could this child be at ciphers that even Athos himself couldn't be sure were ciphers? How far could a boy still in the throes of childhood penetrate the mind and heart of what seemed like a massive conspiracy? But he tried to outwardly show nothing of his doubts.

"Monsieur Planchet," he said.

And the boy raised his head to look at Athos. In that one glance, that momentary stare, Athos discovered eyes as dark and as sharp as D'Artagnan's own. And his spirits lifted. Perhaps there was hope. Perhaps the child really was a wonder at ciphers.

Planchet bowed and tugged his forelock at them.

Athos hesitated, his hand within the sleeve in which he'd concealed the letter. Feeling it crinkle beneath his fingers, he hesitated. Was he about to put the fate of France, the fate of the Queen, the whole future of his monarchy, into untrust-worthy hands? Truth be told, the child didn't look important enough to be a pawn in a game of politics. But then again, as Athos had learned early, sometimes appearances could be grossly deceiving.

And yet, what choice did they have? They might hold onto the letter—true—and hold onto it long enough that if that corpse in the alley had truly been Anne of Austria, all would be lost. And if it had not been Anne of Austria, then all hope of solving the anonymous girl's murder would be gone.

Suddenly, making a decision before he knew he'd made it, Athos plunged his fingers into his sleeve and brought out the much-folded paper. It occurred to him belatedly that they should have made a copy of it. He must learn to think of these things in advance. He must learn to think more care-fully, now that his business was not solely his own.

"Here," he said, extending the paper to the boy with trem-bling fingers. "Here." Heaven knew he'd made enough of a mess of his own business.

The boy took it to the shelf nearest the candle, and un-folded it with the reverent gestures of one for whom paper is a rare and precious substance. Looking at the care with which the boy's thick, stubby fingers unfolded the paper and smoothed away its creases, Athos thought that Monsieur Co-quenard must keep his clerks on a very short leash indeed.

He could well imagine the cane mercilessly applied to the shoulders of a clerk who wasted paper or ink, and the thought made him shiver. His life, such as it had been so far, had at least escaped such narrow restrictions, such spend-thrift care.

Planchet looked at the letter a while. From the side, be-neath the lock of swinging dirty red hair, he looked wholly blank. Puzzled. He stood like that a long time and Athos started wondering again if they'd come on a fool's errand.

And then the boy's face lit up. To say it that way seemed too easy. It was the difference between darkest night and brilliant sunrise, as his eyes opened wide, his lips turned up-ward, his pimply, dejected countenance became so ani-mated, so full of expression and life that it was hard to believe he was the same ill-attired clerk.

"You know what it is, then?" Porthos asked, clearly having observed the same transformation.

"Yes, monsieur, it is a simple cipher. A substitution cipher. Not words, because if it were words that were meant to signify something, it would be impossible for me to decipher unless I had a code book. But this is simply one in which you give each letter a number, then substitute a number for the other and thus a letter for another, which is why some of the words are atrociously spelled and others make no sense at all. It will take no time at all. Mistress . . ." He looked toward Madame Coquenard, who stood there in her nightgown, candle in hand, like a supernatural visitation. "It will only take a minute."

It was indeed a very short time, as Planchet's lips moved, and his fingers flickered in the motions of a fast calculator. It seemed to Athos that a piece of paper and a pen would make it all much easier, but he'd already guessed those were rare items around here.

Planchet turned around. "Most of these words are filler and mean nothing. It is only these two sentences in the middle that are ciphered properly. And they . . ." He closed his eyes. "They say that someone referred to as M. is supposed to meet B. down on Saint Eugenie Street by the Seine on the second floor of number 28, two hours after sundown . . ." He opened his eyes for a moment and looked like someone making an effort to remember something. "Today."

Saint Eugenie was not too far from where they'd found the corpse. And two hours after sunset meant the girl might just have left the assignation when they'd seen her and she'd been murdered. Athos felt disappointment and elation all at once. The message was less enlightening than he could hope for, considering someone had gone through the trouble of setting it in code. On the other hand, it didn't say anything about the Queen.

Of course, what would it say about the Queen of France? What could it say, even in code? And Athos was none too sure that the M. might not refer to her. After all, lovers often had nicknames for one another, and who could know what hers was? A whole slew of tender words beginning with M. came to Athos's mind, and he frowned. He did not like the B. At all. B. For Buckingham.

Madame Coquenard nodded to them, then said, "If you have found what you came to know, then, monsieurs, I'll let you out and go back to my bed. Planchet, put that candle out. You know what your master says about waste."

Was it Athos's impression, or did Planchet cast him a look of mad despair before he blew out the candle?

The memory of that look, the same look he'd often seen in battle and duel when a comrade needed assistance, bothered Athos and nettled him.

It had long been his training to give assistance when such a look was turned his way. How could he now ignore it?

He swallowed hard, as they started out toward the dark hallway, following the meager light of Madame Coquenard's candle. Planchet fell into step behind them.

Porthos was looking at Athos intently, with the sort of expression that meant that he also had seen Planchet's begging stare. Porthos lips formed, "The devil," and his huge hand closed on the pommel of his outsized sword.

Athos smiled. It was all he could do not to laugh. Surely Porthos didn't mean to challenge his mistress to a duel, nor even his mistress's husband. Surely. Attorneys weren't known for their wild ways and contravention of the edicts. And if Porthos dueled against such an old man, it would surely mean murder. And yet, Porthos's instincts reacted to the exploitation of others as they reacted to attack on battlefield or field of honor.

Not sure himself, of what they could do, in this arena so different from his accustomed exploits, Athos looked back at Planchet, and saw another anguished look from behind the young man's unruly lock of hair. What did it mean, and what could Athos do about it?

Oh, Athos had caught on that this was a house of extremely frugal habits, of customs and manners such as the musketeers could barely fathom. But he knew that attorneys and the like had a different way of life, and that a clerk like Planchet could easily go from his present oppressed state and, by virtue of apprenticeship and learning, grow to have a house of his own as large as this, and live a life . . . a life of frugality as austere as that of his master—because from the look of the candles, the spartan feel of Madame Coquenard's room, Athos didn't imagine that the master lived much better than the servants.

He looked back over his shoulder again, and the look on the boy's face was more urgent. It appeared, Athos thought, much like he remembered one of his childhood friend's looking, once, when he had jumped into deep water, only to realize, afterwards, that he could not swim.

Back then, Athos had jumped in. But, right now, Athos didn't know how to jump in, how to save this young man from drowning in a way of life that Athos didn't fully understand.

"Monsieur Planchet," Madame Coquenard whispered, and opened a door on the right side of the hallway.

Through the open door, Athos's dark-adapted eyes could just see a room scarcely any bigger than that of Madame Coquenard but filled with many narrow beds, side by side—ten or so. They were so close to one another that if an inmate turned in the night he would be likely to touch another. Beyond the bed, the light of the moon came through a window that . . . Athos blinked and flinched. The window had bars on the outside.

As Planchet went meekly into the room, Athos thought that the bars were surely to protect the room from burglars coming in. But think about it as he might, it was hard not to perceive the claustrophobic room as a prison, and those in it like prisoners.

Planchet went in with the same look with which Athos had often seen men advance toward the gallows and their doom, his shoulders bent and his head down.

Madame Coquenard closed the door, and, walking almost soundlessly, led them down a further flight of stairs and to a door at the bottom. This door led to the alley through which they had originally come in.

Athos got out first, onto the cold street outside, onto the shine of moonlight, the smell of muck underfoot and orange trees from the nearby garden. Somehow, being outside felt cleaner, and relief flooded him, but then his throat constricted at the remembered look on Planchet's face as the youth went into that miserable prison of a room.

Porthos came out, his shoulders bent, almost like Planchet's, and looking much like a dog that has been whipped by someone he trusts.

Athenais Coquenard was no fool. Standing there, in her

nightgown, she looked both embarrassed, vaguely guilty and—gazing up at Porthos—fearful, as though she thought she might never see him again.

"Monsieur . . ." she said, but stopped.

"Athenais," Porthos said, at the same time. Then, when she stopped, they looked at each other a long while in silence.

"Damn it all," Porthos finally said. "How do you feed a family from that storeroom? I could not feed myself from it for half a day."

The lady cackled, a cackle of half embarrassment, half surprise, as though she were shocked at someone speaking his mind. Surely not a common thing in her world. Not all that common in the musketeers' world either. But at least, in their world, if the speaker were willing to pay for it with his life should it become necessary, it was possible to speak the truth now and then.

"My husband," she said. "You must understand, Monsieur Porthos, that he is very old and set in his ways. When I married him . . ." She hesitated. "When I married him, he had already buried two wives and, as such, he was set in his ways. He did not change those for me, and I must keep house in the same frugal conditions his first wife kept it."

So, it was as Athos had thought. The master lived in as strained circumstances as the servant.

"But," Madame Couquenard said. "My husband is very old and will not last forever. I will contrive to be a good wife—as good a wife as he requires—to him while he lives. But when he dies . . ." She let the words drop into silence.

Porthos said nothing, but Athos could hear, in his mind, plans for rebuilding his ancestral estate and for showing Athenais a better life.

And who was Athos to judge? Surely after this a life with Porthos would seem to her like being let out of prison.

Athos looked away while Porthos kissed his mistress, then back again, as the door closed, with a soft click.

They walked along the alley, slowly.

Porthos sighed. "Damn it all," he said, under this breath.

Athos nodded, in agreement, without knowing what else he could do.

"Damn it all," Porthos repeated, and gave one of his sighs

whose volume and force would have burst the chest of a normal-sized man. "The devil take it."

Athos realized they were walking along the alley the opposite direction from the one they'd come. But, after all, it made no difference. It should make no difference. He walked on, in the dark night, breathing the cooler air of the outside.

He tried to think of the note. Aramis would be disappointed it hadn't told them much of anything. Only, presumably, from where the woman came. D'Artagnan would be upset too. He wondered how D'Artagnan was doing. How would he and Aramis get along, with each trying to outplot the other?

But in his mind, the whole time, was the image of that darkened room, those beds so narrow and so close together that none of those men would be able to turn without falling off the bed and each of them would have to be very careful on rising, lest an arm or a leg hit a neighbor.

His own adolescence had been a time for hunting and riding, for long, free, lazy days by streams and in the middle of fields, just himself and his white horse, Ajax.

Thinking about it, he could almost smell Ajax's clean scent and feel his hide beneath his fingers now. Ajax had been left behind, as he must be, in Athos's erstwhile domain. What had become of him? Athos could do nothing about it, one way or another. So many things he could do nothing about.

Up a shorter flight of stairs, they walked out of the alley and into the larger street, then along it, to the right, along the wall of the Coquenard house, the one with the bars on the lower floor.

Porthos stopped outside the third window they passed. "Isn't this it? Wouldn't you say? The room where the apprentices sleep?"

Athos nodded dumbly, thinking that the same image must be haunting Porthos, the same feeling of prison and narrow containment.

"This one?" Porthos asked, and put his hands on the thick iron bars, as though to be sure.

Athos nodded.

Porthos's hands were huge—easily twice as large as

those of a normal man. For such huge hands, they were not ugly—just solid, and sturdy, with massive fingers and strong knuckles. The huge ruby ring on one of the fingers was almost certainly glass, and yet it looked neither cheap nor out of place, glinting under the light of the moon as Porthos gripped one of the middle bars securely in each hand and pushed. Hard.

For a steadily held breath, nothing happened, then the bars bent, as they would have under the heat of a forge and the steady hammering of an ironsmith.

Porthos massive strength was enough. The bars bent, till his fingers hit the next set of bars, and then those bent too, till there was enough space in the middle for Porthos to reach and, with a push and a muffled crack, open the shutters.

Athos wondered if everyone within would wake at the crack, if they would have to explain to the assembled apprentices of Monsieur Coquenard what they were doing. Faith, he barely knew how to explain to themselves what they were doing.

But as the shutters swung gently inward, only one person appeared in the opening. Planchet looked like nothing on Earth, in his voluminous knee-length nightgown, intelligent eyes wide and alarmed, his greasy red hair on end, as if he'd grasped each side of it as the noise roused him.

Planchet's mouth, open to scream, closed as he recognized them. He tilted his head slightly sideways as he looked at them with the curiosity of a bird beholding something he's not sure is either food or a predator.

"Come, boy," Porthos said, his whisper still retaining some of the boom of his normal voice.

Planchet looked behind himself, at the beds where his comrades did not stir. One of them snored loudly Then, back at Porthos and Athos. It was as though his eyes wanted to escape, but the rest of him hesitated. "My father gave me as apprentice to Monsieur Coquenard," he said. "Who has paid him a good fee."

"So?" Porthos asked. "Do you want to live like this?"

Planchet shook his head, but his eyes narrowed, in calculation or in fear. "But how else am I to live?" he said. "My father is only a farmer, and he has six sons. There isn't enough land to feed us all in the future. There is barely enough land to feed one family now. And if I go with you, what will I do? I cannot earn my living in any other way."

A farmer's son, Athos thought, whose life up until being sent to apprentice with the attorney had probably not been all that different from Athos's youth. Oh, he'd have worked more, doubtless. And harder work, in the measure that wielding a hoe was harsher than learning to use a sword.

He realized Porthos was looking at him with some anxiety. Porthos, kind-hearted Porthos, could not walk away and leave the boy in the kind of prison that would offend Porthos's sensibilities even more than it offended Athos's.

On the other hand, neither did he know what to do with Planchet.

"I already have a servant," he whispered apologetically, half to Planchet and half to Athos. "As do you."

Athos nodded. Porthos had Mosqueton, who agreed to work for almost nothing for the sake of wearing Porthos's exuberant cast-off clothing. Athos had brought the inimitable Grimaud with him from his domain, where Grimaud's family had served a long time. And Aramis had Bazin. No one could replace Bazin, whose ability to whisper pious nothings while carrying love notes to duchesses made him ideal for Aramis.

But D'Artagnan . . . Athos was willing to bet D'Artagnan had no servant, and intelligent Planchet would suit cunning D'Artagnan very well indeed.

"D'Artagnan," he said, looking at Porthos. "The boy, D'Artagnan. He has no servant."

"D'Artagnan!" Porthos said, as though he had just hit upon something wonderful. "Of course." He hesitated a moment. "Of course, the boy doesn't have a post, yet. . . ."

Athos waved that away. He'd taken D'Artagnan's measure with a glance and the boy's future did not worry him in the least. "Yet; but he will. He will go far. And any man at arms needs a servant."

He looked at Planchet, who was looking at both of them with something like nascent hope. "There is a friend of ours," he said. "Scarcely older than you. Just arrived in town where, doubtless, he shall be a great success as a soldier. He will need a servant." The hope in Planchet's eyes grew, and the boy took a step toward the window, but Athos felt he owed him full disclosure. When he was young, he himself had dreamed of adventure and battle, all without knowing what it entailed.

"If you become D'Artagnan's servant," he said, "you will no doubt have times when you'll be hungry. You will almost for sure accompany him to battle sometime, and you might be hurt. You might be wounded. There will be days of very little food, and there will be months of famine."

The boy looked grave. He stared from Porthos to Athos. "I can take famine," he said. "I've known little else. But if I understand the life of a soldier, there will also be victory, and celebration, and days when food and wine will be plentiful."

"Oh, often," Porthos said. "As often as we can contrive it."

"And there will be interesting events that beat routine, and counted candles, and carefully-accounted-for paper," he said.

Athos nodded at that.

Planchet turned back, and for a moment, Athos thought that he had somehow said something to scare the boy, to turn him away. Then he realized the boy was pulling woolen breeches over his sleeping shirt, tucking it in. Heading for the window.

He was so skinny that there was more than enough room on either side between him and the bars that Porthos had bent. He'd somehow got his feet into worn-looking slippers, which hit the pavement with hardly any sound.

They walked away, the three of them, Planchet following a couple of steps behind, as a good servant should. When Athos looked back, he never saw the boy turn to look at the place he'd left.

When they were a couple of houses away, Athos said, "We shouldn't tell D'Artagnan we helped Planchet escape from his master. We'll tell him we met him by accident. At the bridge over the Seine."

"Right," Porthos said, and was silent for a moment. "We'll tell him he was spitting onto the water, which is a sign of a contemplative nature."

Athos nodded. He wondered where Porthos had heard that or if his friend, who thought with his huge hands, his sturdy legs, his outsized body, even understood the meaning of contemplative. But it wasn't worth asking.

The small smile that played on Athos's lips for a moment vanished as he thought they'd still done nothing to solve the mystery of the corpse in the alley. They were no closer to finding the identity of the woman than they'd been at the start of this expedition. Or even to assuring themselves she wasn't the Queen.

Perhaps Aramis and D'Artagnan had fared better. Athos would have to hope so.

The Labyrinthine Jealousy of Kings;
D'Artagnan's Peculiar Cowardice;
The Pearl Bracelet

D'ARTAGNAN was having trouble breathing. His breath caught in his throat as if a big lump had lodged itself there and refused to let anything through.

"What do you mean?" he asked this fine lady, this woman who looked as if she were made, whole, of spun sugar and rose petals and who had just uttered the unthinkable. "What do you mean, if she is not the Queen, you expect us to kill her?"

His voice must have sounded very shocked indeed, vibrating with a mixture of surprise and fear.

Violette glared toward Aramis, a look of half curiosity and half censure, as if wondering why he'd brought a child into serious affairs.

Aramis shrugged. She turned to D'Artagnan. "My dear monsieur, surely you must know this is the only way. After all, if the queen has been replaced—if there is someone else in her place—there must be a reason for it. And the reason cannot be simply to be there, in her place. Finding someone who looks that much like the Queen, who can act the part that well, would take time and effort. Surely you realize that. There will be bigger things at stake, and higher .heads involved in this web than the impostor's. Why is she here? Think. By pretending to be the Queen, she might well bring war on Europe, by . . . having an affair. Or sending secret letters to milady's family in Europe. She can convince the King that she was betraying him all along and sink the fortune of the empire, in the King's eyes." She shook her well-coiffed head, vehemently. "No," she said. "If she is an impostor, you must kill her and not let her complete her plan."

"But if she's found killed," D'Artagnan said. "If the Queen is found killed . . ." He looked at Aramis in mute appeal. Truth was, he couldn't think past the fact that he might be asked to kill a woman. Ever since D'Artagnan had been able to toddle, his father, with the gallantry of an old soldier, had told him that he must never hurt a woman—that women were the reasons men fought, that protecting them was the highest calling of a soldier.

Coming to Paris, D'Artagnan had been ready to kill or die. Kill men or die at the blades of men. He'd never thought to hurt a woman. Women were frail and small and naturally weaker. And very few of them ever brandished a sword. What would his father say?

"If the Queen is found killed in the palace, there will be alarm," Aramis said. "But since she will be thought to be the Queen and in her proper place, it shouldn't be worse than that." He gave D'Artagnan a serious look. "So, if you must do it, take care to do it quickly and not to get caught. All the rest should fall in place by itself."

How could Aramis speak thus? Unless D'Artagnan missed his guess on Aramis's wounded look at this lady, this *seamstress*, Aramis loved her truly. In fact, unless D'Artagnan missed his guess at Aramis's character, Aramis loved all women. Oh, not as much as he loved this one, to whom, if D'Artagnan guessed right, the musketeer's soul had knit itself. But he liked all women and appreciated everything pertaining to females. So, how could he so casually speak of killing one of them, of snuffing out life in a frail body, of stilling movement in a graceful frame?

D'Artagnan didn't know. And he didn't know that, should he be called to do it that he would be able to. He swallowed hard. In fact, he wasn't sure that he wanted to do it, wanted to live with the memory of killing a woman. What a time to find out he was a coward.

He strove to make his face impassive, though, and must have succeeded, because Violette looked seriously at him a while, then nodded, as though satisfied.

She lifted high the oil lamp that rested by the chaise upon

which she had lain. Holding the lamp in her small, delicate hand, she confidently walked ahead toward what seemed to be a huge mirror in the wall. She pressed a point in the elaborate gilded frame that surrounded the mirror.

D'Artagnan couldn't avoid jumping a little in surprise as the mirror swung out on an hinge with but the slightest squeak.

Aramis looked over his shoulder at D'Artagnan with a look of amusement. In that moment D'Artagnan could have killed him for it, but he only looked away. Killing might come soon enough. Too soon.

Violette didn't notice, at any rate. She slid ahead of them into the broad tunnel ahead. The tunnel was wide enough to accommodate two people side by side, and was paneled inside in dark wood, lit only by the lamp in Violette's hand.

D'Artagnan went in, uneasily, behind Aramis. He jumped again as he heard the mirror-door click shut behind him.

"Worry not, Monsieur Gascon," Aramis said, a tone of amusement in his voice, perceptible though the sound carried only barely louder than breath. "Worry not. You'll be allowed out again."

"What—" D'Artagnan said, trying to match the volume, but his voice came out louder than he expected. Violette turned back, finger against her lips, and Aramis waved his hand furiously up and down.

"But—" D'Artagnan started again, and again the same flurried requests for silence followed.

Violette must have guessed that he wished to ask where they were and what it all meant because she spoke, in the same barely audible tone. "The father of our present king did not trust his wife. Some say with good reason. Now, there are many men who mistrust their wives, but kings have the means to make sure. The former king had a network of secret passages built throughout every royal residence. They are accessed by disguised doorways hidden behind mirrors or pictures."

"But—" D'Artagnan started.

"But you wonder how this allows the King to make sure?" Violette asked. "Look to the wall to your right; now and then you'll see a shutter. If you open that shutter it will allow you to look through the holes on the other side, which are cunningly disguised in the fretwork of a frame, in the eyes of a statue, or in another such way that no one sees it." She smiled slightly. "Almost everyone who has lived in the palace long enough knows some of these, but no one knows all of them. The Queen happens not to know of this one. It leads behind her praying room and the holes are concealed amid a design on the cloak of her statue of Our Lady of the Sorrows. Through it, we can look at the Queen. Or rather, you can look while I go in to speak to her."

Again she turned and led them along the winding corridor, past many closed shutters, and D'Artagnan wondered what rooms these would show, and what would be happening there.

But Violette never slowed down and, at any rate, it seemed to D'Artagnan that such an endeavor would not be within the scope of a gentleman's conscience. But then, neither should it be the killing of women.

He followed the other two uneasily, and it seemed to him the corridor doubled back upon itself.

At long last, Violette opened a shutter. "Here," she said, in an almost-soundless whisper. "Here you can see the Queen and observe."

The shutter was big enough for the two men to stand side by side and look, though the view into the room constricted into two piercings that—from the frontal view of the woman kneeling and praying, her face bathed in tears—must be within the statue to which she prayed.

As for the woman . . . It was like seeing the girl in the alley come alive again and move and cry. As though time had unspun itself and suddenly he were looking at the dead woman praying to God to allow her to live.

Though the features were exactly the same, she looked more beautiful in life than in death—her rounded cheeks tinged with color, her sky-blue eyes overflowing with tears, her lips pink and trembling.

Far more beautiful than the woodcuts of the Queen that D'Artagnan had seen. And yet undeniably the same person. The resemblance to the dead girl was remarkable.

D'Artagnan became aware that Violette had been talking when he heard her whisper sharply, "Pay attention, please."

He turned and did so, as she pointed toward the end of

the hallway and said, "That door leads to a small hall. It opens behind a portrait of Francis I. And opposite it opens another door, that one a real door, which will allow you into milady's praying chamber." As she spoke, Violette played with the heavy pearl bracelet at her wrist. "Mark this," she said. "If I unfasten this bracelet and lay it upon milady's praying table, it is proof that in talking to her I found she is not the Anne of Austria with whom I grew up, but an impostor. It will then be up to you to trace the same path I'm taking, come into the room and kill her before she can damage France or France's fortunes."

Never had D'Artagnan's heart beat so fast nor, seemingly, so deafeningly, as it did now.

Aramis was all composure, looking through the aperture in the wall, his face no more than civilly interested, and D'Artagnan tried to imitate him, but his hand that rested upon the pummel of his sword trembled, and it seemed to him as though everyone must hear the sonorous echoes of his heartbeat.

Every sound seemingly amplified and magnified, he heard Violette's retreating steps, then somewhere the soft hiss of an opening door. From inside the room came the sounds of a woman praying—a soft whisper of pleas in a language that D'Artagnan almost understood, but not quite.

If anyone had asked D'Artagnan if he spoke Spanish before this moment, he would have undoubtedly answered yes. But the Spanish he spoke was that of the border towns around his own—the Spanish of peddlers and farmers who lived and worked, indifferently, on both sides of the arbitrary political divide separating the two countries.

The Spanish this woman spoke was near enough for D'Artagnan to recognize it as having some similarity to the tongue he understood, but just that. One word in ten seemed familiar. One sentence amid five gave him the impression that if only he thought about it for a few hours he should know what she'd said. Other than that, he was wholly ignorant.

It seemed to him an eternity till the polished wooden door behind the woman opened, and Violette came in. The praying woman who might or might not be the Queen, got up and greeted Violette with the greatest of effusions, hands extended. Taking hold of both of Violette's hands, she kissed her on each cheek. Not a bad greeting from the Queen of France for the seamstress who supposedly was the niece of Aramis's theology professor.

D'Artagnan grinned at the outrageous lie and realized he must have snorted in his mirth, because Aramis gave him a deadly glare.

But the women within the room did not give any indication they had heard the sound. They were speaking animatedly to each other in the language that D'Artagnan couldn't quite understand.

Soon, the face of the woman who might be the Queen changed from its tearful aspect to a smile, and she brought out a little embroidered handkerchief to wipe away the marks of her former grief.

Here and there, she would interject a word or two into Violette's merry flow.

When Violette's hand went to her bracelet, D'Artagnan surged forward, his mouth dry, his heart louder than ever, his hands trembling. It seemed he'd waited to the age of seventeen to find out he was a coward.

Should this woman prove not to be the Queen, he might very well faint like a shy maiden before he could help Aramis. She was so beautiful, to kill her would be a sin as well as a crime.

Within the chamber, Violette's hand dropped from the bracelet.

D'Artagnan wondered if she did this—playing with the jewel—as an unconscious gesture and if it meant nothing. In which case, what if she unfastened it without meaning? Would he and Aramis become regicides?

Through the thundering of his heart, his tongue like cork, his vision wavering, he realized that the women were hugging and that, two steps away, Violette curtsied to . . . it must be the Queen.

It felt as though someone had dropped a bucket of blessedly cool water over D'Artagnan's overheated mind. It was the Queen after all.

He stepped back and leaned against the other wall of the corridor. It seemed to him as if his legs could not be trusted to do their job of holding him up.

That Aramis turned and gave D'Artagnan a faintly amused look, that Aramis himself seemed unaffected by the whole episode, made D'Artagnan wonder about the mind and life of this seemingly mild-mannered musketeer. Did he often find himself in the position of considering regicide?

Presently, Violette came back, holding her lamp, and motioned for them to follow her. They walked all the way back to her chamber.

And then Aramis betrayed anxiety for the first time, grabbing at his *seamstress's* arm. "Violette. It is the Queen, then?"

"It is," Violette said. A small, hesitant smile appeared on her lips and only the slight shaking of her hand as she put the lamp back on the tambourette betrayed how scared she'd been. "It is the Queen, and France is safe. The Queen."

"Are you sure?" Aramis asked.

Violette gave Aramis a stern look. "On the day that I am not sure of Anne of Austria's identity—on the day that I can't tell for sure if this is the woman I played with in the nursery—on that day, I will have lost my mind completely."

"She could have been schooled."

"In childhood escapades only the two of us know about? And who would have picked my brain without my noticing it, Chevalier?" Violette threw her head back and looked very much Spanish, despite her blond hair and blue eyes.

Aramis smiled a little in response, a smile quickly suppressed. His eyes shone with mischief.

Letting go of Violette's arm, he bowed deeply.

D'Artagnan wouldn't even venture to speak. It seemed to him there were claws beneath the velvet that was Violette, and that those claws could come unsheathed at any moment and cause far more injury than a musketeer's sword. Fortunately Aramis seemed to enjoy his lady's temper.

"But listen," Violette said. She extended a well-manicured hand and lay it upon Aramis's velvet sleeve. "There is danger here. Even if the corpse isn't the Queen, there is some great treason here. The Queen cries because she got a letter from Buckingham. That much I knew. But I did not know *all* the letter said." Violette took a deep breath. "Now she has told me. The letter says that Buckingham is in town, *having been summoned here by a letter from the Queen.*"

"Why did she summon him?" Aramis asked.

Violette swore under her breath, a string of Spanish words that, for once, fell within the scope of the words D'Artagnan knew from peddlers and farmers.

Before he could recover from hearing them drop from the lips of a well-bred lady, Violette said in French, "You are not stupid, monsieur, so don't play the fool more than you have to. The Queen did not summon him. She would not. Whatever feelings she has for him . . . Well, she is a woman, isn't she? But whatever feelings she has for him, she knows the duty she owes the King and crown and the whole land of France. She knows too, how unsteadily the crown rests upon her head. The King has been convinced to shun her company. If he should ever get a pretext, a reason to put her away, he would do it without flinching. She would never dare give him such a reason.

"Only, Buckingham is in town and he thinks that she did—that she has written to him and interrupted his preparations for the royal conference that's to take place in Callais, in a few days, to summon him here because she cannot wait to consummate that love of which they have only spoken."

Violette shook her head, perhaps at the foolishness of mankind in general. Or at least of the half of it that happened to be male. "If the King finds out or even suspects that the Queen wrote to Buckingham and begged him to come . . . Well, it will no more occur to him than to Buckingham that it might be an impostor. And all will be lost."

"But," D'Artagnan said, "who would do such a thing?"

Aramis looked at D'Artagnan as if wondering where and how he could have grown up so naive. Violette's expression was almost exactly the same.

"The Cardinal," Aramis said at last. "Who else?"

"But . . . why?" Back in his distant province, D'Artagnan had heard that the Cardinal was as powerful as the King, perhaps moreso, and controlled all the King's actions behind the scenes. But why should this translate to hating the Queen and seeking her downfall, something that both Violette and Aramis seemed to think was obvious?

"Some say," Violette said, "because he loves the Queen so much and knows that she will never succumb to him. Some say the love and desire that he once felt for her turned into bitter hate."

Aramis smiled, a smile that slid onto his lips and off them almost instantly. "But that's the talk of women," he said. "The truth is he hates her because she is not the princess he would have chosen for the King. She was chosen by the King's mother; but the Cardinal, given a choice, would rather have looked for a bride for our king somewhere in Italy. Or perhaps Holland. And therefore, he hopes to get rid of Anne of Austria so that he is free to make a new alliance for our king, one more to his liking."

Violette shot an irritated look at her lover. "Be that as it may," she said, "and whatever the reason, he seeks to bring about her downfall, and this affair looks likely to do it." She stretched out her hands to hold Aramis's. "My friend, you must, with all haste, find out who the corpse was, and who wrote to Buckingham in the Queen's name, and what turns upon this plot. The fate of France as well as my own peace of mind might rest on it."

Before Aramis could answer, D'Artagnan bowed. "Milady, we are your humble servants and will seek to fulfill your wishes."

He didn't know why he spoke so quickly, nor why so gallantly. From Aramis's face, he'd surprised the musketeer as well. As far as he could determine, D'Artagnan thought as they made their way through servants' passages back to the cool night air of the inner courtyard, as far as he could penetrate his own motives and impulses, he'd done as he had because he was so relieved at not having to kill a woman.

It was time to go back, and hope that Athos and Porthos had better luck with the breaking of the cipher.

Hiring a Servant; Where Aramis
Has to Speak Plainly; Why the Plot
Might Still Involve the Queen

ＡTHOS and Porthos, along with Planchet, waited outside
D'Artagnan's lodgings, at the Rue des Fossoyers, as they
had agreed to, before D'Artagnan left.

Athos was reluctantly impressed with the boy's choice of
lodging. After all, most of the young men who came to the
capital, if they found rooms at all, found narrow hovels at the
bottom of some smelly street. And more often than not, had
to share it with three or four other young men in like circumstances.

D'Artagnan, by contrast, had secured these rooms in the
second floor of a respectable lower-middle-class home, in a
street lined with respectable middle-class homes. He'd told
Athos he lodged there alone and it was therefore a good
place for all of them to meet.

Of course, Athos thought to himself, this would make
perfect sense if D'Artagnan's appearance of just having arrived and utter poverty were being financed by the Cardinal.
For what purpose, Athos couldn't imagine, but he knew that
half the time his mind, cunning and learned such as it was,
could not penetrate the thoughts of Richelieu.

To oppose his suspicions, he had only his impression of
D'Artagnan, and that was that the boy might be cunning but
he was honest, and certainly not capable of such elaborate
and constant duplicity.

"The devil," Porthos said, as he stomped his big boots.

"Where has Aramis gone for his seamstress? At this rate he could have crossed all of France."

Athos smiled, knowing that Porthos was only venting his impatience. He noted, however, how Planchet's eyes widened, and wondered what the boy made of this talk of seamstresses.

It was just as well. He'd soon develop suspicions about the identity of Aramis's paramour. For now, let him believe her a seamstress.

Aramis and D'Artagnan came into view.

Aramis walked as he did when he was upset, stretching his long legs to the limit with each step. D'Artagnan, with shorter legs, had to trot to stay by his side, but trotting he was, valiantly. Athos suspected the youth would rather die than admit he had trouble keeping up with any of them, in any capacity. He walked with his shoulders back, his head up, pride and determination on every feature.

They stopped, both at the same time, a little space away, and stared at Athos and Porthos.

Aramis looked enquiringly at Planchet. D'Artagnan followed his gaze and raised his eyebrows.

"This is a servant for D'Artagnan," Athos said. "His name is Planchet."

"And he will serve admirably," Porthos said, "for you must know we found him at the bridge, spitting into the Seine below, an activity that indicates a fine and contemplative character."

D'Artagnan looked at Porthos. His eyes widened, his mouth dropped slightly open. "Contemplative?" he said.

Porthos nodded, clearly quite happy with this description of Planchet.

It was easy to assume Porthos was stupid, and Athos understood why many among the corps of musketeers thought just that. But Athos knew the man better than other people. He would wager Porthos knew what *contemplative* meant and that, for reasons of his own, he thought the word applied to Planchet and made him the ideal servant.

"A . . . servant?" D'Artagnan stared at the redheaded young man, who bowed and nervously tugged his forelock.

Aramis shifted on his feet, transmitting the impression of impatience with every line of his body. "Come, man, you must have a servant," he said. "I'm surprised your parents didn't send one with you." He pressed his lips in disapproval of such carelessness.

Athos wasn't. If he judged the wealth of D'Artagnan's paternal abode correctly, then D'Artagnan had grown up with maybe three servants, one of them his old and crabbed nursemaid and the other one a young maid-of-all-work. There would be only one manservant, who would doubtlessly act as the valet for the man of the house—but who could not be spared to follow the young master to Paris.

Before D'Artagnan said something that would give his situation away to the other two and thus embarrass himself, Athos intervened. "Aramis is right, D'Artagnan. You must have a servant. It is unseemly for a musketeer to run about town, performing his own errands and to lose his day buying bread and wine, when he can be much better employed in His Majesty's service."

"But I am not a musketeer," D'Artagnan said.

Athos waved his hand and smiled from his certainty that D'Artagnan, with his energy drive and intelligence, couldn't fail to succeed. Besides, Athos knew Monsieur de Treville well enough to guess he'd only failed to give a place to the only son of his old friend because of the lack of any proof that this boy was indeed who he claimed to be. Once D'Artagnan had lived in town for a little while and shown himself not to be a plant of the Cardinal's . . . "Oh, but you doubtlessly will be a musketeer soon enough. You already have, as you said, a musketeer's heart."

D'Artagnan looked at each of the three friends in turn, then at Planchet. He frowned slightly until the young man looked up and met his gaze. In that moment both the youths seemed to recognize the other as one of their kind. "Well, then," D'Artagnan said, "if you think I must and that he'll be useful, I'll hire this young man."

Planchet's features changed along a continuum of expressions, from relief, worry and fear to tentative joy. The reaction of an intelligent young man facing a new and uncertain life. Planchet was too smart not to realize that this life of adventure came laced with danger. He bowed quickly.

"And now that he's your servant," Porthos said, reaching into his purse. "He can make himself useful by finding us a pint of wine." He tossed a coin at Planchet.

Planchet looked at it, goggle-eyed, then at Porthos. "But . . . in the middle of the night?"

"There are taverns aplenty open even at night," Aramis said, as if unwilling to believe someone didn't know this. "Go down this street and to your right, and you'll find the Velvet Glove. It will look closed, but mind you, if you knock at the back door, you'll find many people in there, and they'll sell you a pint easily enough. Tell them it is for me."

As the bewildered boy went down the street to the right, Athos wondered if they'd see him again. For a boy in Planchet's position, after the attorney's tight rein on the purse, the coin Porthos had handed him—which was probably ten times what he needed—might look like a fortune. Porthos seemed oblivious to this danger. He turned to D'Artagnan, "Right. We must now go to your home, and discuss our findings."

D'Artagnan led them up a rickety flight of stairs and opened the door at the top. It shrieked as it unlocked, then again as he flung it open.

Inside was a spartan salon, furnished only with a set of long benches and what looked like the kitchen table of a farmhouse. A door at the back led presumably to the bedroom. The room was like a hundred other boarding rooms in Paris and, not surprisingly, considering when the boy had arrived in town, betrayed not the slightest personal touch and no hint at all of its inhabitant's tastes.

D'Artagnan waved them to sit on the long benches around the table, and they did so. Athos took care to position himself so he could see D'Artagnan's eyes. After all, all he had to go on was his opinion of the boy's honesty, and if he couldn't observe D'Artagnan's eyes while he talked, Athos would be unable to detect any furtive or ill-at-ease looks.

But the boy looked open enough as he said, "The corpse is not the Queen."

Aramis scowled, as if D'Artagnan spoke too early. Or, Athos thought, perhaps too simply. No doubt Aramis would have dressed the same conclusion in *whereas* and *whiles* and hemmed it in with *perhaps* and *nonetheless*es. However, the fact, unvarnished, probably remained that the dead woman was not the Queen of France.

Athos felt relieved—as if a hand that had been clenched

around his middle constricting his breathing had let go. He took a deep breath.

"Are you sure?" Porthos asked before Athos found his voice.

Aramis shrugged. "My . . . someone who has known the Queen from earliest infancy has questioned her and says that she responds to everything as Anne of Austria would. It is therefore highly unlikely that anyone has managed to substitute a look-alike for the Queen. Had they done so, doubtless, they would have coached the girl on well-known facts but hardly on early childhood adventures. However . . ."

"Is the woman in the palace the Queen?" Porthos asked impatiently.

"I don't believe that—"

"Yes or no, Aramis?" Porthos asked.

Aramis hissed out a breath between clenched teeth. "Yes," he said.

"How sure are you?" Porthos asked. "No pretty words."

Aramis frowned at Porthos. He hated to state anything outright and Athos doubted anyone but Porthos, with his impatient forthrightness, could get Aramis to come to the point.

"As sure as I hope to be of salvation," Aramis said, still frowning.

Which, considering Aramis's lifestyle, Athos thought, could be argued was not sure at all.

"How?" Porthos said. "And speak clearly."

"Violette, the . . . the niece of my theology professor—"

"The seamstress?" Porthos asked.

"The exact one," Aramis said. "The seamstress has talked to the Queen and by means of shared reminiscence and incidents only the Queen would know from their childhood—"

"The seamstress's childhood was passed with the Queen?"

"Porthos, what do these questions tend to?" Aramis asked, his impatience growing.

"Nothing, nothing. I am surprised, that is all," Porthos said.

For a moment, Athos wondered if it were possible that Porthos had missed, over all these years of acquaintance, that Aramis's lover was not anything so coarse as a seamstress. But then he saw the glimmer of mischief in the huge musketeer's eyes, and had to hide his own smile behind his hand. Porthos often took advantage of his huge size and seeming awkwardness with language to pretend to be a fool. It allowed him to amuse himself as—were his true intelligence known—he would never have leave to do. And though this was hardly an appropriate time for him to be annoying Aramis for sport, it had been a long and tension-filled evening, and Athos could not blame him.

"Then keep your surprise to yourself," Aramis said. "At any rate, Violette says that she would swear it is the Queen. So we are left with an unknown corpse in our hands, and oathbound to find out the truth of her murder."

Porthos nodded. "Oathbound we are," he said. And slammed his fist on the table. Then paused for a moment. "Of course, has it occurred to you that Violette is perhaps a look-alike? That she too was replaced when the Queen was? True, such resemblance would be harder to find in a woman than in two. But the Cardinal's hand is everywhere."

"Oh, for heaven's sake, Porthos, she called me . . . She knows who I am and what our . . . our accustomed mode of address. She is herself."

Porthos nodded his huge head sagely. "In situations such as this," he said, "I find it is always good to verify."

"So, you did not find out the identity of the corpse," Athos said, thinking it was time that Porthos's amusement was cut short. Otherwise he was quite capable of going on, goading, till the younger musketeer ran out of temper and became unable to make any sense.

Aramis shrugged. "Well, not as such," he said. "But the truth of it is, well, there might be something. The . . ." He looked at Porthos. "Well, you see, the truth of it is—" He blushed visibly.

"Aramis's acquaintance informed us that Buckingham is in town and that he thinks the Queen summoned him," D'Artagnan said, earning an exasperated look from Aramis. "He expects to meet with her."

"So he could be the B. in the note," Porthos said.

"B.?" Aramis asked.

"The B. in the note that we found and which Planchet decoded," he said.

Aramis looked baffled. Athos couldn't help but smile. To Porthos, the direct thinker, it would appear that what he knew everyone must know. And he didn't realize that he had just contradicted his own story about how they'd met Planchet.

"Porthos means that in the note, which we took to the home of Porthos's . . . friend to translate. There we found a clerk who interpreted the note for us."

"Planchet?" D'Artagnan asked.

Very little escaped the young Gascon.

"Planchet has nothing to do with this," Athos said, managing to keep a straight face. "But the clerk who deciphered the note told us it was to remind M. to meet B. at a certain address."

"A certain address?" Aramis asked. "Where?"

"At a town house on Saint Eugenie Street. By the Seine."

"Number 28. The second floor," Porthos said.

Aramis stood and made sure of the fastening of his sword belt. "Let us go to that house, then," he said. "Now. It's not far from where we found the body. Perhaps the murderer is still there."

Athos shook his head. "Wait," he said. "Not yet. I doubt the murderer is there."

"Why?" Porthos asked.

"Because if the murderer had reason to suspect a note with this address was on the corpse, he would have searched more carefully."

"But the person at that address might know something about the corpse. Someone might tell us who she is, and that might tell us who killed her."

"True," Athos said. "And yet would you tell all to someone you've never seen, who wakes you in the middle of the night? We'll be viewed with suspicion. We might get in a fight.

"We will do that in daylight and the four of us will go together, but I can tell you from past experience that word of our duel with the guards will have spread and that Monsieur de Treville will want to see us." He saw a flicker of panic in D'Artagnan's face and said, "To congratulate us, D'Artagnan. We didn't let ourselves be arrested this time. And we won victory over the guards. He'll only want to congratulate us. In fact, His Majesty, the King himself, will want to congratulate us. It is not often he gets something he can gloat over the Cardinal about." Before he could see the panoply of wild hope and pride flow across D'Artagnan's face, he looked away. Seeing it would remind him that he himself had been young once, and foolishly hopeful. He'd learned to expect nothing from the King's gratitude, save now and then, some pocket money.

He spoke ahead, in a rush, to avoid D'Artagnan's having time to ask him anything. "We should wait and go to that house all together. Until then, I say we should make other investigations, try other avenues to find out who this woman was and why she might have been killed."

"And who did it," Porthos said, clenching his huge head.

"And who did it," Athos said, nodding at his friend. It crossed his mind, like a dark flash that he would be punishing someone who hadn't done anything worse than he himself had done, so many years ago—killing a defenseless woman in cold blood.

"I could try to find out about the medal," Aramis said. "St. Jerome Emiliani sounds foreign—Italian, and it can't be a widespread local devotion, so it might be a way to trace her. Perhaps she is Italian. I know a man—"

"Another one?" Porthos asked. "The Devil! Aramis, you want to be careful, or you'll soon be known for knowing more men than women."

Aramis clenched his teeth. Unclenched them. "I know a man," he said again, "who is an expert on saints and their medals and pictures. I can visit him and ask about it."

"And I can find out if there's some way she got hold of a musketeer's uniform," Porthos said. "If some seamstress . . ." He looked slyly at Aramis.

"The uniform did not look new," D'Artagnan said.

"No, so—perhaps I can ask around the corps if any of our comrades is missing a uniform?"

"Or if he sold one," D'Artagnan said.

Porthos gave D'Artagnan an appreciative look. "Or if he lost one."

"What I don't understand," Porthos said, "is why Buckingham would want to meet with this woman if she wasn't the Queen."

Athos looked at Porthos's brow, furrowed in worry, and felt suddenly humble. He and Aramis and probably D'Artagnan had simply assumed this must still involve the Queen, just because the girl looked like her. Porthos had gone along with it, but had just shown the flaw in their reasoning.

"It's possible he wasn't," Athos said softly. "It's possible that while alive and talking, this woman was nothing like the Queen and that she was killed for some other, private reason.

"Or it's possible someone noticed she looked like the Queen and planned to replace the Queen with her and that this is part of some deep plot," Aramis said. "And the murder was a way to stop it."

Athos nodded. "Yes, that is possible also."

At that moment someone knocked at the door, and Athos went to open it. Outside stood an out-of-breath Planchet, holding a pint of wine in a cheap jug. "I walked very far," the boy said. Then belatedly bowed.

"Regretting your bargain?" Athos asked.

"Not in any way, monsieur. This is by far more interesting than my former employment."

He came in with the jug of wine, and after D'Artagnan found cups, they poured five of them, including Planchet in their round. It seemed to Athos that someone with Planchet's talent should be cultivated.

They discussed no more crimes or crime solving, except that, as they were taking their leave of D'Artagnan, Aramis said, "If we see His Majesty and if he does give us some reward, perhaps we can have a banquet, which will allow us to question a lot of our musketeer comrades. About their uniforms."

Athos saw Planchet's eyes widen at the word *banquet,* and he smiled a little. Athos hoped he would like his bargain and life as the servant of a musketeer. But then, he was not the person to advise anyone on bargains. The bargain he himself had sealed had left him with nothing but a blackened heart and an empty life.

Truth was, he thought, he had thrown himself into the investigation of this crime heart and soul, because he felt as though by catching the man who had killed the anonymous woman, he would be eradicating the guilt that never left him.

Outside, he parted from his friends and walked away, under the moon, with nothing but the ghosts of his past.

Hear Paris by Night; Where Curiosity Takes the Apprentice Musketeer; A Man Who Speaks in Riddles

AFTER the three friends left his lodging, D'Artagnan found himself alone with the servant he had just hired. He didn't quite know what to make of the young man who spoke little but smiled a lot. Planchet's hair was a shocking shade of red, which D'Artagnan had never quite seen in human hair. And he was only maybe three years younger than D'Artagnan.

Though D'Artagnan had often seen his father order his own servant around, his father's servant was a middle-aged man who had followed the elder D'Artagnan into war. And the women servants just giggled a lot and left whatever room D'Artagnan happened to enter.

He eyed his own servant dubiously, noting the worn shirt and breeches and the suggestion of too-prominent ribs beneath the worn shirt. "Planchet, is it?"

"It is, monsieur."

"Oh, call me Monsieur D'Artagnan." He was dubious. He knew his lodging consisted only of a single bed and a couple of blankets. But he had some idea the bed might have two mattresses. "I don't think that the people here counted on my having a servant," he said.

He went into his room and surveyed the bed, finding that indeed it did have two mattresses. Taking one of them, he and Planchet set up a nest for Planchet in the receiving room before D'Artagnan retreated to his bed.

He took off his outer clothes, extinguished his candle and lay down in his shirt. But sleep, which the country boy had always been able to summon as soon as he lay in his bed, eluded him. He turned one way and then another. His sheet rumpled and creased under him.

His blanket felt alternatively too hot and too thin. He thought of his father's house, and of his room at home, the broad, oak-floored, whitewashed room, with the window open to the summer night. At this time of the year, the smell of cut grass, the smell of ripe grapes would be drifting through the window. And were he at home, he would be able to hear crickets in the fields, a calming lullaby.

He got up and opened the window of his room. But the smell that came through the window was not that of freshly cut grass, of ripe grapes, nor even of flowers and pines. Instead, there was an effluvium of garbage and horse manure, or wine and too many people living too close together. And the air itself seemed too hot and too sticky. He went back to bed again and tried to sleep.

But the open window also let in the outside sounds. Nearby, some man screamed, followed by gales of feminine laughter.

Somewhere, probably within a nearby house, a newborn cried. Down the street, a dog barked. Farther on, there was a long, inventive string of curses.

D'Artagnan sat up in bed.

Was that the sound of rapiers crossing nearby?

The events of the day, confusing as they were, from his aborted duel to his fight with the Cardinal's guards, to the corpse in the alley and, finally, to his excursion to the royal palace. And now Athos said that tomorrow they might have a royal audience, they might meet the King in person.

He struggled to listen for the elusive sound of metal on metal. It seemed to him that it had come from a few blocks away.

What a mad day it had been, and what might it not foretell for his future. In fact, his only disappointment this day was that he hadn't made it into the musketeers. But then, all the musketeers seemed to believe it would happen sooner or later.

He got out of bed and paced back and forth.

He wondered what the address at which the woman was supposed to meet . . . someone . . . was like. The musketeers hadn't told him anything about the area. And he didn't yet know enough of Paris to imagine it.

He imagined it, nonetheless. He saw opulent town houses with ornate, sculpted facades. There, the dead girl would have met a velvet- and silk-clad lover who was perhaps Buckingham and who, perhaps, loved her for her resemblance to the Queen of France.

Next, he imagined it a squalid tumble-down neighborhood and the girl meeting a cutthroat ruffian for a dangerous plot.

His overheated imagination would not let him rest. He could go to the address, just to see what the area was like, just to study it, to figure out whether the neighborhood gave him any ideas about the woman. He wouldn't wake anyone or cause any trouble. But he must see the address.

When the imagination of a seventeen-year-old takes hold of his brain, both have a way of moving his body before he can stop it.

In this way, D'Artagnan found himself tiptoeing past the sleeping Planchet and out onto the street, fully dressed, walking under the moonlight, as a pink color appeared in the east to presage dawn.

Down one street and then the other, following the idea that the street was near the Seine. The city climbed down gradually to the river side, and D'Artagnan followed through streets and staircases, thinking that he'd never find the street or the house on his own, but not caring.

And then to his surprise, he looked up at a plaque on the wall of the house in front of him. It was the right street. He counted the houses down the street, looking at the numbers, till he found the right house.

The street itself, and the tall, narrow buildings lining it, weren't far above the Rue des Fossoyers in either appearance or prestige. The houses were perhaps better built and more freshly painted. The balconies sported vast vases of flowering plants. Small gardens overflowed in roses and trees. Ivy covered some of the houses.

The house mentioned in the note was in a little better upkeep than the others, and it had two rounded balconies in the front with stone parapets, one on the first floor, the other on the second. Ivy grew up the left side of the building, extending to the left half of the front facade.

The first-floor balcony showed an open door with light spilling through. Lots of light, as though there were more than a lamp in there. The letter had been addressed to that first floor.

D'Artagnan's imagination took over again. Images formed of himself climbing to that balcony and finding out some miraculous clue, or overhearing something that solved the whole case and delivering the solution and the villains' names to his friends tomorrow. He could see himself meeting his friends to go to the Hotel Treville and telling them all he knew who'd murdered the beautiful young woman who looked like the Queen of France.

He could imagine Aramis's envious admiration, Athos's calls for a drinking celebration and Porthos's saying he was proud of D'Artagnan.

His imagination having thus seized hold of his mind, D'Artagnan's strong hands seized hold of the ivy that climbed the building. A foot on a carved stone detail, a hand holding onto the ivy, D'Artagnan hoisted his slim and agile body up the side of the building, up and up and up, till he rested his foot on the edge of the balcony, and his hand grasped the stone surround of the open door.

Where he was standing, he would be invisible to anyone in the room. The open shutter hid most of him. What protruded—about half of his face, and his hand—would be hidden by the exterior darkness in contrast to the brightly lit interior.

But he could have stood in the balcony, in full view of the interior, and not have been seen. The two people within the room were far too busy with their own argument to notice him, or anything beyond themselves.

She was a tall, gracefully built woman, with long black hair. With her back to him, he could not see if she was young or old, beautiful or ugly. But there was something to her bearing, some impression of nobility that made her look like a duchess in exile. And he could see she was angry.

The man facing her looked noble and well dressed also. In fact, he looked like Aramis. So much so, that for a moment

D'Artagnan thought that it was Aramis taking care of yet another seamstress.

But the woman yelled, "I want you to tell me—I want to know where . . ."

The man's handsome face contorted in anger. He too put his hands on either side of his waist. "I don't know who you are. I don't understand your questions. I just want you to leave."

"Not until you tell me what you were doing."

The man took a step forward. The woman rushed forward too and shoved on his chest with both hands.

He stumbled across the room, fetched up against the bed, straightened himself and took his hand to the ornate pommel of the sword at his waist. "Why you . . ." he said.

D'Artagnan couldn't stand by and watch yet another woman be murdered. For all he knew, this man was the murderer of the woman in the alley and would now repeat his crime.

He charged into the room, jumping off the balcony edge with such a leap that he tripped into the bedroom. By the time he managed to keep himself from falling headlong, he was halfway to the two people arguing.

In the blur of righting himself, he heard the woman shriek. He had the impression of wide-open eyes, a pale face, a woman's mouth yelling something at him. And then she was gone, behind him. D'Artagnan heard her feet hit the stone balcony as though mid-leap.

D'Artagnan straightened to face the man who looked like Aramis and whose hand was resting upon his sword. By the time D'Artagnan was fully balanced, he was no less than two steps away from the man.

"What were you about to do to that woman, you villain?" D'Artagnan said.

The man looked bewildered. His eyes opened wide, his mouth dropped open. He looked like he was having trouble understanding D'Artagnan's words. His lips moved as if he was about to speak. He took his hand away from his sword.

D'Artagnan grasped his pommel. The stranger looked at D'Artagnan's hand and frowned. "Are all Frenchmen mad, then?"

Thrown off balance. D'Artagnan was not sure what the man meant, but he was sure the man didn't intend to attack D'Artagnan. The young Gascon said, "What do you mean?"

The man chuckled once, a dry sound with no humor. "What I mean is that while I was here, packing my own bag and minding my own matters, a beautiful woman flung herself through my window, as you did, just now. She wanted to know what I was doing in Paris." He shrugged elaborately. His French was impeccable but had just a hint of the wrong emphasis, which gave the impression it was not his native language. But his shrug was wholly French, native or learned. "What does one answer to such a madwoman? And she started screaming at me, as only a madwoman would."

He looked up at D'Artagnan, his gaze open and clear. Then he opened both hands, palms out in a show of helplessness. "And then you came bursting through my window, yourself. Perhaps it is overkill to put shutters on doors and windows in France? Perhaps you should content yourselves with curtains, so you don't have the trouble of breaking in?"

D'Artagnan swallowed. What he'd seen through the window had looked so clear. There was a woman who was angry at a man, and there was a man who looked like he was about to hurt the woman. This after they'd found this address in the pocket of a dead woman.

It had seemed obvious that this man was the murderer.

But now, looking at the man's clear green eyes, which might be the color of Aramis's but didn't seem to hold half of Aramis's guile, D'Artagnan wasn't so sure he was a black-hearted, murdering villain.

His eye took in details that he hadn't at first noticed—the fine lace at the man's wrists, which made Aramis's fine lace look like worn rags. The well-cut doublet, above, the well-fitted hose and boots. And that open expression—puzzled and angry but not concerned, as if he didn't know what was happening.

D'Artagnan realized that this man was of far better birth than D'Artagnan, of far better birth than Aramis—in fact, so far above them that it seemed impossible their lives should ever cross.

But if he was so noble and so powerful, why was he packing his own clothes? That part of the story, D'Artagnan could see was true, as an expensive-looking valise lay open on the bed and, within it, hints of lace and velvet.

And yet, the man was clearly telling the truth about his lack of interest in the brunette woman. She'd been the one to run, as though she were trespassing. And he'd stood there and watched her run with no more than a bewildered expression and an exasperated remark on the nature of Frenchmen.

And now, while D'Artagnan stood there, staring at him, hand on sword, the man backed up and resumed his packing. From his desk he retrieved a golden ring with a curious-looking heart-shaped red stone. It reminded D'Artagnan of the equally curious little braided ring in the dead woman's pouch, but there was little to link the two rings, this one being several degrees of magnitude above the other in quality and style.

As D'Artagnan watched, the man kissed the ring and lay it, reverently within his valise. The valise was leather and shaped in such a way that long-distance travelers could strap to their saddles.

"You mean to travel soon," D'Artagnan said.

The man smiled, an ironical smile that might have befitted Aramis. "What a curious country France is," he said. "Where a stranger can come through the window and interrogate me about my own private affairs."

At this, D'Artagnan's gorge rose and his spine went reflexively up. "My name is Henri D'Artagnan," he said. "And I apologize if I broke into your room without warning or invitation. I beg you to believe I had my reasons, which I am not at liberty to disclose to you, since the secret does not belong to me alone. However, I'm ready to give you satisfaction on the field of honor if that's what you wish."

The man smiled wider and waved D'Artagnan away. "I could say I am not a child killer, but that would only, doubtlessly, make you crazier. If I'm not mistaken, you are a Gascon and I know your kind."

"My—"

"Monsieur, I do not wish to fight you. Were my life mine, I would gladly face you on the field of honor. But my life is pledged to my liege, for a work bigger than myself, a work that I promised I could help him achieve. As such, I must decline the honor of killing you or letting you kill me." He bowed slightly. "It is a pleasure to know you, Monsieur D'Artagnan. I am not able to give you my name for the same reason I cannot give you my secret. In this case, and at this time, that name does not belong to me, nor is it mine to give."

The fact that the man had admitted that, should they face off, there was a good chance D'Artagnan would kill him, mollified D'Artagnan's wounded feelings. Somewhat. But the affair was still dishonorable. This stranger had insulted him.

He took his hand from his sword. He put it on his sword again.

"You insulted me. You cannot refuse my challenge."

The stranger looked back at D'Artagnan and smiled. "I can and I do. I did not mean to insult you. You have my apology. A man who's been as near to heaven as I have shouldn't fear apologizing."

Heaven? Was the man insane? D'Artagnan couldn't duel someone who was wandering in his wits.

"Will you answer my questions, monsieur?" he asked, as gently as he could. "Will you tell me if you are to leave in the morning?"

The stranger gestured toward the bag. "Clearly I am. As long as you don't ask where exactly I am going and are willing to take my word that I am returning from whence I came."

"And where were you yesterday evening, at the hour taverns close?" D'Artagnan asked.

The man shrugged, and a strange smile played upon his lips. "I was as close to heaven as I ever hope to be."

D'Artagnan blinked. But there was just that hint of evasiveness about the man's answer that made him wonder if the man would find heaven in killing a woman. "And where was this heaven?" he asked.

The other man frowned. "In this very room," he said. "But again, it is not my secret to give."

If it wasn't his secret, then the woman involved must be alive. And yet . . . "Monsieur, I am not so young that I can't see you must have met with a woman. Is that woman still alive and well?"

The man looked shocked. A point in his favor, because he looked as if it had never occurred to him that she might *not* be alive.

"Monsieur," the man said at last, the same little smile plying upon his lips, "here on the witness of God, I swear to you that she is alive and hale."

"Are you sure? If you saw her yesterday something might have befallen her since."

"If she were not alive or if something had happened to her, I would know it by now." The man hesitated. "And in any case, under heaven and God's eye I swear to you I'd rather be cut into pieces than harm a single hair on her head."

D'Artagnan looked at this man's wide-open green eyes, his expression of beatific remembering and his heart sank.

There went all his dreams of solving this case all by himself, this evening. He would like to believe the man was lying, but truth be told he didn't think he could do so. There was such sincerity in his words, such open-eyed honesty in his look that, with the worst will in the world, D'Artagnan could not doubt him.

He removed his hat and gave the man a deep, flourished bow. "I apologize for disturbing you, milord, and I leave you to your rest."

The man waved him away with a grand gesture as though, normally, he were a commander of men, at whose hand armies marched and enemies trembled. "Oh, never mind the rest," he said, and his lips convulsed with mirth. "I but doubt that before you're fully down from that balcony another lunatic French will come through to ask me something I don't understand. And this shall continue till morning and I will get no rest."

With those words ringing in his ears, D'Artagnan made his way to the balcony and down the ivy to the ground. Of the brunette woman, he saw no trace.

Spending the King's Largesse;
How Musketeers Celebrate;
Porthos's Subtlety

IF D'Artagnan had imagined a lot of things flowing from the fateful duel at the Barefoot Carmelites, he could never have imagined a chain of events as confusing as the next two days would prove to be.

In fact, despite the musketeers' eagerness to resolve the case of the anonymous dead woman in the alley, all of their investigations came to an absolute standstill.

When D'Artagnan, bone tired, dragged in to his lodging on the first dawning of that April morning, he still could not sleep. He kept thinking of meeting the King in the morning.

It never happened.

The private congratulations by Monsieur de Treville were followed by that worthy man's hastening to the palace.

He was too late. The King was already closeted with the Cardinal and it wasn't till the evening that Monsieur de Treville could prevail on the King to hear his version of the events instead of the Cardinal's account, which branded every musketeer a criminal. This was followed by a visit to the tennis court and a taunt D'Artagnan—stinging from his encounter with the stranger who was not Aramis—could not ignore.

This led to D'Artagnan and his friends being involved in a duel with several guards of the Cardinal during the course of which D'Artagnan almost killed Monsieur Bernajoux, the most fearsome duelist in Paris, while the musketeers lay siege to the home of Monsieur de Tremouille and threatened to burn the house down.

Suffice it to say that when Monsieur de Treville had made his case to the royal ear, the musketeers had two victories over the guards to their credit.

It was therefore in some glory that they made their way to the royal gaming room, where he was surprised to find the King an amiable small man, somewhat overweight.

He paid them numerous compliments on their swordsmanship, suggested a place for D'Artagnan in the Corps of Guards led by Monsieur des Essarts, since Monsieur des Essarts was Monsieur de Treville's brother-in-law, this was easily arranged, and gave them forty gold pistols.

Then he dismissed them because he must speak with Monsieur de Treville about guard shifts and which musketeers to take on a journey.

The Kings of England and France—or rather, their ministers, Richelieu and Buckingham—had arranged to meet. It was not to be a meeting for any substantive policy discussions, but rather one of those meetings in which kings reassure one another of eternal friendship, which doesn't mean they won't declare war the next week.

Because neither the King of France nor the King of England trusted the other enough to meet in their respective capitals, a meeting had been planned for the fields at Calais, where the entire company was to lodge in tents. Very sumptuous tents, of course, such as the ones that had been set up almost a century before in similar circumstances, for the Field of the Cloth of Gold.

The King would be taking some musketeers with him, and some would stay behind to guard the palace.

Normally the three friends would have been chosen to go, but since Athos's shoulder was bleeding again after all his exertions, the three were to stay behind.

Even the King could not think of coming between the three inseparables.

Coin in hand, the musketeers left the palace by a more impressive gate than the one D'Artagnan had used before with Aramis.

Monsieur de Treville had stayed behind with the King, so once a few steps from the palace, the friends could speak as they wished.

Feeling slightly let down—at not having been received into the musketeers—but happy with a commission in the guards and his share of the forty pistols, D'Artagnan said, "It is time we got back to solving the murder."

He was relieved when Athos agreed.

"Indeed," the oldest musketeer said. "After your foolhardy expedition in the night, we have done nothing."

Aramis looked contrite. "I must ask my friend about Saint Jerome," he said.

"And I don't suppose we could give a banquet," Porthos said. "And thus interview our comrades about their uniforms."

"Without calling attention to it," Aramis said, with a warning look at Porthos.

"I shall order the dinner," Athos said. "At the Fleet Hare in St. Germain."

And thus the dinner was ordered, at which Planchet would be taught to serve at table by Mosqueton, Bazin and Grimaud.

Only when D'Artagnan entered the Fleet Hare, he found there was no table as such. The Fleet Hare was a very upscale tavern, not the sort at which the musketeers routinely got drunk.

Three floors high, it looked like something out of the Orient, with curtains and cushions made of red brocade, heavily embroidered. The curtains created little nooks and niches, where small groups could arrange themselves in relative privacy.

The four friends immediately installed themselves at one of these nooks, with Porthos sitting on a sturdy-looking tambourette covered in leather ornamented with polished golden nails. Athos sat on the floor, leaning slightly over the small table in the middle, for ease of access to the wine jug and cup. Aramis reclined against pillows, managing to look fully relaxed and yet somehow regal.

D'Artagnan himself was left with the option of sitting on pillows also, but felt he did it with far less aplomb than Aramis. More like a drunkard than a lord.

In the other nooks and around other small tables, musketeers gathered in a splendor of blue uniforms and polished swords.

Rabbits and other game were served while others of their kind roasted merrily at hearths throughout the tavern.

A stream of wine, served by comely wenches, poured into their cups or table jugs.

In the walls, here and there, torches added to the blaze, and to the smell, since the candles seemed to be made of rendered tallow.

It was almost unbearably hot. But that didn't deter the people assembled in groups and bands everywhere. Most of the musketeers sat at ease, their doublets unlaced, their hats set aside. One of them, whom D'Artagnan had never seen, sat in a corner, playing the guitar. A couple of women similarly unlaced in a rather more substantial manner than of a doublet, leaned on each of his arms, listening to the music which, it seemed to D'Artagnan, who'd often met with itinerant musicians in his town, was very ill played indeed.

D'Artagnan soon grew dizzy and it seemed to him as though he were either falling asleep at intervals, or as though the succeeding moments came like a stage play, with scenes shifting in and out of focus as if obscured by a curtain.

One moment it seemed to him that all his friends were sitting around him, talking of wenches and drink. Well, Porthos and Aramis spoke of wenches, and Athos spoke—if at all—of drink.

Then Athos, who had drunk more than any of them, sat up straighter and seemed to shed any appearance of drunkenness. "I think it is time we looked around," he said. "And talked to some of our comrades. Common courtesy as hosts, and besides, it might help us track that uniform."

After that, the scenes seemed to flicker, as though various actors left the stage or came back on it in response to some coordinated sign that D'Artagnan could not see. Sometimes all three of his friends were around him, trading stories of the people they'd talked to and what they'd said. And at other times, there was only one.

He must have dozed because he suddenly found himself alone in the nook—bereft of Athos, Porthos and Aramis— while a slim, small musketeer sidled up next to him. The man was far more indecently good-looking than any man had the right to be. No, not good-looking; he was beautiful, from his small, triangular face to the curly black hair carefully arranged around his pale-skinned features.

"So," he said, by way of introduction, "for whom do you work?"

Half asleep and stupid with it, D'Artagnan blinked.

"I beg your pardon," he said. He managed to rouse himself enough to mutter, "I don't know what you mean."

The unknown musketeer gave an amused titter and covered his mouth with a smooth hand. "Oh, come. You ride into Paris one day, manage to make friends with the three inseparables the next? Do you know how many of us have longed to be one of their circle? But none of us are good enough, till some little Gascon comes out of nowhere, and somehow becomes their best friend? And then I am expected to believe that a Gascon boy, little more than a child, wounded seven of the Cardinal's fearsome guards in two days? It is too much. It's clear your identity and all these events are a cover, so tell me, for whom do you work?"

"Work?" D'Artagnan said, his tongue moving torpidly while his mind tried to evaluate what he should do. And what he could do, according to honorable rules. Since he and his three musketeer friends were the hosts of this banquet, was this man his guest? And if this man were his guest, was D'Artagnan obliged to not cut his tongue out of his uncivil mouth because of those insulting words? Or did he need to put up with it for the sake of hospitality?

More important, after all the wine he'd drunk, could D'Artagnan wake enough to make a go of it in a duel? Or should he ask the man to meet him later, outside some conveniently isolated religious house? And would this postponing of reckoning be enough to answer to social niceties?

And would Athos, Porthos and Aramis be upset if D'Artagnan fought another musketeer?

The musketeer looked at D'Artagnan with incredulity, not so much as if he doubted D'Artagnan's answer, but rather D'Artagnan's very existence. "Come," he said. "In this court, all are enmeshed in some intrigue or other, for court or Queen or Cardinal or something. Someone as odd as you cannot possibly have landed in the middle without knowing it." He grinned, the smile transforming his triangular features into the satisfied expression of a cat. "So, tell me, for whom are you working?"

"De Termopillae," a booming voice spoke, from above D'Artagnan, "you are an ass."

The young man looked up and blinked, and D'Artagnan looked up also, to stare at the serious, watchful face of Porthos.

Porthos acknowledged D'Artagnan with a mere glance, then turned to the other man again. "Is that a new uniform?" he asked.

Looking confused, probably startled by the transition from Porthos's insult to his sartorial comment, De Termopillae looked up and stammered, "Yes, yes, it is."

"What did you do with the old one?" Porthos asked. "Sell it?"

De Termopillae's mouth fell half open, as though completely confused by that line of enquiry. But no one, looking up at the redheaded giant with his stern expression so reminiscent of a master's scolding an errant pupil, could have withheld an answer. "No. No," De Termopillae stammered. "It was stolen from the line. At my laundress's. Forced me into getting this new one."

Porthos harrumphed deep in his throat, as though not quite believing the explanation but choosing not to dispute it at that moment. "You may go," he said, stern and dismissive. "Unless you want to make an appointment to meet me somewhere quiet and private soon . . ."

De Termopillae scrambled up, a scared cat clawing at the cushions on which they sat, finally standing and sliding out of the nook the four friends had claimed for themselves.

Porthos sat down on his tambourette, which buckled under his mass of lean muscle. He frowned and gestured toward a waitress, asking to have his tankard filled.

D'Artagnan had managed to fight off the effects of wine so that his normal vision came back, save for a slightly glowing aura around persons and objects. The aura around Porthos's red hair made him look as if his whole head were on fire.

D'Artagnan blinked, looking at him. "I didn't know if it was proper to challenge him," D'Artagnan said. "My father said not to tolerate insults from anyone, except the King and

Queen," and, changing the truth a little to fit the moment, he changed the Cardinal to a personage that Porthos would approve of, "or Monsieur de Treville. But that man was our guest, and besides, he is a musketeer."

Porthos hissed air out between his teeth, without denying that the man was a musketeer and yet seeming to cast it all in doubt. "De Termopillae is an ass," he repeated. "Monsieur de Treville only found him a place in the corps at the King's own request and that because his cousin is one of His Majesty's good friends. Feel free to invite De Termopillae to meet you in any secluded place for an affair of honor and I'll gladly be your second." The giant musketeer quenched his indignation in his tankard, then wiped his red-stained lips on his sleeve. "I avow, all this subtle questioning will be the death of me."

"Subtle?" D'Artagnan asked, thinking of Porthos standing there, glowering, asking direct questions of De Termopillae.

"Yes. All this, 'Did you lose a uniform?' questioning. It would be so much easier to simply identify the few capable of it, like De Termopillae, and ask if they sold their uniform to an agent of the Cardinal." Porthos sighed. "But Athos says we have to be subtle, and that usually means *not* slapping people till they tell the truth."

He took another draught of his tankard and looked pensive.

D'Artagnan collected himself enough to sit up straight and notice that his own tankard was half full. Under the sound principle that if wine had made him dizzy, it might just as well cure it, he took a draught. "Did you find anyone else, other than De Termopillae, who has a new uniform recently?" he asked.

"Oh, three or four," Porthos said. "But all the others are trying to sell their old uniforms." He chewed on the corner of his lip. "One almost has to, you know, with the extortionary amounts that tailors charge these days."

"But only De Termopillae can't account for what happened to his old uniform?" D'Artagnan asked.

"That's right," Porthos said and suddenly cheered up. "Hey, since it's De Termopillae, perhaps Athos will let me slap him till he tells the truth."

He would doubtless have expanded more on this pleasant prospect, but just then, a singalong started. Much to D'Artagnan's shock, it was about the Cardinal. Well, he wasn't so much shocked at its being about the Cardinal. That wouldn't be so unusual considering these men served Monsieur de Treville.

No, the amazing thing was that this figure, feared and revered in equal amounts in the provinces and spoken of as more powerful than the King, here was derided for his bandy legs, his crooked back and his relationships with his mistress, Madam d'Aiguillon and *his niece*, Madame de Comablet.

While trying to sing along with the unknown and quite shockingly explicit verses, D'Artagnan thought back upon what he'd heard.

De Termopillae might or might not be lying about his uniform being stolen from the line at his laundress's. Fact was that very few would steal a musketeer's uniform, or at least that's what D'Artagnan thought. Considering the musketeers' reputation as madmen more than ready and willing to kill anyone for the wrong word or a wrong look, who would be cavalier enough to steal a uniform from one of them?

On the other hand, clearly, the guards of the Cardinal might have.

And, yes, De Termopillae had looked as if he were lying. But then, it seemed to D'Artagnan, someone blessed with Termopillae's features, with his triangular face and slanting green eyes, would always look as if he were dissembling even while speaking the absolute truth.

And Porthos's hope notwithstanding, if De Termopillae had such high connections at court as to get the King himself to exert pressure on his behalf, D'Artagnan very much doubted that Athos would allow Porthos to slap the truth out of the other musketeer.

So, there was only one solution for it. In the three days D'Artagnan had been a member of the group he'd taken a measure of its members, to a certain degree. If he was not wrong—and he rarely was—then Porthos knew an amazing number of working-class women. Not the ones who sold their bodies, but the ones who truly worked with them, at washing clothes or sewing, cleaning or doing another of the hundred unsung tasks that were needed around any large city everyday.

D'Artagnan leaned over to Porthos and said, "Do you know who his laundress is?"

"De Termopillae's?" Porthos asked. "No, but I can find out. There are only so many women who wash the uniforms of the corps." He grinned, suddenly, unexpectedly. "I should ask the source and verify his story, should I not?"

D'Artagnan nodded. "I will go with you," he said, before joining into the song about Madam d'Aiguillon.

Later, after the party was done, he poured out onto the crowded street with the three musketeers and their noisier female companions. He'd noticed that three of them had congregated around Aramis by the end of the banquet. He noticed also that Aramis, while being charming to them all, did not encourage their advances nor their interest in him.

Remembering the woman Aramis called Violette, he couldn't really be surprised. It would be like drinking cheap, soured wine after the best liqueur.

He was thinking about this—thinking about Aramis, who charmed all women but who seemed to have interest only in the one he couldn't marry; about Porthos, whose mind preferred the concrete and the tangible and who was in the midst of this tangled affair with Aramis; about Athos . . . Athos who . . .

D'Artagnan became aware that the four of them were now alone, walking in silence along one of the broader boulevards. Their servants had stayed behind to package the leftover food and wine—which they had paid for in advance—that should feed all of them for several days.

Athos walked slightly ahead of them, his features serious, his brow a little wrinkled.

Without having paid attention, D'Artagnan was willing to bet Athos had drunk twice as much as even Porthos, who was much larger. He also knew that Athos's drinking worried his two other friends. Porthos and Aramis would often exchange looks of concern and sometimes of confusion, as Athos embarked on his fifth—or tenth—bottle of the evening.

D'Artagnan had seen enough habitual drunkards to know what they feared. Even in his small town in Gascony, he'd

seen men old before their time with rheumy eyes and unsteady, trembling hands. He'd heard them struggle to recall
events and people of whose memory alcohol had robbed
them.

Oh, he saw none of those signs in Athos. But then he
didn't know how long Athos had been drinking or how
steadily.

What he did know was that the wine that seemed to make
so many men jolly and talkative plunged the older musketeer into unshakeable melancholy and made him more quiet
than ever.

He looked at Athos's chiseled profile under the moonlight, took in the musketeer's furrowed brow, his frowning
countenance, and wondered what in his own past Athos was
frowning at.

He could look at Aramis and Porthos and see what might
have sent them into hiding under presumed names, in an outfit such as the musketeers; it would have been some indiscre-
tion of Aramis's, some notorious brawl in which Porthos's
great size and his ready courage would have made him remarkable.

But what could have caused Athos to hide? And what was
he hiding from? Oh, he fought like a demon, and he was possessed of as much courage as any of them, perhaps more.
But he lacked that sudden, emotive capacity for acting without thinking that was so obvious in his other comrades.

It was easy for D'Artagnan to imagine Athos in his natural element—striding about some provincial domain, attending to every aspect of governing it with knowledge
derived from a voluminous library harking back to Rome
and Greece. He would fight, yes, if needed, if someone
threatened one of his servants, offended one of his serfs or
in some other way injured him or one of those under his
protection.

D'Artagnan could not imagine Athos as he clearly was
now, fighting at someone's wrong word, someone bumping
into him the wrong way. The fact that he had seen Athos like
that now didn't destroy his impression that this was not only
wrong but impossible, a perversion of nature and disposition.

Athos turned to D'Artagnan as if noticing his stare, and
D'Artagnan, trying to think of an explanation for looking so

long, realized suddenly and with a shock, that in this life they lived, Athos was looking for death.

The same oblivion he sought and failed to find in wine, he also sought at the end of the blades of strangers whom he challenged to duels. And there too he failed to find it.

But why did Athos wish to die?

Before he lost his mind enough to ask Athos the question—and it would undoubtedly have happened, had they continued to frown at each other the way they were—Aramis spoke from behind them. "I found out where the medal came from."

"Oh?" D'Artagnan said, looking back, glad for the distraction.

Aramis hesitated a moment, then nodded. "It's a medal given to orphans . . . orphan girls, raised at a convent, at the edge of town," he said. "The orphanage of St. Jerome Emiliani, which is run by charitable nuns."

Porthos smacked his lips audibly. "They give the medal to every orphan? Wealthy orphanage they must be to give a golden medal to—"

"No," Aramis said. "They give it to . . . to orphans who are not quite so orphaned as others." Aramis's voice betrayed his embarrassment and, looking over his shoulder, D'Artagnan could see Aramis blush.

"What?" Porthos asked, no doubt thinking he was displaying great tact. "Do you mean that there are orphans who are more orphaned than others?"

Aramis pressed his lips together and looked exasperated. "Porthos, imagine that a gentleman, a man of noble birth behaves in a way against the law of chastity with a woman who is not his wife. A . . . seamstress or an attorney's wife."

Aramis's blush had now become a raging red, like a fever. "He might not want to condemn the product of his mistake to poverty and eternal shame, but neither would he want to call it his and display it before polite society."

He lifted his hand to forestall a protest that Porthos's expression must have announced. "I know, I know that some people do, but those are usually only in the highest society, or alternately, the lowest wrungs of nobility, where such an eccentricity might easily be tolerated. But for your average nobleman, with a wife and relations . . . well, it is just not possible. It is then that he might approach the nuns or monks—depending on the gender of the child—of such a house as St. Jerome's and hand the child over. And with the child, to avoid its being raised as a common orphan, a stipend, a payment for the maintenance of the child as befits the father's estate."

"Oh," Porthos said. "Almost like borders, then?"

"Exactly," Aramis said, his blush subsiding somewhat.

And then D'Artagnan noticed out of the corner of his eye, that Athos, still frowning, was now flushed as well—as though all the wine he'd drunk through the evening had finally made itself felt.

Only not quite that, because the flush on his cheeks was accompanied by a worse frown than ever, by eyes hastily averted from D'Artagnan's searching gaze, and by a look of . . . embarrassment.

What did Athos know about such places that raised such orphans who weren't orphans? Was that the secret that had sent him into hiding?

D'Artagnan wanted to ask, but did not dare.

"I know where this orphanage is," Aramis said. "It's a few hours out of Paris, on a decent horse. And I was thinking of going there tomorrow and seeing if we can find the identity of our corpse that way."

"I will go with you, Aramis," Athos said.

And D'Artagnan wondered if Athos was going with Aramis to preserve a secret he didn't want anyone guessing.

Where We Learn of the Province of Several Saints; From Inconvenient Children to Repentance; The Story of a Lost Girl; An Old Enemy in a New Place

$\mathcal{T}$**HE** next day was spent sleeping off the celebration. In the late afternoon, Athos and Aramis set off. It was a balmy afternoon, still bright and full of promise. The sort of day that always made Athos glower and bristle. Aramis was prepared to find his companion in this mood when—on a horse borrowed from Monsieur de Treville's stable, since Aramis didn't keep a horse in peacetime—he made his way to Athos's lodgings.

But Grimaud, Athos's servant, opened the door looking even more sullen than usual, and when Athos appeared he was silent and pensive, a combination of worry and anger and whatever else it was that drove him on and fueled his drunken binges.

He did not wear his uniform. Neither did Aramis, who was glad to see his own decision endorsed by Athos. A musketeer's uniform was hardly the right calling card at an orphanage that specialized in raising abandoned female waifs. That is, unless the musketeer were leaving behind a baby.

Aramis had chosen one of his good suits in decent ecclesiastical black, which was sure to bring out the bright color of his green eyes and the gold in his blond hair. The cut was in the latest stare of fashion, with German breeches that tied below the knee, and were slashed at the back to reveal pristine linen undergarments. As for the doublet, it was cut loose, as the new ones were, and hung down to mid-thigh. It had fewer ribbons and lace than Aramis preferred, but it looked fine. And, of course, made him look respectable.

All in all, he'd been very pleased with his choice. Until he saw Athos.

Athos's suit was nothing so fine as Aramis's. One of his old-fashioned Spanish doublets—which had to be at least ten years old—tightly laced; and riding breeches of the same period, far too tight—in dark, subdued blue. They looked old and the velvet had thin patches where the under weave showed. And Athos had no lace at all: not at cuff, not at collar.

The belt he wore, with his sword, was the same he wore with his uniform, an undistinguished affair of wear-darkened leather.

And if Aramis owned a sword half so fine as the one on the wall of Athos's lodging, he would have brought it down from the wall to wear on this day. That sword would have been enough to bring the whole outfit out of its present shabby category and give it the look of understated nobility.

But once, when Aramis had asked Athos to borrow the sword for a particularly important occasion, Athos had emptied his purse, his jewelry pouch, thrown in his dagger and told Aramis to take all of it or whatever he wanted from it, but not the sword.

The sword would stay on that wall until its owner left this lodging.

And apparently Athos himself would not bring the sword down.

With all this, Athos should have looked shabby and down at heel. At best, he should have resembled a provincial lord lacking the wherewithal to make an impression in the capital.

Instead, he looked like a lord too fine for expensive velvets and too good for new silks and, with his appearance, made Aramis feel overdressed, effete and garish.

It made Aramis tug impatiently at the lace on his own sleeves, adjust the jeweled pommel of his sword and generally behave ill-at-ease while Grimaud disappeared and then returned leading a pure black horse, the one Athos normally used when the occasion demanded it.

Neither Aramis nor Porthos knew if it was Athos's horse

or if he borrowed it. It was stabled at Monsieur de Treville's, but no one rode it except Athos. This same animal, called Samson, appeared whenever Athos needed to ride somewhere.

When Athos mounted it, he looked more than ever the grand-seigneur. And more grim than ever and vaguely threatening.

They rode in silence, out of the city and into the countryside.

Whenever—rarely—they had the occasion to ride through the countryside in time of peace, Athos had a way of speeding ahead, by himself, in his own world. And then, as though suddenly remembering he had company, stopping and allowing the others to catch up with him.

This time was no different, except that, after letting Aramis catch up with him, he slowed down so he fell well behind the other musketeer, before noticing and rushing up well ahead of Aramis again.

During all this he wasn't very good company, and it did not improve when they stopped at a tavern for dinner where Athos ate in silence and drank a great deal more than any man who is going to meet with nuns should. He complained of his shoulder wound once, which might have provided some excuse but not enough for such uncivil behavior.

A few hours' ride later, they came within the domain of the orphanage, which was endowed as a noble house would be, with fields and vineyards and animals.

The prospect of the fields was pleasant and well tended, and the servants looking after trees and vines or pasturing flocks in this verdant countryside seemed happy and well fed.

Then the orphanage itself appeared, atop a hillock.

It was white. That was Aramis's first impression of it. Then he thought that it looked oddly fortified, with tall, blank walls facing the outside. He assumed the house itself was somewhere within that protective shell, but he could catch no more glimpse of it than a hint of slate roof.

"How like a fortress," he said. "I'm amazed they don't have watchtowers in every corner."

This was at a moment when Athos was, fortuitously, right at his side, and the older musketeer gave Aramis a surprised look, which quickly turned to amusement. "It would look like a fortress, to one of those who wish they could scale its walls and steal one of the jewels it shelters, would it not?" he asked.

"I didn't—" Aramis started.

But Athos smiled, one of his brief, ironical smiles, as if he knew what Aramis thought better than Aramis himself did. At moments like this, Aramis felt a great deal of annoyance with his older friend.

"I think it is very pleasant," Athos said firmly, as they came to a gate, where an old man stood in attendance. Aramis didn't hear what Athos said to the old man, but he bowed low and addressed them both. "If you would leave your horses with me, I'll see them stabled. If you go to the front room and ask to see the Mother Superior, someone will call her."

Leaving their horses behind, they walked up a winding path between tall trees. Beyond the trees, they could barely glimpse broad gardens and on the gardens, here and there, like flocks of wild birds, groups of young women in white.

It was too far away for Aramis to discern their features, though he tried to imagine them as beautiful, unspoiled nymphs in a paradisaical setting, completely innocent of the wiles of men or the world.

When he felt Athos's gaze upon him and turned to see the quizzical look on his friend's face, he shrugged and disciplined himself into looking at the building that now showed itself at the end of the straight stretch of lane. It was huge and as square and white as its external walls. However, so many windows pierced its looming exterior, and such a broad staircase led to its wide, oak front door that it could not fail to give a welcoming impression.

They climbed the staircase, two steps at a time, and at the top found an elderly nun in a white habit. She had the sort of features—from her prominent cheekbones to her faded blue eyes—that gave the impression that she'd once been a great beauty, and Aramis wondered if she'd grown up and lived here, all the while, never knowing anything but this house and her vows. If so, what a waste for any man who might have been enamored of her beauty.

And then Aramis caught his own thought and scolded himself for it. Who could have a higher use for beauty, but to use it in the service of God?

But she looked at both of them as though she knew well enough men and the hearts of men, and asked, "May I ask what your business is, gentlemen?"

Athos leaned close and whispered once more, something Aramis could not understand. Was he just using his real name, his real identity to open this door, or did he know this place better than he'd told anyone? Had there been, perhaps in Athos's past, the sort of incident that led a gentleman to become acquainted with orphanages?

The nun looked up at Athos, eyes wide, as though trying to divine the truth of what he'd told her. "Monsieur Comte de—" she said.

Athos shook his head, and took his finger to his lips, but his mouth had twisted in one of the very rare smiles of his that showed no trace of irony. He bowed to the nun, "Sister, we come only to enquire about a baby that might have lived here, some years ago. We have a medal she used to wear and . . . I'm afraid we . . . we must know if she grew up here."

The nun looked concerned now. "Only one of our girls left recently. She hasn't done anything scandalous, has she?"

Athos handled it better than Aramis could have managed. He shook his head gently. "Not that we know. But she might be involved in something very dangerous, and I won't know till I establish whether she grew up here or not."

The woman looked up at him again, as though examining his innermost thoughts and evaluating his reliability. Aramis felt her gaze fall on him, and looked down, afraid she would find something objectionable in his eyes.

"Very well," she said. "I'll go get the Mother Superior."

Having had some experience of abbesses and convent mothers, Aramis expected a worldly woman, perhaps in her later years, perhaps dressed in the best fashion of the court. It was not unusual for a noble family to dispose of a second daughter by making her a devotee in an abbey—and in fact by convincing the King to make her an abbess sometimes as soon as she took veil.

Well, either she'd be worldly or very old. In Aramis's experience, great age and saintliness had a way of going together, usually after a very-well-lived life. In fact, Aramis thought he himself might be able to manage some modicum of saintliness if he lived to a ripe old age. If there was an age ripe enough.

But the woman who came in proved all his cynical assumptions wrong. She was middle-aged and dark haired—at least judging by very dark, arched eyebrows and a few straggles of black hair that escaped her white coif. She wore an ample habit like that of the elderly nun. And she had not a trace of makeup on her squarish, sensible-looking face. Her mouth pressed close, in the expression of someone who has a lot to do and doesn't have time for whatever interruption these two strangers might represent.

The elderly nun, having summoned her superior, stayed near the door, obviously as a chaperone.

"Madame," Athos said, advancing and taking the hand she extended, to kiss. "I don't know what to call you?" he said.

She smiled, a tight smile, admitting his impotence. "My name in this house is Mother Clementine. Sister Prophirie said you wish to see me about Madeleine?"

"Madeleine?" Aramis asked, and Mother Clementine turned toward him, her dark eyes attentive, her gaze sharp.

"You don't know—" she said.

"Her name," Athos interrupted. He looked reproachfully at Aramis, a glance that was a definite warning to keep his mouth shut. "We don't know her name, Mother Clementine. We know nothing, in fact, except that she . . . how can I say this . . . she bears a strong resemblance to . . . well, there is no other way of saying it but that she looks very much like the Queen."

Mother Clementine gasped and took a step back. "Madeleine," she said.

"Madame," Athos said. "We must know who Madeleine is and how she came . . . how she came to this convent. And how she left."

The Mother Superior looked on the point of denial. She looked at Athos, then at Aramis, then at Athos again. Her eyes searched Athos's features as though they might contain an answer to a question she did not know how to ask.

"Sister Prophirie said you were . . ."

Athos nodded. "I go by Athos," he said. "But yes, I gave Sister Prophirie my true name. The name I use now is not unlike your name in the convent, my existence before the musketeers having been wholly submerged in it."

"But then surely you know . . ."

"I know nothing. Or at least, it is as if I knew nothing. I never learned the details of the case. I only suspect it because of a little ring we found on her."

Again the sharp gaze examined Athos's features, while the mouth seemed to become firmer, the chin more square. At last, she nodded.

"Seventeen years ago," she said. "When I was but a novice in the house. She was left at the door, in a basket, but she was . . . Her clothing was finer than we're used to seeing and she was wrapped in a little silk blanket. Clutched in her hand was a braided silver ring, with a pinkish stone. And in the basket was a note saying that this girl should be called Madeleine, in memory of her mother's straying and repentance.

"Every month on the anniversary of the date she was abandoned, a packet of coin was received, marked for the keeping of Madeleine. The packets had the seal of a noble house. You know which. We were given to understand this came from her mother. This allowed us to engage a private nursemaid for the girl and keep her in some style in the back parlor. Besides . . ." the Mother Superior hesitated. "Well, she was a good child and obedient, and we had her learn her letters and her numbers and even a little Latin. It wasn't until recently that someone realized she looked a lot like the Queen, which was bound to cause talk, and which is why we were so relieved when . . ."

"When?"

"Well, normally our girls don't leave unless they get married or take the veil—in which case, they might not leave at all—or, in the case of the very poor, destitute, truly orphaned ones, they might leave to positions as nursery maids or servants. But last month a man appeared who could tell us, without hesitation, when Madeleine had been abandoned here, and what the note said, and even the description of her braided ring. He said he believed himself to be the girl's uncle, and asked to meet her." She fidgeted nervously with the beads that hung at her waist. "We allowed it, though heavily chaperoned, of course. The moment this gentleman saw her, he said she was very like her father who, we were given to understand, was a nobleman of some stature. And then he asked us to let him take the girl and raise her . . ."

She hesitated and cocked her head sideways. Her hand continued nervously fidgeting with the beads. "I hope I did not sin," she said. "As I prayed earnestly on it, and saw no reason to doubt the man or his story. He sent Madeleine an extensive and very complete wardrobe and, after meeting with him several times, and discussing the matter with him, I allowed her to leave, with the promise that she would write very often. She left a week ago, in a very grand carriage. Surely nothing bad can have happened to her. Surely . . ."

Athos had gone deathly pale. Aramis tried to summon words with which he could or would wish to puncture this woman's serene certainty that nothing could have gone wrong with her ward, but no words came.

"Let us hope nothing has gone wrong," Athos said. "I shall pray nothing has gone wrong. But . . . if you would tell me, what did Madeleine's uncle look like?"

"He was a dark man, noble and looking very much like a lord. And he had a dark patch over his left eye."

Rochefort. Despite the vague description, Aramis felt sure it was Rochefort, the Cardinal's right hand. The eminence grise to the eminence grise. Only the almost physical weight of Athos's glare on him kept him from saying something.

He could tell, from Athos's expression, that Athos too thought he knew the man.

Outside they collected their horses, and started back on the road to Paris, riding companionably side by side.

But Aramis could not stay his tongue long. He had seen too much in there. The nun had almost called Athos Comte de something. And there was, definitely, a funny constraint about the whole interaction between Athos and the Mother Superior. If Aramis didn't know better, he'd think the two knew each other.

He cast Athos a long sidewise glance and said, loud enough to be heard over the horse's hooves at a canter, "Athos, you must tell me, was the girl your daughter?"

Athos looked back at him and for the first time in Aramis's acquaintance, he looked truly shocked. So shocked, in fact, that it took him several minutes to summon a simple monosyllable. "No."

"Then who was she? Why did your true identity matter? Does the Mother Superior know you? What does it all mean?"

Athos looked gravely at Aramis. "I can't tell you."

"You must tell me. How can we solve this crime if you, of all people, will hold secrets? You must talk to me. Surely you know I'm as silent as a tomb."

Athos smiled, a cold, fugitive smile that showed no teeth. "Aramis," he said, "the only people as silent as a tomb lie in one. I trust you with my life, my friend, but do not ask me to trust you with secrets that involve my family or its honor."

"I have kept a thousand secrets for you, a thousand secrets that would have seen you hanged had I spoken."

Athos allowed his unnerving half-smile to slide across his lips. "Yes. But I have not allowed you to keep secrets that would ruin the reputation of a whole branch of my family, involving innocent people in a plot even they can't guess."

"Is this all the explanation I can expect you to give me?" Aramis asked.

"It is all you have the right to expect," Athos said. "And, Aramis, you and I have seen enough to know that, thrown in the Bastille and tortured, just about anyone can confess to anything."

"I? I would never. You know I have my faith and my—"

"Why tempt the Lord?" Athos said. "You cannot confess that which you do not know."

Aramis had been Athos's friend for years. He'd been his second in countless duels, and had had Athos second for him in countless more. Together they'd brawled and drunk and wenched. Or, at least, Aramis had talked to and romanced wenches while Athos stood by, smiling his unnerving smile.

But this last week had been trying. Far too trying. First there was D'Artagnan, and the enigma that was D'Artagnan and Athos's seeming insistence in taking D'Artagnan at face value and allowing him far deeper into the musketeers' friendship than was prudent after such a short acquaintance.

Then there were all the silences and omissions with which Athos hemmed in their investigation of the corpse in the alley and the sullen silence in which Athos had ridden here as if he couldn't trust himself to speak to Aramis.

And now Athos was acting as if Aramis—Aramis of all people!—could not be trusted with secrets. What good, then, was their friendship of so many years standing?

If Aramis hadn't possessed a nervous and irritable nature, he'd never have got into a duel and dispatched a man who had interrupted his first idylls.

And if he weren't sensitive to insult, he would not have fought countless duels throughout the years.

Alas, now those characteristics spurred him on, and he in turn spurred his horse on, pushing it to a canter, a gallop, distancing himself from Athos. Let him ride in silence and alone, or strive to catch up in vain.

Aramis had had enough of Athos's suspicious behavior and sullen silence.

A Rider in the Night; Athos Faces
His Fears; Where a Young Man Is
the Same As a Young Woman

ATHOS sometimes remembered that he was the oldest of the musketeers. Sometimes, but not too often. Porthos, slightly younger than himself, and Aramis, yet younger than both of them normally managed to fill in what they didn't know of life, with unwavering honor and empathy for those in need or danger. In that way they often seemed to be Athos's own age.

But this was one of those times when Athos felt terribly old, as he watched Aramis spur his horse on, away from him down the fast-darkening road. What did Aramis think? That Athos would cry for fear of riding in the evening with the moon his only company above? That he would strive to catch up with Aramis out of fear that someone would think he couldn't catch up?

The folly of youth was unfathomable.

Athos continued to ride his horse at a trot through the verdant slope lined with trees. Somewhere ahead, when the road was straighter and better lit he too might gallop at least for a while, but with as long a ride as they had ahead of them, galloping on heedlessly would only tire Samson.

If they didn't make it to Paris till morning, it didn't signify much to Athos. Instead, he was thinking of what they'd found back there, in the convent. He wondered whether this girl, tragically dead so early, had been a relative of his. Surely not. It would be too much of a coincidence. And nonetheless, all signs pointed to it. All signs save that Madeleine looked nothing like the family of La Fere, Athos's family, all of whom tended to have a certain, obvious resemblance to each other.

But, of course, she might have taken after her father. Who was some Spanish Lord of the House of Hapsburg. For once, it might have happened.

Yet he couldn't doubt that Madeleine, the good child who'd lived in some comfort at St. Jerome's was the girl found dead in an alley in Paris. He also couldn't doubt that Rochefort was the man who'd taken her from the convent.

Did this mean her fate was of his making? Or had she died not as a result of Rochefort's—and the Cardinal's—plan but as a way of foiling it? Had someone killed her to stop her from doing what she'd been brought to Paris to do? And what *had* she been meant to do?

Whatever it was, and however it was, was there any reason for him to let Aramis know what Athos knew? He could find none. Knowing to what extent the family of La Fere was involved in this would only bring up the matter of Athos's other life, his former identity. It would in no way help solve this poor waif's murder.

Thinking about this, Athos had allowed his horse to slow even more as he passed under the branches of a tree which overhung the road.

He heard fabric rustle. A snap echoed, as a branch overhead was pulled. Leaves whispered frantically.

Instinctively, Athos ducked forward and looked up. What was it overhead? A bird? An animal? A bulk fell. A weight in the saddle behind him made Samson tremble.

A warm body pressed against Athos's back.

"God's blood," Athos said, his hand at his sword. He was too late. Cold metal touched his throat on the right side. He could just see a small, pale hand holding it there. The arm that held the dagger snaked over Athos's shoulder.

He swallowed hard. It was a devilish situation, almost impossible to escape without getting one's throat slashed.

"Do not move, monsieur," someone whispered from behind him, low and viciously. "Not a scream, not a sound, or it's the last one you make."

The metal flashed silver under the moonlight. Aramis's horse was a dot in the distance, in the darkened lane. The sound of his hooves was almost inaudible. And besides, did Athos need to ask for help? Aramis's help?

Something within Athos bridled at the thought. But there was that blade at his throat. And yet that was the reason that Aramis would be no help at all. Before Aramis could reach them—even if Athos cried out now—chances were that he would be dead, his throat ripped out by the sharp blade he could feel nicking his skin. And if Athos fought back . . . No, again, he would be dead, before he had the chance to throw his attacker off.

The way the attacker wrapped himself around Athos, Athos's superior strength meant very little. Unless the attacker didn't mean to kill Athos. But attackers who dropped onto the back of horses and held daggers to strangers' throats usually meant business.

"What do you want?" he asked.

The light of the moon allowed him to see the hand; it was small and well formed. Together with what he could perceive of the body behind him, and from its weight, which did not slow the horse down at all, the attacker must be a small, very young man. Certainly no match for Athos once he could find an advantage and a way to press it.

For one, if Athos himself were trying this daring maneuver, he would have removed the other man's sword by now. This boy was clearly not in the habit of jumping on the back of horses and attacking people in the dark.

"What do you want?" Athos asked again in a whisper. "What am I to do?"

"Lead the horse there," the youth said, and pointed with his free hand toward the right side of the lane. "Among those trees."

A prickle of unease stung the back of Athos's neck, matching the prick of the blade in the front. Among the trees it looked pitch-black and secluded. Though this lane seemed deserted enough, with no other riders, it was still possible that someone might by pure chance pass by and see them. But not within the cluster of trees. There, Athos could be murdered with very little notice from anyone.

Not that he intended to be murdered. If that was this young ruffian's intention, he'd find that plans don't always turn out as one hoped.

Thinking of ways to escape this position, he led the horse slowly into the cluster of trees. Soon, Aramis would notice Athos hadn't followed. Would he turn back for Athos, or would he continue on, stung by Athos's pride and his refusal to share secrets?

And if Aramis came back, would it endanger them both? No. No use hoping and wondering. Athos must deal with this on his own.

He felt a cold stab of fear and realized the irony of the situation. He'd been ambushed while riding in the dark, thinking himself safe. Just as he'd once . . . But he forcefully banished the thought of his dead wife. If he let himself feel guilt and get mired in it, he would get himself killed.

And while his death would be a relief from the haunting guilt, the burning shame of his present position, he owed something to his friends—to Aramis who might ride back and fall into a trap, and to Porthos and D'Artagnan in Paris, caught in the midst of a mystery that might prove lethal for all of them. At least, if the Cardinal truly was involved.

Instead, he thought of what his captor's plans could be. He could just intend to kill Athos, with a quick thrust of the dagger from right to left. But if that were his intention, why lead Athos to the dark space among the trees? It would have been easy enough to do it on the open road, then tip Athos's corpse off the horse and gallop on before anyone saw or connected the attacker to the murder.

In fact, judging from how empty this lane was, it would probably be daybreak before anyone came by and found Athos's corpse.

Asking Athos to ride to a secluded place meant something else—some lengthy process that must happen away from even the most improbable of prying eyes.

But what? Robbing Athos? This was likely, as just tipping the corpse off the horse might both startle the horse and force the murderer to stop ahead and backtrack to get Athos's purse, jewelry, sword and dagger.

Or it was possible that the person now pressing close against Athos's back, holding the dagger poised to his neck, worked for the Cardinal? In which case, he would want to tie up Athos, or in some other way render him immobile, so he

could take Athos to Paris and the Bastille, to interrogate him
about his involvement in this confused affair.

In either case, Athos judged, he would be asked to dismount. And his captor would need to dismount.

Which made the chances of this being an agent of the
Cardinal's almost none. No agent of His Eminence would be
so incompetent as to not have removed Athos's sword already. And searched him for a dagger besides. Because when
they dismounted, the captor would have the blade away from
Athos's neck long enough for him to escape.

All this Athos thought as he carefully rode his horse
down a descending, irregular slope, then over rocky ground
that felt like a dry creek bed, toward the darkest space amid
a cluster of oaks, a space that felt cool and smelled verdant.

There, just as he pulled on the horse's reins to stop it,
Athos decided to chance all. Fortunately the attacker was using his left hand, not his right, so Athos need not exert force
on his left shoulder. Pulling on the rein, he let his elbow go
back just a little too far, very fast, straight into the solar
plexus of his captor.

It could go either way. Startled, the attacker might finish
his motion, draw the knife across Athos throat.

But instead, he made a sound of shock, and the delicate,
small hand opened, letting the knife drop to the ground at the
same time Athos vaulted off his horse, in a motion he'd used
at the battlefront to avoid being crushed beneath the weight
of a stricken mount.

Jumping clear of the horse, Athos jumped farther back
yet, to get a clear look at his captor, while with one hand he
reached for his sword and, with the other, for his own dagger. His right shoulder hurt like the devil's fire, the sudden
jump having unsettled it. He gritted his teeth and ignored the
pain.

A man on horseback almost always had the advantage.
And Athos did not intend to kill or injure Samson, an animal
of whom he had grown almost as fond as of his long-lost
Ajax. So he needed plenty of distance, and his weapons at
the ready. He turned, half crouched, his hair loose from its
binds and falling down to the middle of his back. Sword in
his left hand, dagger in his right, Athos faced his attacker.

But the man on Samson's back was making no move to

retaliate. He looked less injured than Athos expected. A hand reflexively rubbed the place where Athos must have hit him, but he was not doubled over. Instead, he was frowning at Athos from beneath an unruly mop of black hair untidily tied back into a ponytail. And he was a mere boy.

Not a youth, not a man, as Athos had thought, but a boy too young to have any beard growth. So young, in fact that, by the light of the moon, his face looked soft and still carried what could be called baby fat.

The cheekbones were striking, prominent, and the eyes might be black or as dark blue as Athos's own. They studied Athos with an unflinching expression. There was, Athos noticed, no sword sheath hanging from the belt.

As the attacker's face contorted in an expression of distaste, something about the features struck Athos. Despite the almost chiseled beauty of the face, there was a rounding that couldn't be expected in a young man, unless he were barely out of the cradle. And the lips were soft and full, the chin pointed and small.

Athos let his gaze stray down to the person's chest, and his own face contorted in shock.

Mort a Dieu! This was why his hit had hurt the attacker less than it should. There must be a wealth of ligatures where it hit, which had cushioned the blow. Because despite what was, undeniably, good binding and men's clothes—a tight black doublet and hose—there was no way around the fact that Athos was facing a woman.

Athos did not like women. Oh, not in the way that some men—some of them members of the royal family—had of not liking women. It wasn't as though he loved men instead. His were more the feelings of someone who, being passionately fond of candy, eats a poisoned one and thereafter is forever wary of sweets.

Rationally he told himself that he had demonstrated the worst of judgments in choosing his wife and he couldn't, therefore, be trusted to choose or fall in love with a woman.

But rationality had nothing to do with it. Looking at this woman dressed as a young man, appreciating the soft symmetry of her features, the flattering disarray of her hair, and unable to believe that she was anything but a female, he felt his throat close and his hands tremble.

Curse it all. He didn't know if he could kill a woman even if he needed to. Another ghost by his bed and even barrels of wine might never dull his senses enough to allow him to sleep.

He stepped back and back and back, as if the woman were a serpent. In fact, in his experience, women and serpents had much in common. The most beautiful ones were the most poisonous, and this woman was very beautiful indeed.

She looked at him curiously, as she dismounted from the horse, and tied it to a tree. Bending, she picked up the dagger Athos had caused her to drop.

Curse it all. He was going crazy in his dotage. He should have retrieved that dagger before she had a chance to.

But she slipped the dagger into her belt, making no attempt to come at him. Which showed that perhaps she might be daring, able to drop onto the back of his horse without warning. But she was not crazy. Only someone insane would attempt to use a dagger to attack a man holding a sword. Particularly when that man looked as desperate as Athos.

Of course, the fact that she was not insane probably made her more dangerous. Probably. Sane people as adversaries had at least this for them, that they would not willfully attempt to get themselves killed.

The girl stood where she was, near Samson, who whinnied softly and looked at Athos in confusion.

She looked pale and scared as she stared at Athos. No. Pale and angry. Or somewhere between scared and angry, a brew of emotions that few people could control and which women were notoriously bad at controlling. "What have you done to Madeleine?" she asked. "What have you done with her?"

The Horrible Truth; An Angel of
Mercy in She-Devil Guise; When to
Accept Female Company

"**I** have done nothing with Madeleine," Athos said. And even as he said it, he remembered the little frail body, the innocent face, both lying hidden in a coffin in a priest's basement. Without name, without honor, without vengeance.

But how could he explain things to this woman who still looked more ferocious than any other woman he'd ever met? No. Than *most* women he'd ever met. That one he'd loved madly enough to marry and to make lady of his domain had shown the same fire, the same ardent passion, like a flame kept too long banked that longs to burst out and devour everything around.

In memory of his great love, of that woman whose fire had consumed his soul, and whose betrayal had destroyed him, Athos tried to be gentle and to indulge the fury of the creature facing him without hurting her. Without bringing himself to a point where he'd have to kill her. Anything but that. He didn't think he could endure it. "Who are you?" he asked gently, keeping himself well away from her, keeping both hands in sight, and both clearly away from his sword and dagger.

She looked surprised, as though everyone should know her and be able to recognize her on sight. "I'm Helene," she said and, on those words, looked like she expected recognition or apology.

He looked at her blankly.

She pulled a stray lock of pitch-black hair back from her

pale oval face, and looked peevish. "Helene. From the orphanage."

At his continued lack of comprehension, she was further tempted to say, "I was raised with Madeleine. We were like sisters."

"Sisters?" He couldn't imagine anything less like the blond woman dead in a Paris alley than this fiery brunette who dressed and fought like a young man.

"Oh, not sisters in truth," Helene said. "Not . . . We are no relation, at least that we know." She flashed a feral grin. "Of course, someone in our position wouldn't know, would we? For all we know we share a father, her by his high-born mistress and myself by some maid he got too close to behind his wife's back. It is not for us to know, is it? It is all a wrapped bundle at the convent door and a note asking the sisters to look after the baby, in Christian charity."

"I—I suppose," Athos said, not scared but shocked, by her vehemence, by her . . . anger? Did she hold him responsible for her abandonment? How could he be? Oh, truth be told until this moment he'd believed it was a humane way to raise and hide a bastard who would otherwise ruin a house. He'd never thought the children might mind. He'd never thought of the children at all. Until the beginning of this adventure, until his glimpsing of the little braided ring in the pouch around the dead girl's neck, he'd thought the whole matter closed the minute the baby was left at the convent door.

Helene tossed her head, as though guessing some guilt that Athos himself couldn't quite discern. "Oh, it is," she said. "But I don't think we were sisters. At least we looked nothing one like the other. And we acted nothing one like the other. But Marie, the nurse they hired to look after Madeleine, liked me. We don't know why. No one knows why. I don't even remember when, don't remember a time when the two of them weren't a part of my life. At some moment, probably while I was still an infant, Marie saw me and took a shine to me and took me to the parlor with Madeleine.

"Madeleine was always kept away from the other children in the orphanage," Helene said. "As though the product of lower-class sin could corrupt her with their touch." Again anger flashed in her expression, but it was gone quickly as she went on. "Madeleine was kept away from all other orphans, but I was allowed near her, I was allowed to know her. And Madeleine is the most wonderful person."

Her gaze softened. "Very nice, and shy, and quiet, and wouldn't talk back to anyone. Not at all like me. But I protected her and we were . . . like sisters. Like dear, close friends." She frowned. "When her uncle came to get her, I was scared. I did not trust him at all. If he was her uncle. He seemed very shifty, with his patch and his underhanded manner. I tried to ask him more about Madeleine's family, and he ignored me as if I were no more than a fly buzzing around him."

Athos could imagine that someone like Helene wouldn't like to be ignored, and he could imagine that Rochefort would need to do precious else to invite her ire. She wouldn't like him because he treated her like a menial. Which she might very well be, but surely didn't look.

"And now you and your friend come around, all very secret, whispering some name to the porter and convincing Sister Prophirie to let you in, all very secret and shaded and behind closed doors—and no one will tell me who you really are or what right you have to enquire about Madeleine."

Athos could tell that he, himself, had been tarred with Rochefort's brush, with the unforgivable sin of not paying attention to Helene, of not informing Helene of all.

He deserved that disdain at least as much as Rochefort did, but he could not say anything, he could not explain himself, and so he looked at her in silence.

"And no one will tell me if anything happened to Madeleine," she wailed distressedly. "I listened at the door. Of course I listened at the door. She's been gone a week and she was supposed to have written to me and told me all of her new life—of her carriages, her jewels and the young men making themselves crazy over her. And she didn't. Not a word. This is not like Madeleine. I'm sure if she could, she would have written." She turned away from Athos, looked at the sky above, at the branches of trees waving in the breeze. "So I listened, but you only said something that might mean Madeleine is in trouble, but not what the trouble is, nor how I can help her. So I left while you were taking your leave. I ran here and climbed the tree. I intended to listen to you and your friend. But he rode ahead, so I dropped onto your horse." She turned again, impulsively, and looked at Athos with intense, pleading despair. "Please, how can I help her? Can you take me to her?"

Athos struggled for words. His mouth felt very dry, his head dizzy as though he were half drunk or as if he had run for hours, without ceasing, without pausing for breath. As he had run after his crime. And his shoulder felt as if it were on fire. He could feel blood seeping out to soak the bandages.

He swallowed, finding very little moisture on his tongue. "Oh, mademoiselle," he said, and in those words, hoarse and inarticulate, he sounded so much like Porthos that it startled him. Perhaps this was what Porthos was like all the time. Perhaps words were as painful to him as this story would be for Athos.

"We found . . ." he started, and realized he'd started wrong. "Five days ago, coming from a drinking spree in Paris, we saw what looked like a musketeer running ahead of us. He was small and slim and not anyone we recognized, by the light of the moon and tavern lamps, fleeing ahead of us. We called and he ran. We gave chase . . . and found him murdered in an alley."

She was looking at him and it was her turn to seem blank, uncomprehending. "Why do you think he was murdered?" she asked. "Musketeers duel."

"Indeed they do," Athos said. "But there is no honorable duel-inflicted wound that consists of a gash across the throat and nothing else. A gash to the throat from right to left, such as can be given with a small knife or a dagger. Never a sword." Talking of this, factually, he'd composed himself. He would bring great pain to this woman, but what else was he to do? He could lie to her, but some part of him knew she would guess he was lying. And among the many things he was sure Helene disapproved of, he would believe lying to her on something this important would rank very highly indeed. Highly enough to discredit him in her mind forever. And though he didn't know why, he couldn't bear the idea of Helene despising him. "We turned him over. Only it wasn't a him. It was a her. A beautiful, young blond woman."

Helene's eyes widened, her mind leaping to the rest of the story. "No," she said. "No." And then, "Madeleine . . ."

Athos nodded. "We believe so. In her sleeve was hidden a pouch with a ciphered letter. Around her neck was a pouch with a little ring and a ribbon with a medal of Saint Jerome Emiliani."

"Madeleine," Helene repeated, slowly, as though by saying the name she could bring life back to her friend. "Madeleine." It was an invocation, a prayer.

Scared, angry, confused, she looked at Athos, her emotions written on her face. "But why Madeleine?" she asked. "Who could have wished to injure Madeleine? And what could my poor goose have to do with a cipher or an assignation? She didn't even break convent rules, and before this shady uncle of hers crawled out of the woodwork, I'd always assumed she'd become a nun. I learned to leave the convent unwatched by the time I was six, but not she. Never."

Helene sounded matter-of-fact, but her eyes filled with tears, which trembled and threatened to spill down her cheeks that had gone from too-pale to feverish red. Possibly with rage. In so many people, grief and rage were close neighbors. Athos took a step back, so he had the room to immobilize her if she came at him with that silver dagger.

But she didn't. She just looked at him, obviously waiting for an answer. He sheathed his own weapons. An image of wiping her eyes with his fingertips surged through his mind and he shook his head to dispel it.

"Your friend," Athos said. "Madeleine looked like the Queen."

Helene stared on at him, as if what he said had nothing to do with her question.

"We think . . . I think she got caught in some plot, some intrigue around the Queen. Perhaps a foreign plot." He rubbed his forehead with his hand, and, doing it, realized his head ached. Not a pounding headache but a faint pain, like what is left after a vat of wine and a restless sleep filled with ghosts and evil dreams.

Helene was quiet for a while.

Athos remembered they were in a dark place, not visible from the road, and that Aramis, having ridden up ahead of Athos, might have repented his hot temper or decided that charity required him to backtrack.

He was quite capable of riding by them without noticing

and riding all the way back to convent, and working himself up to a state of worry over Athos. "I'm sorry," he told the girl, who was still looking at him with a horror-filled, disbelieving gaze. "But you should probably be back at the convent."

Helene shrugged. "It doesn't matter," she said. "No one keeps track of my movements anymore, not since . . . Not since Madeleine left. They won't even know I'm gone."

"No," Athos said. "But that is not what I meant at all. What I meant is that you should go back to the convent. You will be safer there. Strong as you are, and daring, you are still a young woman, and there are dangers . . ." He realized what he was saying and how it might be interpreted in relation to her close friend's death.

She must have read his mind because she nodded. "Yes," she said. "Look what happened to Madeleine. My poor goose."

Athos untied his horse from the tree. Samson walked beside him, as Athos tugged on the reins, pulling him out of the clearing and back through the rocky ground, to the path.

Helene walked beside him. Athos would not ride while she walked. He would walk her back to the path and see her on her way back to the convent, after which he would go on to Paris.

At least he could tell Aramis of this. There was no obvious secret here. He could tell him about Helene, though it added almost nothing to the story, save the knowledge that Madeleine had been easily led and gullible. Something terrible for a young woman who'd fallen into the hands of Rochefort, the Cardinal's evil minion.

At the road, the full light of the moon revealed that Helene's face was far paler than Athos expected. She looked like a ghost, void of all blood and life. Only her eyes shone, living, very wide open. "Monsieur," she said and audibly swallowed. "Monsieur . . ."

He waited. It had been very long since he'd spent any time in the company of a woman. Even longer since he'd faced a woman in grief.

Memories of family funerals flowed back to him, but they were all from when he'd been a small child and not expected to do anything to console the bereaved. Now he was expected to do something, to say something, and he did not know where to find the words to do it.

If he thought of himself as anything at all, these last few years, he thought of himself as a stone, alone amid men, locked in his grief and his guilt. How was someone like him to reach out to anyone?

Helene's gaze looked away from his face. Her eyes lowered. "Monsieur . . ." she said again. "Take me to Paris."

At first, he thought he'd misheard her. "Beg your pardon?" he said.

She looked up, then, her zeal-burned gaze on his face. If it were a flame it would have devoured his flesh. "Take me to Paris," she said. "Let me help you in this investigation. Let me see the corpse and confirm if it is my poor goose's. Let me . . ." She took in a deep breath, then clenched her teeth so that they showed through her slightly parted lips, not in a smile but in something resembling a dying rictus.

She bit her lower lip. Her eyes swam with tears that sparkled in the moonlight. Not one of them was allowed to drop down her pale, pale face. "Let me have my vengeance."

Athos started to shake his head. "You're a young lady," he said. "Your honor, your life—"

She cackled, low in her throat. "Madeleine was a young lady," she said. "I'm just a girl. Born from some tavern wench, no doubt, and her passing-by beau. Madeleine . . ." She blinked and yet the tears didn't fall. "Madeleine had everything to live for—a life amid the gentility, perhaps a good marriage someday. I have nothing. All I had was my affection for her, and now she is gone. Would you deny me my revenge because I was born female?" She took her hand to her chest. "Inside this chest, monsieur, beats a heart brave enough for thirty men."

What could Athos do? He'd never been any good at arguing with women, even in the happy days before his marriage. Women both fascinated and scared him a little, even then— with their sudden passions, their uncontrollable feelings.

And yet, something he knew, learned from his mother and his female cousins: When women were good, they were very good. Their loyalty was stronger, their courage greater, their generosity more freely overflowing that those of men.

If someone had killed Aramis or Porthos, or even his new

friend, D'Artagnan, could Athos rest until he'd had revenge? And if someone had waylaid his friend, made him the center of a plot from which he had no chance of escaping, would Athos not feel an even stronger need for revenge?

How could he deny it to this woman, then?

"Are you sure no one will miss you at the convent?" he asked.

She nodded. "Absolutely. I usually stayed in the back parlor rooms with Madeleine, so no one is used to seeing me around and, since Madeleine left, there has been no one to notice if I'm there or not."

He mounted his horse, and extended his hand to help her up. "Then come," he said. "To Paris. And we shall try to help you have your revenge."

This was how Athos set off for Paris with a beautiful young woman riding behind him, her body warm against his back, the heat seeping through his doublet and making him feel as if he'd been frozen for ten years and was only now beginning to thaw.

Where Aramis Swears He Will Never Understand Humanity; On the Lodging Intricacies of a Beautiful Woman Involved with Musketeers; Honor and Duty

ARAMIS waited on the road, alarmed when he'd realized he didn't hear the sound of Athos's horse behind him. He hadn't backtracked because he was prey to a horrible sin of anger at the time. He reasoned that if Athos was going to play superior, then Aramis was not going to act like a lackey and look like he was afraid of proceeding alone toward Paris.

And so, instead, he'd found a place on the road where it circled what some optimistic soul might term a village—a sad conglomeration of three houses and a stable. Though it was nighttime and all the hovels dark and silent, two or three pigs and a dog roamed around, grunting and snuffling, and Aramis felt the place *must* be inhabited and, if he were lucky, he could call there for help, should it become needed to go.

He could not have, with the best of will, thought of any help these poor peasants might give him beyond some hard bread and a glass of water, but perhaps if Athos delayed too much Aramis might ask the families here for help in backtracking. In case he needed to carry Athos back.

Waiting like that, in the dead of night, he'd shivered with horror at the thought that Athos might be injured or dead.

And in the next second felt his heart speed in righteous anger because, if Athos were dead, then he would have taken his secret knowledge about the orphanage with him, and he would have made a fool of the rest of them.

He waited by the side of the road for very long, and might have dozed on horseback.

When he heard hooves, he felt as if they were coming from very far away. He took his cold hand to the pommel of his sword. Who knew who might be coming. If he was lucky, it was Athos. But what if he wasn't?

In this investigation, they might very well be dealing with the security and kingship of France? What if some shadowy behind-the-scenes play demanded the deaths of Athos and Aramis both.

His hand on the pommel of his sword, Aramis straightened on the horse and tried to see, down the road, the approaching rider.

Soon, the approaching horse was visible and it looked like Samson, from gait to color to reins and saddle. But there were two people on the saddle. It couldn't be Athos. Aramis's hand closed hard on the sword.

The horse galloped closer. He pulled the sword out a little. The first rider had Athos's broad shoulders Athos's dark hair, now loosed and Athos's pale skin. He was Athos, but who was the young man riding behind him? Where and why had Athos picked him up? Could he have anything to do with Athos's dealings at the orphanage?

In Aramis's mind, a story unfolded. Some paramour of Athos's had left a child at the orphanage years ago. But Athos had just discovered the child and it wasn't a girl, but a boy, who had been raised as a gardener's assistant or . . .

An orphanage devoted to raising girls would not have taken a boy and raised him, gardener or not. It was all nonsense.

Closer still and Aramis saw that his friend's expression was set in grim determination. And also that Athos gave no appearance of intending to stop. Samson kept at a steady gallop as he was drawn parallel to Aramis and then continued down the road.

Athos did not even turn to look in Aramis's direction.

As the madman galloped past Aramis, with only a hand wave to indicate Aramis should follow, Aramis seethed.

Sangre Dieu! What had come over Athos? And what had

Aramis done to deserve being treated in such a way? Even a lackey would bridle at this sort of aloof haughtiness.

But he would not be thought too weak or indecisive to follow his friend. He turned his horse around and spurred it on. The animal, glad to finally have his head, rushed forward, soon overtaking Athos.

At a gallop there was no way of talking, but Aramis felt free to look. The boy looked too well dressed to be a gardener and, even in the fugitive glimpses caught while they were both riding, side by side, too high-bred to be a commoner of any sort.

There was a fineness to the feature, a look of elegance to the leg and the arm and the setting of the head that made Aramis think that this was no peasant boy, that it wasn't just a commoner picked up out of charity by the wayside as Porthos and Athos seemed to have found D'Artagnan's new servant, Planchet.

While Aramis stared, the boy faced him fully and smiled. And in that smile, Aramis realized the error of his ways. This was no boy, but a woman. And a devilishly beautiful woman, yet. As beautiful in her dark-haired, wild way as Violette was in her softer, more pampered manner.

A woman. It took more than a moment for the thought to make its way from Aramis's realization to his understanding.

Ventre sangris! Athos was riding with a woman. It was unbelievable. The man who scolded them for wenching, the man who looked with narrowed eyes at the most beautiful of courtesans, the man who—particularly when drunk—went on about the perils of women and the dangers of romance had a beautiful woman riding behind him on his horse.

Whatever remained of Aramis's faith in humanity, and in his friends in particular, vanished.

You'd think when you'd been as close to anyone as Aramis had been to his two friends all these years, you'd know what they were likely to do. Truth be told, Aramis would have been less surprised had Athos shown up with a lion riding behind him.

Athos—continuing his behavior from before—rode too fast or too slow, or in other ways avoiding a canter in proximity to Aramis when Aramis might have asked questions that Athos clearly wished to avoid answering.

Slowly, Aramis's irritation grew, as he looked at the woman and gathered, even beneath the male clothes and binding of breasts, that she had a small waist and probably large breasts. He admired the soft, gentle curve of her long leg within the male boot and stocking. The gracefulness of her position as she leaned into Athos's back bespoke not just natural limberness but probably a long and intimate acquaintance.

And suddenly Aramis smiled. What a pharisee Athos was. Always scolding them for their interest in loose women, always saying that in women lay the way to perdition. And all this time—how long?—Athos had this woman . . . somewhere.

Aramis had to assume that Athos had this girl near the orphanage, that perhaps she was one of the orphanage's maids. But it didn't seem right.

Athos scowled, and it wouldn't be just the pain of being discovered. Also, Athos looked confused and disoriented, as though what was happening had escaped his control, as though he were none too sure where he was headed or why. A suspicion grew in Aramis's mind that Athos was attempting to overcome a sudden attraction. Athos had somehow become stricken with a chance-met woman?

Aramis could not imagine it.

Well—Athos would have to talk to Aramis when they reached Paris. They had agreed to meet their friends at Athos's lodging by noontime. And sure enough, when they rode into Athos's street, they could see Grimaud and Bazin, who'd been told to meet their masters so they could care for the horses.

As Aramis dismounted and handed the reins of his hired horse to a reproachful Bazin, he enjoyed the look of surprise in Bazin's and Grimaud's eyes at Athos's feminine companion. Even the unflappable Grimaud looked shocked, set back, perhaps even a little afraid as he looked up, with his watery-blue eyes at the raven-haired beauty dismounting from his master's horse.

But Athos didn't seem to notice any of their looks of surprise, or care what they thought. Instead, he turned and, in silence, started up the steps to his lodging.

Aramis, about to follow Athos, paused and gestured for

the girl to follow ahead of him. After all, even in these very strange circumstances, a lady should be shown courtesy.

She behaved as if she expected it all along, as if deference were her due. With only the slightest of smiles to them, she made her way up the five steps to the front door of Athos's town home.

In the front room, Athos dismissed Aramis. "You must go home," he said. "And get some sleep, as Porthos and D'Artagnan shall meet us here at noontime."

"But . . ." Aramis said, and looked at the girl.

"Oh, Helene will stay in my guest room tonight," Athos said. Then with a grimace at the growing light showing the windows. "Or rather, this morning. We'll discuss her role in this tomorrow."

Helene? Aramis thought. And she was to stay here, was she? "Is that quite respectable?" he asked.

Athos frowned. "Do you accuse me of lechery? Or Grimaud?"

Aramis shook his head, confused.

"Well, then she will be perfectly safe here," Athos said. "And I will see you at noon."

Thus dismissed, Aramis left Athos's home.

A Landlady's Tale; Where D'Artagnan
Feels Like a Newcomer

AFTER spending the previous day sleeping off the celebration, Porthos appeared at D'Artagnan's lodging so early
that Planchet himself was still asleep in his comfortable nest
in D'Artagnan's entrance room. From which he took some
time to drag himself, leaving Porthos in the landing pounding on the door, until D'Artagnan's landlord—a greasy little
mouse named Bonacieux—called up the stairs for Porthos to
stop disturbing decent people. And then, on looking up the
stairs and glimpsing Porthos, Bonacieux ducked away into
his own doorway downstairs and disappeared.

Porthos was tempted to follow him and teach him a les-
son, but at just that moment, Planchet opened the door. He
grinned at Porthos. The last few days had been good to the
lad, who now looked as if he had some meat on his bones,
and had washed his shockingly red hair. Tied back with a
ribbon of uncertain provenance, it left Planchet's eyes uncovered.

His clothes were D'Artagnan's old suit, which probably
meant that D'Artagnan had acquired new clothes, and been
generous with the old ones.

Planchet bowed to Porthos and let him into the front
room, then went inside to wake his master. While Porthos sat
impatiently at the rickety table, protests issued from within
the room. The first, in a plaintive adolescent tone was, "Still
sleepy," followed by, "You villain, you."

Planchet yelped.

"Planchet?" D'Artagnan's surprised tone meant that the

villain hadn't been meant for his servant. "I apologize. I didn't realize—"

"Monsieur Porthos is here," Planchet said in a strained voice.

"What, already? Fetch me some water, Planchet. And see if there is anything for breakfast."

Planchet ran through the antechamber and down the stairs and returned with a pitcher of water.

Various monosyllabic exchanges followed, from their tone relating to stockings, breeches, underwear.

Eventually, Planchet disappeared down the stairs again.

D'Artagnan emerged. He looked quite different from the young man who had come into town less than a week ago. The face was the same, with its olivine complexion and dark hair, the intelligent eyes and sharp gaze.

But the clothing was now probably only secondhand velvet, in a shade of blue that was the right color for the guards of Monsieur des Essarts. And the hat had been recovered and outfitted with brand-new plumes.

A mug filled with red wine materialized in front of Porthos, and Planchet, with a shy smile, ducked away. He set a plate of bread and cheese and another mug of wine on the table and D'Artagnan sat and wolfed it down with the quickness of a seventeen-year-old.

"Come, come," Porthos said. "I had to wait while you made yourself pretty. And all just to go talk to laundresses."

He was gratified to see the young man blush. Athos and Aramis so rarely responded to his teasing anymore. He took a pull of his wine, emptying the jug, then stood up. "If you're done, we'll go. At this time, they will be by the river with their fresh loads of clothing."

D'Artagnan stood up, nodded and followed, but his brow was furrowed and it seemed to Porthos as if the youth were deep in thought.

Even Porthos could not be oblivious to that kind of mood for very long. Oh, he pretended to be talking of this, that and the other thing as they walked along the silent streets early in the morning.

There were very few people about. Only a straggle of servants of noble houses, hurrying here and there, who knew why. And a few housewives, rushing about for bread and wine and other necessities of a waking household. One or two children passed them too, clutching a satchel of books, their faces suspiciously shiny from washing, their steps as slow as possible.

But the main roads were deserted, and Porthos liked Paris in the early morning. It held the same kind of delicious thrill as walking in on a pretty woman at dawn before she was dressed.

He pointed out some of the best taverns—the few they hadn't covered in their whirlwind tour of drinking spots on D'Artagnan's first day in town. He even pointed out his favorite brothel, La Rosette—the establishment of Madame Pointu.

The boy only nodded, absently, as though his own, provincial town, could have boasted all these marvels and more.

It went on till Porthos had to ask, "D'Artagnan, what is bothering you?"

And then the boy looked at him, surprised, like a sleeper awakening from dream. He blinked confusedly up at Porthos and said, "Why would you think anything is bothering me?"

"Either that or you're a very poor man in early morning," Porthos said. "And having seen you in the early morning, at that duel outside the tennis courts, I refuse to believe that is the case."

D'Artagnan sighed. "I keep thinking back on the house by the Seine, and the gentleman and the brunette. I'm not sure . . ." He shrugged. "I'm still not sure what to make of it all. It could all have been as the man said, or I could have made a horrible mistake one way or the other. It is possible that woman truly intruded on him, or it is possible she was his accomplice, and equally possible that she had been lured there by him, for purposes of his own. Perhaps to kill her." He sighed again. "In fact, there is nothing I can say about the man or his intentions, save that at the time I felt that he was being truthful. But I could be wrong."

"I doubt it," Porthos said. "Such impressions, particularly when they go against that which you expected, are usually right." He walked a while in silence, thinking of what D'Artagnan had told them of the meeting in the night. "You said he was foreign?"

"Yes. He had an accent, though he spoke French as well as any native."

"A Spanish accent? Or German? Or English?" It seemed to Porthos that was the first thing to establish, as everything else would flow from it.

"I don't know," D'Artagnan said. "It could have been any of them, as it was so slight it was hard to tell."

"Well . . ." Porthos said. "Which of those nationalities did he look? Because I find it very rare that a man won't look like the land he comes from."

D'Artagnan chuckled at this and, before Porthos could enquire why, said, "Porthos, you, yourself, look far more like a wild German or a Swede than a Frenchman."

"Ah," Porthos said, and grinned.

It was good, for once, to have a friend who would tell him what he thought. Aramis and Athos would have smiled at his pronouncement too, but would never have gone so far as to contradict him. They appeared to believe he only said these things because he lacked a discerning intellect. In fact, Porthos said a lot of things because he preferred the sound of his own voice to silence. But the boy hardly needed to know that.

"Perhaps in my size and coloration I do," he said, smiling. "After all, plunderers from Sweden and Denmark raided French coasts not so long ago, or so my tutor told me, though to own the truth he was a great bore, and it's possible I'm confusing this with something else he told me, about the coast of England or the Plantagenets or anything like that."

Porthos tried, for a brief moment, to recapture what his tutor, a kind Franciscan, had tried to put into Porthos's mind once and for all. But history held little interest to this man of senses. It was dry as dust, lacking taste, smell and sound. All Greeks and Romans, Phoenicians and whatnot, and not one of them having decent manners or ways of dressing. He sighed, giving it up for a bad job and, instead, allowed his hand to go up and twirl the corner of his abundant red moustache. "But anyone looking at my face would know I was a Frenchman," he said. "And at my clothes. Germans aren't very fashionable."

D'Artagnan laughed, an easy, open laugh. "Probably as you say," he admitted. But then he fell silent again. "Truth is," he said at last, "the man looked French, or as close to it as doesn't matter." He shrugged. "He looked a lot like Aramis, only perhaps a little older."

Porthos frowned. "Like Aramis?" He scratched his head. Aramis was a deep and tricky one. Porthos had been devoted to the young man as if he were his own younger brother since the day he'd traipsed into Porthos's fencing studio— all meek and mild, full of soft words and quotes from the New Testament.

Back then, Aramis had never held sword nor foil, he said, but he'd been challenged to a duel and he had accepted and would like to learn the sword.

Porthos remembered looking at the young man and thinking he had neither the stamina to fight a duel nor the sheer natural anger needed for killing someone. A child like that, raised by a pious mother, brought up on the idea that he should never commit violence, might be very well suited to the church, but he would hardly be suited to anything else, and certainly not to distinguish himself on the field of valor.

But the boy had proved so adept, and such a fast learner, that Porthos had offered to second him at his duel. Which, as Aramis had proved him wrong and killed his opponent, had led to their having to go into hiding, in the corps of musketeers, together.

They'd been friends ever since. But Porthos wasn't such a fool that he didn't know that Aramis was always in the midst of some intrigue or another and had his fingers in more pies than most people even knew how to count.

"Could it be Aramis?" he asked. "That one never tells us everything he knows. He might be running some deep plan."

D'Artagnan shook his head. "No. He was older. But he had the same air as Aramis, and the same color hair and eyes."

Walking at a comfortable pace, they'd left the middle-class neighborhood where D'Artagnan rented his lodgings, and edged, by degrees, to the Seine and progressively tighter and narrower alleys. But Porthos remembered the address in the Rue Saint Eugenie and he didn't think it was that far from where they were.

"We could go and look," he said. "Now. Perhaps your stranger is still there. Yes, yes," he said. "I know he told you he was leaving in the morning. But men accosted in the middle of the night by a stranger who comes in through their window are often untruthful." It occurred to him as he said this that he'd never gone through a *man's* window in the middle of the night. Women were not all that different from men, though. So he would still be in the right. "And even if they are truthful, their plans might fail. You know Athos always said we should go back, together, in the light of day."

"I think he meant all four of us together, in the light of day," D'Artagnan said.

Porthos shrugged. "Athos might have meant that," he said. "But if so, Athos has strange ideas. Athos often does, reading as much as he does. He doesn't spend enough time in the real world. Four of us showing up together and, if the man has left, his landlady is likely as not to be scared of us and tell us she knows nothing about him. Two men, alone, on the other hand, and we can easily say he's been recommended to us by someone—like . . . Monsieur de Treville— and that we're just coming to get him to go drinking with us, or something like that."

D'Artagnan looked at him dubiously. Porthos knew that, in addition to lacking the ability to think using words and abstractions, he also lacked the ability to persuade with speech. And D'Artagnan had known him such a short time that he probably had no idea of Porthos's real intelligence. No doubt he thought Porthos a simpleton.

"The street is just down there," he said, pointing. "I think. Down this alley and to the right. Come. What harm would there be in knocking at the door and asking for the renter of the first floor?"

D'Artagnan laughed. "I'm finding that in Paris, the most unexpected actions have the strangest consequences. Getting enmeshed in a stranger's doublet and seeing that the inside of it is not as fine as the outside, for instance, can get one challenged to a duel."

Porthos laughed. It was good, he thought, that the boy was feeling comfortable enough with him to make jokes. "Ah, that," he said. "Indeed. If you don't know that said stranger is often teased for his clothes not being quite so fine as they look." He grinned. "I swear it looked like you were trying to get a peek inside my doublet."

"I was trying to catch the man from Meung," D'Artagnan said and, in reply to what must have been a very blank look from Porthos, "a man who attacked me and stole my letter for Monsieur de Treville."

"Ah," Porthos said. "A villain who should be killed. When you catch him, I hope I am with you. I'd like to cut off his ears and make a display of them. Depriving a man of becoming a musketeer should count as a capital crime."

Another dubious look from D'Artagnan as if he weren't sure how much of this was Porthos's idea of a jest.

Then the Gascon nodded, as though reaching a decision. "Very well," he said. "Let's go there."

The road was even closer than Porthos thought, and the house looked very respectable, with its stone balcony and ivy-covered front. Looking closely, one could see, amid the ivy, pulled off bits, broken-off branches, and the scuff marks of D'Artagnan's boots against the facade. D'Artagnan's and the woman's, if the stranger's tale had been right.

Porthos couldn't imagine climbing up to the balcony the same way. The ivy would never support him. In any case, even if the stranger were still there, he would likely tell nothing to yet another madman who came in through his window. So, instead, Porthos marched to the front door and pounded on it.

After the third knock, the door opened a sliver, and a woman's face showed in the opening, peering out.

She looked like Athenais. Or rather, she looked as if she were the same class as Athenais. The poorest of poor nobility married into the merchant class, or the other way around. Of good enough upbringing to feel constrained, but not of enough worth to live comfortably.

Her hair was grayer than Athenais's though, and her wrinkles more obvious and far beyond the laugh lines that Athenais showed. And her gaze was nowhere near as direct or intelligent as Porthos's mistress.

Still, Porthos knew exactly how to deal with this class of people. In many ways, considering the scant worth of the house he'd been born into and his mother's merchant relatives, it was his own. He removed his hat and bowed deeply. "Madame, I'm sorry to disturb you, but we are musketeers and we have come at the behest of Monsieur de Treville for the gentleman lodger in your first floor?"

He realized a little too late that his words could be misinterpreted. She could think they had come to seize the gentleman lodger and arrest him.

For a moment it looked like this was in fact what she thought, as her small, worried, wrinkled face, stared up at Porthos. Then she cleared her throat. "I saw musketeers here, with him, while he was here."

Porthos smiled. "There you go. He's apparently some connection of Monsieur de Treville's who wishes him to be properly treated while he's in town."

The woman cleared her throat again, and the door opened a fraction more. She looked beyond Porthos to D'Artagnan and seemed reassured by D'Artagnan's obvious youth and smaller stature. "Well . . ." she said. "A bit late for that, isn't it?"

"Is it?" Porthos asked, hoping the man wouldn't be dead. Not yet another corpse to deal with! Corpses should be killed the proper way, in duel or brawl, with nothing at all mysterious about their demise. Well, either that or, he supposed, they could die in their beds, quietly, of course, though that option always seemed rather boring to Porthos.

"Why, yes," the woman said. "He left two days ago, didn't he?"

"Did he?" Porthos asked, confused by the woman's seeming habit of asking questions he couldn't possibly answer.

"So he left in the morning as he said he would," D'Artagnan interrupted.

The woman shifted her gaze toward him. "Yes."

"Oh, that is too bad," D'Artagnan said and sounded so disappointed that Porthos almost said they could still investigate the uniform and have something to tell Athos, but he bit his tongue in time, remembering that didn't fit with their story for the landlady. Truly, he hated secrets and conspiracies.

He bowed to the woman, preparing to take his departure,

when D'Artagnan said, "Well, tell Monsieur de Treville that Monsieur . . ." He looked blank and fumbled. "Porthos, my friend—" He slapped his forehead. "Bless me, what did Monsieur de Treville say his friend's name was?"

Porthos, admiring the ingenuity of the lad, was barely able to mutter, "I don't remember."

"Neither do I," D'Artagnan said. "And now Monsieur de Treville will think we weren't truly attending and that we didn't really come to look for his friend."

"Oh, don't let that worry you," the landlady said. "I don't think there's any secret about it. He was the Chevalier D'Herblay."

Porthos jumped at the name. He remembered the Chevalier D'Herblay. "Are you sure?" he asked, shocked. And then, pained at lying, "I thought that Monsieur de Treville had said a different name."

"No," the woman said, and shook her head. "It was the Chevalier D'Herblay. He gave me his name right when he came a week ago, and he responded to it. I did think it was odd, what with him being British. But he was a very gentlemanly man, and these big houses often have holdings in both countries, so perhaps his father was French and his mother English and he, poor thing, brought up on the isles."

Porthos didn't remember what he said, or how he got himself out of that situation. All he knew—for absolute truth—is that he said something and gave the woman a couple of sous for which she was extravagantly grateful, curtseying and smiling.

As they walked away, along the narrow street, D'Artagnan held his tongue till a hasty look over his shoulder showed him that the door behind had closed, then said, "This D'Herblay shouldn't be hard to trace if he's truly from one of those families big enough to have holdings both here and in England."

Porthos heard himself groan. Oh, curse it all, he knew who D'Herblay was. He knew it all too well. "Devil take it," he said. "We forgot to ask her what he looked like."

"I told you what he looked like," D'Artagnan said, looking a little puzzled. "He looked like an older Aramis."

Porthos stopped dead in the middle of the street, staring down at D'Artagnan, trying to remember, trying to imagine what to tell his friend that wouldn't give away knowledge he shouldn't divulge. "That," he said aloud, "is a very bad joke."

"What is?" D'Artagnan asked.

Porthos shook his head. With murder done, how important was loyalty to one's friends? And if D'Artagnan was one of them, a friend, couldn't Porthos trust him with the secrets of the group? Why would D'Artagnan give Aramis away, anyway?

But they'd known D'Artagnan such a short time and knew so little about him. What if he wasn't who he said he was? What was Porthos to do?

He'd seen Aramis cast looks of doubt and distrust at the young man. And, of course, that clinched it. If Aramis didn't trust him, then Porthos couldn't confide in him. Not in this case, at least.

He sighed. "D'Artagnan, I have reason to believe that D'Herblay is a fake name, a name of convenience, that this Englishman made up to hide his true identity."

D'Artagnan blinked up at him. "What reason?"

"I cannot tell you," Porthos said. "The secret doesn't belong to me."

D'Artagnan frowned. "Then how can you be sure that this person was not D'Herblay?"

"Because I know . . . knew D'Herblay. Knew him very well. And he looks—looked—nothing like what you described," Porthos said.

He wasn't happy lying and he knew his countenance gave him away every time he tried. But this was not lying. This was treading a fine path between truth and lie. And Porthos was telling the absolute truth, if you looked at it the right away.

He had known D'Herblay five years ago. A boy of all of seventeen, with blond hair who spoke in little polished words, in a meek voice, like a convent girl's. He'd worn a monk's habit, as though he were already professed, and he'd approached Porthos because he'd been challenged to a duel.

He wanted to learn to fight with the sword so he could defend himself against the man who threatened to kill him for reading the lives of saints to his sister—and Porthos now knew enough to suspect—while illustrating many of the points in which the saints' virtue had been attempted against.

There was only one person in the realm who knew D'Herblay's family and might have noticed the resemblance. Cardinal Richelieu.

Porthos's Talent;
A Laundress's Honor;
Porthos's Ethics

D'ARTAGNAN knew clothes were washed. At least once a month his mother set about a great bustle and would take the clothes off his body, if he let her, leaving him shivering in his room till she was done washing.

He had a vague idea it involved water and steam.

Nothing prepared him for the place where Porthos took him.

When Porthos had said the women did laundry down by the river, he had imagined bucolic women beating and rinsing the clothes in the water, as he'd often seen—from a distance—the young women of his native town do.

But this was completely different. It started with their approach to a low-slung building, which could have been a Greek temple had it been more open and its proportions better.

Like a Greek temple, it had columns surmounted by a roof with a triangular facade. Only here, walls linked the columns, and only a few doors and windows pierced those walls.

What D'Artagnan first saw was smoke poured out of every opening. Walking down the street beside Porthos, he thought that the building was on fire. Only Porthos didn't look alarmed.

As they got closer, D'Artagnan noticed that the smoke did not smell of burning. Instead, it was wet and hot to the touch. It wrapped around him like a cold sweat and it smelled, vaguely, of olive oil and boiled pork.

They walked into a cloud of steam, in which Porthos became no more than a half-glimpsed ghost—a bulk, walking beside D'Artagnan. Were it not for the sound of the musketeer's movements, the heavy footfall beside his own, D'Artagnan would think that the rest of the world had disappeared into this fog, and that he remained, alone, in nebulous confusion.

They passed through a door—not that D'Artagnan could really see the door, but there was the feeling of crossing a threshold, and the light dimmed. Now there was a slight smell of burning wood. A chatter of women—too many to tell any individual voices, filled D'Artagnan's ears as much as the steam clouded his vision.

Had he not heard, here and there, loud, happy laughter and the occasional bit of song, he would think he'd been plunged whole, headfirst, into one of the circles of hell.

He was aware of Porthos grasping his sleeve and guiding him around in the hot blindness.

Little by little, though, his eyes adjusted, as did his ears. What faced him then was a wide building filled with women and clothes. They boiled clothes in large cauldrons at the back, stirring them with stout poles. Other groups knelt by a huge canal that crossed the building end to end, and beat and scrubbed clothes with far more vigor than D'Artagnan had ever thought needed for such an activity. The clothes were either beat with flat pieces of wood, or raised well over the women's heads, to be brought down, full force, upon stones placed by the side of the canal.

D'Artagnan supposed the canal was a part of the river, deviated and roofed over for the comfort of the women doing all this laundry.

What shocked him most, though, was the crowd and the immense variety of women—from little girls who were probably no more than ten, to women so old that their faces were masses of wrinkles and their backs crooked from a lifetime of labor. There were beautiful ones and horribly ugly ones, and D'Artagnan found himself wondering what Aramis would do faced with that immense variety of womanhood. And how they would react to him?

But then he saw how they were reacting to Porthos. It seemed to him as though the minute the large musketeer entered the laundry room, through the mist and the steam, every woman turned to face him like a flower turning toward the sun.

Oh, D'Artagnan knew it could not be so. But looking around, it seemed all the faces he could see clearly through the steam were staring at Porthos. The bolder ones actually smiled. One dropped a piece of cloth into the water, letting it float unheeded down the stream while she smiled at Porthos, white teeth flashing.

There, a blonde girl, her hair escaping in all directions from the dark scarf she'd wrapped around her head, stirred the pot over the fire with renewed vigor, and tilted her hips slightly, just slightly, forward, toward Porthos. Another one, arms raised to beat the cloth upon the rock, stayed like that, while the cloth hung from her uplifted hands, her gaze followed Porthos's every movement and her tongue went quickly, nervously, across her lips.

Porthos, in his turn, squared his shoulders and threw them back, responding to their admiration perhaps without even noticing it. He pulled at his magnificently gilded belt; he adjusted his sword; he smiled just a little and then, as if he'd identified the most likely person through some kind of mysterious power, advanced, smiling, on a woman by the river—a matronly creature with graying hair and a plump face crossed with laugh lines.

D'Artagnan followed, as an apprentice would in the wake of a master, as an enlisted soldier following an officer.

The woman, seeing Porthos approach, stood straighter, and, at first, looked panicked, as if she were afraid he was going to ask her a question she couldn't answer.

But Porthos smiled, his genial, friendly smile. And the woman smiled too in return, a joyful smile. Her green eyes sparkled. She looked a good twenty years younger.

As they stopped before her, she seemed to remember, at the last minute, that she must look busy, and started wringing the cloth that had been forgotten in her hands.

Porthos removed his hat, as if he were about to address royalty. Perhaps, D'Artagnan thought, that was Porthos's magic and what held these women spellbound to his every expression—that he didn't understand or make distinction between a duchess and a laundry woman.

"Madam," Porthos said, and bowed. Somewhere, nearby, a young girl tittered. "I don't suppose you know who among your friends does the laundry for the corps of the king's musketeers."

The woman grinned, "I do, monsieur," she said. "Myself and Marie and Sofie."

"Ah." Porthos smiled at her, appearing to give the impression that she had solved a particularly difficult puzzle. "Ah. But you wouldn't be able to tell me . . . It would be too much to ask, surely . . ."

This big man's acting hesitant emboldened the laundress. She put her hand out. She grabbed at Porthos's shoulder. "Monsieur, really, it is no trouble. Tell me what you need to know. I'll be more than happy to tell you."

Porthos shook his head. "It is unlikely you know this, but perhaps I could . . . If it's not too much trouble, perhaps you could tell me, that is, if you know . . ." He tilted his head sideways, managing to play the part of the hesitant big man to perfection. "You could not tell me, by any chance, if you know who does the laundry for a gentleman by the name of De Termopillae? I mean . . ."

"The musketeer? Little man, with a face like a cat who's been at the cream?" she asked. She smiled at Porthos, and such was his act of hesitation and shyness, she patted his arm in reassurance.

It seemed to never occur to her to ask Porthos why he would need to know that. His hesitation made her unable to question him. Instead she reassured him as if he were a shy toddler, a diffident child.

"There's no reason it should be so difficult," she said, looking stout-hearted and full of confidence to his hesitant manner. "I am the one who does his laundry, sure, but we all know . . ."

As if to confirm it, two other women had closed in, one a young, bold-faced creature, probably no more than sixteen, with sharp features and knowing, golden eyes. She smiled at Porthos, a knowing smile. "De Termopillae. That gentleman has more lace than I've seen in many a bridal trousseau."

The other one, a dark-haired, tanned woman of maybe twenty, who had approached on the other side of the first woman, nodded, as though she too, knew all there was to know about De Termopillae's laundry.

"And many uniforms?" Porthos asked. "You know, the tunic and breeches of the musketeers." And he pulled on his own exemplars of the kind, to make the point, though his tunic was half-hidden beneath a magnificently embroidered doublet.

"Two," the matronly woman said. "Two. Or at least, three, since he usually gives two to wash at once."

"And the one that was stolen?" Porthos said. "Is that part of the count?"

At the word *stolen*, the laundress drew herself up. For the first time she seemed to shake the spell of Porthos's curious charm, to look him in the eye, sternly. "I have never stolen even a handkerchief . . ."

"Oh," Porthos said, and bowed and again acted abased, humble, small. "Oh, madam, I'm sorry. I didn't imply . . . I didn't mean . . . I'd never think you'd steal a uniform from one of the musketeers," he said. And his expression was so sincere, the flaming blush in his cheeks so obvious that the woman's look of offense subsided, though her hands still held the cloth a little harder than needed, still clenched, ready for anger.

"Madam," Porthos said, "De Termopillae told us his uniform was stolen from the line at his laundress's . . ."

The laundress threw the piece of cloth—by the looks of it, a shirt—down. It fell atop a pile of others. She put her hands on her hips.

"Why, that dirty, sneaking rat," she said. "No clothing has ever got stolen while under my responsibility," she said. "I do all the clothing I contract myself." Narrowing her eyes, she looked around and lowered her voice. "Not like some I could tell you about. And there is no one here who can say I've ever lost a piece. I dry them in my own yard, behind my house and always under my watch. I'm very careful."

Porthos nodded. "You'd say, then," he said, "that it was impossible for someone to have stolen the uniform while you had it?"

"Two uniforms he gave me, regular as always every two weeks," she said. "And two uniforms I gave him back. Every time." She glared. "I cannot believe he would utter such a calumny."

Porthos shrugged. "Well, Monsieur De Termopillae comes from a big family, with much power and influence. He probably can't find his uniform and so blamed it on the first person he could think of."

"A great family." The woman made a face. "Well, I'll tell you, his lace is not of the best, and his embroidery is often on one side only, or just the little that will show through the slash in the sleeves. If he comes from such a great family, I suspect he gambles, or wines, or wenches, or in some way disperses the money they give him."

Porthos raised his eyebrows. "Many of these great gentlemen—"

"Gentlemen," the laundress said, her ire still not appeased. "Gentlemen. Well, he's no gentleman then. Heaven only knows how he found the money for the brand-new uniform he gave to wash two weeks ago. In fact," she smiled, "I'd wager he won it at gambling."

She looked away from Porthos for the first time, to glance at D'Artagnan with the expression of someone who makes an undefeatable point, seemingly unaware of any irony in her words.

He hoped he looked appropriately credulous. Porthos certainly did, as he bowed and scraped and bowed some more, and said, "Thank you so much. Such a great help. I cannot begin to tell you what a help you've been."

He complimented and bowed, and smiled, till all three of the women started smiling, and then he kissed their hands, one by one.

Such was the effusiveness of their goodwill by then, that even D'Artagnan was allowed—required—to kiss their cold, water-wrinkled hands afterward.

It was not till they were outside that D'Artagnan dared voice his admiration of Porthos's technique.

"That was extraordinary in there," he said, looking up at Porthos. In the next breath he wondered whether Porthos would even know what was extraordinary, whether Porthos would realize he had done anything out of the ordinary. After all, this was the man who thought that asking someone about his new uniform and what happened to the old constituted subtle and cunning interrogation.

But Porthos grinned knowingly. "Wasn't it?" he said.

"Yes," D'Artagnan said. "Had you gone in there and questioned them normally, and asked what they knew of this or that, they would have told you that their clients and their laundry was none of your business, and you would have walked away empty-handed."

"Ah," Porthos said. "But look, I'd never walk in there and question them like that. Those women have enough grief and enough trouble. Most of them have children, and many of them have husbands who are not much good because they're sick or in some other way . . . well . . . you know, not good. They work to feed themselves and their children, and they are treated little better than animals by most people who meet them. I would not dream of questioning them in a way . . . I would not dream of treating them like animals. Learn this, my young friend: If you treat those who serve you well, you will get much further than if you stand on pride and circumstance."

All of a sudden he looked alarmed and hurried to explain. "It is not that I think that Athos or Aramis act wrong, mind you. Athos is not so much proud as he is noble as a Scipio. He is, you know, or so I hear, from a very ancient and powerful family and such things are learned in the blood, in your mother's womb, when you're so young that you'd barely notice it. But he's not proud, you know, not as such. He's . . . he just has a way of making anyone else feel baseborn and ill-mannered."

"But he wouldn't be rude to the laundress," D'Artagnan said. "Nor would Aramis."

"No," Porthos said. He grinned suddenly. "Though Aramis would try to abjure her for the sake of her immortal soul and tell her all these things that she has to do and will be forced to do if she wants salvation. Which might not be quite the best way to go about it."

"No," D'Artagnan said. "Your way was the best way." He meant it. "You put her completely at ease by acting shy and hesitant."

Porthos shrugged. "It is not," he said, "that I am shy and hesitant, but I learned early on . . . Look, I was the largest

child in my town, the largest young man of anyone's acquaintance. If I acted strong and full of purpose, people
were scared of me. And you don't want someone like that to
be scared of you. She'll just shut up."

He walked a while longer with D'Artagnan, down the
brightly lit street. "Do you think she told us the truth?" he
said.

D'Artagnan nodded. "I'd wager on it." He smiled at the
memory of the laundress denouncing gambling and wager-
ing in the next sentence. "I'd wager on it, heart and soul. If
she had lost the uniform while she had it—she would have
told you. And if someone had stolen it, she would have been
full of stories about how it had been stolen despite her best
efforts to defend it. You were acting as if you'd admire her
either way."

"She might have sold it," Porthos said. "Might she not?"

"I don't think so," D'Artagnan said. "She looked indignant when she thought you were accusing her of it, but also
surprised, as if she knew of no missing uniform. And besides, De Termopillae is still contracting his laundry to her.
Do you believe he would do that if he knew she had stolen or
lost a uniform?"

Porthos shook his head, then brightened up. His step acquired a new spring. "But that means that De Termopillae
lied. Which means he might very well have sold it, himself,
to someone . . . And if we get him to tell us to whom he sold
it, half of our work is done."

"We'll at least know someone who is involved in this,"
D'Artagnan said.

"And," Porthos said, his disposition now fully recovered,
"Athos might very well allow me to slap De Termopillae
once or twice in the bargain."

D'Artagnan doubted it, but he was not about to ruin his
friend's day by saying so.

"Speaking of which," Porthos said. "Athos said we
should meet at his lodgings at noontime today. We'd better
hurry."

The Measure of a Man; A Lady's Distress;
Where Our Heros Make Assumptions

BY the time they got upstairs, Athos remained standing by his usual chair, at the head of the table. Behind him, on the wall, was a portrait of a cavalier from the time of Francis I and above that, on the wall, the sword that Aramis envied.

The girl had sat down at Athos's right hand, as if by natural right.

The other musketeers, disturbed at this intrusion in their councils, arrayed themselves on the left side of the table. First Porthos, then Aramis—who had had quite enough of Athos's company for a while and who, furthermore, did not want to get in an argument with the older musketeer and his old friend, should Athos refuse to explain anything.

But as soon as D'Artagnan took his seat by Aramis, Athos himself sat down, and, taking off his hat and throwing it on the table, with the gesture of someone ridding himself of a burden, he said, "Gentlemen, permit me to present to you Mademoiselle Helene. She has no other name, having been raised in St. Jerome's, the orphanage in which the fair unknown—apparently named Madeleine—whom we had the misfortune to find only after her death, was also raised. Helene considers herself Madeleine's sister, and, as such, I'll let her speak after I tell you what Aramis and I found at the orphanage."

He narrated their meeting with the Mother Superior with his normal spareness of words. When that was over, he said, "Aramis chose to ride ahead of me and I was riding behind, being mindful not to tire Samson, when someone fell on the back of my horse."

He proceeded to tell a tale of high adventure, of being attacked on the highway, of being forced into a dark space amid the trees. Of this girl, Helene, threatening Athos with drawn dagger.

While he spoke, he unlaced his doublet, familiarly, and lowered it off his right shoulder, so that Grimaud, armed with a pot of grayish salve and fresh bandages could tend to his wound.

Aramis wondered if Athos had simply not taken in account the woman in their midst, and was, therefore, behaving as he did when it was just the musketeers. Or if his shoulder was paining him so much he did not care. Or if, perhaps . . .

But no. As Athos turned a little sideways, to allow Grimaud better access, Aramis could see that Athos's right shoulder was caked with blood, which had stained the bandages and his doublet. Only above the shoulder did his skin remain white, at the very top, where the arm started. Well, not wholly white, since Athos had a triangular birthmark there, a curious, dark shade and defined shape.

The quantity of blood did credit to Athos's story of a fight.

In any case, Aramis couldn't really imagine that Athos was lying. Athos had never, in the past, demonstrated an ability for imaginative lies. His sins were usually of omission rather than of commission. He preferred to say nothing at all rather than to make up a fable. If this were not the truth, he would simply have said, "This is Helene, who was raised at St. Jerome's."

And this was not at all Athos's type of story, anyway. His was more likely to be a story of an encounter by chance, of two people realizing they had common cause. The idea of resisting an assault on the highway was very much a Porthos story. But Athos was telling it . . .

While Aramis tried to think through the maze of his thoughts, and while D'Artagnan and Porthos looked at him as though for confirmation, the girl stood up. She really was very beautiful, far more beautiful than she'd seemed in the dark of night on the back of Athos's horse.

For one, her eyes were dark—but a very dark blue, not black. And her naturally pale skin had an even, creamy complexion highlighted by the pitch-black hair that fell, now loosened, to her shoulders. The man's suit barely disguised what, in women's attire, would be a very interesting figure indeed. Aramis imagined her in court dress, and felt his throat tighten and his palms sweat when she spoke.

"Monsieur Athos agreed that I have a right to my vengeance," she said. She spoke with a plebeian accent but with such calm dignity that it raised both the accent and the words above the ordinary. "And so he agreed to let me come to Paris and at least present my case to you."

She held her small, white hands interlaced in front of her, in a position no doubt learned from the nuns. "Because I was the closest thing to family that Madeleine had growing up. While she might have a family somewhere, and while her family might have several other people entitled to speak for her, I do not know if that is true. I know she received money for her keeping, but that might have been left in the care of a family servant, long after all her family perished. And while the man who got her from St. Jerome's claimed to be an uncle, I was never sure his claim was true."

She raised her head defiantly and managed to look even more heartbreakingly haughty and beautiful. "Madeleine might have strong brothers aplenty, ready to avenge her death. But if so, they either do not know or do not care about their wayside-born sister. And therefore it is left to me, who was as good as her sister, to defend her and protect her in death as I did in life. I ask only that you shall let me follow your investigations, that you let me help if I can, and that, in the last instance, I can be there to see the murderer punished."

She spoke very prettily and though very much aware of the dangers of a woman in Paris and of the trouble it could cause. Aramis could not but bow his head and say, "I have no objection."

Porthos and D'Artagnan too, vowed to help the girl.

"But where will she stay?" Aramis said, having some vague idea of recommending her to Violette for her service, an arrangement that would protect Helene.

"She will stay with me," Athos said. And in his gaze, leveled at Aramis, was the sternest warning, the most absolute decision. "Grimaud and I are both respectable men of good reputation and, at any rate, I'm the only one who has a spare room. Beyond all of which, we live here alone and she won't be exposed to the gossiping tongues of a landlord or the landlord's daughters." This with a final glare at Aramis.

The *but* Aramis had started to voice died in his throat. Athos might not have known the woman before. He might not know anything about her. But Aramis was a man with some experience in affairs of the heart. And the one thing he could guarantee was that Athos's heart had already allied itself to this girl.

He smiled, despite himself, and watched Athos frown in response. But Aramis could not help it. This was what came from Athos's habit of living like a monk. A soft touch, a woman leaning into him through a long ride, and the man was lost beyond recovery.

One thing Aramis could be sure of: Despite her beauty, which lent something of nobility to her features, and despite her pride and her self-possession, this girl was not nearly noble enough for Athos. And if Athos were foolish enough to marry her, his family would have reason to regret it. Beyond her tainted birth, there was something slippery and strange about Helene, from her haughty demeanor to her ability to escape the orphanage while wearing male attire.

But perhaps, Aramis thought, always ready to self-examine, he simply resented that Athos seemed to be at an advantage when it came to winning the heart of this girl.

The thought shamed him, and he looked away from his friend, feeling his cheeks heat and concentrating on what a selfish person he was and how the sin of self-love and self-admiration had thoroughly corrupted him.

Which was why he was totally unprepared to hear, "D'Herblay," hurled across the table in D'Artagnan's voice.

He looked up and the "Yes?" he'd formed his mouth to say died on his lips at Porthos's warning expression and at D'Artagnan's continuing to speak, "Though we don't know who he is."

"I beg your pardon?" Aramis said, to justify his having looked up. "What is this?"

"The landlady at Rue St. Eugenie said that the foreigner—probably English—who lodged with her was named Chevalier D'Herblay," Porthos said, his face wooden.

"Did she, now?" Aramis asked. The devil! There was no other Chevalier D'Herblay. He'd inherited the title when his father died, and he had only been two years old at the time. His father had been an only child, as had his grandfather, the D'Herblays not running to large families, at least not large, legitimate ones.

D'Artagnan nodded. "Yes. And he looked somewhat like Aramis, though he was older."

Who would know what Aramis looked like and what his true name was? Beyond the identity of the man, who would spot the similarities and think this was as good a disguise as any?

Monsieur de Treville did, but Aramis could no more think of his captain being involved in this than he could suspect himself. But there was someone else; someone who, once, in the midst of a confusing adventure involving duels and defeated guards, had given Aramis to understand he knew his true identity very well because he'd known Aramis's father in youth. "The Cardinal," he said, loudly, before he could stop himself.

The others—Athos included—all stared at him. Grimaud finished tending to Athos's wound and Athos pulled his doublet closed and laced it while frowning.

"Aramis, while I'm the first one to blame His Eminence for everything," Porthos said. "I don't think we can accuse him of looking like you, only older."

"No, no," Aramis said, thinking fast. "But I've been told, often, that Buckingham looks like me, only older. And I think this is too likely a plot engineered by the Cardinal. Did not Athos and I tell you that we think that the man who played Madeleine's uncle is none other than Rochefort? I think Rochefort got Madeleine from her convent and had her meet Buckingham. Perhaps he meant to have her become Buckingham's mistress, in place of the Queen or—"

D'Artagnan was shaking his head violently. "That could not be it," he said. "Because D'Herblay told me that if the woman he'd seen had been injured or killed he'd know it and everyone would know it. This would only be true if he thought the woman *was* the Queen. So he could not have known it was not Anne of Austria he met."

Athos gave D'Artagnan a small smile of approval, which

further piqued Aramis, who felt left out, kept in the dark about Athos's knowledge and ignored in favor of this new-comer. And to add insult to injury, His Eminence had chosen to use Aramis's name for his nefarious plans.

"Be that as it may," Aramis said. "D'Herblay sounds like a name the Cardinal would know, a name he would use for—"

"What do you mean, a name the Cardinal would know?" D'Artagnan asked.

"I mean an old name, the name of an established family. Probably one with no descendants or with only one obscure descendant." He stared at Porthos, trying to convey with his gaze that his plain-spoken friend was not to ask questions.

"But," Porthos said, despite Aramis's glare, "That explains the musketeer uniform."

And while Aramis's mind skittered in fear of what Porthos might say, Porthos added, "If Madeleine was being set up to look like the Queen by His Eminence, nothing of the Cardinal could be around the meeting place. And therefore, no agent of the Cardinal—whom Buckingham might chance to know—could accompany her. And she could not walk the streets of Paris at night without some protection."

"So they put her in a musketeer uniform," Aramis said, feeling a sick relief that his secret was safe after all. And realizing, with a pang, that Athos's own jealously guarded secret might be of the same nature.

"Which they probably bought from De Termopillae," Porthos said. "D'Artagnan and I questioned the laundress and neither of us thinks she stole or lost the uniform, so De Termopillae, who is abominably vain." This was spoken without the slightest hint of self-consciousness by the musketeer in the gold-embroidered doublet, with its gold-emblazoned sword belt. "Must have sold the uniform so he could buy a new one."

"Selling a uniform is not a crime," Athos said. "He might have sold it to a secondhand shop, and whoever bought it—even the Cardinal—might have bought it there."

"Yes," Aramis said, feeling once more obliged to point out the obvious to his friends who, between the two of them could neither conspire nor sort out any type of conspiracy. "But if De Termopillae had sold his uniform to a secondhand shop, he would have had no compunction in telling us so. After all, other men told us they had sold their uniforms to secondhand shops, though too long ago to make any difference to our case."

Athos nodded. "Yes, his evasion does indicate a guilty conscience. I shall talk to him again. Before we go so far as to involve ourselves in the Cardinal's affair and try to find out what he meant by it. Will you come with me, Porthos?"

Porthos nodded and started to rise. "Wait," Aramis said. He looked toward Helene. "Should we not verify that the woman who died is indeed Madeleine?"

"Aramis, you cannot mean to subject—" Athos said.

"No. I wish to. Of course. I'll go," the woman said, and rose gracefully from her seat. "I will come."

Athos nodded, but his look at Aramis was full of suspicion and mistrust. "Take D'Artagnan with you," he said.

Aramis smiled and nodded. He didn't mind taking D'Artagnan. The truth was, he had not the slightest intention of subverting Athos's relationship with this woman. But Athos's jealous reaction had told him all he needed to know about Athos's feelings.

It only took a cup of wine to topple an abstinent man.

Aramis Defers to a Lady; Body in the Cellar; Body in the Church

D'ARTAGNAN wasn't sure what game was being played. The whole meeting at Athos's quarters had made him uncomfortable and he wasn't even sure why. He had some idea that Athos was not normally seen in the company of women.

From some cryptic remarks the musketeer had made when drinking—not while drunk, because Athos rarely *acted* drunk—D'Artagnan assumed some great grief or disappointment lay in Athos's past, and that a woman was at the root of it.

But he still could not understand the silent tension between Athos and Aramis. He could see that Porthos was troubled by it but said nothing and allowed the others to believe he was oblivious.

With the woman, Helene, D'Artagnan and Aramis set out, back to the place where they left the body. Before they left, Aramis insisted that she wear a large hat, which hid her features. This, at least, made the fact that she was a woman more difficult to realize.

"You should dress as a woman," Aramis said. "You would be less noticeable."

But she had set her chin forward, failing to show that instant attraction to Aramis that D'Artagnan had grown used to seeing from women. "I do not have a dress, and besides, it does not matter what I wear since all I want to do is see Madeleine and identify her body. She is dead and she would not care what I wore, at any rate. And at night, the male attire affords me some protection."

To which Aramis, perhaps recalling how one should deal with women, had removed his hat and bowed deeply in silence, refusing to start an argument.

The truth was, with Helene's face hidden by a hat, hardly anyone gave them a second glance. Or if they did—as they left behind the middle-class neighborhoods, with their shops open on the bottom floors of homes, and children, husbands and wives often all laboring at the family business, be it shoemaking or pastry—and walked into the humbler parts of town, the narrow streets and the noisy metalworking or sewing workshops filled with many, many children and young men, they called attention to themselves only by reason of one of them being a King's musketeer and better dressed than most.

Most women's eyes still gazed at Aramis and filled with astonished wonder, as if shocked at seeing someone that handsome amid them. So, D'Artagnan reasoned, if Helene showed no intention of being smitten, it wasn't that Aramis didn't still attract women. It must be something else about Helene.

She walked behind them, head down, looking at her feet. D'Artagnan's glances at her went unmet.

He wondered what she was truly like, what she was truly doing here. Oh, he could well imagine that in her position he too would like to avenge an adopted sister. But what woman grew up in an orphanage and grew to have such fire and make such a decision?

D'Artagnan knew about orphanages, at least from hearsay, and he imagined them as regimented and exact as convents and their inmates as quiet as nuns. He dodged a group of children walking toward him, and looked back again. He could not ask Aramis about Helene, of course, not with her right behind them. So, instead, he asked Aramis, "Why is it that Athos thinks our problem might lay with the Cardinal? Other than, of course, because the Cardinal is the enemy of the Queen?"

Aramis looked at him, his green eyes narrowed, as though taking stock of D'Artagnan and his motives. "Well," he said at last. "When we were speaking to the Mother Superior, we were told that the uncle who came to pick up Madeleine was tall and dark, with a look of the nobility about him, and that he wore a patch over his left eye."

"A patch?" D'Artagnan asked. Like the man who had laughed at his mount in Meung, the man he had challenged to a duel and who had knocked D'Artagnan unconscious and stolen his letter to Monsieur de Treville. He punched the open palm of his left hand with the closed fist of his right hand. "The man from Meung."

Aramis raised his eyebrows in mute enquiry.

"He was the man I was pursuing when I collided with Athos and made him bleed, and caused him to challenge me to a duel. At least, I refused to apologize because I was in such a hurry, and I believe that is what caused him to challenge me."

Aramis laughed. "So there truly was a man who stole your letter to Monsieur de Treville?" he asked.

"What?" D'Artagnan asked in turn, putting his hand on his sword. "You thought I lied?"

Aramis smiled. "Please," he said. "Don't be such a hot-headed Gascon. I hadn't given it much thought one way or another, but so many people claim to have letters of introduction to the captain. And so many of them have creative excuses for why they can't present them." He inclined his head. "I am glad you told the truth, since we've never admitted any of those other types of people to our friendship."

They walked on down increasingly narrowing streets, until they came to the neighborhood that D'Artagnan recognized as the working-class area where the church of Father Bellamie was.

During the day, the place looked better. Not that the houses looked cleaner or better painted, but there were clothes hung on ropes stretched across the streets, giving the area the look of a place decorated for a festival.

But something was missing. D'Artagnan expected to see children skipping through the streets and women talking in the doorways. But except for the flapping laundry overhead, the area appeared quieter and more still than in the middle of the night.

He knew something was wrong even before the afternoon air filled with the heavy, dolorous tolling of bells. Funeral bells.

Aramis stopped. He looked at D'Artagnan, then back at Helene, with a look of confusion. "Perhaps we shouldn't go into the church. If he's conducting a funeral . . ."

D'Artagnan nodded. He had no interest in intruding upon the funeral, doubtless—judging from the silence and the prolonged tolling of the bells—of some beloved neighborhood figure, someone everyone around here would be mourning.

"We can go to the cellar," Aramis said. "I know the way, and you know, he never locks it, in case a relative wishes to come claim a body while he's asleep."

He led them through a little wooden gate set in a brick wall and through a walk that D'Artagnan had crossed only at night and which now, in daytime, he could tell ran through a meager vegetable patch with some wilted cauliflower and yellowing cabbages.

Aramis led D'Artagnan and Helene to a small door with peeling red paint set in the wall of the house. Opened, the door revealed a narrow stone staircase, which D'Artagnan remembered. He also remembered the faint smell of decay and death from below.

This time, however, there was no candle and no oil lamp. Aramis left the door open and they climbed down into the increasing dimness.

Before D'Artagnan's eyes had adjusted to the dark, he heard Aramis gasp. Then he saw it: The coffin was not where they had placed it. Instead, it was in the middle of the floor. And it was empty.

"Madeleine," Helene said softly behind them.

"Perhaps . . ." Aramis said. "Perhaps he has moved her?" He swallowed audibly. "Perhaps we should look?"

D'Artagnan felt bitter bile climb to the back of his throat at the thought of opening those coffins, of looking . . .

But there was nothing for it, and a brave man could not quake from seeing the horrors of the death he was willing to cause in duel and on the battlefield. He thought that Aramis trembled, but then he wasn't sure that he himself didn't, as the two advanced on the pile of coffins against the wall.

The first five were empty, but the sixth was occupied, as they could easily tell by lifting it.

Looking at each other, the two men nodded. Helene stood nearby, looking paler than normal, twisting her hands together.

Softly, gently, as though they feared waking the person inside, D'Artagnan and Aramis lifted the lid. But the creature inside, though his features were unrecognizable and gray, could never have been Madeleine. For one, it was much larger, probably male—it was hard to tell, as the corpse had clearly been in the water for too long—and definitely dark-haired.

Holding his breath, D'Artagnan helped Aramis put the lid back on the coffin, and they stepped back. Helene, to her credit, did not look as sick as D'Artagnan felt. Of course, she hadn't looked at it as closely as he had.

He bent over, momentarily, controlling his desire to vomit, then straightened and helped Aramis continue the search.

How could Aramis look so untouched, so composed still? What was the man made of?

The other coffins proved empty as well. The three of them studied one another in the dim cellar.

"Perhaps someone claimed her," Aramis said. "Perhaps her uncle, or Rochefort playing her uncle, claimed her and . . ."

D'Artagnan nodded. "We'll need to talk to the priest after all."

Up the stairs and into the fresh, clean air outside, D'Artagnan took deep breaths that felt as though they could never rinse from his nose the awful stench of the water-logged corpse.

They crossed the vegetable patch.

The church was on the other side of the street from the little garden, the same squat building that D'Artagnan had noticed before and which had reminded him of the church in his native town. Like that church it had a small field beside it filled with a forest of tombstones.

D'Artagnan followed Aramis into the narrow door of the church and took off his hat, at the same time that Aramis and Helene removed theirs.

But they didn't get very far inside the church. They couldn't. The church was full. Men and women and children of all sizes and descriptions packed every inch.

The man saying mass was a tall, lanky man who looked nothing like Father Bellamie.

Ahead, by the altar, a coffin was set upon a pedestal. By the light of the candles burning all around, D'Artagnan noticed the little priest who had led them to the basement the first time. In the coffin.

"Father Bellamie?" D'Artagnan asked in a whisper, to the nearest woman.

The woman, who had been frantically praying under her breath, turned. "Yes," she whispered back. "A horrible murder. Someone broke into his house, early morning six days ago. They found him dead in that little cellar where he kept the bodies of poor unfortunates. With his throat cut from side to side. From right to left, straight across."

The woman crossed herself and, reflexively, so did D'Artagnan. He felt as if a sudden torrent of icy water had cascaded upon his soul. The priest had been killed. It could only have been because of them, because of Madeleine's body.

But who had done it? The Cardinal could just as easily have thrown the priest into the Bastille. It would have been easier, and it would have called less attention to his comings and goings.

So, who could be responsible?

A Heated Council; Why Even Gray Eminences Need the Benefit of the Doubt; One Final Verification

ARAMIS knew there was going to be a confrontation of some sort. When they returned from the priest's funeral, they met Athos and Porthos, who'd just questioned De Termopillae.

Their meeting had that crackling quality, as they all gathered at Porthos's home—or rather, the small, tiled antechamber furnished with magnificent velvet settees, which was all anyone—even his close friends—were allowed to see of Porthos's home. Beyond that, only Mosqueton was permitted to walk and whether it matched the antechamber in splendor or was a place of squalid economy, no one could tell.

They sat—Aramis, with D'Artagnan next to him, and then Porthos, on one of the settees. Helene, remarkably composed for a woman who had just found the body of her friend missing, sat across from them, her lips trembling, her eyes filled with tears. But she was neither crying nor screaming, and Aramis knew enough of women to think this was a show of great courage. Even most men in Helene's position would not have been able to control themselves.

But Athos . . . Athos who was normally quiet and laconic, Athos who was older than the other musketeers and in many ways had always played the father to the group, was pacing nervously, back and forth, behind Helene, like a caged tiger.

Aramis thought—no, Aramis knew—it was because of

emotions roiling in Athos's chest, emotions Athos had thought he'd forsworn, emotions he was not ready for and would not acknowledge. So he paced, while within him impulse warred with reason. And his body, left to its own devices, showed its unease, in a nervous flexing of fingers, in teeth that showed too much through lips parted in a grimace.

Through his teeth, Athos spoke. "I think," he said, "that it is time we sought Rochefort out, time we asked him questions. There is too much mystery in this, but of one thing only we're sure—that somehow the Cardinal is involved in the murder."

Beside Aramis, D'Artagnan tensed up. "We know no such thing."

Athos rounded on D'Artagnan. "How not?" he asked. "What other power in France can orchestrate such a conspiracy?"

Aramis tensed, alert. He, himself, was still not yet sure that D'Artagnan wasn't the Cardinal's agent, and what would be more in keeping with this suspicion than D'Artagnan's defense of His Eminence?

But D'Artagnan didn't seem to be afraid of giving his partiality away. He stood up to face Athos—though even standing he didn't reach Athos's shoulder—and threw his head back to match Athos's expression. "We don't know there is a conspiracy." Anger or nerves put a stronger than ever accent upon his tongue, the lilting tones of Gascony singing in his words. "We don't know that anything has been orchestrated. Oh, we know that the girl was—perhaps—being used for one of the Cardinal's plans. Maybe. But do we have proof even of that?"

"You never let me tell you," Athos said, still speaking through clenched teeth and managing to convey the impression that he was keeping inordinate anger barely under control. "You never let me explain that Porthos and I talked to De Termopillae. And he confessed that he had sold his uniform to a beautiful woman. He doesn't know her name, but he suspects she was an agent of the Cardinal, because he later saw her with Rochefort."

"So the Cardinal intended to conspire to replace the Queen with Madeleine, perhaps," D'Artagnan said. "But why would he kill her? It makes no sense."

"Perhaps she rebelled," Porthos said, shifting in his seat. "Perhaps she rebelled and threatened to expose his whole plan."

"Mademoiselle," D'Artagnan said, sharply addressing Helene. "Would your friend be likely to rebel?"

Helene looked surprised, then shook her head. Athos looked outraged that D'Artagnan had addressed her.

"Gentlemen, from what we heard," D'Artagnan said. "This woman was pliable, obedient, a good girl always ready to conform to the whims of those in power over her."

"People change," Athos said. His voice was heated, with an edge of madness, like the voice of a man who speaks out from a fever. "People change. Sometimes in a moment. Sometimes they don't know themselves that they are going to change until they do it."

Aramis wondered if either Porthos or D'Artagnan knew of what Athos spoke. He very much doubted it. Insight into other men's emotional state was never one of Porthos's strong points, and D'Artagnan's acquaintance with them was too slight for him to guess Athos's plight.

He cleared his throat, and both D'Artagnan and Athos looked toward him, breaking the intensity of their angry gaze at each other.

"Athos," Aramis said, using his ecclesiastical voice in as low and soft a manner as he could command. "Athos, still there would be no reason for the Cardinal to kill her. He has other powers at his command. And if His Eminence is no longer able to intimidate an orphanage-raised girl, he will sure enough lose control of the country."

"Are you siding with him?" Athos asked, darting a glance at D'Artagnan. "How long have you known me, Aramis? Long enough to trust my judgment?"

Aramis sighed. "In most cases, yes," he said. He bit his tongue, afraid of what might follow on his declaration. "But as you said, men can change in a moment."

Athos's hand rested on his sword pommel. "Do not force me to challenge you to a duel."

"You have," Aramis answered with a slight smile. "Upon meeting me."

He was vaguely aware of D'Artagnan's looking at Porthos, and he heard Porthos's booming whisper—Porthos could never whisper in a discreet way—answering the un-spoken question. "They fought themselves to a standstill," Porthos said. "And then they swore friendship. And I, who was Aramis's second, swore it along with them."

But even Porthos's booming whisper had a hint of uncertainty. Since that day, five years ago, none of them had confronted the other. Oh, they'd bickered and they'd argued, but not like this.

However, Athos had also heard Porthos. His hand withdrew from his sword, slowly and with every appearance of effort. "Aramis," he said. "While the Cardinal might have other means of silencing a woman, I don't think that this means every one of his henchmen has sworn off murder." He looked at the three of them. "Who else could reach into a little parish and kill the priest? Who else would do it?"

"Why would he kill the priest?" D'Artagnan asked, in his turn, standing to the full height of his inconsiderable stature. "Why? What sense does that make? The Cardinal would not need to kill the priest."

Porthos stood in turn. He didn't look upset like the rest of them. Or rather, he did, but Aramis judged his giant friend's uneasiness was composed of fear for their argument and fear that his friends were at the point of dueling. "Perhaps the priest caught the Cardinal's agent looking for something on the body? Perhaps the priest was about to raise the alarm?"

D'Artagnan looked at Porthos, no less intimidated by the musketeer's giant stature than he was by Athos's feral anger. "Porthos," he said. "Killing someone with a knife by slitting his throat is not the act of a man surprised in a crime. Think about it. Oh, I know people can be killed in a duel by being stabbed through the neck. But that is not how the woman described Father Bellamie's wound. She said his throat was cut straight across from right to left."

Aramis noticed Helene's uncomfortable twitch at these words, and he was glad of it. It proved she was human and not so strong as to dwarf even their strength as musketeers.

"No one gets their throat cut in that way with a sword—or at least, if they did it would be in the middle of a duel, and I can't see Father Bellamie dueling anyone," D'Artagnan said.

"What he means," Aramis said, once more breaking in

and diffusing Athos's angry glare at the youngest man. "Is that if Father Bellamie had interrupted someone who was searching the body, perhaps for the notes and medal we found, they would be facing each other. While whoever cut my friend's throat did it from behind, it had to have been someone he trusted. Someone he trusted enough to let get behind him. Because he was a saintly man doesn't mean he was a fool. In fact, those who are blessed by the Lord often have a very keen intellect. He would not have let some armed man get behind him," he repeated. And like that, it came to his mind the priest's last words, that he who lived by the sword died by the sword. But poor Father Bellamie was the one dead by the sword. The Lord worked in unimaginable ways.

Aramis shuddered.

It took him a moment to steady himself and in that moment, Athos had found his footing. "Doesn't mean anything," he sneered. "The Cardinal has many agents, and many of them are beautiful women who look as mild as lambs. Look at how De Termopillae sold his uniform to someone he said was a beautiful woman, but whom he later found was an agent of His Eminence."

"But it is unlikely that any agent of the Cardinal would find a need to kill the priest. They could disappear. They could overpower him and run. What would poor Father Bellamie do? Denounce them? What good would that do him?"

"Don't be a fool, Aramis," Athos yelled. "There are many who kill for the pleasure of killing. And those who do it on a wave of anger and bitterness, and think not at all." His yell was ragged, full of uncried sobs, and his eyes were wide and maddened like the eyes of a horse that has bolted.

Even in the wave of his madness, he looked noble, but it was the nobility of a Zeus gathering the thunderbolts, of an Ephestus beating out the storm on his forge.

They were all now on their feet, yelling, except Helene, who remained sitting, her hands interlaced on her lap, her eyes closed, giving every impression of praying.

"Stop," Porthos yelled.

They froze. In the silence, the ceiling and walls vibrated with Porthos's shout. The redheaded musketeer, normally the mildest of them all, not needing anger to augment his powerful physical presence, looked angry. It was not uncontrolled anger, like Athos, but a cold fire burning in his blue eyes, a paleness on his cheek that contrasted all the more with his red hair.

"Stop," he said again, though they already had. It was as though he wanted to reiterate it in a calmer voice. He looked at each of them, in turn, even D'Artagnan. "I am ashamed of you. It was not so long ago we swore, we always swore, one for all and all for one. And this is what it comes to? Why? Because we disagree about what to do next? Because we don't know who killed this woman? Can we not talk rationally? You, Athos, are the one forever going on about logic and the disciplines of the Greeks. And you, Aramis, with your training: Didn't they teach you logic and rhetoric in seminary before they let you out? I'd wager they did. And you, D'Artagnan, young as you are, I thought I saw intelligence in your eyes at our first meeting."

The three of them looked at Porthos, only to be met with the stern glare of a teacher disappointed in a favorite pupil. Aramis looked down again. He remembered how Porthos had scared him, when he was young and had come to Porthos for fencing lessons. He remembered Porthos, using just this tone when Aramis forgot the right movements, or parried when he should have seized the moment and thrust.

He was still looking at his feet when Porthos said, "Aramis, you think that this woman was killed for private reasons, is that it?"

And Aramis found that he knew nothing at all. He had gotten so heated in arguing with Athos that he'd forgotten he failed to have a theory to counter Athos's.

"I . . ." he said and hesitated, casting a quick glance at Athos, who looked equally dumbfounded. "I don't know," Aramis finally said. "There are many reasons she might have been killed. I find it unlikely that the Cardinal would order the murder of a simple priest."

"I too find that unlikely," D'Artagnan said. "Perhaps it is coming from my province and having always heard of the Cardinal as being so powerful, but I think if he wanted to get rid of a man he could easily enough get him thrown in the Bastille with a letter of cachet. He would not need to kill anyone."

"Very well," Porthos said. "And what do you propose to do to solve the rest of the murder and find out who might have done it?"

Aramis and D'Artagnan—admittedly and knowingly the only truly cunning ones in this group, the only ones who could see their way through a plot or create one—looked at each other.

Aramis felt at a loss for words. "Well," he said. "It is difficult. We have Helene, and I'm sure if there were any reason in Madeleine's past or upbringing to cause her murder, Helene would know. So . . . if the Cardinal didn't do it, whatever led to her murder must have happened after she came to Paris."

"And her uncle looked like Rochefort," Athos said. "Or at least the description did. And we have reason to believe Buckingham was in town, and was convinced he'd met with the Queen. But Aramis's friend"—he cast Aramis a quick glance, as though afraid Aramis would be upset—"the seamstress, who knows the Queen, says she didn't leave the palace to meet him at that time. So, this leaves us to believe that he must have met Madeleine. And there is no one else who could have made Madeleine pass as the Queen and who could have arranged this meeting. No one but the Cardinal. Add this to the description of the man who picked her up from Saint Jerome's and of course there is some plot— though the plotters might not be the murderers."

"So what do you propose to do?" Porthos said.

Athos looked up. "We should arrange to get Rochefort."

"How?" Porthos asked. "He's the Cardinal's creature, who comes and goes at his command only."

"That I don't know yet," Athos said. "But we should capture him and question him. My lease of this house extends to the cellar, where I keep my wine, and where it's dark and secluded enough no one will hear Rochefort. We can imprison him and question him."

"It will be very dangerous to do that," Porthos said. "We will be making ourselves the enemies of the Cardinal."

Aramis cackled. He couldn't help himself. "A great change, as we've been daily earning his friendship by wounding all his guards."

He was gratified to see one of Athos's fugitive smiles at this statement. Athos was, after all, still himself, even if his newly rediscovered interest in the fairer sex had made his temper irregular and difficult.

"We won't kill him," Athos said. "Or hurt him, because that would truly set His Eminence against us and make him thirst for our blood. If I ever kill Rochefort I want it to be done in public, and I want it to be known that it was a fair fight." He paused for a moment. "Though we should make him believe we might kill him."

"But how to attract him to a trap?" Aramis asked.

"I've been thinking," D'Artagnan said. "As you know, he is my man from Meung." And to Athos's and Porthos's blank looks, he explained. "At Meung, when I came into town, a man made fun of my horse. So, I . . ." He blushed like a child. "Well, I had been advised that I should fight well and fight often. . . ." He hesitated. "My father said I should never pass up an opportunity to fight. Which I'm afraid explains my would-be duels with you."

He smiled, a sudden, fugitive smile that made him look much, much younger, a mere schoolchild playing at being a man. "So when this dark man with a patch over his left eye laughed at my horse, I challenged him to a duel."

Aramis, having seen D'Artagnan when he'd first come into town, had all he could do not to giggle at the image of that young scarecrow challenging Rochefort in all his majesty, secure in his position and the Cardinal's protection.

"I take it he didn't fight you," Athos said.

Helene had opened her eyes and was looking at them attentively, as if the story interested her very much. She probably didn't feel it so keenly now that they weren't talking about her dead friend.

D'Artagnan shook his head ruefully. "No," he said. "He had his servants seize me and knock me unconscious. And then he went through my pockets, and stole the only thing of any value that I had."

Athos raised his eyebrows and D'Artagnan nodded. "A letter of introduction from my father to Monsieur de Treville," he said. "A letter that would have got me a commission to the musketeers that very day."

"So he robbed you and inconvenienced you," Athos said. "I fail to understand how this gives you the opportunity to bring him to a trap."

"Well," D'Artagnan said, "I'm not exactly friendless now. I have the three of you, and Monsieur de Treville, and I've met the King."

Aramis saw the look of amusement in Athos's eye, at the idea that anyone thought meeting the King was an advantage. But Athos said nothing, and D'Artagnan, who was looking at Porthos, probably hadn't noticed anything.

"I propose to write Rochefort a letter," he said. "Is there a place I might send such?"

"He lodges at the Cardinal's palace," Athos said. "It is well known."

"Well, then," D'Artagnan said. "I shall send him a letter there, remind him of his dishonorable behavior, demand the return of my letter and challenge him to a duel. If he shouldn't show up for the duel, I'll let him know the three of you heard the whole story and will be more than glad to let it be known around town that the Cardinal's henchman wouldn't meet and fight a mere boy from Gascony."

"Could work," Aramis said. He had one quick spasm of fear that D'Artagnan had been able to concoct this plan and could answer for Rochefort's falling for it because he was, in fact, an agent of the Cardinal's himself. But what agent of the Cardinal would invent such a story of previous acquaintance with Rochefort? The story made D'Artagnan seem foolish and helpless. Were it a lie, he would have made up a better one. "We'll need a closed carriage to transport him in, though. So we can do it in secret. I'll borrow one. I know a man."

"Will work," Athos said. He gave Helene a quick look. "But it is cursedly dishonorable for us to entrap a man who comes for a duel."

"Murder is cursedly dishonorable also," Porthos said reasonably.

"Yes," D'Artagnan said. "And I'll gladly cross my sword with him first. If I win, perhaps we can capture him and question him then."

Aramis smiled at that. Yes, D'Artagnan would gladly cross swords with anyone. And having seen the young Gascon in action, Aramis was none too sure he'd fail. In fact, he was tempted to feel sorry for Rochefort.

"You do realize," Porthos said, "that we'll be running an

enormous risk, in kidnapping Rochefort like that? That we'll be sticking our hand in the asp's nest?"

"Haven't we run risks before?" Athos asked. He seemed calmer now that they had agreed on a plan. Or perhaps, Aramis thought, he looked calmer because Helene looked almost hopeful.

Athos put his hand forth, palm down. "One for all," he said.

One by one, their hands came down on top of his: Porthos's, Aramis's and D'Artagnan's. "And all for one," they said.

Helene watched it all, wide-eyed and then gently, softly, her small hand came to rest on top of D'Artagnan's and she smiled. Athos smiled with her. A genuine smile, not his fugitive glimmer of amusement.

In the Dark of Night; Monsieur Athos's Wine Cellar; What Rochefort Knew

✑

*T*HEY arranged to meet Rochefort in one of those locations around Paris well-known for duels, this one on the other side of town from the Barefoot Carmelites—a location to which D'Artagnan feared their previous exploits might have called attention.

This was next to the King's hunting preserve, within some orchards. To hear Athos's description of it, the fruit in these orchards were more commonly picked by sword point than by hand, and the trees were scarred by thrusts and cuts. But the farmers who owned the vineyards cared not at all for the damage done to the property, because most of their money came from tending to the wounded noblemen. And from promising to hold their tongues about only injuries or deaths and their cause.

In fact, Athos said that the greatest risk they'd run was of having another pair of duelists be there and witness the whole thing.

But as it turned out, the orchards were deserted under the full moon. It was one of those very pleasant nights in spring where the warm, dry air already feels like summer, but without the heaviness of damp heat.

The orchards were silent and covered in flower, which looked like lace upon the trees and shot a heady smell of apple into the air.

There was nowhere to hide, and at any rate, they had long ago decided that they weren't going to hide. What they were doing was dishonorable enough without their worsening their consciences.

Grimaud, driving a closed black carriage, had brought them here. Helene, in feminine attire provided by Athos, sat beside him in uneasy silence, her features veiled by a scrap of lace.

Carriage and occupants sat within a copse of trees near the hunting preserve, invisible from the orchard.

They crept in through a portion of the wall that had caved in. Bricks and bits of masonry littered the ground. Pieces of broken swords glimmered here and there, and torn scraps of clothing fluttered in the wind like flags of defeat and surrender.

"What if he brings a second?" D'Artagnan whispered. A second would greatly complicate things, as it was another person to kidnap or somehow immobilize.

"He won't bring a second," Aramis said, full of man-of-the-world assurance. "Rochefort does not have a single *friend*. He has lackeys and servants, but no friends and no one he can trust with his life. Most of the people who work for him would be more likely to turn against him should he be wounded or weakened."

But D'Artagnan still felt nervous and scared. After all, his father reverenced the Cardinal almost as much as he reverenced the King. And here was D'Artagnan, ready to kidnap the great man's right-hand assistant.

Then he started to fear that Rochefort wouldn't come at all. It seemed to him, as the moon rose up in the sky and the way the shadows of walls and trees crept along the ground, that Rochefort was very late indeed.

Looking at the three musketeers, he saw them leaning casually against the wall, talking.

Athos glanced toward the hidden carriage now and then, as if to reassure himself Helene was well.

Porthos and Aramis were behaving as though it were a proven fact that Helene would marry Athos after this was all through, and D'Artagnan didn't know the gentleman in question well enough to have an opinion. In fact, it seemed to him they were very well suited. Two of a kind, both their calm exteriors masking great passion.

He started pacing, until Athos stopped him with a pat on

the shoulder. "Be at ease, D'Artagnan," he said. "He will come. Someone like Rochefort cannot afford to have it said that he missed an affair of honor."

Indeed, as soon as Athos said it, they heard the sound of hooves down the road, and a horse and rider appeared in sight through the collapsed part of the wall. The horse was the same white dappled gray animal that D'Artagnan remembered seeing in Meung, tied to a post and ready to carry his master on his journeys.

The man too, as he dismounted from the horse, was strikingly familiar. Now, more used to the capital, D'Artagnan discerned what he hadn't seen before—that Rochefort, despite his missing eye, was a handsome and well-dressed man who exuded class and comfort from every movement and gesture. His soft, pliable doublet, his long breeches, both bristling with fluttering gray ribbons, were as fashionable as Aramis's attire.

He advanced on them, removing pearly white suede gloves and putting them in his pocket. The gloves made a fine contrast with his silvery-gray doublet and well-cut breeches. Two steps away from D'Artagnan, he removed his hat and bowed.

"Monsieur," Rochefort said. His voice was frosty but not unpleasant. "You will forgive me for having discounted your attempts at a duel in Meung. You see, I thought you were but a child and I don't kill children. But now that I've heard of the terrible wounds you've inflicted upon Jussac and Bernajoux, I can no longer consider you a child, and as such, I'll be glad to cross swords with you. Though I would prefer if you returned my letter."

Rochefort made a gesture, as though disavowing knowledge of any letter. He looked around at the three musketeers. "I see you bought the three inseparables as your seconds. I regret I did not bring a second." He smiled, a smile all the scarier, for it was almost ridiculously affable. "However, fear not: There is not much chance you'll kill me or even injure me seriously. And, as such, a second will scarcely be necessary. As for your seconds, I'll dispatch them with the same happy goodwill I will dispatch you." He bowed again, then replaced his hat on his head.

D'Artagnan removed his hat in turn, and took a deep

bow. "Now that I have the honor of knowing who you are and how powerful you are," he said, "it is all the more flattering to cross swords with you."

"I do not know who you believe I am."

"Why, I hear you are the one who holds the confidence, and perhaps dictates the policies of the greatest headway of life in the world, in fact, of the man who is king before the King."

Rochefort smiled but said, "I do not have the pleasure of understanding you."

"I hear you are the right hand of His Eminence, the Cardinal Richelieu."

At this Rochefort bowed again. "I have that pleasure," he said. "And that consideration alone should caution you on how you deal with me."

"I shall be very cautious indeed," D'Artagnan said. "And now, let's allow our swords to speak."

He pulled his sword out while he said the last words. Rochefort took his sword out also, and tossed it from hand to hand, playfully. D'Artagnan remembered Athos's saying that like himself, Rochefort was equally good with both hands.

There was no formal interlude. Rochefort came at D'Artagnan with full fury and the intent of a man who means to make short work of this.

D'Artagnan stepped back and back and back, led to almost fleeing by his opponent's strength and rage. But lacking experience, D'Artagnan had a surplus of theory. And his theory told him he could not and should not flee forever.

Instead, he leapt up onto higher ground and from there, jumped to the side of Rochefort, making use of his greater agility. From that side, then, he renewed his assault on Rochefort, on his own terms, and the older man was hardpressed to defend himself.

As far as D'Artagnan could see or notice, as he passed one or the other of his friends, they all watched him thoughtfully. None looked worried. Sometimes Porthos moved his arm, or tapped his foot, in what seemed like a desperate desire to enter the fray or improve on D'Artagnan's style or technique.

But even though the two combatants passed sometimes

within a mere finger's width of the three spectators, none of the musketeers moved or said anything.

D'Artagnan thought that this was to avoid disturbing him, and for this he was grateful.

Rochefort managed to gain the upper hand, by sending D'Artagnan's sword flying with a swift parry. They both ran for it. D'Artagnan was faster. With the speed of youth, he threw himself across the intervening space, arm extended. He grabbed it. Rochefort was on him before D'Artagnan could straighten. The young man was forced to parry a pin-down sword thrust while lying on his back.

He pushed Rochefort's sword away, somersaulted to a standing position and swung his sword with force. It sent Rochefort's sword flying. Making use of his greater agility, D'Artagnan leapt to the sword and placed his foot on it.

Rochefort looked surprised. He stood, his hands on either side of his body, as the three musketeers closed in on him. "You have my sword," he told D'Artagnan. "What more do you require? I freely acknowledge you carried the best of this dispute and won over me."

D'Artagnan rose, holding the sword. "Unfortunately, to-day, more than that will be required."

"Today?" Rochefort asked. "But . . ." His face contorted in a grimace. "You want my life? You will kill an unarmed man in cold blood?"

"Not now, not in cold blood," D'Artagnan said. "But for full satisfaction of your offense, I require you to accompany us, and that you answer some questions."

Rochefort blinked, looking, for a moment, innocent and unguarded. "Questions?" he said. He looked around, behind him, and noticed that the three musketeers had closed in. "What is to prevent me from screaming?"

Porthos was exactly behind Rochefort. Porthos's hand went up like a hammer, and came down on the back of the man's head.

Rochefort's eyes widened, then closed, as he made a sound halfway between a whimper and a sigh and crumpled to the ground.

"Porthos," Athos said. He knelt and felt for Rochefort's pulse. "What have you done?"

D'Artagnan too knelt by the man, and reached for his

pulse, but Athos said, "He's alive. And his being alive, perhaps Porthos's impulse was not the worst."

"It was not an impulse," Porthos said. "How did you mean to transport Rochefort—Rochefort, yet, and His Eminence's right hand, through Paris otherwise? Even bound and gagged, even in a carriage, he might very well have found a way to call attention to himself. The agents of the Cardinal are full of tricks."

"But you could have killed him, Porthos," Aramis said.

Porthos looked surprised. "No one dies of a little tap on the head."

D'Artagnan decided not to challenge this. He'd learned from his week with the three musketeers that they had their ways of relating, a lot of it involving meaningless arguments that left their friendship undimmed.

Tired and sweaty from the fight, D'Artagnan ran his sleeve across his forehead. He sheathed his sword as well as Rochefort's, then helped Athos bind and gag the still-unconscious man. They had borrowed a carriage from a man who Aramis knew, and now they loaded the unconscious agent of the Cardinal into it.

Helene looked at the unconscious man's face and gasped. "It is him," she said. "The man who claimed to be Madeleine's uncle."

She came into the carriage and sat by Athos. After a while, Athos spoke. "You know what we did, it wasn't quite honorable."

Aramis nodded. "We knew at the beginning. Sometimes honor must bend to catch those without it. If he tells us what we need to know—or rather, *when* he tells us what he needs to know—we'll take him back to the Cardinal's palace with not a scratch on him. None the worse."

"Except us," Porthos said. "The Cardinal will seek his vengeance on us as soon as he can after this."

The way the three musketeers accepted this in the quietest and most matter-of-fact manner made D'Artagnan realize they had the highest of honors—the ability to take actions that were dangerous, and to pay for them when the bill came due.

A Henchman's Loyalty;
The Orphan's Story; Another Danger

❧

$\mathfrak{I}$T took only a day. Athos had expected it to take longer. But almost exactly a day after Rochefort had awakened, tied to a chair in Athos's cellar, unable to move or to make himself heard no matter how much he screamed—and under guard night and day—he'd decided to speak.

Part of this was the result of Athos's cunning, something he hadn't been aware he possessed till a few moments ago.

Athos was the one on guard, sitting at a little table with a single candle and a bottle of wine. He hadn't bothered with a glass because it seemed a waste of time when drinking alone.

Upstairs, in his comfortable guest room, Helene was presumably asleep. And in the space in between—that receiving room the other men knew so well—the other musketeers had lain down for the night, once more proving to possess that army-man quality of army men of being able to sleep anywhere at any time, on any surface.

Somewhere upstairs too Grimaud would be asleep and Planchet, who, left alone too long, had come in search of his young master, slept under the table in the front room.

And Athos was drinking and staring at the prisoner. Rochefort looked hardly the worse for the wear. They had fed him and given him water, and the bump on the back of his head—left by Porthos's quick, devastating blow—would not kill him. In two more days no one would be able to feel it.

Before Rochefort had awakened, they'd discussed whether or not to use certain techniques to intimidate him into talking. Techniques such as the Cardinal himself used on prisoners in the Bastille.

But they didn't have at their disposal the instruments the Cardinal had in that notorious hellhole. No wheel upon which to break the prisoners, no pliers for the removal of nails. They could have managed with candles and knives. Except that, in the dark, cool cellar, surrounded by Athos's almost impossibly large collection of wines, looking at the tied Rochefort, they could not even think of doing it.

After all, they knew—were certain—that Rochefort had participated in torture sessions before. They were sure, by the virtue of his position with the Cardinal, that he had terrorized and intimidated common people, merchants and peasants foolish enough to say a word against the Cardinal, or poor victims caught in the middle of His Eminence's schemes.

But they still could not face doing it. Porthos's words summed up and decided the situation. "It would make us like him," he said. "It would make us worthy of working for His blood-soaked Eminence, the Red Duke, and nothing more. And we, though we might bend it, are men of honor."

And so as men of honor, they had taken four shifts, sitting with the wily agent of the Cardinal. Athos didn't know for sure what the other ones did on their watch. From overhearing it, though, he suspected that D'Artagnan had asked the same questions over and over again, with Gascon boisterousness, demanding that Rochefort tell him what he had done with Madeleine and why.

Aramis seemed to have appealed to the best in Rochefort, reading the Scriptures to him and praying, then reading the Scriptures again.

Porthos had ranted and cursed and talked nonstop about the scourge of the Cardinal upon the old, honorable families of France and about the need for Rochefort to come clean. His rants and threats and screams had sometimes made the rafters over his head, and the floor underneath his friends' feet upstairs, tremble.

All of the friends' different techniques had exactly the same effect: none. Rochefort had alternately smiled or frowned at them, and stayed mute as the tomb.

Athos had volunteered to take the night shift. He hardly

slept anyway. And he'd sat at the stool next to the little table, on which sat his candle.

The wine was good, a ten-year-old red from Provence, tangy on the tongue, sweet to the palate, burning on the throat. Athos took measured sips and looked at Rochefort.

Rochefort was, Athos knew, of a family as old and as honorable as Athos's own. He wondered what it took for someone raised, as Athos had been, on obedience to the King and royalty to serve the man who manipulated the King and who was, behind the scenes, the true king of France.

And he wondered what it took for someone like that to accept that the Cardinal's will was the best for France and that they should, now and always, crush all opposition in the Cardinal's way.

He thought he could almost understand it. Almost. Doubtless, Rochefort's family property was in the same state of penury and ruin as Athos's. The last two centuries hadn't been kind to the small nobility. Their crafters and better-skilled farmers left the provinces to flock to the cities in search of a better life. Left behind were those peasants with no initiative, serving Lords with smaller rents and barely the money to support a brood of children. The only reason many noble families survived at all was enough strong sons to hunt food for the table.

If Richelieu promised to Rochefort the rebuilding of his domains, and enough in rents to keep his family going, to keep his children and grandchildren—or alternately, his brother's children and grandchildren, if Rochefort was the second son—in style well into the next century, well . . .

Even so, the acts that Rochefort had doubtless tainted himself with were despicable. Though Athos had never asked the man personally—nor had he any intention to—Athos had heard too many stories of kidnappings, murders and torture for some of it, at least, to surely be true.

He looked at Rochefort's face. Even his features were not all that different from Athos's. Both had strong chins and high foreheads, sharply chiseled cheekbones. Only Rochefort's skin was darker, and the eye looking out at Athos with something between horror and examination, was dark brown to Athos two dark blue ones.

Athos blinked. He suspected even their expressions right

now were similar. Looking at Rochefort was like looking in
a dark mirror, at a pathway of ruin and dishonor entered into
for the sake of his family's honor, for the sake of keeping his
family unstained.

They were not different. Not different at all. Why had
Athos killed his wife, except to keep his family honor unstained? That had been his first step on the same path
Rochefort was treading. One more step and Athos himself
would be lost.

He thought of Helene, sleeping upstairs. He wasn't quite
sure what he felt for her. He read in the girl signs similar to
those he'd read in his wife when he'd first met her—the vul-
nerable need to be protected coupled with a wild, unquench-
able, repressed fire.

Only Helene was too young to have done whatever it was
that Athos's wife had done to get marked with the fleur-de-
lis upon her shoulder—the mark of a harlot and murderess.

And Athos thought that perhaps if he could marry Helene, if he could marry her now, and keep her unstained—
protected—if he could allow her fire to shine through in
hunts with him through his semi-wild domain, and in travels
of exploration wherever her fancy called her, with him by
her side, she would never have a chance to suffer whatever
fate had inflicted on Charlotte that had made her turn . . .
That had made her tread the path leading to the gallows and
the branding with the fleur-de-lis.

He took a sip of the sweet, burning wine, and he imagined his life with Helene—imagined it much as his life with
Charlotte had been, the wild hunts, the wilder rides through
the fields. Without the horrible discovery in the morning . . .

There would be two sons. No, three. One to inherit, one
to be a musketeer, and one to send to Aramis—who by then
would be the superior of some Jesuit monastery—to train to
the church.

He smiled at the mad rashness of his dreams, then
abruptly realized that he was smiling while looking at
Rochefort and stopped it, making his face impassive again.

Before any or all of his dreams could come true, he must
find out who had killed Madeleine so that Helene could be at
peace with herself and with the world once more.

He drank some more wine, and stared at Rochefort, wondering what was on his mind, what he had done that involved him in the death of the girl.

"How long do you intend to keep me here?" Rochefort asked.

Athos shrugged and took a sip of wine. There was something to the way Rochefort asked, as if time mattered. On a wild hunch, riding upon a feeling that that the Cardinal's scheme was timely and that if Rochefort thought it had already come off he wouldn't worry about revealing it, Athos allowed one of his slow, disdainful smiles to cross his lips. "How long do you think you've been here?"

Rochefort's eyes showed wild panic. His lips moved, as if he were counting. In the dark cellar, it would be hard to tell time, as Athos knew all too well.

"A day?" he hazarded, surprising Athos with his accuracy.

Athos smiled again. "No. Almost two. You were unconscious almost a day."

A blatant lie, as Rochefort had awakened as soon as they tied him to the chair in the cellar. But Rochefort had no way of knowing. And the pain in his head would make it seem like the injury was that severe.

Rochefort's eyes flickered, first in alarm, then in triumph.

"Oh," he said. "To the devil with it. If you'll not let me go till I answer your questions, I'll answer them. I'll talk. It's too late for you to stop it anyway."

Athos raised his eyebrows, putting his glass down.

"The plot that involved the girl, the whole of it is in motion now, and far too late for any of you to stop, so whether you know it or not makes no difference to me. You could never prove it anyway."

"Murder is not the sort of thing you can hide that easily," Athos said.

"Who said anything about murder?" Rochefort said, puzzled. "This has nothing to do with that. But I will tell you to the extent of my ability how I found out about the girl and how I got her and why."

"You'll speak, then?" Athos asked.

Rochefort nodded.

Athos reached for the bell pull above him. It was a strip of leather, almost invisible in the shadows of the cellar, but he used it to call for Grimaud when he was down here and discovered a strong need for food or a book. Or, of course, when he'd drunk so much that he couldn't trust his own legs, unaided and unsupported, to take him up the stairs to his room. This was a state in which he never allowed his musketeer friends to see, but Grimaud had seen it often enough. It was sometimes what Athos required to be able to sleep.

The strip of leather was attached to a wire that ran upward and was in turn attached to a chain from which hung a large, pendulous bell, designed in such a way that it could be heard in every corner of the town house, even in Grimaud's attic room, should he be asleep.

Athos pulled vigorously on the leather and heard the muffled tolling of the bell upstairs, followed by scuffles and steps from his friends, and what sounded like a long and particularly creative oath from Porthos.

"I suppose you want witnesses," Rochefort said. "But none of your words is worth more than the others."

Athos nodded. "Oh, I don't expect the Cardinal will believe any of my friends' words more than mine," he said. He took a final sip of his wine. "On the other hand," he said, "this will save my having to repeat the story."

As he spoke, the other three came trooping in, clambering down the stairs to the cellar—Porthos with his hair unbound and messed, so that it stood almost on end and made him look like a primal Tor, the god of fire worshipped by some primitive, savage people; D'Artagnan with his face marked from sleeping on his cloak folds, and his eyes half closed and looking much like a young child disturbed in the night; and Aramis, with every one of his golden hairs in place and pulled back into a bind, and looking as if he'd awakened hours ago and had the benefit of a valet and all the implements of a barber's art.

Which merely confirmed Athos's impressions that Aramis could be dragged backwards by his heels, through flaming hell and icy flood and emerge looking fresh and calm, and as at ease and perfumed as if he'd just finished dressing for a royal audience.

The three of them piled at the end of the stairs, with Aramis in front, D'Artagnan behind him, peering over his shoulder and Porthos at the back, glowering over his friends' heads.

At a gesture from Athos they stopped there, and Athos said, "Monsieur de Rochefort is going to grace us with the story of his exploits that pertain to our poor murdered orphan, Madeleine."

It was only as he finished saying these words that he saw Helene. He had, some days ago, spent money on two dresses for her. She was wearing one of the two now—a dark-green velvet affair with a white collar that framed her already pale face and made her look even paler and more lost, like a child walking alone in the woods.

It allowed her to unbind her breasts, which swelled the upper half of the dress in gentle curve. They were not large, but large enough, and shaped in gentle, upward-pointing curves.

He looked away from her breasts quickly, and at her face, framed by dark hair that seemed to have a life of its own, curling in tendrils around her face, like solid, dark smoke.

Her eyes, weary and tired, looked into his. But most of all, she looked attentive. Attentive. Ready to listen to Rochefort.

"Speak," Athos told Rochefort.

Rochefort licked at his lips, a nervous gesture. "Some years ago . . ." he started and sighed. "Well, as you know, the Cardinal, my master, has agents and friends in all countries, and a great part of France's relationship with other countries depends on his interest in them and his working with them to establish the policy he wishes."

Athos nodded once, refusing to be baited into a discussion of those policies. He believed that overall, Richelieu had made France more respected and prosperous abroad. The fact that this was not his business, not his place, but the business and place of the King, who the Cardinal seemed to have forgotten was master of them all, was a minor problem, an issue Athos was sure would not at all affect Rochefort. Rochefort was too far gone down his path to see the lack of honor in it.

"Well, in Spain, my Lord the Cardinal's friend found a gentleman . . . minor nobility, but related to the our Queen through a . . . less-than-legitimate connection. This man looks a lot like our King's lady. When the Cardinal heard that this gentleman had a child he'd sired upon a noble Frenchwoman, the Cardinal got . . . interested.

"Oh, we couldn't have known, in any way, that the girl would look like the Queen. The chances of that were scant enough. But we thought that she might look noble enough to use on some missions, in return for status and for knowing who the father who'd abandoned her was." He looked at all four faces on the stairs, then at Athos's, and shrugged as though in answer to the disdain he read in their expressions. "People who have been raised as embarrassments have no loyalties except to those who rescue them from such a situation. As such," he said, "we thought the girl would be pliable. We also had reason to hope she'd be intelligent and spirited. After all, we knew her relatives on her mother's side." His gaze rested on Athos with something of knowing mockery. "The family is old, very old, having been noble before France was France. And all of them are intelligent and spirited, even the women.

"Imagine our surprise when we found the girl. She wasn't stupid, not exactly. But she was meek and mild as a summer's day."

A sound from the stairs, which might have been a repressed sob, and Athos looked up to see Helene covering her mouth.

"On the other hand," Rochefort went on, his gaze taking it all in, "she was, even two years ago, almost the image of the Queen. Which suggested to us another way of using her."

He smiled very slightly, as if remembering long hours of discussion and debate. "After much talk, the Cardinal thought the best way to do this was to use the girl, Madeleine, as a double for the Queen and get her to do something that would compromise the Queen."

There was another sound from the stairs, which was, doubtless, an exclamation of shock. Since Athos knew Helene had heard of the conspiracy from them, he could only imagine that her shock was at the casualness with which Rochefort referred to her dead friend.

"However, we needed to do something with the girl when the conspiracy was through—" This time, Rochefort himself looked up at the muffled sound from Helene. He frowned at her, as he went on. "So, for years in advance, we cultivated her father. As it turned out, her father's legitimate wife was deceased, and he had no heirs. So this one girl, girl though she was, would be useful to him. And we convinced him of such. In his name, I got the details of how the girl had been abandoned, and what I needed to get her out of the convent, as well as a stipend for her to acquire a proper wardrobe and to arrange for her travel to Spain. On her way there, we planned to keep her in Paris for a week or two to execute our plan, and then she would vanish, to Spain, where her resemblance to the Queen would never be noticed. Or if it were, would be no more than was expected of a cousin. And so we set it up."

He looked away from Helene and toward Athos. "I don't know how the Cardinal planned it or worked it, but he arranged to have a letter written in a handwriting that looked just like the Queen's. This is not difficult when you have all the contacts he has. And with this letter, he summoned Buckingham, and told him that Anne wanted to meet him, in a first-floor room, in Rue de Saint Eugenie. He was to rent the room under a false name. And there she would come to him, in disguise."

"Why . . . why D'Herblay as a false name?" Aramis asked, hesitantly from the stairs.

Rochefort looked up, visibly surprised. "I have no idea. It appears the Cardinal knew some of the family when he was young, and he thought it was a convenient name. He suggested the name in the letter he pretended was from the Queen."

"And she used musketeer attire," Athos prompted, taking yet another draught from his bottle and savoring it.

"Of course. This allowed her to walk, unmolested, through the streets. Also allowed her to not be fully seen by Buckingham."

Athos thought through it. It was as they had thought. Rochefort had got Madeleine from St. Jerome's to impersonate Anne of Austria for Buckingham. "But why?" Athos asked. "What I mean to ask is, if she yielded to him, who would know it? No one caught them, and therefore it does no damage to the Queen."

Rochefort shook his head. "It was not a matter of her yielding to him. In fact, I don't think we could have convinced Madeleine to do it, had we tried. She had been brought up in the convent and her morals would not allow her to give herself to a man before marriage. As I said, she was a good, obedient girl. We convinced her she was acting in a play. And while I suppose the Cardinal considered leading the King to the house where the rendezvous happened, to observe it all undercover, it would not have answered.

"His Majesty can have an intemperate mood, and if he'd broken into the room, he would quickly have discovered that Madeleine was not Anne of Austria. Though we coached Madeleine so she would have the right accent in the few words she said to Buckingham, her unschooled gestures and language did not at all resemble the Queen's."

He was quiet after that, and Athos regarded him, equally in silence. "You said it would be too late for us to stop the plan, so there is a plan, beyond making Buckingham believe he had seen the Queen, I believe?"

Rochefort sighed, then inclined his head, not so much nodding as a reluctant admission. "The Queen . . . that is, Madeleine, gave Buckingham something that the King gave Anne of Austria, amid other presents on her wedding day. That something was stolen and Madeleine gave it to Buckingham as proof of her love."

Suddenly Athos's mind cleared. He remembered, days ago, hearing that the kings of England and France were to meet, as they had met almost a century ago, in the fields at Calais. There, the King of England would come, with his retinue, which would not fail to include Buckingham.

Athos had felt slighted that—because of his wound—he'd not been chosen to be part of the King's guard. In fact, the King had left right after his audience with the musketeers. It was to be a grand event, in tents, with much feasting and dancing—one of those things the nations of the world did instead of negotiating peace. The sovereigns would meet and reassure each other they meant peace and understanding, and then in a few months war would erupt.

Athos rose from his chair. "It is too late, because the King and Queen are already there, and Buckingham is there. Buckingham is an intemperate man and he might very well wear the jewel the Queen gave him, right in front of the King. And if not, at any rate, he'll never part with it. It will be in his luggage. Which means if the Cardinal . . ." Before he realized it, Athos was heading for the stairs, only to find his way blocked by Aramis and Porthos. "The Cardinal might already have suggested to the King that the Queen's ring was given to Buckingham. They might already be searching for it."

He stood very still and felt as if his chest were encased in ice. His father had taught him loyalty for the royal family of France. He'd been taught to respect and revere them. He stood there, watching centuries of honorable Counts de la Fere look at him out of the pages of history.

He'd failed to stop the disgrace of the Queen of France. "The Queen might already be lost," he said.

A Live Queen's Honor Trumps
Dead Woman's Murder; Where Athos
Must Be Made to Stay and Aramis
and Porthos Must Go

"**W**HERE are you going?" Aramis asked, interposing himself between Athos and the rest of the stairway. A daring move, as Athos was the more substantial and taller of the two and, if in a passion, quite unstoppable. "What can you do?"

"Nothing," Rochefort said. "He can do nothing. Even if he got to the place where they're meeting and found his way through the maze of tents before the Queen's supposed perfidy is exposed, he could do nothing. He can tell de Treville what happened. He can tell the King what happened. But the King will believe the evidence of his ring in Buckingham's hands more than he'll believe anything a mere musketeer might tell him."

Athos, pale, tried to get past Aramis again, and again Aramis blocked his path. He'd known—he'd always known—that at the base of Athos's laconic and self-controlled behavior, was an impulsive man. But whatever he felt for Helene, whatever was happening now in his heart had brought it out in a way that Aramis didn't expect. He was making a fool of himself.

"The Queen is lost," Athos said again.

"Perhaps," Aramis said. "Perhaps not. In any case, you are not the one to save her."

Athos looked at Aramis, uncomprehending. Clearly,

Athos had no idea how impulsive, how uncontrolled his behavior had become. In his present mood, the older musketeer was quite likely to march into the tents of the high dignitaries of both countries and challenge Richelieu for a duel. But Aramis couldn't tell him that.

"Athos," he said, "you cannot go without taking Helene. You can't leave her here without your protection. And she would not be safe going with you. Let me go, with Porthos. I know everything about the Court. I have friends and acquaintances through my friends. I can make way through tents and dignitaries faster than any of you."

Athos's hand remained extended and his eyes looked dully at Aramis, all the while looking like someone trying to translate something from an odd and arcane language.

His lips moved as if he were repeating Aramis's words to himself, to understand them fully. And then he said, "You will need horses."

"We'll go to Monsieur de Treville's stables," Porthos said.

Before Aramis had time to draw a proper breath, he and Porthos were being pushed outside, into the star-filled night, in search of horses.

The Ghost and the Living; The Uses of
a Broken Heart; Murder No More

ॐ

ATHOS woke up in the night with certainty that D'Artagnan had fallen asleep.

He did not know whence the knowledge came, nor how it had lighted upon his sleeping brain. He sat up in his room, in the dead of night, listening to the familiar sounds of the house, and he knew—knew for an absolute fact that D'Artagnan, who was downstairs, supposed to be guarding Rochefort, had fallen asleep.

Had he been dreaming of . . . her again? Had her ghost wakened him, as it so often did? But his mind could not conjure the image of the beautiful young blonde who'd been his wife for all too brief a time.

That face, which he'd remembered too long, too exquisitely, in dream and memory, had disappeared from his mind altogether—vanished like a painting left out in the rain and shedding its color till nothing was left but a blurred outline and a suggestion of colors.

His room looked as it always did. The bed was one which he'd managed to have brought from his domain. Oh, not the count's bed, not the bed that was rightfully his, not the bed in which he'd slept with *her*. No. That was still in his house, waiting his return, if he ever returned alive.

But this one was a broad, comfortable bed from one of the guest rooms. Its gilded headboard, sculpted all over with cherubs and angels would have surprised his friends, and would doubtless have caused Porthos great envy. But for Athos it meant security. This was the bed in which he'd slept as a child, the headboard the one he'd traced with much smaller fingers, back in the day when the world was simple, life made sense and he still believed in angels watching his every move from above.

The rest of his room reflected the sparseness in gesture and manner that his friends had come to see as part of Athos himself. There was a trunk, by the window, in which he kept his spare clothes. It was unadorned, raw wood, and capable of being closed quickly by two leather straps, so it could be carried into battle if its owner needed. In the corner a camp table, which could fold away and be carried with the trunk, supported a tin basin and its ewer—which sufficed for most of Athos's daily washing.

The only other furnishings in the room were curtains—gauzy curtains of some lacy material, which had been in the room when Athos rented it. They now billowed full, in the breeze and, the moonlight on them, seemed to Athos to take the shape of a beautiful blonde woman.

He looked away from the curtains, with a shiver, and pulled his sheets up around him. The blanket which, with the bed, he'd had brought from his domain, was tossed over the foot of the bed, obscuring a footboard that matched the headboard. He'd felt hot when he'd gone to bed.

But now the sheets were insufficient to keep his shivers at bay. And he doubted that even his blanket could make him feel warm again. And besides, there it was, still, the intuition, at the back of his mind, that D'Artagnan had fallen asleep downstairs.

Or perhaps it wasn't intuition. After the others had left, they'd had wine there in the cellar, D'Artagnan and Athos and Helene. They'd even given some to Rochefort. And after the wine, D'Artagnan had seemed . . . drowsy. Confused. Which seemed strange, considering that the boy came from near Spain, where the wine was plentiful and strong enough.

He had to have a better head for wine. Surely.

But the boy was young. While Athos thought this, his feeling of cold and unease had got him up, got him on his feet, got him searching for his breeches, which he'd tossed with careless disregard uncharacteristic of him, and which seemed to have fallen behind the trunk.

He pulled them on. Yes, the boy was young. And that

might mean that before he came to Paris he was used to going to bed very early. Earlier than anyone in Paris did. Which meant . . .

Which meant that D'Artagnan was asleep. This shouldn't matter. Rochefort was tied up. And he'd looked as sleepy as D'Artagnan.

But there was something about that unusual sleepiness . . . something.

In Athos's mind, the image of Helene's hands formed. Helene serving the wine. Those elongated, delicate fingers, those pale hands that could ply a dagger and serve wine with equal delicacy.

There was a movement he remembered—her hand dipping into her sleeve. Her back turning. The suggestion of a white bag, of white powder . . . He didn't know what to think. Had he dreamed it? Had he seen it happen? Could Helene, the orphanage girl, raised by nuns, have poisoned the wine for the prisoner? And for D'Artagnan?

Athos could not believe it. And yet, the memory was there. The white bag, the quick movement, her back turned when it shouldn't be. And then both men sleepy. So sleepy.

Athos opened the door to the hallway, from his room.

The hallway outside was silent, bathed in shadows. It was long and narrow and most inconveniently illuminated only by a tall, elongated window in the middle of the outer wall. The light of the moon coming through that narrow hole put an almost unreal, bluish glow upon the opposite white wall. No curtains, since there hadn't been any here when Athos rented the dwelling. And he had never bothered having them put in.

At one end of the hallway, the staircase went down, past Helene's room, to the main hall, the receiving room with which his three friends were so well acquainted—the setting for war councils, for feasting, for mad planning. At the other end, the staircase went up as well as down. Up to Grimaud's garret apartment, a residence of the uttermost comfort, even if absolutely spartan. And down, to the kitchen, where Grimaud daily produced culinary miracles that defied both the musketeer's tight budget and more constrained imagination.

Athos hesitated, not knowing which way to go. The idea of why he must go, why he must creep downstairs in the dark of night and check on D'Artagnan and the prisoner was still just a half-formed imperative, something his subconscious had got hold of in his sleep, and which was propelling him forward, despite himself.

If Helene had poisoned the prisoner, and D'Artagnan, then Athos would be . . . bereft. There was no other word for it. The desolate, arid landscape of his heart for the last ten years would be nothing compared to the desolation to follow.

But he could not imagine Helene doing that. Then why did he feel the need to go downstairs? Even if D'Artagnan and the prisoner were both asleep, why would it matter?

Because Helene had made them sleep? And why would Helene want that?

Suddenly he knew. He remembered Helene saying she wanted to come with him to Paris, she wanted to be present at the investigation, she wanted to be there when justice was done.

When justice was done.

Without realizing he'd made a decision, Athos slid down the hallway, headed to the service stairs and to the kitchen below. He knew he had to be stealthy and silent.

He did not want to startle her. He did not want to give her a reason to hurry.

He slid, as fast as he could, as soundlessly as he could, down the darkened hallway, found the stair step with his bare foot, then the next. For someone who could not see where his feet were landing, he moved extremely fast down the steps, till he came to the bottom.

The kitchen was a largish room—larger than his bedroom, but smaller than the area where he often entertained his friends. It was also far more crowded, with a large cooking hearth taking up most of the space. Beyond that there was a squarish ceramic sink, a bewildering collection of plates and jugs and other utensils. In a corner sat a deep wooden box, which Athos knew, from seeing, was what Grimaud used to knead bread.

At the center of the kitchen stood the vast, scrubbed pine table, at which Grimaud cut and peeled and prepared food, and at which Athos ate when it was just the two of them alone, because whether he was a count by birth or not, in his reduced circumstances, in his life in exile, it seemed foolish to insist on all the etiquette.

Because he often ate there, he knew exactly how many knives were supposed to be arrayed near the top of the table. There were usually ten. Now there were nine. Because Grimaud was scrupulous about setting his knives in the proper order and the exact same arrangement every time, Athos knew that the knife missing was the second largest. A sharp knife, used for cutting meat.

Helene. He could not allow Helene to do this. It came to him, like a shiver, like an uncontrollable impulse, that he couldn't care less if she killed Rochefort. D'Artagnan, yes. D'Artagnan's death, he'd mind. He'd taken to the boy, who was almost young enough to be his son and who in many ways reminded him of his young, guiltless self.

But Rochefort? Helene was welcome to kill Rochefort and the hell with him. Except that Athos knew the darkness and the guilt that would descend on her soul afterwards. And he could not allow that. He could not allow her to destroy herself.

He skirted around the table, and started down the stairs to the cellar.

The cellar was all dark and he could hear two sets of breathing. D'Artagnan and Rochefort. They were both alive, then, and from the depth of the breaths, asleep.

It was too dark for Athos to discern anything down the stairs and in the cellar.

He stood in place, and blinked, trying to get his eyes adjusted to the lighting.

Ahead of him, he saw something move. Not a person, just the movement. The movement, and something else. The hint of fabric whispering on fabric. The barest trace of a scent. Roses. Helene.

He plunged forward, on a feeling, a sense, the idea, that she was there, somewhere, ahead. And grabbed at her arms, in the dark.

She exclaimed in surprise. She must have been so intent on what she was doing and where she was going, that she hadn't heard him approach.

As he pulled at her, she struggled a little, thrashing in his arms.

"No, Helene," he said. "No."

At the sound of his voice, she exclaimed again and he heard something fall from her hand. From the sound of metal and wood hitting the stone stairs, he thought it must be the knife.

She turned, both hands closed in tight fists, beating at his chest. "I must," she said, in an urgent whisper. "He killed Madeleine. I must. I must."

"Shhh," he said, and held her tight, tight, her body warm and pliant and soft against his own taut body, separated only by his shirt and some sort of thin shift that must have been what she was sleeping in.

Her feeble attempts at fighting only served to remind him that he was human and that she was a woman. And that he hadn't held another human, much less a beautiful female, in very, very long.

"Shhh," he said again.

She stopped pounding his chest and relaxed within the hold of his arms. She smelled like a rose garden in the moonlight, and she felt warm against him.

He pulled her gently up the stairs and to the kitchen, closing the door behind him.

The Advantages of an Aching Head; How to Add Two and Two and Get Five

D'ARTAGNAN woke up in the dark. He had a feeling that someone had just closed a door upstairs, and he didn't know where he was.

His head hurt, a dull ache, distant and nonetheless throbbing, as though someone had snuck up on D'Artagnan in his sleep and filled his head with wool. Ears and eyes gave him dim, distant sensations, and his left ear crackled and wheezed. His eyelids felt as though they were glued with paste. And he was sitting, tilted against the wall, upon an uncomfortable stool. Moving his hand, he hit a small table that resounded like wood.

The cellar. He was in Athos's cellar, and he was supposed to be watching their prisoner. Had Rochefort escaped?

No, even through his dimmed hearing, he could just perceive the regular, deep breathing of a sleeper nearby. So, Rochefort too had fallen asleep.

All the same, D'Artagnan thought, standing up and balancing himself with his hands on the small table while blood returned to his legs and feet in a torment of pin-pricks, he'd just proven himself unworthy of the trust his new friends had placed in him. If he was unable to stay awake when he was supposed to be on duty here, why would they believe he could stay awake while on duty as a musketeer?

Annoyed at himself, he felt on the table for the candle, which he expected had burned itself out in its candlestick.

To his surprise, he found that the candle was still there, almost the length it had been when D'Artagnan had sat down, but the flame had gone out. He picked up the candlestick—with the candle in it—and started a tentative trek up the stairs for light. He had some memory of banked ashes in the kitchen, and he thought he could use one of those to light the candle again.

On the stairs, he tripped on something that sounded metallic against the stone. Farther up, he opened the door to the kitchen.

And, by the light of the moon coming in through the broad windows and washing over table and hearth, he saw two people, in a tight embrace.

Athos. Athos and . . . In the confusion of his headache, he couldn't remember the girl's name. He could only think how much she looked like Athos—the same dark hair and pale skin. Same blue eyes so dark they might almost be black, same square shoulders and proudly set head.

D'Artagnan blinked. Aramis had said that the dead girl seemed to be in Athos's family, but . . .

While he was watching, Athos led the girl—Helene— toward the stairs leading to Athos's room.

D'Artagnan stood in the kitchen, holding the unlit candle. His head still hurt and so his thoughts weren't as rational or straightforward as they usually were. Instead, they sparked in the dark of his headache like so many fireflies shining in a dark night.

He thought of Athos's reaction to the talk of the orphanage and of the girl. D'Artagnan remembered too, Athos flinching at seeing the ring in the dead girl's pouch and even though he could not and would not believe the girl was Athos's daughter—his embarrassment bore no trace of guilt—he had suspected that she was perhaps a relation. The girl hadn't looked anything like Athos. But this one did. Were both of them, then, the relation of whatever noble family Athos came from?

Swaying slightly on his feet, aware of their retreating steps, D'Artagnan thought that he should be going back to guard Rochefort.

And then he thought that Rochefort had confessed very easily to the whole conspiracy. Except to the murder—to that he had not confessed. On the contrary, he had denied it most vehemently.

After all, Madeleine was well born. Rochefort had her father's complicity, and her mother was either dead or in another marriage.

Why kill her? And why would Rochefort kill the priest?

Their minds had been so taken with the conspiracy to ruin the Queen that they had not thought to wonder exactly how that implicated Rochefort. Still tied. Below the stairs.

D'Artagnan got hold of a brand from the hearth and touched it to the wick of the candle till it caught. Then he dropped the brand, blew on his scalded fingers and, protecting the flame of the candle with his hand, started down the stairs.

The object on which he'd stepped was a knife. It looked like one of the knives from the kitchen upstairs, haphazardly dropped on the step. Looking at it, D'Artagnan shivered. Why was it here? He thought of Athos and Helene, retreating, up the steps. Had Helene thought to take revenge? D'Artagnan shivered, again.

Down the steps to where Rochefort was still tied and sitting up in a position that had to be uncomfortable after more than twenty-four hours. Why, then, was he still sleeping?

The wine. Helene had served them all wine. And three of the cups were still there, on the table. Athos had finished the bottle from the bottle, unlike his normally fastidious self. Perhaps because he drank so much and so often, he had learned to dispense with smaller containers and drink directly from the source.

D'Artagnan took one look at Rochefort—sleeping, abandoned, his head tilted back, his mouth open, an unearthly snore escaping through his loose, sagging lips.

Picking up the three cups, D'Artagnan smelled them. One of them smelled like normal wine, but both the others had a sharp, slightly vinagery smell. It smelled like the sleeping powder D'Artagnan's father used. A sleeping powder. Helene had given them a sleeping powder. But why?

D'Artagnan couldn't quite put his finger on the reason— perhaps she had meant to take revenge on Rochefort? But revenge for what, if he hadn't confessed to the murder? He might have murdered Madeleine, but how could they be sure?

And there was something else here, a feeling of shadowy

play behind the scenes that made D'Artagnan's hair stand on end and put a shiver down his spine. He had to know. He had to ask Rochefort.

Grabbing the bottle, he found it still had some wine in it, and he did the first thing he could think of: He dumped it over Rochefort's head.

The older man snorted mid snore, and made a sound that turned to a low scream, as he opened his eyes and saw D'Artagnan standing over him holding a bottle.

D'Artagnan realized it looked as if he were about to bash the bound man's head in. "Relax," he said as he put the bottle aside. "I only wanted to wake you."

"With wine?" Rochefort said, shaking his head, sending droplets of wine flying in all directions.

"I didn't have any water," D'Artagnan said, while Rochefort's narrowed eye and furrowed brow implied this was not a sufficient excuse. D'Artagnan shrugged. "I must ask you some questions."

Rochefort's bound hands made an effort, as though to reach into his pocket. Seeing this, D'Artagnan reached in the pocket and got out a plain linen handkerchief, with which he wiped the wine running down the other man's face.

If they'd both been drugged, why had D'Artagnan woken earlier? Perhaps because he was younger? In better health?

"Rochefort, tell me the truth," he said. "Did you kill Madeleine?"

"Mad—the girl from the convent?" Rochefort looked genuinely surprised at the thought. "No. As best I can imagine she fell victim to some cutthroat or cutpurse. We should have followed but we were afraid Buckingham would spot us and we'd give the game away."

He shook his head and looked genuinely saddened. "We should have protected her better. I still don't know what we'll tell her father."

"And her father is truly a nobleman."

"Yes. Yes, from the House of Austria."

"And who was her mother?" D'Artagnan asked.

Rochefort shrugged. "French noblewoman, from an ancient and respected family. With better pedigree than purse, if you know what I mean. Very proud. Their name is de La Fere, though the woman came from a sideline, being the daughter of a daughter of the house. But all the same, very noble, very proud and full of dignity. They couldn't brook the kind of dishonor that an illegitimate birth would bring upon them, and so they forced the woman to send the girl to be raised at St. Jerome's while the mother was sent to a convent for the rest of her days. Which turned out not to be many."

He spoke sincerely, and there was a hint of sadness at wasted life. It was a shock to D'Artagnan who, in his short time in the city had come to view the camp of the Cardinal as people who would stop at nothing to get their way and win victory.

But that, perhaps, didn't mean they would stop at nothing when there was no victory involved. Wishing to win at all costs didn't—D'Artagnan supposed—mean inflicting pain for no reason. In fact, even in his young and untutored state, D'Artagnan had a suspicion that too much sadistic delight in suffering might mean lack of victory, lack of success. If you stooped too much to hurt those who were not in your way, sooner or later one of them would trip you on your journey.

In any case, he could not tell himself that Rochefort felt nothing for the girl or her mother. The reverse was clearly true.

"What about the priest?" D'Artagnan asked.

"The priest?" Rochefort asked, and blinked, clearly bewildered. "What priest?"

"Father Bellamie. Of St. Peter the Fisherman."

Rochefort shook his head. "Never heard of him. How does he come into this?"

The surprise and confusion didn't seem to be faked. For one, from his own aching head, from Rochefort's slightly squinting eyes, D'Artagnan suspected that the man had a huge headache and was thinking none too clearly. If Rochefort knew of the priest, given his current situation, the normal thing would be to say something about how it wasn't his fault.

"Isn't that one of the parishes where all the seamstress shops are?" he asked. And shook his head. "I rarely go there, except to shop, and even more rarely attend church there." He paused a moment. "Or anywhere."

"He was murdered," D'Artagnan said. "And the body

we'd given into his keeping was stolen. The body of the girl. Madeleine."

Rochefort's mouth dropped open, in surprise. "I didn't know," he said. "We thought . . . We knew she had been killed. The way she disappeared, we knew she had been killed. But we thought that she'd been hidden, somewhere. The corpse. In the way cutpurses and thieves hide their victims. Particularly comely young women." He shook his head. "The Cardinal worried someone would give the alarm that a woman who looked like the Queen had been found."

"The priest was killed the same way she was," D'Artagnan said. "His throat was cut."

And, as he spoke, as he watched Rochefort's shocked reaction and shaking head, a monstrous idea formed in his mind.

He set the bottle down on the table, and started toward the stairs, at a gallop, not pausing to explain why to Rochefort.

"Monsieur D'Artagnan," Rochefort said, at the same time that D'Artagnan reached the middle of the stairs and again tripped on the knife.

He backtracked quickly to the cellar again and said, "Monsieur Rochefort, I am going to lock the door at the top of the stairs, to ensure your safety. Be so kind as to endure it. I shall be back by daylight."

Thus speaking, he blew out the candle, and rushed back upstairs.

The great big key was on the outside of the door. D'Artagnan turned it. Most cellars had good locks, to prevent the household help drinking the house owner's wine, since not all servants were as trustworthy as the good Grimaud.

D'Artagnan pulled the key out and slipped it into his sleeve. He would not part from it till he returned. Hopefully that would be enough to keep Rochefort safe.

A blackguard he might be, and he might have committed many crimes. But D'Artagnan would not have him killed on his watch, and not while he was helpless.

He ran to the front room and shook Planchet awake. Finger to his lips, he led the servant out of the house to the street.

Outside, he said, "Planchet, can you ride a horse?"

Planchet nodded. "My father's landlord had horses and I often helped with them."

"Good, because I need you to go to Monsieur de Treville's stable, and tell him you need two horses for Athos. They've seen you there with us, and they'll probably give them to you, while I doubt he'll lend horses to a future guard."

"Why horses?" Planchet asked.

"We must go to the orphanage and talk to the Mother Superior to whom Athos and Aramis have spoken. There is a monstrous idea in his mind and he wanted it laid to rest."

Planchet nodded.

"And we must be back as soon as possible," D'Artagnan said. "Lives might hang on it."

The Advantages of Knowing
a Man; Where Porthos Wonders
at Aramis's Web of Contacts

ᘒ

THE road to Calais went by like a dream. They'd picked the best available horses, the ones that Monsieur de Treville's groom had assured them were the fastest—two white horses with the fine legs of Arabians.

But after two hours at full gallop, the horses' pace was growing slower and they were beaded in sweat. Porthos wondered if they would have to walk the rest of the way.

This was probably a quixotic endeavor, and useless, as what Rochefort had said doubtless held. The Queen was doubtless already lost and soon rumors, that bird that flew faster than all other creatures on Earth, would fly back to Paris and announce that she was being shunned, divorced, exiled.

But Porthos remembered the look on Athos's face, that pasty-white, scared face, the eyes bulging as much as the eyes of a hanged man. And he was not about to return to Paris and to Athos and tell him that they hadn't even tried to save Her Majesty. Were he to do that, Athos might lose whatever little control he had upon his reason and sanity.

Oh, Porthos admired Athos. Who could but admire a man who, wearing faded velvet cut in the style of ten years ago, could look more noble and, indeed, better dressed than Porthos, who always took care to wear the showiest clothes and the first glare of fashion.

Or at least that's what Porthos would have said, were he questioned. He would have answered like that, and grinned, and hoped that no one guessed there was a deeper-thinking, more guarded Porthos beneath the facade of brash and thoughtless *bien vivant*.

But Porthos admired in Athos everything he himself wasn't. The ability to be quiet for long stretches of time while, somehow, remaining at the center of the situation and fully aware of all that was happening. The ability to control himself, so that if he showed rage or calm it was not necessarily what Athos was feeling but only that which he wanted to show. And—Porthos sighed on thinking about it—the ability to read the philosophers of Greece and Rome not only without falling asleep, but also being able to extract from such reading maxims and rules of conduct.

But even though Porthos, in his mode of addressing the world often gave the impression that he was stupid, he most certainly was not.

He noted that Athos was distracted and confused, and acting so little like himself that he seemed, at times, to be close to losing control.

Porthos being Porthos, and always the direct man, thought that Athos should bed Helene already and stop baying over her like a dog who stood outside the fence and cried out at being barred from his prize. After all, Athos was a man, not a dog, and all such fences were of his own making.

Porthos had never understood an honor that consisted in treating women as inaccessible jewels, both more and less than human—things to be seen but not enjoyed, admired but not touched. For Porthos, women were flesh and blood and joyful touch, and if he sinned in the way he enjoyed them, then it was why, no doubt, the church had seen it fit to institute the sacrament of confession.

Athos's honor had led him astray and perhaps he, himself, didn't know what he wanted with Helene. Porthos sighed again, as Aramis signaled they should slow down.

Which was a good thing, because from the way his horse was breathing, Porthos was very much afraid that the animal would die under him. Always a difficult situation—which he had experienced in campaign—jumping from the horse without getting caught under its weight. And also not something he wished to do to one of Monsieur de Treville's horses.

Aramis was looking around, even as he slowed down his horse's pace.

They had just emerged from an area of even, flat ground, cut here and there by islands of trees. For miles and miles— though they'd been going far too fast for more than a casual impression—there had been no homes. If anything, only an isolated farmhouse here and there, and nothing that Porthos could register as inhabited country.

But now, just ahead, was a tavern. It was dark and silent, but also large. Very large. The size of Monsieur de Treville's residence in Paris, including the vast stables at the back.

Porthos thought that such taverns, with lodging rooms overhead, often contained large and well-appointed dining rooms as well. His stomach rumbled. He'd had nothing to eat since he'd grabbed some bread and cheese on the way to the duel.

He did not believe in eating before a duel—even a duel in which he was only the second—and they'd not thought of it afterwards as they questioned Rochefort. Though there had been wine. Lots of wine.

As Aramis brought the horse into the silent inn yard, Porthos closed in alongside him.

"What are we doing?" he asked. "It's empty."

Aramis shook his head. He looked over at Porthos, and he looked as tired as Porthos felt. Even his normally impeccable hair was in disarray, escaping in tendrils and whorls from beneath his hat, which hung back on his head and was prevented from falling only by what remained of his ponytail.

He tied his horse to one of the many stone poles—with rings—lining the yard, and stretched to relieve what Porthos knew from his own experience was overwhelming soreness in every muscle and joint, and deep-seated pain in each bone.

"Aramis, are we just going to rest?" Porthos asked, imitating his friend's actions, but not understanding what good it did them to stop at a closed inn.

Aramis again shook his head. He absently patted his horse on the head, while the animal, covered in sweat, shivered and panted. Then Aramis removed his saddlebags, slung them over his shoulder and started toward the main door.

Looking over his shoulder at Porthos, who was removing his own saddlebags, he said, "I know a man. I'm going to see that man about a horse. Two horses."

Porthos was too tired to make one of his customary jokes at this declaration. He merely nodded, in acknowledgment of the fact that Aramis usually did know someone, somewhere.

Aramis's repeated, loud knocks at the door brought out a meek and mousy-looking cleric, who blinked at them in the confusion of one who is barely awake.

"Call your master," Aramis said.

The boy shook his head.

And Aramis, the normally mild musketeer, who never even raised his voice to his inferiors, reached forward and grabbed the boy's grimy shirt front. "Listen, you will go wake up your master and you will tell him that the Chevalier D'Herblay is here, and he needs help, now."

The boy, let go, bowed hastily and ran into the shadows of the house.

The door was open a slit, large enough for the two musketeers to look into a dark and smokey interior that smelled of old food and of too many people sleeping in insufficient accommodation.

"You know," Porthos said, making his voice as low as he could and as nonthreatening as possible, because with Aramis in this mood, he had no idea what the reaction would be. "You have no guarantee that he'll actually go and wake someone. You might have scared him too much, in which case he'll disappear into the dark never to be heard from again. It might have been more advisable—"

Aramis had removed his hat and loosened the leather bind that kept his hair confined at the back. His hair, wavy and blond, fell over his shoulders in all directions, while he made largely unsuccessful attempts to comb it with his fingers. He shot Porthos a venomous look from beneath this golden curtain. "Monsieur Porthos, this comes nicely from you," he said. "Who never speak unless you're going to scream and who wouldn't know self-control even if you were exerting it."

Porthos bit his lip to keep back his immediate reaction, which was laughter attempting to bubble up from his chest.

If he laughed now, with the mood Aramis was in, they would likely be embroiled in a duel if and when the householder came for them. Which wouldn't do at all, because Porthos had no intention of killing Aramis or even wounding him. And a duel in which one of the participants is fully intent on murder, while the other one is calm and composed, can go one of two ways but always ends up in one death or the other.

Instead, Porthos spoke in his newly found low and calm voice—which nonetheless reverberated around the yard and raised echoes from the walls. "This is why I speak," he said. "Because I have so much experience with the behavior you have just shown," he said. "And I know it not to be the type of action conducive to getting obedience."

Aramis had managed to pull all his hair back from his face, and was trying to tie it back with the leather strip, blind, and struggling with bits and pieces of hair that refused to stay still. "Well and good," he said. And Porthos would swear that if Aramis had his own booming voice, he would, right now, be waking people up for miles and miles. "Well and good, but if they do not answer my request, I shall presently resume knocking till the whole house is awake."

Porthos had visions of massed ranks of servants, which these large inns normally kept to keep miscreants under control, coming boiling out of that door in the light of the moon, in response to the behavior Aramis described.

But before Porthos could decide whether to warn his friend, the door to the kitchen opened, and a man appeared in the doorway.

He was a large man, dark and florid of face. His expression of extreme skepticism changed at the sight of Aramis, who had finally got his hair under control, though not as impeccable looking as was his usual.

"*Dents Dieu,*" he said, grinning broadly. "It is little Renee D'Herblay," he said. He put his hands forward and grabbed both of Aramis's with the greatest of familiarity. He looked Aramis up and down. "And a musketeer. I'd always thought the lady, your mother, intended you for the church."

Aramis inclined his head. "The lady, my mother, did, but events happened that postponed my taking of vows."

The man looked shrewdly at Aramis's uniform and the

businesslike sword strapped to his side. "Indeed," he said, managing to cast aspersions of doubt on the idea that Aramis would ever subdue his bellicose manner into the church. He stepped back, letting go of Aramis's hands. "And how can I help you?" he said. And then, with the look of someone who can't resist one more comment, "I'd have known you anywhere. You've grown into the image of your father. You could be him, come back from the grave."

Aramis nodded. "I need fresh horses," he said. "Fast. I will return them to you on the way back. Until then, if you would, lodge these horses and have your grooms care for them, so they are fresh when we return."

"And when will you return?" the hosteler asked.

"Probably before next morning," Aramis said.

"Should I ask where you're headed? Or is it a secret?"

"I'm afraid it is a secret," Aramis said demurely, looking at his nails.

"Indeed," the hosteler said again. "Ah, you're such a one just like your father, always involved in some secret dealing with some lady or another. Those were the days, Chevalier, those were the days. Now let me get my lazy grooms to care for your horses and get you fresh mounts."

While the man went into the house and shouted something into the smoke-scented darkness, Aramis turned to Porthos. "Monsieur Amarrez-du-Large was my father's valet in my father's young days."

Porthos nodded.

"He lived with us till my father's death, so the appropriateness of behavior of a servant to a nobleman was never impressed upon him. He views me, and treats me, as the toddler he used to know."

Porthos smiled. Was Aramis truly apologizing to Porthos, of all people, for allowing familiarity from people of the lower classes? Then again, Aramis knew nothing of Athenais.

Grooms came out of the kitchen—now fully revealed to be a kitchen, as the door was thrown open to the moonlight—and surrounded the horses from Monsieur de Treville and led them into the stable to tend to their needs.

Two other grooms brought out two slick, black animals that had something of Athos's Samson to their heads' set and the look of their eyes.

Aramis and Porthos threw their saddlebags over the saddles and clipped them in place.

"Chevalier," Amarrez-du-Large said. "Would you do me the honor of taking a light meal with us?"

Porthos drew in breath to say yes with all his heart, and could not believe Aramis's answer. "No, I'm afraid we have no time, Amarrez."

The large man's face fell. And looking at him, Porthos noticed something he'd have passed over another time—while the man was larger than Aramis, broader of shoulder and waist, and while his hair was a completely different color and his skin darker, there was something very alike about the two men, something that the expressions of both echoed and reflected.

The devil? What was here?

"But, will you allow us to give you some food, then, for your journey?" Amarrez asked.

Porthos almost shouted yes, and was relieved to hear Aramis say, "Yes, Amarrez, that would be good."

Which proved, Porthos thought, that the young man was not quite mad. And knew that Porthos was likely to gnaw off Aramis's arm at their next stop if Aramis didn't allow him some food.

A moment later, they were on the road again, this time on the black horses, and their saddlebags had been augmented by one that contained wine, bread and cheese.

Of necessity, they went slower while they ate, and Porthos was thinking of a way to say something about the resemblance between the innkeeper and Aramis. A way, that is, that wouldn't end in a duel with his friend.

"I think Amarrez was my father's brother. His mother was my grandmother's maid, and Amarrez was raised in the household with my father," Aramis said, out of the blue, startling Porthos.

Porthos laughed. "That explains the similar features," he said while he thought that clearly all of D'Herblay men had similar interests. To wit, interests ones with petticoats.

Aramis cast Porthos an amused look, and permitted himself a little smile. "I thought you might be wondering," he said.

"Porthos," Aramis said after a while. He took a sip from

his bottle and put it back in his saddlebag. "What are we doing, riding like madmen through the night, to save a Queen who is probably beyond rescue?"

Porthos shrugged. To him it was all very simple. "Are you going to go back to Athos and tell him you didn't even try?"

Aramis shook his head and leaned over his horse's head. In the next moment, they were both spurring their horses on, hurrying down the still-darkened road lit by the splendorous light of the full moon.

The Story of an Unfortunate Count;
The Wages of Hatred; What Comes
After Confession

❦

ATHOS led Helene up into the hallway. By the time he got there, to the narrow, darkened space lit only by the little window, he was shaking. And he didn't know whence the shaking came, except from knowing how near she had come to committing murder, how near he had come to losing her to the same sort of dark regret that engulfed him.

She leaned against him, seeming boneless and pliable, and looked at him with a look of trust and wonder.

"Helene," he said. "I must talk to you, I must . . ."

If they stayed here, in the hallway, with her leaning against him, he was afraid of what he would do. And their talk could easily wake Grimaud who would be shocked, and possibly afraid.

Athos was not in the habit of explaining his everyday affairs to his servant, but someone who had lived so close with him, in such proximity and obedience as Grimaud, would be worried if his master didn't explain. And Athos did not wish to tell him that Helene had planned to kill a defenseless and tied-up man.

He must take Helene somewhere he could talk to her without the fear of being overheard or waking up anyone. And besides, he had wine in his room. And, for Athos, emerging from his long-imposed silence was something always facilitated by wine.

"Come," he told her, and taking her by the hand, led her gently down the hallway and into his room.

She went, pliably, obediently, her white underdress float-
ing behind her like a cloud.

When they got to the room, with its large windows
through which the moonlight spilled, he gestured for her to
sit on the bed, while he went and leaned against the wall, between the windows.

She sat on the bed, pale and still, and folded her hands
upon her lap in that oddly proper convent-girl manner. The
underdress, thin and of good silk—Athos having ordered it
so—fell clingingly around her body, hugging the strong,
square shoulders, the small, high breasts, the tiny waist. Below the dress, her ankles showed, thin and well-shaped, and
below them small, pink-and-white feet.

Athos's words deserted him, taking his thoughts with
them, and he would have been content to remain there forever, looking at her.

"How did you know?" she asked. She tilted her face up to
look at him. The moon bathed it in an eerie glow, making her
pink lips seem very defined, almost pouting, and making her
eyes shine.

Her forehead wrinkled, her eyebrows raised, and she
looked for all the world like a child trying to solve a difficult
arithmetic problem. "How did you know what I was intending to do?"

Athos shrugged. "It was the ghosts." And then he realized
what he had said, as her mouth opened a little, in shock.

He did what he could to rescue his reputation for sanity.
"What I mean," he said, "is that there are two kinds of
ghosts. The ones people talk about, of having seen in the
moonlight, sliding silently along unused houses." He
shrugged. "It is largely accepted that those aren't real and
that only insane people see them." He didn't add that he often saw them, or rather, he often saw the ghost of his wife
when he opened his eyes in the dark of night, and before
sleep had fully fled him. He never knew if those were truly
ghosts or scraps of wakening nightmare and guilt. And he
did not intend to tell the girl his life history. Or, at least not in
truth.

"And then there are ghosts of the mind," he said, his voice
gaining confidence. "Those born of experiences you've had
or . . . or experiences your friends have had. Things you

know, things you've learned the hard, painful way. Those ghosts dwell at the back of your mind and sometimes emerge into the conscious before you even know they're there. And they tell you things. Things you should know. Things you've attempted to hide from yourself."

Helene was still looking at him, still appearing puzzled. A strand of pitch-black hair fell forward onto her face, and she pushed it back. "I don't understand," she said, "what your ghosts could possibly have to do with me? Or how they could possibly have let you know what I was intending to do, or the vengeance I sought."

Athos shook his head. "Because revenge knows revenge, and anger knows anger."

This was going to be almost impossible without drink. Months ago, at a time when Porthos and Aramis had been especially concerned about Athos's drinking and determined to edge their noses where it was none of their business, they'd gone so far as to worry Grimaud with their talk.

Grimaud had said nothing about it. Of course Grimaud hadn't. Athos had trained the man to be practically mute, responding to gestures and movements and, with gestures and movements, giving whatever answer he could.

But his looks of pain and vexation every time Athos, went to the cellar for a bottle had so gotten to Athos's conscience that, in the middle of the night, he'd gone down there, retrieved fifteen bottles of the best wine and carried them back. He'd put them in his clothing trunk, beneath his two spare suits—in case he needed a true binge without worrying poor Grimaud.

He was fully aware that Grimaud knew they were there too. He must, since he always took care of Athos's clothing. But he didn't mention it, and Athos did not comment on it.

Now he opened the trunk, reached in, brought out a bottle, opened it, and took a swig. "The story I'm going to tell you pertains . . ." He hesitated. He'd half meant to tell her that it was the story of a friend of his. But now it came to it, he didn't know how to do it. He didn't know how to lie to her. So instead of telling her how he knew this, or how he'd come by the story, or even when or where it had all happened, he took a deep breath, and started. "There was once an old, respected family. Counts. They weren't rich as such things are respected among the great of the land. They had domains enough, but these weren't domains that abounded in trading cities or great mercantile villages. No, they were domains of fields and forests and streams, and this family lived quite well enough and quietly."

He turned away from her, because looking at her, he could not think. And so he instead looked out the window, down at the street below, silent in the moonlight.

He lived in a quiet and solidly middle-class neighborhood, so the street below was deserted in this dead hour of the night. In other parts of Paris, drunkards and partygoers would infest the shadows, but not here. Here the bustle would not start till two hours before dawn, when apprentices, bakers and others who needed to rise early would start creeping out of their still-darkened homes, and head for their work or business.

Right now it was all whitewashed stony facades and closed shutters, or shutters opened into darkened rooms. He set the bottle on the windowsill and said, "In the present day that family, never very numerous, came down on its legitimate, male line, to a single man, the heir of all the lands and of the titles and dignities that went with it. As the heir, he could have married any woman in the land, because though his line had almost no money, it had dignity aplenty and many a duchess or countess with great income would be glad to unite her fortunes with him."

He took a swig of the wine, feeling its warm sweetness on his tongue. "Alas, the man was a fool." He didn't want to turn back and look at Helene. He rather suspected she knew very well he was talking of himself, but if he turned back and saw that knowledge in her gaze, he would lose all power to continue. "He was a fool who had read too much poetry and spent too much time with Virgil's eclogues. Instead of going to court in Paris, when his father died and left him in possession of title and lands, this man decided to stay in his village and immerse himself in the running of his domain."

Another swig of the bottle gave him the courage to continue. "Which was why he was so lonely and so inexperienced that he fell in love with the priest's sister."

He thought he heard the rustle of her nightgown, behind him, but he refused to turn around. "The priest was a new one. A very young man, very pious. And his sister was a blonde beauty, all meek mildness who soon became beloved by the villagers for her kindness in assisting them with food or herbal remedies in their distress.

"Seeing him so holy, seeing his sister so beautiful and pious, the count fell and fell hard, for her beauty and seeming innocence. He could have had her, of course." Without turning, he shrugged his shoulders, signifying he wasn't an idiot and he knew that people of a certain stand in life could have whoever they wanted without the benefit of matrimony. "But he was in love, he was romantic and he wanted to do things properly. So he married her. And for a while their marriage and their love was idyllic. And then one day . . ."

There needed to be more wine, and Athos took a drink before he continued. "One day, a beautiful spring morning, he went riding with his countess. It was a sport both were fond of. Oh, they called it hunting, but it was rarely such. When he wanted to hunt—as was often needed for providing the table—he went alone. When he went riding with her, she would ride ahead and he would chase from behind."

He could see the scene in his mind—his younger and more innocent self enjoying himself in an innocent game, Charlotte, riding ahead, laughing, looking over her shoulder at him.

"She wasn't looking at where she rode," he said. Because she'd been looking back, temptingly, at him. "And she got thrown from her horse."

He saw in his mind as she fell from her horse and lay there, immobile, pale. He'd thought she was dead then. And how much better for him it would have been, had that been the case. He would still have shame, but no remorse.

"The count rushed upon her, to give her assistance. He hurried forth and he cut at her dress, which seemed to him to be too binding to allow her to breathe."

A deep sigh threatened to escape his lips and he stopped it with more wine. "Which is when he saw, on her shoulder, branded, the mark of the adulteress and the murderess who escapes the gallows and is condemned to imprisonment—a fleur-de-lis." He shook his head, as tears came to his eyes. "The count was young, and he was proud. He could not, would not, be able to live with such a secret. She was not who he thought she was. He'd thought he was lowering his line by marrying a poor woman, young but honest and possessed of all virtues. Instead, he was staining that noble line, filled with old traditions and rightfully proud of his position in the world, by bringing into its fold a murderess, an adulteress, and who knew what else.

"Assuming that she had escaped from whatever her decreed confinement was, in either prison or convent—and she must have escaped, since she was here. If she were caught, she would have been hanged. But if the count turned her in to the authorities, he would have had to reveal his monstrous deception. For the rest of his life, in public, it would seem to him that people would laugh behind their hands at his naivete. And so, he did what he could do—as lord of his domain. He judged her there and found her guilty. Before she gained consciousness, he put a rope around her neck and strung her from one those flower-bedecked bows."

He stopped, feeling tears in his eyes, and wishing he could go back to that moment. Now the perceived dishonor of a public trial seemed as nothing. He found himself trembling, lightly, with the effort of containing his emotions. "He rode away," he said. "He rode away, but still, the memory of that day, the memory of . . ."

His voice faltered. He finished the rest of the bottle. It seemed to him he heard rustles behind him. She was going to leave the room. She was going to run away. She was going to tell all he was a madman. And he couldn't blame her. He wasn't sure he *wasn't* a madman.

"Sometimes," he said, his voice harsh, raspy and low. "Sometimes I wake up in the night and she is there, by my bed, looking at me with those innocent-looking blue eyes. And sometimes she tells me it was all a mistake, that the fleur-de-lis was put there, in revenge, by a spurned lover. Sometimes she tells me . . ." He shook his head. "I didn't want you to have to carry that burden. I don't care about Rochefort. It is said he's ambushed and even killed people enough. But I didn't want you to—."

He felt warm hands on his shoulders. She pulled and pushed, turning him around.

He gave no resistance. In his state, he could barely remain standing, much less resist her.

"I understand," she said. "I understand, Monsieur le Comte. I understand your remorse and how you wished to save me from the same torment. But I do not think you committed any crime. I think you acted as any man of honor would have acted."

She wiped with her fingertips tears that he wasn't aware of having let run down his face. Her fingers were warm and soft.

Then she stood up, on tiptoe, and kissed his lips, lightly, in absolution. Then she got hold of his shoulders and lifted herself more, planted her lips firmly upon his, and pushed her tongue between his unresisting lips.

Her kiss was passionate, maddened, and his body responded, while his mind was still in a haze. He wrapped his arms around her shoulders, lowered his face to hers, and kissed her with the thirst of a man lost in the desert many years who has finally come upon an oasis.

How One Breaks into a Convent;
Waking a Nun; Stories of Murder and Fear

❧

"IT'S no use," D'Artagnan said, looking at Planchet.

They were outside the gates of the outer wall of St. Jerome's. For half an hour now, perhaps more, D'Artagnan had been standing at the gate, knocking heartily on the metal, and calling inside for all he was worth.

"Holla," he'd called. And again, "Holla within."

But no one answered from within the quiet precinct, and, in fact, the house itself was placed so far beyond the walls that it was unlikely they would hear him at the house.

"It is no use," he said. And in saying it, tried to give up the horrible idea that had formed at the back of his head in the house, the idea that had sent him out, riding like a madman, through the dark, to this orphanage that Aramis and Athos had talked about. To ask the question they hadn't asked. So he could sleep at night.

"Monsieur," Planchet said, speaking so quietly that he was almost inaudible. "In the house . . ." He stopped, his face contorting into a mask of indecision. "Where I lived, before . . ."

D'Artagnan guessed the boy's scruples. From Athos's and Porthos's contradicting stories, he had long ago guessed that Planchet had not been found by the Seine, spitting contemplatively into the water. He now took a wild guessing stab to put the boy at ease, "I have guessed, Planchet," he said, "that you come from the house of Porthos's mistress and that you were the one who broke the cipher for us." And to put the boy further at ease, "Porthos tells us this lady is a duchess."

A smile slid across Planchet's lips, but it was the only sign of his amusement. When he spoke, his voice sounded serious and somber. "In the house of the duchess, they didn't always treat apprentices very well, so I know how to get in and out of a well-guarded house, silently. We often had to . . . to . . . Well . . . Sometimes we had to steal bread or . . ."

D'Artagnan raised his eyebrows, but said nothing. His first reaction was shock at having hired a thief for a servant, but then again, he could well imagine the conditions of that house if it had goaded Athos and Porthos to help the boy escape. "I'm glad my friends brought you out," he said instead to Planchet's anxious face.

Planchet nodded. "I could have got out before. I did get out before. But I had nowhere to go and no way to survive if I just got out. So I always went back in the end. I didn't want to become . . . I didn't want to be breaking into houses to steal food the rest of my life. It's a path that ends on the gallows." He looked up at D'Artagnan and, at last, not reading any signs of disapproval on his face, went on, "I can go up over the wall and go inside. And once inside, I can find someone to talk to and to open the door for us."

A confusion of adventure's possible outcomes—none of them good—tumbled through D'Artagnan's mind. "You might get into one of the girls' dormitories by accident," he said. "Or one of the nun's cells. You could be seized, beaten, thrown down into some dungeon."

Planchet shrugged. "I very much doubt it," he said. "I know how to walk into a house silently, how to move about in utter darkness and get my bearings. I will not go in through the first window that gives me entrance. I shall scout the place. Remember, monsieur, in my other expeditions, in the night, I risked swift death if caught."

D'Artagnan looked at the boy. He had already grown in D'Artagnan's service and far from looking like a scarecrow, had some meat on his bones and some heft to his appearance. His shoulders had started broadening and they had lost their curious hunched-over look, trading for a more squarish, military bearing.

He'd inherited the suit in which D'Artagnan had arrived in Paris and though D'Artagnan now understood that he'd cut a sorry figure as a gentleman, the suit looked good and almost opulent for a servant, given the wealth of lace that D'Artagnan's mother had scavenged from his father's old suits and which D'Artagnan himself had sewn over every inch of it upon arriving in town.

Planchet looked self-confident and full of decision. And yet D'Artagnan felt responsible for him, and wasn't sure he wanted to throw the boy into such a dangerous situation.

Risking his own life was one thing, and D'Artagnan did it often. Risking someone else's life at his command was something else entirely, something that D'Artagnan couldn't muster the resolution to do.

"Think, monsieur," Planchet said, his sharp gaze on D'Artagnan. "You haven't told me what you wanted to do here, save that you wanted to confirm or dispel a suspicion. I don't know all the facts you know, and I could not hazard a guess as to what that suspicion is. But I'm guessing it is strong enough to send you up from a relatively comfortable house and riding madly through the night." He paused for a moment, and D'Artagnan nodded. "If that's the case and we don't go into this house, then you will forever be bedeviled by this suspicion, right or wrong. Monsieur, is this the type of suspicion with which you can live in easy company?"

D'Artagnan opened his mouth. A welter of images ran through his mind, from the girl killed in the alley to the priest with his throat cut. He thought of Rochefort, whom he'd locked in Athos's cellar—half stupid with sleeping powder and wine, and probably asleep again. Utterly defenseless. He seemed to be telling the truth, but was he, in fact, a murderer?

He thought of Athos, going up the stairs with Helene. Athos, whose noble mind and impassive exterior seemed to hide such a sudden fury, such a fiery temper ready to explode. He thought of the knife on the stair step. Of Aramis and Porthos, riding through the night to save a queen and crown that might already be lost.

Even if all of it came out according to the best hopes and plans, could D'Artagnan live with his suspicion?

Grant that Rochefort was alive when D'Artagnan arrived, and allowed himself to be freed with a minimal of resentment. Grant that Aramis and Porthos, through a daring miracle, reached the camp of tents on time and there managed to hold the crown on the head of a threatened queen. Grant that Athos married his Helene or—if his principles allowed such—made her his mistress. Would everything work out fine, then? Or would corpses still be turning up, with their throats cut? And would D'Artagnan be able to sleep at night, with his doubt in his mind?

"Devil take it," D'Artagnan said. It was only partly words, and mostly a sigh. "Yes, Planchet, go. Go."

The boy took off like a shot toward the seven-foot-tall white wall that, from Athos and Aramis's description, enclosed the convent grounds. He climbed the wall like a cat, leaping and finding support on surfaces that should never have supported weight, human or otherwise.

At the top he looked around, then took a leap toward the nearby tree, where he grabbed onto the branch, before swinging down and out of D'Artagnan's sight.

For a few minutes, D'Artagnan heard rustling and the sound of leaves or a sound like feet on gravel.

Then for a long time there was nothing, and D'Artagnan started pacing outside the wall of the convent. He shouldn't have let Planchet go. It was too dangerous. Even now, the boy would be falling prisoner of some attentive guard, being mauled by a dog, or perhaps cudgeled to death by a vigilant cook.

But there were no sounds from within to justify these thoughts.

And then, at long last, there were steps. Steps from more than one person, D'Artagnan judged. He untied both horses from where he and Planchet had left them by the convent wall, and took their reins in his hands.

If the person who soon started fumbling with the latch on the other side of the gate was friendly, then D'Artagnan wanted to be ready to go into the precinct, and he couldn't leave his horses behind.

And if the person there wasn't friendly, granted he had Planchet with him, D'Artagnan wanted to rescue Planchet and get both of them on horseback and away from danger as soon as possible.

The gate swung open to reveal an impossibly aged man and, behind him, Planchet, looking rather smug and pleased with himself.

"Are you this young man's master?" the old man asked in a reedy voice. "Because he tells me a fantastic story of murder and treason and deception and he says you must talk to the Mother Superior or lives must be at risk. Is any of this true, or is he one of the most fantastic liars who ever walked the earth?"

D'Artagnan had removed his hat as soon as he saw the old man. He now held it against his chest as he swept a low, low bow. "It is true," he said. "Or at least, it is true that we are concerned with investigating a murder and that this murder involves such treason and deception—if my suspicion is true—that other lives might well be at stake.

"Whether or not Planchet is also one of the most fantastic liars who ever lived, I can't hazard, though so far he has shown no signs of such extraordinary talent."

And, strangely, it seemed to D'Artagnan that Planchet looked wounded at this assessment. But the old man cackled and nodded. "Very well. If you need to speak with the Mother, you shall speak with the Mother. I am Damien, the porter, and I'll wake someone who shall wake her. Will you tell me, though, whose murder and why our little house should be involved in crimes in faraway Paris?"

D'Artagnan had thought that this moment might come and he felt relieved to be telling it to this man and not to a nun. If he had to tell it to a nun who'd raised the girl, and see the woman cry, he wasn't sure at all he could endure it. So he said, eagerly, "We found a murdered girl in Paris, in an alley. We think she was Madeleine, who was raised here."

Damian looked startled, but nodded. "Madeleine. Little Madeleine. What fate." He nodded again. "I shall tell Prophirie to tell the Mother. Meanwhile, follow me. It is not seemly that you, being men, should enter the main house at night. Even I, who am a ruin of a man and, at my age, present as my sole danger the ability to stare and long, will only enter it for a few minutes, to wake Prophirie. But I live in a spacious room above the stables. Let me take you there. You can tend to your beasts and then wait while I go see if Mother Clementine will speak to you."

Planchet and D'Artagnan took the horses to the stables and worked in silence, side by side, rubbing down their animals and feeding and watering them, before climbing the little staircase that Damian had indicated, to the loft above.

The loft was set up at least as well as D'Artagnan's city quarters, with bed and chair, table and a curious pedestal holding a basin for water. On the wall hung two spare suits.

The bed was roiled, the covers thrown back. D'Artagnan guessed Planchet had awakened the man suddenly.

D'Artagnan sat on the rickety chair, and Planchet sat by his side, on the floor.

They did not wait long. Soon, Damien's slow steps, followed by two sets of quick, light steps, sounded downstairs in the stables. The horses made sounds of recognition or welcome. Sounds of people climbing the stairs followed.

Damien was first up the ladder and, despite what D'Artagnan would guess was a very advanced age, he climbed with the same agility Planchet showed. Perhaps in his past too, there lay the household of a stingy *duchess* and expeditions for food.

Behind him appeared the face of a woman at least as old as him, wearing a wimple and a voluminous black cape. Damien gave her his hand to help pull her onto the loft and she came up, unsteadily, and stood beside Damien.

After that came a middle-aged woman, not so much large as of an imposing figure. She too wore a wimple and a long black cloak, but her feet showed, bare, square and sturdy, beneath. They were the feet of a peasant's daughter, accustomed to going barefoot in the stable and still untroubled by it many years later.

From this woman's look of authority, D'Artagnan judged her to be the Mother Superior. He took off his hat once again, and bowed a low curtsey to her. When she extended her hand to him, he genuflected and kissed the ring in sign of respect for her union with the church.

"Damien and Prophirie tell me that you wish to ask me questions about Madeleine," the Mother Superior said, her tone firm and only slightly wavering, perhaps with grief at her pupil's death. "He tells us she came to a bad end in Paris, something I suspected since the other two gentlemen came by to enquire. I've prayed many a bead on her behalf, but though the Bible tells us the Lord can restore life to the dead,

it is hardly likely he will do it on the behest of a simple orphanage director. And she was dead already, when they
came, was she not?"

D'Artagnan nodded. "She died eight days ago, in an alleyway in Paris, with her throat slashed."

And because the eyes of the Mother Superior were at
least as intelligent as D'Artagnan's own, he felt as if he'd
found an ally, and he told all, in an unwavering voice, dis-
closing, for the first time to someone outside their associa-
tion, what they'd done and everything that had happened.

At the mention of Madeleine's death, the Mother Superior crossed herself.

Then when D'Artagnan described Helene's dropping
onto the back of Athos's horse, the Mother Superior exclaimed, "She was always impulsive that child. If she had
been brought up in a common room, with the other girls, she
would never have remained so stubborn. We have strict discipline that tends to break the will of one's such as her. But
Marie, poor thing, Madeleine's nurse, took such a shine to
Helene that she wished to have the girls brought up together.
She told us that it wouldn't be good for Madeleine to grow up
with no playfriends. And then, you know . . ." She blushed a
little. "Marie appeared at our door, asking for a job on the
same day that Helene was found. She said she was a widow
and that her child had died, but I always suspected that Helene was Marie's own and that Marie, may God forgive her,
had conceived from some passing stranger." She looked
down, as if to avoid his gaze. "So Marie brought Helene and
Madeleine up the same way, and while Madeleine was sweet
and obedient and needed little restraint, Helene never got that
much more strict guidance she needed." She smiled a little.
"I'm glad, at least, the impetuous fool decided to drop onto
the back of your friend's horse. He is an honorable nobleman, the last of a dying breed. Had she dropped onto the
horse of some ruffian it might not have ended well with her."

D'Artagnan nodded and went on to describe further what
had happened to them. At the mention of the priest's death,
Mother Clementine again crossed herself. And D'Artagnan
looked away as he described their kidnapping of Rochefort,
because he couldn't stand the expression of reproach he was
sure he would find on her features.

"And so, I have come," he said. "And I would like to talk to Marie, if I may?"

The Mother Superior looked surprised. "Marie? Poor Marie. I wish you could talk to her, but that will not happen until the day of judgment. The day that Madeleine left, Marie went to the village as she usually did, to get some supper for herself and her charge—who was then only Helene. I don't know if Madeleine's uncle had given Marie some money in reward for years of faithful service. This is possible, though, as we know she lingered at the village, and chose ribbons and bows as well as a better grade of wine and some treats for herself and . . . the girl who is probably her daughter." The Mother Superior's features set into what could only be described as stern grief. "And then, when she started back toward the convent, it was already dark. Someone must have overtaken her at the gates. She did not have time to cry, because Damien was just within the gates, as he is until he retires. And he heard nothing. But in the morning we found her, her throat cut from side to side."

"The day Madeleine left?" D'Artagnan asked, his voice horrified. "But Helene didn't seem . . . I mean, if the girl is her daughter, surely Marie would have found a way to convey this, sooner or later. But then, Helene should have looked more . . . grieved." Even as he said it, D'Artagnan had a feeling that the anger Helene displayed might be her way to show grief. He wasn't so naive that he didn't know this was the way of many people.

"I don't even know if Helene knows, because since then she hasn't been at any of the communal meals and I don't know how much time she has spent here. I'm surprised she intercepted your friends after they left here, as I haven't seen her at all these days, and I don't think anyone has. We were watching for her particularly, because we thought she would experience a particular grief and pain." The Mother Superior looked sad. "The rumor around here was that Marie had her by some foreign soldier during one of the many skirmishes twenty years ago. I wouldn't know for sure, but since Marie is not from these parts, I would assume any rumor was propagated by ill-considered confidences of hers."

D'Artagnan nodded. "How old were the girls," he asked, "when Marie took Helene in?"

"Oh, no more than a few months," Mother Clementine said.

D'Artagnan nodded. For all he knew, the girl could be the child of one of Athos's male relatives. *Foreign soldier* was a relative term when applied to armies full of noblemen, where half of them might very well have the blood of several nationalities in their veins.

He blinked. Then he bowed, suddenly, sweeping up his hat in a big arc. "I think I have my answer," he said. "I thank you."

"You're not going to tell us what your doubt was?" Mother Clementine said. "Or what the answer might be?"

D'Artagnan shook his head. "I wouldn't want to malign an innocent by accusing him or her of murder, when it might all be to naught."

The Mother Superior considered this, then nodded. "It is as well not to want to spread calumny. Murder is such a heinous crime."

"Yes," D'Artagnan said, and bowed again, starting toward the ladder. "Come, Planchet."

Planchet hopped to follow him.

"But you'll come back and tell us how it came out, won't you?" the Mother Superior asked.

D'Artagnan had already started down the stairs, and only his head protruded up into the loft but he could see everything in there. He nodded. "If you wish me to," he said, "I will."

"I will count on it," the Mother Superior said.

An Encampment of Kings;
The Perils of Thin Tents; Where
Sometimes the Fate of a Queen Hangs on
the Swiftness of a Seamstress

"**H**ALLO, who is there?" the guard standing by the fire outside the perimeter of splendid silken tents called.

His voice was familiar, as was his bearing. Aramis had no trouble at all in recognizing him. In fact, part of the reason he and Porthos had decided to approach the circle here was because Aramis recognized the man. They'd circled the encampment once, with their horses, before deciding to approach.

The man's name was De Perplus; he was a guard in the regiment of Monsieur des Essarts, the same regiment D'Artagnan would be joining after the meeting of kings. And he was one of those often placed in that part of the royal palace where he was known to give access to Aramis for visits to his seamstress.

Right now, Aramis said, "Aramis," and stepped out of the shadows with Porthos behind him.

"Oh, Aramis," the man said, and relaxed, resting his lance back down, and grinning. "Couldn't stay away from her that long, could you? And you dragged poor Porthos with you too. . . ."

"Porthos came to keep me company on the ride," Aramis said. "But we have to be back by morning to stand guard," he lied. "And so this must be a hurried affair."

"Well," De Perplus said. "A good thing, for once, to be

known for one's speed." He grinned inanely at his own joke, then pointed within the forest of tents—all beautiful and even under the moonlight and by the scant light of camp-fires, a miracle of color and ornamentation. "You'll find her down this alleyway, and then to your left at the next, and she is on the third tent down, the one embroidered with roses and violets."

Aramis nodded.

"And Porthos can stay with me and entertain me in a game of cards while you go," De Perplus said.

Aramis hesitated. But given his stated reason to come here, dragging Porthos with him to Violette's tent might not be the best of ideas. Porthos was highly recognizable. Any-one who had ever seen him walk past would remember him. And there was really no good explanation for why Aramis would need to take a friend with him.

He looked at Porthos and nodded. "Do, Porthos. Stay with De Perplus. See if you can find someone to tend to our horses, and maybe exchange them for fresh ones, since we'll be leaving very soon. I shan't be long."

With De Perplus still laughing at this declaration, Aramis made his way down the alleyway and through the directions the guard had given him. And stopped.

Violette's tent was silk, which is to say, it was somewhat transparent, in the dark of night, with light shining from the inside. All of which would be fine in normal circumstances, Aramis imagined.

But right then, the shadow play inside the tent was quite easy to read. Violette—it could only be Violette, judging from the shape of that body, a shape that Aramis knew all too well from traversing it with lips and fingers through countless nights of passion—stood on a recurved tub of wa-ter, and another woman—dressed, probably her maid—was pouring water over Violette's head from a ewer.

Aramis stopped, his mouth going suddenly dry, his head dizzy, his hands clenching each other, as if one could sup-port the other against temptation. But there was nothing for it. He was not here—so much the worse—to satisfy his im-pulses and needs. Those were sinful enough when they didn't stand in the way of far more important business. Now, they would be criminal.

If Aramis took the time to enjoy Violette's charms, and that wasted time led to the loss of a Queen, how much would Aramis regret it, and how could he ever expiate it, even given a lifetime in a monastery?

He advanced toward the tent and leaned in. His forehead and hands sprang in sweat. He wanted to go in, dismiss the maid and . . . He wanted to . . . But instead, he called from the tent flap, "Violette, it is I."

From inside came an exclamation of surprise, and the silhouette on the tub stepped hastily out. "Chevalier?" she called.

"It is I," he said, and, as if to remind her of what she should never have forgotten—that he had a secret identity that hid his more noble one, he added, "Aramis."

"Aramis," she said, partly exclamation but mostly sigh.

He heard her whisper hurried instructions to her maid, then there was a confusion of forms, as some fabric was passed back and forth and—from the shape of the silhouette, something was done to Violette's hair, probably pinning it up and back.

Aramis consoled himself with the thought that if Violette was here, if she was bathing and primping, then the Queen must still be well. Because Violette was so close to the Queen, because her only status at court came from the Queen, if the Queen were in disgrace, Violette too would long since have been bundled off to parts unknown. Or she would be following Anne of Austria on a trail of infamy.

By thinking of such politics, Aramis had almost managed to recover his control when Violette opened the tent flap and showed herself.

She smelled of roses at the fullness of summer, and her hair, pinned hastily up atop her head, looked in more delicious disarray than ever before. Her dressing gown—a white affair that tied in the front with multicolored silk ribbons—like the tent, would have been opaque under more normal circumstances. But now it clung to her body, here and there, revealing creamy pink skin beneath.

Aramis sucked in breath and put his hands behind his back, lest the traitors should entertain notions of reaching for those heavy breasts, pulling at the silk of the gown, or of caressing those creamy shoulders, which the gown left uncovered.

His lips were something else, as he could only bite them together for so long and would eventually have to talk.

"What is it, Aramis? Why are you here? And don't tell me it is only that you missed me because you know well I don't condone such nonsense."

As she spoke, Violette waved for her maid to leave. The girl did, walking backwards and keeping her eyes on them the whole while.

Aramis tore his eyes away from the darker shadow of the nipple that tipped the dome of her breast. He swallowed an amazing amount of saliva that had followed upon the unnatural dryness of his mouth. "It is about the Queen," he managed to say.

"The Queen!" Violette said, alarmed, and stepped back, holding the tent flap for him to pass. "Come in, Aramis, come in. Tell me all. We must not delay. I can tell from your arrival at this hour, and from the state of your hair"— Aramis's hair had turned into an unruly mop on the ride here—"That it must be a matter of life or death."

"It is," Aramis said, and by thinking of the girl in the alley, the pitiful, murdered corpse sacrificed so that the Queen could be dishonored—by thinking of Father Bellamie, his much more pious friend, so suddenly departed—Aramis managed to keep himself from straying. Instead, he told Violette all while she undressed and dressed again.

For a moment there, when she was totally naked and bending over her travel trunk to retrieve a gown, he had to clench both trembling hands upon his belt, and mutter, "Ave Maria, Gracia Plena—"

Violette turned around, looking puzzled. "Chevalier, this is no time to pray," she said. "Tell me, instead, what did Rochefort reveal?"

And Aramis told, thinking of Rochefort and of the cellar and of the ugly truth the man had told them. Anything, anything to distract from this light-headed feeling, this heat in his veins that made him feel as if he had a fever.

If he didn't learn to control himself better, he'd never be a priest. On the other hand, if he controlled himself through the display of Violette's flesh, as she got dressed not more than an arm's length from him, he might well have earned his crown of martyrdom.

She asked him to tie her corset, as he finished explaining the plan and that one of the Queen's rings, part of her trousseau, was now in the hands of Buckingham. And how this ring might incriminate her forever and cause her to lose the crown and her marriage.

"We have not a moment to lose," Violette said. "I can get you to Buckingham's tent, but we must go now."

Aramis's shaking fingers tied the corset, and Violette said, "That dress over there." She pointed to the dress she'd thrown over a screen earlier. "Would you put it on me?"

And he did, but not without putting a hand forth, first, to touch her breast whose fullness had been pushed upward by her stays. The skin was as soft as the inside of a newly unfolded rose petal.

He retained the memory of that softness against his fingers, as he helped Violette cover her hair and figure with a dark cloak. Then she handed the like to him and, relinquishing his musketeer's hat behind, he did likewise.

They slipped as anonymous shadows through the night. Twice, they were challenged, and twice Violette answered with some word Aramis couldn't quite understand. Else, leaning forward, she would explain something to the person on guard. And then they would be allowed to pass.

Soon, they were at a place where the British tents started. They did not look so different from the French, save that they had perhaps less embroidery. But the division was marked by two rows of campfires, watched over by the French on one side and the British on the other.

Violette slid among the men as though she knew what she was doing and approached a guard on the other side, to whom she whispered a few words.

The guard looked alarmed, then nodded, then looked up at Aramis and motioned for him to follow.

As the guard started amid the tents, Violette whispered to Aramis, "It is Buckingham's servant. It was lucky we found him having a talk with the guards. He knows me as one of the Queen's creatures, and I told him this is an affair that pertains to the Queen and that if Buckingham would not see us, the Queen was surely lost. And if she were lost, he would surely punish his servant, because I would make sure his failure was known."

This explained the agility with which the man walked through the maze of tents to the center of the encampment.

At the very center there were two very large tents ornamented with cloth of gold hangings, and clearly belonging to the Queen and King.

But to the side a while, and only slightly less splendid, was another tent. The young servant went into it. A lamp was lit or, more likely, from the speed of it, a cover was lifted from a lamp. A man's silhouette appeared; he had, clearly, been asleep.

When the servant came back to admit them to Buckingham's presence, the British nobleman, perhaps more powerful than the King himself, was far more decent than Violette had been when she admitted Aramis to her presence.

He wore a dressing gown, it is true, but it was a dressing gown of brocade, its collar surrounded by ermine, which seemed rather too warm for the summer night.

Aramis's first impression was one of shock. He'd seen Buckingham before, from a distance, at state occasions and diplomatic meetings. But he'd never seen him like this, close by, with his hair in disarray from sleep—though still far more neat than Aramis's own—and his features devoid of that dignity office confers.

For the first time he understood why everyone said the two of them resembled each other. He wondered if some forgotten ancestress united the two houses.

Buckingham was looking sternly at Aramis. "Milord," Aramis said. "I bring you alarming news."

"So my servant says," Buckingham said, looking at his servant.

"Yes, milord, and I must explain to you why the encounter you thought you had in Paris, the one that you believed made all your happiness, wasn't truly so," He saw the alarm in Buckingham's face and, despite knowing the impulsiveness of such a character and how dangerous it was to scare the powerful, he went on, "The woman you met wasn't who you thought she was. She was an agent of those who seek to bring down the one you love."

Buckingham looked like a man having trouble controlling his expression. And his voice sounded harsh as he said, "Explain!"

Aramis explained, quickly. He knew he had proven his point when he spoke of the unlikelihood of the Queen—though never mentioned by name—walking around Paris, dressed as a musketeer and alone. In that sentence, he knew he had fit in to some uneasiness that Buckingham had already been nursing about the affair.

Buckingham, not a stupid man, had believed because he wished to believe. And Aramis confronted him with evidence he could not dismiss.

"I would rather part with a piece of my own heart," the British nobleman said. "As it is all I have of hers, even if purloined. But I cannot risk bringing harm to her head."

He reached under his bed and pulled out a beautiful ornamented gold chest inlaid with pearls. He opened it with a key he kept on a gold chain inside his shirt.

Inside the chest was the ring D'Artagnan and Rochefort had described. Buckingham started to hand it to Aramis, but Violette reached over and took it. "I will make sure it's returned," she said.

With this, the two men bowed to each other.

"I never thought I would be grateful to a Frenchman," Buckingham said.

"Life is strange, milord," Aramis answered, perfectly composed. "I never thought I would be able to talk reasonably to an Englishman."

They smiled at each other, conscious of their great likeness despite the disparity of their positions and the enmity of their kingdoms.

And then Aramis was back outside, again following the servant through a maze, till they got to the dividing line, where Violette said something to the guard, who allowed them through.

Outside her tent, Aramis could stand it no more. The smell of her, the feel of her next to him, even involved in that all enveloping cloak, was more than he could endure.

He reached for her and crushed her to him, kissing her lips with feverish, mad hunger. She went limp and whimpered against him.

"Monsieur," she said, but struggled on feebly as his hands parted her cloak and bunched up the skirt of her gown. She wasn't wearing underwear beneath.

And then he was pushing her against one of the tent poles, their bodies merging.

He became aware of noises, of exclamations from a few tents down.

And then a peevish, wavering voice that Aramis knew all too well as the voice of the King of France said, "What do you mean, the Queen has lost this ring. We must find it, wherever it may be. *Ventre san gris,* I gave it to her. How could she lose it?"

Violette pulled herself abruptly away from Aramis, leaving him bereft and cold. "I must go," she said. "I must go."

He was still arranging his own clothes when he heard her voice, from the vicinity of the royal tent. "I beg your pardon, I couldn't help overhearing, and the ring isn't lost, it is just that Her Majesty lent it to me . . ."

Aramis let his frustration out in a long sigh, ducked into her tent to retrieve his hat and headed for the periphery of the camp, where Porthos had just won three pistols off De Perplus. He had also, somehow, managed to secure fresh horses.

With the pistols he'd won, Porthos had made arrangements for one of the guards to take the hosteler's horses back later and to retrieve these.

Aramis and Porthos transferred their luggage to the new horses, and rode, as fast as they could, back to Paris, to put Athos's mind at ease.

A Matter of Shoulders; Athos's Taste
in Women; D'Artagnan's Arrival

ATHOS woke up with a throbbing in his shoulder. Still immersed in the lassitude of sleep, he shifted around, trying to relieve the pain and to resume his dream.

But the shoulder hurt still, with a dull ache that pulled him unavailingly toward consciousness.

He sighed and stretched, and yelped at the pain in his shoulder and opened his eyes.

Sun streamed into the room, bright midmorning sun. It had been very long since Athos had overslept. And it had been even longer since he'd slept well. He blinked at the light, and felt an odd calm that he hadn't known in years.

Then he looked to the side and saw the source of the calm—Helene, who still slept on his bed, his sheet pulled up to her neck, her hair falling all around on the bed like a silken spread. There was only a little bit of her face showing among the hair—peaked little chin and high cheekbones, and the eyelids closed, allowing a wealth of dark eyelashes to rest upon her cheeks.

Athos wondered what she had thought was happening— if she'd thought anything. He understood that she had felt sorry for him and perhaps it was all an effect of the night and of their proximity, and she'd given it no more thought.

In which case, when she woke she might have regrets and wonder what he intended with her. He stretched a hand to touch the soft, silken, black hair, running his fingers along it.

Helene needn't worry. Athos had no intention of taking advantage of her innocence, deflowering her then sending

her out into the cold beyond with no protection and no bene-
diction.

He didn't even, he thought looking at her, intend to make
her his mistress, on the side. No. She had awakened him
from a long and desperate sleep of loneliness. He would not
part with her willingly.

It had been years since he'd . . . since his wife had died.
Probably no one would remember the scandal of finding the
countess hanged in the forest. He could go back with Helene
and marry her, and raise children to inherit domain and
honor after him.

He smiled, toward the window and the new day already
in full bloom outside, under the dazzling sun of spring.

A scent of flowers and herbs came through the window,
overlaying and dimming even the stench of manure, of
horses, of people, that was Paris.

There was some noise below in the wakening house.
Doors opening and closing. Athos thought poor Grimaud
might very well be awake, in which case he would be
shocked not to find his master equally awake and about the
house.

On a normal morning, Athos would already be up and
drinking, quietly, in a corner of the kitchen.

This wasn't a normal morning, but Athos did not wish
to goad his servant with such worry that poor Grimaud
found it necessary to come bursting through the door. Smiling at the closed door, he reasoned that would not be a good
thing, at all.

He touched Helene on the shoulder. "Wake up," he said
gently.

He tugged at the cover over her shoulder. And stopped.
Because there on the shoulder, was a mark that looked almost exactly like the large, triangular birthmark on his own
shoulder.

A characteristic of the De la Feres.

He jumped back as if he had been stung by an adder, and
Helene woke.

She sat up in bed, and looked at him, worried.

The sheet fell to her lap, revealing her high, firm breasts.
He remembered the feel of them in his hands, and his mind
shied away from the memory.

Who was she? How could she be related to him? This beauty mark, on the right shoulder, in a triangle, was exactly the mark of Athos's family.

"Are you well?" Helene asked. "You are so pale."

He shook his head. "My shoulder is bothering me," he said.

"Oh. Do you wish me to dress it?"

He shook his head. "I'm afraid that will only make it bleed," he said.

She got up, wrapped in the sheet, and went to the window, to look out. "It is a glorious morning," she said.

"Yes," he said.

She tossed her head, which uncovered her beauty mark. Was she trying to allow him to see it clearly? Making sure he couldn't miss it? Why?

Athos's cousin, Xaviere, had—when they were both so young that Athos had never even thought of love or of falling in love—had an affair with a Spanish noble of the house of Austria. A Hapsburg.

From that affair a baby girl had resulted. To save themselves from the shame attendant on such a birth, the family—a collateral line to the De la Feres—had the girl left at St. Jerome's and the mother sent to a convent.

But that girl was Madeleine, the girl who had died in the night.

Or was she?

Athos's hair stood on end at the back of his head. He could not think it. No. He could not.

But he thought of how expertly she had put sleeping powders in Rochefort's and D'Artagnan's drinks. And she might well have done the same to his own, had he not drunk from the bottle.

Athos's hands were shaking. "You should go to your room," he told Helene. "And dress before my servant sees you."

She turned around, beautiful, looking like something out of classical antiquity, with her bare breasts and that sheet enveloping her lower half. "We are going to keep it secret, then? What happened?"

He shook his head, but he felt slow and dumb. "I don't . . ." he said. "I haven't thought about it." Which was a horrible lie because of course he had thought about it. About Helene in his bed, Helene in his house, Helene as the mother of his children.

But Madeleine and the priest, both, had been killed with a knife, and Helene had crept down the stairs, yesterday, with a knife in her own hand. Not her dagger, but perhaps even she didn't wish to give herself away that far by showing how sharp her dagger could be.

He shook his head again. "We will talk."

Anything, anything to have her out of his room. He wished for something, some miracle, that would prove her innocence to him, but the feeling at the back of his mind was that she had killed both her friend and the priest. And he couldn't endure that feeling.

D'Artagnan had seen Buckingham argue with a dark-haired girl. He looked up at Helene's dark hair, glossy, on either side of her face. A dark-haired girl who dressed as a man.

His head hurt. He swallowed. "Please, go dress, first."

But she didn't move, standing by the bed and looking at him with a wondering gaze.

He got hold of his dressing gown, wrapped it around himself and almost ran out of the room and down the stairs.

Old Crimes and New; On the Sameness of Babies; Retribution and Forgiveness

❧

D'ARTAGNAN came into Paris early morning and took the horses back to Monsieur de Treville's. It was only after that that he made his way to Athos's home.

Part of the problem was that he felt so aghast at what he'd discovered. He thought Athos was safe—or would be safe—until D'Artagnan returned.

But, more important, if Athos was not safe, how could D'Artagnan warn him? He'd seen the fits of temper, the sudden mood swings the oldest musketeer had displayed recently. And he did not wish to face them alone.

He would prefer to wait till Aramis and Porthos were in town, but there was not much chance of that happening before mid-morning. And while D'Artagnan was away from Athos's home, Rochefort at least would be safe. A villain, he might be, but D'Artagnan didn't wish Rochefort's blood upon his hands.

It so happened when he opened the door to Athos's home, that Athos was coming down the stairs, very fast, and wearing only a blue dressing gown—a thing of brocade and velvet that looked like something only a nobleman would wear.

But more than his sumptuous attire, what called D'Artagnan's attention was Athos's paleness. Always pale, the musketeer had now turned curdled-milk white.

"What is wrong?" D'Artagnan said, looking for any signs of blood on the dressing gown, and failing to find it. "What happened?"

But Athos only shook his head and motioned for D'Artagnan to follow him. Which D'Artagnan did, all the way to the receiving room, in the front, where they had held their councils before, and where the picture of the ancient cavalier hung above Athos's favored chair.

Athos fell into the chair now, and motioned for D'Artagnan to sit, which D'Artagnan did, too confused by trying to think how to break his news, and too scared by his friend's appearance.

Athos looked around, before speaking in a whisper, "There was a count," he said. "A friend of mine, forced to abandon his position to avoid greater dishonor. This friend comes from a great and ancient family. A family that always has, on a particular part of their body, a beauty mark." He blushed, doubtless remembering his own unusual beauty mark, upon the shoulder. "Not everyone in the family has it. But those who do, have it in the same place and the same exact shape."

D'Artagnan nodded, more to indicate that he didn't wish to pry upon Athos's past life and that what Athos was telling him made sense, than to encourage his friend.

Athos nodded in turn. "Yesterday . . ." He blushed darker. "I shared my bed with Helene." He bit his lower lip hard enough to leave marks visible upon the skin. "And she has that beauty mark."

D'Artagnan raised his eyebrows. "I don't understand," he said.

"My friend," Athos said. "From my talk with the Mother Superior at the convent, I determined that Madeleine was supposed to be descended from that family."

And now, D'Artagnan's tongue loosened. He need not fear telling the truth to Athos, who suspected it already. "I woke up, last night, after you . . . While you were going up the stairs with Helene. I realized that both Rochefort and I had been given sleeping powders. I saw the knife on the stairs. And I thought that both the girl and the priest had been murdered with a knife. And that when Helene dropped onto the back of your horse, she threatened you with a knife. Also, she is left-handed, and the cuts were all clearly made from right to left— as they would be by someone left-handed standing behind the victim. But I could think of no motive, except . . .

"Well, no one seemed to have an explanation for why Madeleine's nurse had chosen to take Helene in and raise her as her pupil's equal. And I thought I would like to talk to the nurse. Also, I had seen you go upstairs with Helene, and I surmised that . . . that you looked alike. I had thought already that perhaps Madeleine was related to you, but not Helene. So I took Planchet and borrowed a couple of Monsieur de Treville's horses. We rode to the orphanage and there we found . . . that the nurse too had been killed, by having her throat slit the very day that Madeleine left. And after that, Helene was not seen at the orphanage again. So her saying that she knew something had happened to Madeleine because Madeleine hadn't written to her, made no sense. None of it did, unless . . ."

"Unless?" Athos asked, going paler.

"Unless the nurse had exchanged the babies. The Mother Superior thought the nurse was Helene's—or perhaps we should call her Madeleine, since I think she was the dead girl—mother, by some dead soldier."

"Two babies always look much alike," Athos said.

"Yes, and a woman looking after two babies has a unique opportunity to exchange them, before they know their own names."

"I wonder who she . . . how Helene found out who she really was, and the relation to my—to the family?"

D'Artagnan shrugged. "We know she started leaving the orphanage at a very early age. Perhaps she stumbled on some portrait or something. Perhaps there is . . ." He looked over the chair, at the portrait on the wall, which could have been Athos dressed in antique attire. "Perhaps there is a great resemblance between all members of this family. And perhaps she noticed the resemblance to herself. Then after that a very little investigation would suffice: Visits to the holdings of the family and getting gossip from old retainers who might be gratified by her resemblance to those of the blood."

Athos nodded. He was paler than ever. "And she probably knew she was not treated the same as the other girl. No woman would treat her daughter and her charge the same, no matter how much she tried."

"She must have followed Madeleine that day," D'Artagnan said. "And found out where she was staying in Paris.

And perhaps visited later—after she'd killed the nurse. She would visit Madeleine—"

"Perhaps she had no plan yet, just the stinging rage of having her future denied and her honors stolen," Athos said.

"Perhaps," D'Artagnan said. He didn't add he doubted it. He, himself, thought the murder of the nursemaid had been the beginning and that from that point on Helene had been bent on revenge and on reclaiming her position, somehow. "She followed Madeleine, talked to her. The other girl was pliable and obedient. Helene knew about Madeleine's meeting, but she couldn't guess why. It is possible even, she didn't tumble to the resemblance between Madeleine and the Queen."

"So she killed Madeleine," Athos said. "And then she wanted to kill anyone who'd met Madeleine that night. I think that's why she went to Buckingham." He looked defeated. Tired. "Perhaps she'd followed us then. I'm convinced she followed us *to* the orphanage, not *from* the orphanage. At any rate, she found out about the priest, and she killed the priest and stole the body. I stopped her from killing Rochefort," he said. "I think she meant to kill him, and let him take the guilt." He swallowed hard. "I don't know why she . . . I don't know why she shared my bed. I have a horrible feeling it was just to . . . for me to notice her birthmark and to inform her that she was a long-lost member of my family and that way give her back to her proper station." He paused a moment. "Or perhaps there was real attraction there, but—"

A cackle sounded from the door. "Don't flatter yourself, Comte," Helene's voice said.

She was wearing her dark male attire again, and she had a dagger in her hand. While both of them started to rise, she walked toward them, a smile on her lips.

Mercy and Revenge; The Count's Choice; The Hand of the Cardinal

"**H**ELENE," Athos said. He felt the blood drain further from his face, which was strange because it had already felt cold as marble and it was hard to believe it could pale further.

She did a little step and bowed. "At your service, Monsieur Comte." She smiled at them, but the smile was the feral uncovering of her teeth that promised no joy. "And I'm amazed the two of you managed, between you, to piece together my actions. Even if it took you long enough. You were correct. Marie had told me that Madeleine came from a very great family. It appears that one of the money packages arrived sealed with the family seal, so everyone in the orphanage knew or suspected of Madeleine's family. And Marie bragged to me—to me!—of how great Madeleine would be one day, because, after raising her in such comfort, the De la Feres wouldn't simply ignore her. There would be a time to claim her, and a good marriage. She would be a noblewoman.

"It seemed to me the greatest injustice of all that Madeleine, who was content with anything, should have everything, while I, who wanted so much more than I had, should remain behind, at the orphanage, with no better hope for a future than becoming a servant or a nun. At first I thought I might be able to convince her to take me with her and get some cousin or other of hers to marry me. I found some old portraits." She looked at the one on the wall. "Not unlike that one. And I realized that this family was mine, not Madeleine's. They looked like me. All of a sudden, everything made sense. Though everyone in the orphanage thought I was Marie's daughter and that she was kind to me, I knew better. Madeleine was the one she worshipped, the one she favored. Which made sense, because she was her own. Baseborn whelp.

"From that day on I stewed with hatred for her and for Marie. But for a long time I thought Marie was wrong. They wouldn't come for Madeleine, and our lives were equal. I hid my hatred and Madeleine adored me as always.

"And then her uncle came. And I knew she was going to have a great life, a wealthy one. Are you going to blame me?" she asked, waving her knife. "Are you going to blame me for following her, for striving to claim back what they had stolen from me? They were thieves! Shouldn't thieves be killed?"

"Was the priest a thief?" D'Artagnan asked, in the horrified tone of a child facing a monster.

Athos, himself, was thinking, to his shame, that Helene's reasoning paralleled his when he'd found the fleur-de-lis upon his wife's shoulder. Hadn't he too, swiftly, played judge and merciless executioner?

Helene laughed. "No, not a thief, but a dullard. He would not let me have the corpse. Not, he said, till some musketeers or others came to collect it. Or to swear that I was a relative. He seemed to think he must hold onto the corpse forever."

"Where did you put it?" D'Artagnan asked. He still looked shocked and paralyzed.

"In the Seine. With stones tied to her. She'll never float up. I should have sunk the priest too, but then I would have had to make two trips, and besides, people would notice more if the priest disappeared than if he were killed. In that neighborhood, theft and murder for theft are common enough. And I couldn't take too long. I wanted to keep an eye on you. All of you. I knew who you were. The only thing was, before I went after you and found out what you were doing and what you thought, and imposed upon that fool there." She looked at Athos with such withering disdain that his heart ached. "I had to find out what had happened between her and this nobleman that the Cardinal had arranged for her to meet. I didn't understand the purpose of the meeting, but they might be marriage negotiations, and then the nobleman would be looking for her. So I went to his house, got in through the window—"

"*Sangre Dieu,*" D'Artagnan said.

Again, the feral smile flashed in his direction. "Oh, you only recognized me now? I was afraid you had, from the beginning, but you never seemed to, and I knew you'd never seen my face. Buckingham, whom I now know the nobleman to be, didn't understand my questions. The fool thought he'd seen the Queen. So he yelled at me to get out and that he'd never known any Madeleine, and then you showed up." She nodded to D'Artagnan. "I should have killed you then."

"And now, now, what are you going to do?" Athos asked, to distract her attention. His hands were sweating, his mouth dry. What would he do if she tried to kill them? Neither he nor D'Artagnan could or would sit by meekly while she slit one throat and then the other.

But what else were they supposed to do? He couldn't imagine killing her, and he was afraid that D'Artagnan too looked as if he could never do it.

"Now, you are going to hand over to me all your coins, all your gold." She grinned. "And then I'm going to leave. And you will never hear of me again. Or at least, you should hope you don't."

Athos saw that D'Artagnan would hesitate and might bridle at this, so he reached into his own purse, and brought out all the coin he had on him. Helene turned to D'Artagnan. "You?"

Slowly, meekly, the boy tossed in all his coin, and a dashing pearl brooch that sat on the side of his hat, which he must have bought with the King's money.

As D'Artagnan reached over to hand her the money, his other hand snaked in the belt, for his dagger.

But Athos grabbed his wrist and said, "No."

D'Artagnan looked bewildered and Helene smiled. "Why, thank you, Comte. For that, I'll allow you to keep that relic." She looked at the sword on the wall. "Doubtless worth something but far too recognizable."

Without another word, she turned and started for the door.

Aramis and Porthos appeared in the doorway, come from outside, and took in the scene with raised eyebrows. Helene still had her dagger out. Athos and D'Artagnan were sitting side by side, their empty purses in front of them.

"Holla," Porthos said. "Not so fast, my pretty."

"No," Athos yelled. "No. Porthos, let her go. You too, Aramis. Let her by."

Porthos looked up with openmouthed wonder and, while he was doing so, Helene ran out the door.

Athos heard her run across the kitchen. He heard the back door slam.

"The devil," D'Artagnan said, standing up. "She is a murderess, Athos, a—"

Athos grabbed him by the wrist, stopping him. "D'Artagnan, she is also a very cunning and dangerous woman. It is not worth it. Don't risk your life."

"But . . . what of the lives she will take?"

"I doubt it," Athos said and tried to believe it. "She has just ruined the Cardinal's plan. Rochefort, no doubt, will put it together. The Cardinal's reach is everywhere."

"But what if he fails to catch her?"

Athos shrugged. "Well, then . . . Her provocation here was great. If God wills that she lives, perhaps she will learn to be merciful. Perhaps she will repent." He thought of himself. "Murderers do."

Aramis swallowed, hard. "We'll have to keep it a secret," he said.

Athos nodded. "Yes. Of course. Rochefort will work it out, I think, but we can't tell this story abroad and expose the Queen to gossip. I assume she is still the Queen?"

Aramis looked oddly distracted as he nodded. "Yes, we got there in time and I was just . . . The King just asked for it as I was . . . leaving."

Athos was not sure what the initial end for that sentence was, but he did not wish to ask. Instead he nodded. "Good, then, we will stay secret. The four of us."

He put his head in his hands. From outside came the sound of hooves hurrying away.

Athos closed his eyes, listening, as he lost forever the last woman he would ever allow himself to love.

Almost a Musketeer; More Royal
Largesse; Friendship

✑

D'ARTAGNAN came out of the Palais Royale marching
in an assured step. Outside, he stopped and put his hat on his
head, and looked up at the brightly shining sun.

He'd survived his first month in the capital. No, more
than survived. Thrived. The tunic on his body, the breeches
he wore, were pale blue and bore the emblem of the guards
of Monsieur des Essarts. He would be standing guard at the
royal palace one night a week—honored with the confidence
of the King and Queen.

Though he'd missed his heart's desire of being a musketeer, he trusted Monsieur de Treville's assurance that there
was a musketeer's tunic in his future after a suitable apprenticeship in the guards.

And he had friends.

As he thought of them, he saw them, hurrying toward him
from another of the palace's exits. Aramis looked embarrassed, Porthos looked amused and Athos—still looking distant and wan—had at least lost the awful paleness and the
look that the world had come crashing down around his
head.

"D'Artagnan," Porthos said, "you look very handsome in
your new tunic."

"Almost like a musketeer," Aramis said, his lips twisting
in a teasing smile. "In bad lighting."

"Aramis's friend has passed on forty pistols," Athos said
somberly. "That she sent to us for our service to her."

D'Artagnan nodded. "That is good, because I have need

to go to the orphanage again. I promised the Mother Superior I would tell her all." He felt great reluctance at this duty as he must, yet again, reveal to Mother Clementine something horrible about one of her charges. Even if she might suspect it already, it would be unpleasant.

"We will go with you," Aramis said quickly.

"Are you sure?" D'Artagnan said.

Aramis nodded. D'Artagnan looked into the musketeer's green eyes and found only trust there. And if Aramis trusted him now, he must truly be accepted.

"Of course we'll go with you," Porthos said. "We wouldn't let you go do something so unpleasant alone."

D'Artagnan looked at Athos, but didn't ask the question. He couldn't ask Athos to face his pain that fully, that soon.

But Athos allowed one of his smiles to slide across his lips, and put his hand forward, palm down. "One for all," he said.

D'Artagnan, startled, let his hand fall atop of Athos's and felt Aramis's and Porthos's fall on the back of his, as he said, "And all for one."

Turn the page for a preview of
the next Musketeers Mystery,

The
Musketeer's
Seamstress

Coming soon from Berkley Prime Crime!

The Impossibility of Murder;
Where Aramis Questions His Sanity;
The Impossibility of Escape

THE Chevalier Renee D'Herblay—better known for some time now as the musketeer Aramis—was sure that no one could have murdered his mistress.

A tall, slim man whose long blond hair and elaborate attire normally belied the very solid muscles now on display, he stood naked in the doorway of her room. His numb hands gripped the wooden frame for support, because his knees had gone unaccountably lax. He looked out, unbelieving, at the huge bed that took up most of the bedroom.

The bed was high and heavy and massive—a solid construction of Spanish oak that had probably come in Violette's dowry when she'd married a French grandee. Upon the oak, soft draperies had been heaped, to make the bed suitable for someone of Violette's soft skin and softer habits—there was lace and velvet and a profusion of pillows of all shapes and sizes.

Aramis knew that bed better than he knew his own. He had been Violette's lover for many years and he'd spent considerably more time in her bed than his. At least, time awake.

But now he grasped the doorway hard for support, and stared at the bed, uncomprehending. Because on the bed, Violette lay. Violette who, only minutes ago, had been lively, full of fire, eager for his embraces and inventive with her own.

Now she lay . . . He felt sweat start at his hairline, the

cold sweat of fear and disbelief. And blinking didn't seem to change the scene his eyes showed him.

Because Violette could not be dead. And yet she lay on the bed, motionless, her normally pink body gone the color of cheap candle tallow, her mouth open and her eyes staring fixedly at the canopy of pink satin over her.

Between her perfect, rounded breasts that his hands and lips knew as well as his eyes did, an intrusion—an ivory handle—protruded. And around her breasts, there was blood, dripping into the lace and pillows, the satin and lace.

Aramis swallowed hard, fighting back nausea and a primal scream of grief that wanted to tear through his lips.

His mind, still in control, feverishly went over and over the reasons why the scene in front of him was impossible.

First, he'd left her alive when he'd gone into the small room next to her room, where—out of modesty or high breeding—she kept the *chaise percé* used for calls of nature. Second, he'd taken no more than a moment there. He was sure of it. And he'd heard no doors close or open anywhere. Third, the door to the room was locked—had been locked when they first lay down together. He'd turned the large key himself, watched it click home. Fourth, they were three floors up in the royal palace, with sentinels and guards all around and thick walls encircling the whole structure. And there was only one small window in the room—too small to admit anyone—and a door to a narrow balcony well away from walls and trees. A balcony small enough only for two people to stand close together. The bed was too low to the floor to conceal anyone beneath it.

No one could have come into the room. And Violette was not the sort to commit suicide. Or to commit it with a knife to the heart. No woman was. Aramis, who knew many women, knew. They were more inclined to the poison that would pluck them from life while they slept. Not that he'd ever had any of his mistresses die this way. But he'd heard about it. He'd . . . read.

He struggled to stand, pulling his hands away from the doorway. If Violette couldn't be dead, ergo, she must be alive. And if she was alive this must all be a tasteless joke.

Standing on his own feet, he took a deep breath and inhaled the sharp, metallic smell of blood. But Violette would be as thorough in her jokes as she was in everything else. It would be real blood. Animal blood. Yes, that must be it.

He charged forward, to the bed, and put out a hand to shake her hand resting, half-closed, on the frilly coverlet near a pool of blood that seemed more abundant and darker than he'd have imagined possible. It was soaking into the fabric and probably into the mattress beneath.

"Violette," he said. This close he could see the blade of a sharp dagger plunged into the flesh, and the wound into which it plunged, and the blood . . . Blood was only trickling out now, but it already looked like there was more blood on her than there should be in any human being. "Violette," he said. "I am offended. This is in extremely poor taste. You must know—"

His hand touched her arm. Before he could control himself, he jumped back, his hands covering his mouth, but not in time to hold back his shocked scream. She felt . . . not exactly cold, but not as warm as living flesh could feel. And her skin felt dead.

Aramis knew dead. He'd killed men enough in duel and in combat ever since that day, when he—still known as Chevalier D'Herblay—was barely more than nineteen and a young man had caught him reading the lives of saints to the young man's sister. Well, at least that was what Aramis still told everyone he was doing. The truth was somewhere closer to his having demonstrated to the young lady the biblical intricacies of the word *know*. The young man had objected and challenged D'Herblay for a duel. And D'Herblay, knowing instinctively that his fashionable looks, his command of Latin grammar or even his wielding of sharp rhetoric would not get him out of this situation, had looked for the best fencing master in Paris, Monsieur Pierre Du Vallon. So good had Du Vallon's lessons proved that D'Herblay had killed the prudish young man. Which, since dueling was forbidden by royal edict, had led to D'Herblay's and Du Vallon's going into hiding under the assumed names of Aramis and Porthos in the uniform of His Majesty's musketeers.

Since then, and particularly since making the acquaintance of a disgraced nobleman who called himself Athos and of a young Gascon hothead called D'Artagnan, Aramis had fought more duels than he cared to think about. Between the

four of them, one or another was forever challenging someone for a duel and calling on all his friends to serve as seconds.

He'd killed men, he'd seen corpses—Aramis heard his
lips, loudly, mutter a string of Ave Marias—but never one
murdered like this, in the safety of her room, in the privacy
of her boudoir. And not while only Aramis was present. Not
while only Aramis could have done it.

His hands over his mouth, he'd backed up until his behind fetched up against one of Violette's innumerable, amusing little tables, covered in more lace, velvet and satin, and
stacked high with books she never read, her command of
written French being shaky and her interest in the written
word being far secondary to her interest in other pastimes.

Through the roaring in his ears, he was dimly aware that
people were knocking at the door and at least one female
voice was shouting a string of Spanish names, followed by
other Spanish words. The names were Violette's. Her real
name was a string of proper names, followed by a string of
surnames, all connected by *y* and *de*, which Aramis could
not hope to understand or remember. Ever since, on a cold
night, when he stood guard at the royal palace, she'd approached him and told him her name was Violette, he'd
called her that and nothing else.

But the knocking on the door seemed like a distant worry.
Closer at hand, Aramis was grappling with his soul. Ever
since his father had died, when Aramis was no older than
two, Aramis's pious and noble mother had decided her
young son was bound for the church. So, wherever his path
took him, he dragged with him the excellent, thorough and
insistent religious education his mother had given him.

Even now, in uniform for many years, Aramis considered
himself a priest in training. As soon as he cleared his name
enough for some order to take him.

He was aware of the serious and grave sins he committed
with Violette, who was, after all, married to some French nobleman living in the far provinces. True, her marriage had
been one arranged to match the marriage of the Queen,
Anne of Austria, her childhood companion and friend. Violette, to hear her talk, barely knew her husband, with whom
she had not spent more than the two weeks of the wedding

festivities. He enjoyed rural pleasures, and she'd lingered at court with her friend the Queen. And she'd found Aramis.

And there, Aramis thought, lay the crux of the sin, for they'd sinned often and in very imaginative ways. And had not, perhaps, some angel reached from heaven to smite with ivory dagger the cleft between Violette's perfect breasts.

But the banging on the door grew more insistent and Aramis's knowledge of Latin allowed him to guess that the Spanish-speaking woman wished to know who had screamed and why, and would not be appeased by anything but Violette's voice. A voice that would not sound, again, till the angel of the apocalypse sounded the final trumpet.

Naked, scared, shocked, Aramis stood and stared at the door, which was shaking under the impact of many hands, many fists.

Cold sweat ran down his face. He felt his hand tremble. He'd never trembled on battlefield or field of honor, but this . . . this supernatural retribution, he could not endure.

And yet, if an angel had struck, would he not have killed both of them while they were abandoned to their pleasure? And why would an angel wait until Aramis went to the little room to attend a call of nature?

Despite his education—or perhaps because of it, for, after all, it had included logic—Aramis had an analytical mind, which shouted over the vapors of his fear and the madness of his religious guilt to tell him that a human hand had killed Violette. A human hand, not Aramis's.

Perhaps, he thought, there was a tunnel into this room? After all, any palace of any age had more tunnels, secret passages and hidden rooms than any rabbit warren.

But, looking around the room, he could not imagine where the tunnel would open. Every available palm-length of wall had one of Violette's cabinets, tables, chaises leaning against it. And all of it was solid, heavy Spanish furniture that would not be moved by a simple door springing open behind it.

And now a man was knocking at the door and calling out in French, "Madam, Madam, if you do not open we'll be forced to break down the door."

Aramis, well versed in the art of manipulating palace staff, knew that it would only be a matter of minutes before some sturdy lads were fetched and their shoulders applied to the wall. The lock was solid, but not that solid. It would open. And they would catch him here. Alone. With Violette's corpse.

How long before the gibbet was built and he was hanged? Or would he be lucky enough to be beheaded? One of his long, pale hands went, unmeant, to his long, elegant neck.

It would kill his mother.

He edged toward the balcony door. It was the only way out. And that not a true way out, for what was there, beneath, but the hard ground that would break his body? But at least he wouldn't die on the gallows or the block. He would not bring that shame onto his mother.

His hands, filled with a decision he could only half muster, tore at the door, forcing it open.

The cold air of the evening rushed in on him, a scent of trees and grass and, beyond that, the scent of manure and cooking fires that was the great, bustling city of Paris.

His ears unnaturally sharpened by his fear, he could hear somewhere on the grounds of the palace the rough laughter of musketeers on guard and the sound of die being tumbled. Was Athos or Porthos on guard tonight? He could not remember. Truth was he could not remember when it was and his normally perfect knowledge of his friends' guard schedules had slipped wholly from his mind.

In the end, his wit, which had always been his defense, would desert him. The sound of the knocks on the door changed. Ah. Sturdy shoulders applied with a will.

Aramis stepped out onto the balcony, which was semicircular, built of stone and surrounded with little rounded columns of stone topped by a carefully edged parapet.

The polished stone felt rough against his nakedness as he leaned over to look three stories below, to the paving of an ornamental patio surrounded by flowerbeds. On one of the flowerbeds, in front of the balcony, a lone tree stood, its branches thrust skyward like the hands of beseeching sinners.

If Aramis flung himself out . . . If he threw himself out toward it . . .

He narrowed his eyes, calculating the distance, which was more than that of his outstretched body were he laid in the air between it and the balcony. And it was, worse, a good story below.

His body had been honed through years of duels and sword practice. He knew his muscles could perform amazing leaps in the heat of combat. But here, in midair, with nothing to push against, how was he to reach for the saving branch of the distant tree?

And even if he managed to get down there, how could he save himself, naked and—he looked down—somehow smeared with Violette's blood. How could he escape the palace and its well-guarded entrances? Everyone knew he was in here with Violette. Or, if not, everyone would guess when they found his uniform tossed casually over one of her chaises.

He took a step in the room, not so much intending to retrieve the uniform, but thinking of it, with the image of his blue tunic in his mind.

And he heard the crack of the door, as it gave under the assault of young men's shoulders.

If he jumped, it would be suicide. But if he stayed here, they would kill him. Suicide was a sin.

Without thinking, with no time to plan, he scrambled up onto the little stone parapet. He crossed himself. And then he jumped, somersaulting, his body twisting midair, his arms reaching hopelessly toward the impossible hold of the distant tree branches.

KATE KINGSBURY

THE MANOR HOUSE MYSTERY SERIES

In WWII England, the quiet village of Sitting Marsh is faced with food rations and fear for loved ones. But Elizabeth Hartleigh Compton, lady of the Manor House, stubbornly insists that life must go on. Sitting Marsh residents depend on Elizabeth to make sure things go smoothly. Which means everything from sorting out gossip to solving the occasional murder.

A Bicycle Built for Murder
0-425-17856-0

Death Is in the Air
0-425-18094-8

For Whom Death Tolls
0-425-18386-6

Dig Deep for Murder
0-425-18886-8

Paint by Murder
0-425-19215-6

Berried Alive
0-425-19490-6

Fire When Ready
0-425-19948-7

Wedding Rows
0-425-20804-4

Available wherever books are sold or at
penguin.com